PRAISE FOR
WALK THE MOONS ROAD

"It is always a pleasure to discover a first novel by a genuinely talented writer, and this is one of the most promising such yet. . . . I read it through in a single sitting. . . . Highly recommended."
—*SF Chronicle*

"A delightfully intricate first novel, combining ethereal beauty with dockside humor and bawdy adventure . . ."
—*Locus*

"Haunting and evocative."
—*San Jose Mercury News*

"Who is Jim Aikin, and out of where did he pull such a good first novel as *Walk the Moons Road*? . . . A good, solid piece of action SF, with a good, solid alien planet background with enough originality to make it fresh."
—*Isaac Asimov's Science Fiction Magazine*

Books by Jim Aikin

WALK THE MOONS ROAD
THE WALL AT THE EDGE OF THE WORLD

THE WALL AT THE EDGE OF THE EDGE OF THE WORLD

JIM AIKIN

ACE BOOKS, NEW YORK

This book is an Ace original edition,
and has never been previously published.

THE WALL AT THE EDGE OF THE WORLD

An Ace Book / published by arrangement with
the author

PRINTING HISTORY
Ace edition / March 1993

ISBN: 0-441-87140-2

Ace Books are published by The Berkley Publishing Group,
200 Madison Avenue, New York, New York 10016.
The name "ACE" and the "A" logo
are trademarks belonging to Charter Communications, Inc.

PRINTED IN THE UNITED STATES OF AMERICA

10 9 8 7 6 5 4 3 2 1

For Sharon R.

THE WALL AT THE EDGE OF THE WORLD

Chapter 1

A crowd was already gathering when the first uncertain light of morning stirred among the clouds. The early arrivals stood in small knots here and there across the square, murmuring and shuffling, huddled in their cloaks and hoods against the thin winter drizzle. By sunrise, a semicircle of bodies filled three sides of the square, leaving an open space around the Triple Gate and the block that had been set before it. Sunrise was not sunrise, only a dull and ragged reddening, streaked and clotted with yellow and silver, that leaked out beneath the gray. The richly ornamented façade of the Sharing House was bathed in a dirty pink glow.

Danlo Ree shared a wordless apology as he edged between groups of villagers. The loose ranks in the rear parted courteously for him, but those in the front were pressed tight. Fortunately, he was tall enough to see over others' heads, and he had chosen his angle of approach with care. He was within yards of the block—a solid chunk of gray wood four feet long and two high, stained in irregular dark blotches, the top scarred by deep lengthwise cuts into a saddle-shaped concavity.

The young couple on his right were holding hands with white-knuckled intensity, and ignored him. The plump middle-aged woman on the other side smiled and shared warmth. "Newly come to town?" she whispered.

"Passing through. Travelling counter."

"Not so many travellers come to a Cleansing."

Which was a polite way of asking why he had arisen so early to stand in the rain among strangers. Guilt flashed through him, and her eyes narrowed. "Lost one of my own," he explained. "I come to remember."

"To remember? Olivia's mercy, why?"

"I don't know." That was true, more or less. He knew only that over the years he had attended many Cleansings, and that afterward he remembered things and was glad he had braved the pain. In a day or two, the Guidance took hold again and the memories dimmed. Until another Cleansing came, he remembered only that it was good to fight against the Guidance, to go, to remember.

"Most often," the woman said piously, "the bereaved choose not to be reminded."

Choose. Danlo nearly laughed. The Guided part of his mind had tried to keep him in bed this morning, keep him asleep. He had had to wrestle with himself, as if the tangle of sheet and blanket were inside his skull instead of wrapped around his legs. Oxar kenned his turmoil, and woke, but even on ordinary mornings Danlo cared little for Oxar's sharing, which was full of well-thumbed sentiments but not oversupplied with compassion. Danlo himself understood little enough of what he was feeling, but he could see that Oxar's dull, conventional mind would diffuse it like a wind through smoke. So he brushed aside the other man's inquiry. He gathered his clothing and carried it down the hall to the washroom to dress. After a minute Oxar padded in, in woolly slippers and a purple robe, yawned and stretched, and offered to come along if Danlo wanted company. Danlo managed, tactfully, to send Oxar back to bed, and made his way alone through the misty, empty streets to the square.

The Triple Gate at the center of the square was only a small replica of the towering structure at the Hub of Roads in Serameno. It stood fifteen feet tall—four sturdy posts topped by three horizontal crosspieces. The angles and proportions were standard: the outer posts were set further back, closer to the Sharing House, so that the crosspieces formed half a hexagon. The Gate had been garlanded with strips of colored paper for the ceremony, but the decorations drooped sadly in the drizzle.

The song of the ktess began, a low golden pulse that swelled moment by moment. The crowd fell silent and the fidgeting stopped. They stood as motionless as stones as they opened to one another within.

A figure garbed in blue-and-white motley stepped out of the Sharing House, out of the dark mouth of the doorless portal. He raised a wooden flute to his lips, trilled out a flourish, and pranced lightly down into the square. He passed beneath the Gate, paused just beyond it, raised the flute—and himself on tiptoe—and led the crowd in a slow, reverent chorus of "They Are Among Us to This Day."

At the last notes, this year's Frank and Olivia appeared in the portal. They raised their arms in the eternal gestures, Frank reaching wide all-embracingly while Olivia presented her open palms, fingers curved outward, before her womb. In consideration of the weather, the pair had been provided with cloaks and rain hoods, which hung open so that the traditional costumes could be seen—Frank's black coat and trousers, white ruffled shirt, and red butterfly-shaped necktie, Olivia's long white gown and corsage of roses. The Frank was trying hard to look solemn and important, but his arms were wobbling a little, and his face threatened to break into a smirk. The Olivia darted a glance at him and looked away again. As they walked slowly toward the Triple Gate, their coltishness evaporated. They grew large in the ktess as Frank and Olivia themselves drifted near and settled into the young bodies. Danlo's hair prickled. He could almost see the huge forms of the Immortals coalesce in the air. Being in Their presence stirred him profoundly. But it was not why he had come.

He was on the east side of the square, and the Sharing House was on the north. The proctor station, a lower building with wide glass doors, was opposite him on the west. As Frank and Olivia took up their positions behind the Gate, the doors of the station quivered. The glass reflected the red-streaked, cloud-clotted sunrise, and the reflection twitched, threatening to flow, but congealed again and stood trembling. Then the doors swung ponderously outward and apart, splitting the sunrise so it whipped away to both sides, and from the dim recess marched the procession.

First came the drummer, pacing slowly. The flutist sounded the melody of "Joined Within" in long, unornamented tones, and the drummer struck a halting cadence. Behind him, in pairs, appeared the proctors, their faces hidden within the folds of their tall purple hoods. Six proctors, eight, ten. The crowd parted to let them pass. Twelve, fourteen, sixteen. And between the third pair, and the fifth pair, and the seventh, walked the nulls.

Two of the nulls came quietly, dreamily, their limbs loose and languid in the chains, but the third twisted and dragged at the proctors who gripped her arms. She was wailing in a high, pathetic voice, begging them to stop, don't do this, please, please. Except for the solemn phrases of the flute and drum and the jingling and scraping of the chains, the girl's raw pleading was the only sound.

The girl's voice, or perhaps it was the wet cold, sent a chill rippling down Danlo's neck. He twitched his rain hood tighter. The Guidance shrilled in him. He wished that he were back in his warm bed at the hostel, that he had finished his work here yesterday and been off on the coach to Bearsvill, that he had somehow not learned that there was to be a Cleansing. He turned, wanting to escape, but the villagers had pressed in behind him in a solid wall. Their faces were rapt, their eyes glowing. He quelled his panic and turned back to the square. The song of the ktess was a golden nectar, and he opened himself to it, wishing it could somehow fill him entirely and bear away the terrible discomfort on its tide. Snatches of memory came to him. Julan's voice, the roundness of her arms, the stricken look in her eyes. . . .

Wanting not to disturb the harmonious tranquillity of those around him, he walled up his awakened pain in an inner chamber of his mind, where the ktess could not wash across it. He became, unobtrusively, two-minded. The pleasure of the communal bond flowed through his outer mind, yet because he had withdrawn, it failed to transmute his ordinary sensations—the stiffness where his body protested at being dragged out of bed, the cadences of the flute and drum marching so measuredly beneath the girl's wild sobbing shriek, the sour smell of rain on pavement mingling with the warm dampness of the good folk of Woolich pressed close around him. He felt the same ecstasy he saw reflected in their eyes; he could not help feeling it. The beautiful words of the White Book flowed through the ktess: *In the Cleansing is the renewal of the Oneness of the Body, the unending Oneness of the Body.* He saw lips moving; his own were moving too. Yet in another chamber of his mind he saw that the girl had scratched herself, or been scratched, a long red mark down the side of her face. The White Book said nothing about this sharp and ineradicable irrelevance, could say nothing about it, because the scratch existed only in this particular morning. Nobody but the girl felt the sting of it, and nobody but Danlo noticed.

Behind the proctors came the parents of the nulls. One of the women was swaying or staggering on wobbly legs; her husband had to support her. And bringing up the rear, pacing in a deliberate, halting tread, strode the Hand of Cleansing. The Hand of Cleansing wore a stiff yellow hood and a yellow blindfold, and he bore the great gleaming axe diagonally across his chest. The parents were bareheaded, and the elaborate coils and loops of their hair were sodden and sagging in the drizzle. The nulls, of course, had been shaved. (He remembered Julan's long brown hair, how it hung down in his face when she lay above him. Remembered sweeping it up from the kitchen floor after the proctors came. What had he done with it? Surely he would have kept it. No, they made him throw it away. Of course.)

The drummer took up his position and the left side of the Triple Gate, next to the flutist, and the parents stood at the right. The pairs of proctors who were not escorting nulls formed a semicircle before the Gate. When the music ended, the first null was presented to Frank and Olivia at the Gate of Guidance. The null, who looked to be the eldest of the three, was a lanky, round-shouldered boy of fifteen. He smiled at Frank and Olivia in a vague, amiable way. His parents reached out and implored him, using the words from the White Book: "Lift up the veil! Behold the ktess! Be of the Body!" In the ktess, in loving silence, the whole crowd called the same words. But the boy could make no response. So Frank and Olivia would not let him pass through the Gate, and said in unison, "He is not One with us. We cannot ken him." The proctors drew him back, and brought him forward next at the Gate of Knowledge, where again Frank and Olivia barred the way. Finally he was brought to the Gate of Love, and a third time he could not enter.

The same pattern was followed with the second null, and the third: three nulls, three gates, nine presentations to Frank and Olivia, nine confirmations that the young people were not of the Body.

Julan's parents had both been dead by the time she became afflicted. It had fallen to Danlo and her younger sister to stand beside the Gate. The proctors had given Danlo something to drink; he remembered that. The rest of the ceremony was a buzzing blur. He wondered whether it had been necessary to drug him, or whether the forgetfulness had been the beginning of the Guidance. Anger flared in him: They had stolen his grief. He contained the anger quickly in the hidden part of his mind, and cast about surreptitiously to see whether anybody had noticed.

If anybody had kenned the anger, the joddies should have. Three of them stood in the front row not far from him. But they gave no sign. Their eyes were closed, red-robed arms across one another's shoulders. Other joddies were scattered among the crowd, alone or in pairs. One might be standing directly behind him. He did not dare turn and look. Probably the dense welter of thought in the crowd would cover his feelings. It was vital that he keep them concealed. If the joddies knew he had subverted the Guidance, they would come to him after the Cleansing and renew it.

When the third null had been turned away from the third Gate, they were led toward the block. The girl's sobbing had subsided to a moaning gurgle. She hung like a broken doll between the proctors, legs splayed, head down, her torso racked by spasms. A rope of her saliva trailed on the rain-slick pavement. Perhaps that was why she was unquiet. The proctors would have given her the cup of peace, but she must have spat it out.

She was to be the second to be Cleansed. The proctors holding the first null forced his head down onto the block, and twisted his arms firmly behind his back. He turned his head a little to one side, as if he were getting comfortable on a pillow.

The Hand of Cleansing, still blindfolded, stepped forward and raised his axe. Guided by the eyes of the whole assembly, he swung unerringly. The polished blade arced high against the dreary sky, and with a soft *thwock* the null's head jumped forward off the block, and bounced and rolled.

The proctors lifted the headless body aside. The fount of blood squirted and spattered down the block and across the glistening pavement, and red tendrils coiled among the puddles.

The next pair brought the girl forward, and forced her down. "Noooo!" The scream clawed at her throat. "*Nooooo!!*"

The Hand swung.

Danlo felt wetness on his cheek. He thought it was only a drop of rain that had found its way under his hood in a vagrant gust of wind, but when he put up two fingers to wipe it away, the fingertips came away streaked with red. He wiped his fingers on his cloak. He kept wiping stiffly long after there was any reason to.

When all three nulls had been Cleansed, the nearest joddies stepped lightly forward, and with solemn grace knelt and picked up the heads. Pressing their palms against the ears and holding the heads high and well out before them, they padded gently up to the Triple Gate and presented the objects to Frank and Olivia, who crossed their hands over their hearts and bowed their own heads in thanks. The joddies turned, still holding the awful trophies aloft, and walked in single file along the inner edge of the crowd. As they began their circuit more joddies stepped out to join them, some walking before or behind them and others circling the square in the other direction. They passed one another alternately to the left or right, as if they were trailing streamers and weaving a garland or a braid. At every circuit more joddies pressed forward to join the procession, and the pace quickened. Within a minute, fifty of them were swooping like red birds around the square in a complex and perfectly interlaced pattern, eyes closed, running at top speed, their sandals slapping and pattering on the pavement, bearing aloft among them the dripping, gore-smeared shaven heads.

The villagers around Danlo smiled warmly at one another.

Danlo managed to bring up a smile too, though it felt waxen. The flute and drum started again, this time with quite a different tune, and other flutes were brought out from beneath cloaks. They leaped and frolicked together. Linking elbows, the crowd began to sing softly, the great hymn "Unending Renewal." Danlo took the baritone line. After three verses, with a collective sigh, the crowd began to disperse. Neighbor smiled and nodded at neighbor, wife took husband's arm. Only a few faces were pale and grim. Danlo walked slowly and smiled, while beneath the placid surface his nerves twitched and writhed. He remembered everything—how Julan had fallen ill, how the appeal to the One had been brushed aside, and how, afterward, the matches and kerosene had been pried from his fingers before he could make a pyre of the house and himself in it. He clutched the memories tight in the inner part of his mind while he smiled and nodded agreeably at those around him, and accepted their murmured benedictions in return. The flutes trilled and skirled, and the good folk of Woolich passed out of the square to begin their day, leaving behind them three headless corpses piled in a careless heap and a throng of red-robed joddies running in a double circle in the rain.

Chapter ‖ 2

NEEDING to get away from the crowd, Danlo slipped into a lane between two buildings. His legs were jelly, his eyes half-blinded by tears, but he plunged onward. Down some steps, the lane emptied into a covered walkway, its sides and roof trellises heavy with vines. The walkway was cave-dark, though at this season the vines were leafless, so a little patchy daylight leaked through. The ancient stems, pruned back to rough stumps, wove thick and twisted among the geometrical latticework. He thought he kenned a joddie behind him, and cast a terrified glance over his shoulder, but he saw only a dim, constricted tunnel wrapped in gray brambles.

His step faltered. He clung to the trellis, fingers gripping the rough slats as he gave way to the rush of memory. His love for Julan, undimmed by the passage of years, filled him with a fire of longing and grief. That fire was what the Guidance had stolen from him. Except at times like this, he could recall vaguely that he had once been married, that his wife had fallen ill and died, but he could not dwell on the details.

They had met when they were both seventeen. A tall, shy, awkward boy, Danlo was shocked that a girl so beautiful could care for him. Two years later they were married. They found a snug little house, and Danlo studied to become a counter, working late into the evening with papers spread across the kitchen table. Julan would come up quietly behind him and rest her hand on his shoulder. He would drift back from the wilderness of numbers in which he had been wandering and feel her warmth, and touch her hand. She would lean over and kiss him, her long hair sighing down across his arm and chest, and then he would shuffle the papers into their folders and put the cap back on his pen.

From the first he had known that in Julan the ktess sometimes flickered, dimmed like a light that passed behind a curtain. But it was of no importance. She had been Received when she came into the ktess at puberty, as had Danlo, as had everybody else in the world. She was of the Body, as surely as any adult. A child who failed to come into the ktess when the physical signs of adulthood had become unarguable was a null, and had to be Cleansed. Nulls were rare, and Julan was certainly not a null. The idea that she might be would not have occurred to anybody.

In their third summer together, Julan fell ill. Danlo blamed himself. The Guidance could not absolve him, but it blocked the self-condemnation that might otherwise have poisoned him. She had not wanted to swim in the stagnant water of that blocked-off canal, where things green and unpleasant proliferated and clung, but he was in a playful mood. He dove in and splashed her and made fun of her until she relented. The next day she was feverish, the day after, worse. The doctors brought pills, and took away samples of her blood, and muttered learnedly among themselves, but they failed to damp the fires that raged through her.

Two joddies came, then, and probed for some buried emotional blockage that might be provoking the symptoms. They found nothing. They too shook their heads and departed.

For two weeks Julan hovered in delirium. Then, as mysteriously as it had come, the fever abated. Weak and pale, she could only whisper to her husband through cracked lips. He sat by her bedside for hours, spooning broth, tenderly wiping her face with a damp cloth, reading aloud from her favorite books, reading on even when her eyes were closed and he could not tell whether she was listening or asleep.

In all respects but one, she mended quickly.

He hid the change from himself for as long as he could, and said nothing about it. Afterward he wished he had had the courage. It was Julan, sitting at an open window, the brilliance of afternoon glowing like milk in her white dress, who said, "I have been reaching out. Sometimes at night I can't sleep, so I lie there and reach out for hours, until I think I'll shake to pieces from the strain. But there's nothing. Nothing."

A bread crumb—or perhaps it was a cry of pain—caught in his throat, so that he had to pause and cough. "The healing takes time. We will ask the joddies to summon Olivia." An animal apprehension flickered in her eyes. Her eyes were set deeper in her face now than before the sickness, and her cheekbones stood out more sharply. Her hands were thinner too. The long, delicate fingers picked at an embroidered rosette on her skirt, fussed at it as if to tear it, thread by thread, apart. He put his hand on top of her hand to still the agitation, but she jerked away, and turned her head so he could not see her face.

It sometimes happened among the Body that old people fell away from the ktess, just as they might become blind or deaf. Such unfortunates might no longer be considered quite human, but they were not considered nulls either. They were cared for in special homes where they could fret and clamor in their childish way without disturbing others. But Julan was twenty-three. She could not be kept in such a home for the rest of her life. Nor could she be allowed to live in the community, when she was no longer of the Body. The joddies consulted among themselves, and charged the rememberers to dredge up the precedents of the centuries. Danlo and Julan waited. She grew thinner; she would not eat. She walked in the garden for hours, and by turns clung to him and shrank from his touch.

When the joddies came, he kenned their decision at once. He would have struck them with his fists if one had not taken control of his limbs until the fit subsided. Julan had to be told aloud, as if she were a child. Because her ktess had always been weak, they ruled that she had always been, essentially, a null, that her Receiving had been an error.

After she had been Cleansed, after he tried to set fire to the house, after he shook off the restraining minds of the joddies and tore his clothes and ran though the streets until he fell and scraped his hands and face and bled without feeling the pain, he was taken into a chapel by half a dozen proctors. There, over the course of three days, joddies gave him Guidance.

Solemn and withdrawn but calm and untroubled, the young counter returned to his work. His family thought he should marry again. They arranged, at every banquet, that he should be seated beside an eligible woman. He found that he had little interest in them, though he was not sure why. He talked amiably, and danced and sang, but remained untouched.

A lively wench named Yovi refused to be discouraged. Though he was happy enough to take her to bed, her chatter about their future together made him nervous, for reasons that he could not have explained. He discovered a way to deflect her—a forbidden way. To Guide others was the province of the joddies, who were trained to apply this power with wisdom. But Danlo's aversion to Yovi's attentions was strong enough that it overcame the Guidance given him ten years before at his Receiving, as it was given to them all. He entered the depths of Yovi's mind without her knowledge, and planted there a cloud of reluctance, resistance, revulsion. He was surprised how easy it was. Yovi fidgeted for a minute, stood up, mentioned some errands she needed to run, put on her shoes, and left. She never showed any further interest in him.

After a few years, the women he had danced with were busy with husbands and babies. He wondered sometimes if he had made a mistake. Perhaps he should have married again. But when he first found himself at a Cleansing, quite accidentally, and his Guidance broke open like an egg and he remembered Julan, he knew why the joddies had thought it safest to build barriers around his ability to love. If he loved, he might remember too much. He sought out more Cleansings, as many as he could without arousing suspicion. Each time he was able to recall more about Julan, and retain bits of it even after the Guidance knit itself back together. This last awakening had stirred him to a great depth, as if he had taken a stick and churned the mud at the bottom of a pond. He wondered whether he might, at last, have shaken off the Guidance. He hoped so. He wanted to possess all of himself, to be whole, whatever the pain. But what would the joddies do to him if they learned that his mind was strong enough to undo their careful work? He would have to keep his thoughts well hidden.

At the end of the solitary passage he emerged beside a wide street. The cloud cover had lifted higher, and the snow-draped slopes of the Sernada, the spine of the world, strode down the east, the peaks wrapped in tufts of gray cotton. He was in the commercial district. The flat roofs were inset with domed skylights like the caps of big white mushrooms, and each establishment had a large sign on its front that told, in stylized letters that rippled and swam in many colors, whether food or fabric or furniture was to be had within. Smaller scrolling messages told about the week's special offerings. Though it was early, a few pedestrians strolled with shopping baskets on their arms, and several large electric coaches whispered along on fat tires. The coaches were painted eggshell blues and yellows and pinks, and their upper halves were sleek bubbles of window. One cruised slowly along the curb, and the driver shared an inquiry: *Ride need?*

Danlo stilled the turmoil in his mind. *Walk prefer.* He wasn't sure of the route back to the hostel, but he had no desire for company at present. He straightened his back and strode off purposefully, hoping exertion would lift his spirits.

The streets of Woolich, broad and immaculate, glistened from the recent rain. Small, neat houses and workshops pressed together, yards and gardens set off by hedges and picket fences. At one corner he came upon half-a-dozen shirkers. Under the benign eyes of a joddie, who was sitting on a stool under an umbrella, the shirkers were energetically repaving a rough place in the street. Danlo's pulse quickened. To make the world smooth for everyone—yes! He detoured toward the group, meaning to pick up a shovel and pitch in, but the joddie pushed him away indulgently, affectionately, in the ktess. Danlo's face burned as he trudged on. If he hadn't been distracted by the need to present an untroubled surface, he would never have fallen under the sway of such a simple compulsion.

By nightfall, he knew, the shirkers would have repaired as many as ten potholes, if ten could be found in a village this size. Tomorrow they might be clearing clogged rain gutters or painting a building. After a few days, when they had learned their lesson about contributing to the community, the joddie would release them, and they would return to their normal work.

In such a small village there was no need for street signs, but at the moment Danlo was unwilling to reach into anybody's mind to ask for directions. He was beginning to fear that he had taken a wrong turning, when he saw the ornate wooden porches and peaked roofs of the hostel ahead. The lobby was empty, not even the hosteler behind his desk, but the clink of plates and silverware emanated from beyond a wide archway. Danlo threw his rain hood back and loosened his cloak. He kenned several guests in the dining room, and thought he detected Oxar Blennish among them. Oxar was seldom late for a meal.

Danlo didn't want to encounter Oxar until he had composed himself. The stairs creaked as he ascended. He slipped through the curtain that separated the washroom from the hall. In the cunningly angled mirrors, he was suddenly surrounded by himselves, some of them facing him and some in profile or facing away. He leaned close and inspected one of the other Danlos. A faint brownish streak extended down his cheek; he heard again the tremulous wailing of the girl null, the *thwock* as the axe drove through her neck. He barely suppressed an urge to slam his palm against the mirror and shatter it. Instead he twisted the tap hard, and water gushed into the basin. He slapped water in his face and reached blindly for the soap. When he had scrubbed thoroughly, he stood dripping, his eyes still closed, and took deep breaths to still the trembling.

After groping for a towel, he inspected the cheek closely, stretching the skin taut between his fingers, and found no trace. Reluctantly satisfied, he took out his comb and arranged the careful symmetry of his curls. Close attention to good grooming, the White Book rightly pointed out, helped still the agitated mind. Tight ringlets, now damp, framed a long narrow face that had grown longer in recent years as the hair receded sharply at the temples. His jaw was strong and clean-shaven, his nose prominent but blade-thin, his eyes flat, calm gray.

He pushed the bedroom curtain aside and threw his cloak on the back of a chair. The room was warm and cheerful, with lace curtains and the inevitable portrait of Frank and Olivia smiling benignly down from the wall. He was tempted to crawl into bed, to burrow down under the covers and give way to his memories. The southbound coach wouldn't be boarding for half an hour. But Oxar would wonder if he was ill, and probe for details. If Oxar learned enough, he might report it to the joddies. That was the trouble with travelling with a rememberer. Oxar never overlooked details, and he never forgot anything. Best present the appearance that all was as usual.

But what was the use of being reunited with his memories, if nothing changed as a result? Why not simply be what he pretended to be—a contented, useful member of the Body? Why not let the memories fade, as they had faded so often before? It would be

easier than dissembling, and less painful. Either that, or give way
to the mood, go back to bed, and let Oxar think what he liked.

Neither option attracted him. There was another: He could
simply walk away into the mountains and let the wild beasts tear
him apart. At least he would be done with the pretense, done with
the weary sameness of his life. Of course, if he was ready to do
that, he could easily avoid the pain of being torn apart by beasts.
He could simply curl up in bed and refuse to move until the
joddies came to Guide him. If he was intransigent enough, they
might be persuaded to Renew him. His name would be gone, his
counting skills, even his ability to dress himself. And painlessly.
To be truly one with the Body, after so many years of feeling
obscurely out of joint. . . .   But another part of him clung
stubbornly to life.

The harmonious course, then. Outwardly harmonious, at least.
With a small sigh, he arranged his mind as carefully as his hair,
and went down to breakfast.

The dining room was done in gray and muted violet, with violet
tablecloths and napkins and high-backed chairs with soft gray
upholstery. The windows, spattered this morning with raindrops,
overlooked the tangled greenery of the garden. Four large china
cabinets displayed fine tableware, some of it doubtless centuries
old. The largest cabinet stood in the center of the room; it was
backless and encased on both sides with glass, and the interior was
divided into dozens of cubbyholes of various sizes and shapes.
Antique cups and saltshakers and gravy boats reposed within, each
placed in a cubby whose dimensions fitted it.

Other travellers sat at tables: a young couple with a boy of five
or six; a drab old woman by herself near the window; another old
woman, much stouter and more elegantly dressed, and across the
table from her a wraithlike red-haired girl whose hair swept
upward ten inches or more in a stiff jewelled crest; two young men
with feathered headbands set at rakish angles and tasseled fringes
on their sleeves—and of course Oxar Blennish. Oxar was steering
a last bite of hotcake around his plate on a fork, sopping up syrup.
He was broad-shouldered and thick-necked, with a bland square
face and loosely curled honey-colored hair that hung down his
back. At thirty, he was ten years Danlo's junior. His hand-tailored
white shirt was held closed with two rows of little pearl buttons,
and the buttons above his belt tugged against the stretched cloth.
As Danlo pulled out a chair and sat opposite him, he popped the

bite into his mouth and said around it, "Wondered." *Long walk/drowned?*

Danlo shrugged. "Walked." *Sad/remembering/slow.* The mental emblems of their exchange were not words but compounds of speech, vision, and feeling. *Sad* was gray and heavy below the eyes, *remembering* a peek into a sack whose contents shimmered, *slow* a lethargy in the limbs.

The hosteler himself bustled up to their table. A small man with a well-scrubbed round face, pink cheeks, and long sideburns done up in rows of tiny braids, he rubbed his hands together and beamed at Danlo. *Food serve desire.* "Pleasure?"

Hunger/thanks. "Sweet roll, cup of tea."

As the hosteler turned to go back toward the kitchen, a joddie entered the dining room. Danlo caught sight of the red robe out of the corner of his eye, and felt the sudden warmth and contentment that flowed through the ktess. The hosteler rushed to show the joddie to a window table. He scooped up a wooden bowl of walnuts from a serving table and set the bowl in front of the joddie, and made a second trip for a small glass bowl of spiced butter and a nutcracker. The joddie began cracking walnuts, dipping them in the butter, and popping them into his mouth. He had prominent gapped teeth and bags under his eyes, and could have benefited from a shave. The hosteler hovered over him and fidgeted. "Sorry not cracked," he said softly.

"Travel ready?" Oxar asked Danlo.

Danlo shared a vision of papers being tucked into a valise, and the valise latch being snapped shut. "Done."

One of the joddie's walnuts slipped out of his fingers and bounced and rolled across the carpet. Danlo reached down automatically to retrieve the nut. A brown ovoid, wrinkled, nearly weightless. He could still feel it in his hand after he had put it back in the bowl.

"Tree eggs," the joddie said to nobody in particular. "Don't break like eggs, though. Have to crack 'em." He cracked another.

"Cleansing enjoy?" Oxar inquired, dabbing his lips with a napkin.

Danlo's mouth went dry. "Flutes marvelous. When I was younger, no flutes. We sang unaccompanied. Then one year, overnight almost, demand for flutes rose a hundredfold. For flute teachers, too."

"Like flutes." *Pretty.*

The hosteler swept past their table with a silver-rimmed crystal goblet of amber nectar—Danlo caught a whiff of apple juice—which he set before the joddie with a flourish.

The joddie cocked his head and smiled. The air before the hosteler shimmered, and Danlo sensed, in the ktess this time, a scent of lavender. The hosteler laughed delightedly. ''Ah, Margeth! Margeth! Margeth! So wonderful.'' He reached out both hands toward the gauzy cloud. The cloud floated closer to him, enveloped his face and shoulders, and he puckered his mouth and kissed. ''Of course, of course. Would I neglect? Still the best in Frennau County. Ask any of the guests. Here—these two goodmen.'' He turned toward Danlo and Oxar. *Permission beg intrude.* ''Present Goodman Ree and Goodman Blennish. Goodmen, my wife Margeth.''

The apparition wavered and came into focus. A pretty young woman with large, limpid eyes and impossibly luminous hair smiled gravely at Danlo. *Our service satisfactory?* Her lips moved without sound; he kenned her words in the ktess.

Pleasure/smooth. Danlo inclined his head formally.

''Margeth passed inward last spring,'' the hosteler said. ''Childbirth.''

Oxar said, ''Visit great kindness.''

Danlo did his best to wall off his sudden discomfort in the inner part of his mind. *Agree.* ''Kindness.''

As the hosteler and his wife turned away, she became indistinct. He strolled out of the dining room, one arm extended around the waist of the cloud, his head angled over as if resting on its shoulder.

The joddie took a noisy slurp of apple juice, scratched his earlobe, and reached for another walnut.

Danlo cast his mind in the direction of the kitchen. The cook was already up to her elbows in sudsy dishwater. He pushed back his chair. *Food get.* It was easy enough to fetch himself a sweet roll and a mug of tea. He brought them back to the table, sat, and spread his napkin.

As he was biting into the roll, Oxar returned to an earlier subject. ''Cleansing.'' *Odd.* ''Your wife Cleansed.''

He eyed Oxar calmly. *Thoughts leak? Sorry.*

''Not this morning. Remembering last time.''

Inquire details.

''Last year, in Sancruz. You had nightmares. Then claimed you hadn't. That looks good.''

"Peach jam filling," Danlo told him. A sip of tea. Then, noncommittally: "Nightmares."

Oxar shared a vision/skinsense of hands—Danlo's hands—covered with slimy, dripping green scum. Cold hands closing around a warm throat. "Funny thing. Got the idea you meant it." *About memory loss.* "Wondering. Guidance? Weakened?" *Desire to help.*

Which wouldn't do at all, not with a joddie less than twenty feet from their table. "Inconsequential." *Decline help. Thanks.*

Disagree. "You always go. Think you even plan our itinerary for it. We could have finished here two days ago, been in Bearsvill."

Danlo decided the conversation had gone far enough. He entered Oxar's mind far enough to stir up uncertainty and plant a greasy lump of reluctance. The smooth skin between Oxar's brows knitted; he pressed fingers against his temple and shook his head, trying to clear it.

"We'll be in Bearsvill tonight," Danlo said soothingly. "City banquets and city women. Coach leaving any minute. Packed?" *Efficiency.*

Danlo stole a glance at the joddie, who was leaning back in his chair, rocking slightly, fingers laced across his stomach, eyes closed, a smile playing at his lips. It seemed evident that the joddie was fully occupied keeping Margeth's after-death essence focused in the hosteler's private room, and had noticed nothing. Danlo couldn't be sure of this without kenning more deeply, but it was a bad idea, he felt, to peek into a joddie. It could easily attract attention. In theory, keeping a secret from a joddie was impossible. As the nursery rhyme put it, "They know when you've been sleeping, they know when you're awake. They know when you've been bad or good, so be good, for goodness' sake!" But in practice, there were simply too many thoughts among the Body of Harmony, and too few joddies to keep tabs on them all. The ktess was like the china cabinet in the middle of the dining room—open on both sides, every item in plain view, yet each sealed away from the others in its own little compartment. And I'm a pepper mill, he concluded, and Oxar here is a butter dish.

"Not sure I like that comparison," Oxar said.

Sorry.

The brass bell on the porch clanged mellifluously, announcing the impending departure of the southbound coach. Danlo and Oxar carried their dishes out to the kitchen and went upstairs for their bags. When they came down, the hosteler was back behind his high desk in the lobby, looking dreamy-eyed. "Trust the goodmen found the books of Woolich in good order."

"The best, goodman hosteler. Your counters are well trained, and your proctors admirably thorough."

"Stay with us next year?"

"With pleasure." Danlo inclined his head. *Luxurious. Bed very soft.*

"Wonderful cooking," Oxar added.

The rain had stopped, and the clouds were breaking up. The coach driver, a skinny little man of about sixty whose purple goatee curled outward like a playground slide, was helping the drab old woman climb into the vehicle. Danlo and Oxar stowed their baggage in the rear compartment and boarded. The coach was a twenty-seater, and sparsely occupied—only the old woman and the young couple from the dining room with their five-year-old. The boy was chattering restlessly, pointing at this and that and asking questions. The woman bounced him on her knee.

The husband stood and exchanged formal greetings with Danlo and Oxar. "Taud Makar. My wife Goody. And this is Keven." The little boy scooted down from his mother's lap and solemnly imitated his father's greeting, pressing his upraised right palm first against Danlo's and then against Oxar's. "Teacher," said Taud. "From Bearsvill. Been visiting Goody's sister in Snorr."

"Travelling counter," Danlo said. "From Serameno. Central Counting Office. Oxar is my rememberer."

The two feather-bedecked young men from the dining room entered the coach, chuckling about some joke. They greeted Danlo and Oxar and Taud Makar. A duplet, they shared the same name, Lef Ipiliki. Lef were waterworks inspectors on a tour of the southeastern aqueducts. They took seats near the back of the coach and went back to chuckling and murmuring, their heads bent together. The old woman had taken out her knitting. She admitted that her name was Oevah Cott, but seemed declined to share her background or her travel plans. Oevah was wearing the coarse brown frock of a vacuist, so her reticence was not surprising.

The driver boarded last, and greeted his passengers. His name, he said, was Walf—"Just Walf. Never had another name, never wanted one." Danlo marveled at Walf's curved purple goatee, which tapered to a point a good eight inches out from his chin. The mustache points extended up as well as out. The whole assemblage was held in place by hair thickener, so that it jerked and

quivered when Walf spoke. This effect seemed to delight him, for
he seldom shared silently. He babbled like a child as he set the
coach in motion, often half-turning his head to address his
passengers more directly. "Nice run here, if you've never been on
it. Been?" Without waiting for an answer: "Straight south
through Etter and Porvill. Right along the Bound Wall, for a
stretch. Nice view of chaos. Help you appreciate civilization. Said
you're a rememberer? Remember this run. Pretty stretch of
country, most of it. Nice roadside chapels. Maybe stop at a
couple."

The vehicle moved smoothly through the streets of Woolich,
and once past the edge of town sped up to a breathtaking forty
miles an hour. Danlo watched the countryside roll by. The
foothills rose and subsided so gently that the road seldom had need
to swing wide around their flanks; the coach labored up each slope
and glided whistling down the next. At the top of one rise he could
see the floor of the Serral Valley lying board-flat in the distance,
studded with farmsteads and articulated by a gridwork of fences
and irrigation ditches. To the left, the hills marched higher, and
further off massed the snow-clad crags of the Sernada. On both
sides of the road fields stretched out, some fallow, some bare, a
few already sprouting young winter crops, row upon row of green.
Small, widely scattered bands of workers clustered at the pumping
stations, or followed like seagulls in the wake of the great farm
machines. Plowing and planting, the eternal rhythms of civilization. Danlo felt comforted. Why had he thought of walking away
into the wilderness to die? He was sure he could remember if he
tried, but he didn't feel like trying.

This was his first trip to the snug little communities between
Vaylia and the Sernada. The Central Counting Office sent him out
for several months each year to inspect the books of the local
counters in one region or another. What he learned he passed on
to a rememberer, Oxar or another, who stored it effortlessly
without needing to understand it and carried it back to Serameno
in his head. The ktess did not transmit statistical information
reliably over distances, so the travelling counters and rememberers
were as important, in their humble way, to the continued health of
the Body as the joddies. If too many almonds were being grown in
the north and too many grapes in the south, it was the counters
who must determine the fact, who must order up extra trucks and
the throwing wide of storehouse doors. If too many teachers were

being trained, and not enough dentists, the counters alerted the
Body to guide some teachers into dentistry.

Danlo had seen the whole world in his travels, not only the
carefully tended gardens of the Serral Valley itself but what lay
beyond. He had stood at the river bank in Porlin and looked across
at the brooding expanse of the Northern Forest. He had watched
from a bluff north of Saffersisko as the fishing boats passed out
from the bay into the endless gray of the Passing Ocean. And this
year, before he turned north again, he would catch a glimpse of the
desolate sands of the Mavi Desert.

As the driver had predicted, they reached a point where the
cultivated land actually ended a quarter of a mile from the road.
The ancient stone wall called the Bound Wall, which marked the
edge of civilization, cut across the crest of the nearest hill and ran
southward, more or less parallel to the road, like an immense
snake with neither head nor tail. Where the road was low and the
wall running along a hill, the wall seemed a comfortingly solid
barrier. At other spots the road ran higher and the wall dipped, so
that the land beyond lay spread out in plain view, bristling with
brush and rough outcrops of bare rock. The wall seemed a flimsy
thing then. Chaos itself lapped against it the way the ocean
battered a cliff. Here and there the overhanging branches of wild
trees reached out across it, neatly pruned only at the point where
they would actually have intruded into humanity's domain. Danlo
had read old accounts in which the labor of clearing the land
immediately beyond the wall was undertaken as part of the
maintenance of the wall itself. In this region, at least, nobody had
set foot out there for a long time.

"What's that, Mommy?" Keven pointed out the window at the
untamed landscape. "What's that stuff out there?"

"Hush. Hush. Nothing for you to worry about." Goody Makar
caught at her son's hand and gathered it against his side.

Danlo was charmed by the little boy. He wished he and Julan
had had children. But what if they had proved to be nulls? Would
he have been able to withstand the same pain again? No, he was
better off without children. All the same, he got pleasure from
watching and talking to them. He enjoyed, vicariously, the
spontaneous wildness, the secretiveness, even the open defiance.
We're all like that when we're young, he reflected. We enjoy it for
as long as we can.

Oxar was gazing out the window with a rememberer's blank
attention. Danlo wondered now whether he had made a mistake in

joining Oxar to get him off the subject of the Cleansing. It was another incident that Oxar might notice. Joining another's mind in order to exert influence was a far worse infraction than shirking. And it was getting to be a habit with Danlo. He was amazed that he had never been caught. As usual, he tried to justify the action by telling himself that he had never joined anybody for personal gain, or for pleasure, only in order to get them to leave him alone. But the justification was wearing thin. Joining was joining; there were no excuses. Only joddies were permitted to bend others' will. Their training assured that they would not misuse the power, only wield it in the best interest of the Body.

Danlo knew his ktess was stronger than most. At sixteen he had been considered for the Joddirate, but he was judged too willful and intractable, and he had a skill with numbers that was needed. He guessed that his aptitude for joining was unusual, but since joining was forbidden, no tabulation was kept of how many could do it, or how well. Joining Oxar had definitely been a mistake; in the inner chamber of his mind, he cautioned himself not to do it again.

The driver broke into his reverie. "You're a counter. You like that sort of fiddly indoor work?" He glanced back at Danlo. With every word, the exotic goatee bobbed in and out, and the points of the mustache described little circles in the air.

Pleasure. "Enjoy putting things in order."

"Me, rather be out roamin' around. Know what you mean about order, though. That over there—" The driver gestured at the land beyond the wall. "—that wants puttin' in order. Hate this stretch of road. Always have to look out at the mess. Don't know why we don't clean it up. Move the wall back. Or just tear it down. Not much use. Seen a lion come right over the top, once."

"There's a reason why the size of the world is fixed, goodman." Danlo was not surprised that a coach driver wouldn't know this tidbit of ancient history. He himself wouldn't have known it if his father, a history buff, hadn't enjoyed rattling off such facts to anybody who could be induced to listen. "There came a time, six hundred years ago, when the Body of Harmony grew to a hundred million people. We spread much further east than we do today, and north and south. Today we understand the value of stability and good fellowship, but in those days external monuments and achievements were thought highly of. And of course the most obvious form of achievement is numerical growth. In the end, we spread so widely that the contact among the joddies that forms the One began to grow confused. There were misunderstandings, and strife. Neighbor mistrusted neighbor."

The driver's face paled as he contemplated this awful thing.

"The Joddirate saw that if we continued to grow, the Body would soon split into two, or even more, smaller Bodies. We would no longer be One."

"And that'd lead right back to the Time of Chaos!"

Firm grasp. "So the birth rate was reduced until the Body shrank to its present size. The Bound Wall was built less to keep wild animals out than to remind us of how large it's safe to grow."

"Thought it was because we were running short of water," said one of the interchangeable waterworks inspectors.

"That could have had something to do with it too," Danlo conceded.

"Had to go out one time," the waterworks man said. "Team to repair one of those big old reservoirs in the mountains." "Spooky place," the other one put in. "Dead leaves all over everything." "And animals living in the station. Thought we'd never get back." They shared a vision of a heavy tree trunk fallen across a narrow, pitted road. "Ought to let all the rivers run free down into the valley, say we. Take care of the dams easier."

"Put too much good farmland under water," Taud Makar said.

"Just the same. Scary out there."

They rode along in companionable silence for some time. The driver opened a window, and cool air bathed them. Danlo kept an eye on the wall, fascinated by the way it dipped closer to the road, then receded, then approached again. The sun had broken through the clouds, and it cast ragged patches of gold across the fields.

A sudden surge of alarm crackled through the ktess. They all sat up straighter and looked around wildly. The little boy, unsure what had caused the stir, looked apprehensively at the faces of the adults. Danlo's palms were damp, and his heart raced. "Where? Where?" the driver cried. "What direction?" The coach rolled down another hill. The land ahead lay deserted. A leafless orchard stood between the empty road and the wall, and Danlo lowered the window and peered out into the trees. Something large and shapeless moved among the skeletal tracery of branches, and five or six small dark birds sprang up and wheeled away. He put his hand on the driver's shoulder. "There."

"Only birds," Oxar said.

The sense of panic grew stronger, and confused visual scraps fluttered around it—men swinging hoes, and other things that made no sense. At the bottom of the hill the coach passed the edge of the orchard, just as a field worker in blue coveralls broke from the cover of the trees and ran toward the road. The driver braked. Two weirdly dressed people ran after the field worker, seized him by the shoulders, and bore him to the ground. He shook them off and regained his feet, and again they attached themselves to him. The three spun about as if they were dancing. A dozen more workers were gathered in a loose clump near the edge of the trees. Several of them had fallen to their hands and knees, but others were still standing, hoes raised high or jabbing outward. Facing the workers was a large group of weirdly dressed people. Some of these were holding the ends of long poles in their mouths, and others were swinging hoes of their own. The weirdly dressed people actually seemed to be partially naked, and their hair was appallingly disarrayed.

Shouting came thinly through the open window of the coach, and the clatter of wooden implements striking one another. The ktess boiled with a panicky impression of drowning. The coach jerked to a halt and the doors hummed open. Danlo was first down the steps, but he could ken Oxar and the other men close behind him. He set out toward the altercation at top speed, long legs pumping. The field was freshly plowed and muddy, and he ran awkwardly between the rows of green shoots, his cloak flapping out behind him.

Chapter ‖ 3

THE women had left their homes and children in the spring, and they had walked all summer and into the fall. Now it was winter, and they were still walking. In all that time, they had not found what they were looking for. Linnie wondered sometimes if they ever would. She was sure the other women thought about it, but nobody said anything. She wondered about other things too. The world through which they walked was richly various, yet underneath the changes were things that didn't change. Linnie uncovered those things and turned them over in her mind while she walked. The world, she had learned, was very big, and it was empty, and large parts of it were very dry.

Big meant you had to walk and walk. At home Linnie spent as

much time paddling a canoe as she did walking, but she didn't mind walking. At least, she hadn't minded until she hurt her leg. Walking was painful now, but she was afraid that if she slowed the others up they would leave her, so she gritted her teeth and kept at it. Big was frightening, because she felt in her bones how small she was. But big was wonderful too, because there was always more to see—new kinds of game, stands of unfamiliar trees, exotic, brightly colored bugs that buzzed around the bushes, the shades and consistencies of the soil itself.

Dry was very strange. It parched the skin and cracked the lips, and from horizon to dusty horizon there was no place to plunge in for a swim. In the bayous where Linnie had grown up, the land was an uncertain, temporary thing. A sandbar might be swept away in a storm, and a new one appear further along the channel. The channel itself might give a convulsive shake, like a great snake waking, and seek out a new bed across what had been hard-packed ground. Walking among the vines and creepers, you might stumble into a sinkhole and emerge dripping mud.

In the absence of water, the land stood very still. Or maybe the land was dry, Linnie speculated, because it was too high for the water, which ran away so fast that it leaped from the rocks and crashed into foam far below. In some places the land was very high indeed. She felt a little chill when she looked at the masses of stone marching huge and blue across the horizon. The land heaved itself up, cold and hard, in teeth and spines so high that the belly of Night Sky Mother must surely scrape them every night as She swam across. They had no name for the high places, but Agrom ruminated, and after a while nodded her gray head and said she remembered: The old world for those places was "mountain," because the land was mounting itself, like a pair of pigs in rut.

One mountain was belching fire and smoke. The women understood at once that the fire was coming from one of the tunnels carved out by Uncle Gnaws-at-Rock. The whole world was riddled with such tunnels, like an anthill. One day soon, unless Uncle Fire Spider defeated Uncle Gnaws-at-Rock in their terrible underground war, the ground itself would crack and clatter into rubble, and all the water would be swallowed up. Thinking about the tunnels beneath her feet made Linnie dizzy. The fire must mean that an especially fierce battle was raging beneath the mountain. The women chose a route that gave the fire mountain a wide berth.

Big and dry were difficult, beautiful, strange, sometimes frightening. Empty was sad. In many of the valleys were scattered rows of mounds that showed where the ancestors had lived. Once, the ancestors must have swarmed across the world as thick as bees. But of living tribes the women found not a trace. Twice a small party went up one of the mountains and looked out in every direction as far as they could see, while the rest camped below and made new moccasins and arrows and skin bags for carrying water. When the looking party came back down they shook their heads, and the next morning the fires were put out and the journey began again.

Sometimes as she walked along, Linnie talked to Grampa Gator. "I ain't so sure we're doin' the right thing, Gramps," she said. "Maybe we oughta just turn around and go home." She could see Grampa Gator if she closed her eyes, smiling his toothy smile, lying patiently in the mud. Grampa Gator was old and strong and wise. He could turn mean too, but only if he wasn't treated right. "I don't mean give up—I know we gotta stop Uncle Fire Spider *somehow* from stealin' our men. And I don't know no other way to do it, so maybe this is the best we can do. But even so. I reckon I wouldn't like it if some other woman, or bunch of women, come along and took my man. It wouldn't much matter what they meant to do with him, whether they was aimin' to send him down underground to fight in some war, or whether they just wanted to make a husband out of him. I kinda wonder—if there's more happiness in the world after you do somethin', then maybe it's the right thing to do, and if there's more unhappiness then maybe it ain't the right thing. Even if we do find us some men, and it sure don't look like we're goin' to, and even if we can get 'em home in one piece, and even if it *works* givin' 'em to Uncle Fire Spider, so he leaves our own menfolk alone for a spell, why then we're still tradin' one bunch of unhappiness for another bunch. And what if it don't work? What if Uncle Fire Spider takes 'em and then just comes back for more? I don't know if I could hold my head up after that, knowin' what I done to that other poor woman."

She didn't talk to Grampa Gator out loud. She didn't want the other women to hear. Most of them were children of Grampa Coon, or Grampa Magpie, or Grampa Houn-Dog—or their husbands were, which was the same thing. Were or had been. Linnie's husband had been a child of Grampa Coon too, but after Uncle Fire Spider stole him away Linnie went back to talking to Grampa Gator, as she had when she was a little girl. She figured

Grampa Coon had let Makelvy die, so she wasn't going to have any more to do with Grampa Coon than she had to to keep the other women from spitting at her. She sang to Grampa Coon before they went hunting, but inside she was singing to Grampa Gator. Grampa Gator had let some men die too, including Linnie's pa; she tried not to think about that. Uncle Fire Spider came and stole away their dreams, and after a while they got so weak they could hardly stand up any more, and then they lay down and died.

It was getting so there weren't hardly any men left in Ranoima at all. The ones that were left had their pick of the women. They took seven or eight wives each, some of them, instead of two or three. And they couldn't be bothered to do any work. They lazed around in the shade all day, making lewd suggestions and demanding to be fed, while the women took on more and more of the hunting and canoe-building and house-building right along with the gardening and child-raising. Uncle Fire Spider had been stealing men for as long as anybody could remember, a few at a time, and the women had adapted. Linnie learned from her mother how to hunt and do other things that had used to be men's work. But in the last few years, Uncle Fire Spider had needed a lot more warriors for his war with Uncle Gnaws-at-Rock, and the number of healthy men had dwindled. Even those with wives were too weak to have sex with them, so there were hardly any babies born. Boys too young for sex were being married to households full of women, and getting sick and dying without ever making any children of their own.

It was the same in most of the villages around the mouth of the River of Missopy, though worse in some villages than others. Ranoima was not only the largest village but the hardest hit. At the beginning, Linnie's grandmother had told her, women tried enticing away the men of other villages by promising special favors. As the shortage grew worse, some tried husband-stealing. But the husbands generally ran off as soon as they were untied. Some of the women blinded their new husbands to keep them from running off. This worked, but a blinded husband was worse in some ways than no husband at all.

A group of women went to Nurm, who kept the poles for the dances to Night Sky Mother. They asked her to ask Night Sky Mother for a sign telling them what they should do. That night, Night Sky Mother came to Nurm in a dream. Nurm had no trouble convincing the women that Night Sky Mother had shown the path that they must walk; the hard part was convincing them that some must stay in Ranoima to look after the children, and the gardens, and the remaining men. All the women clamored to come. Linnie had no children, and Makelvy was dead, so she had no need to stay behind. After three nights of solemn prayers to Night Sky Mother, those who were chosen set off. They strode through the middle of the village in a ragged marching column, wearing their best leather vests and knee-length trousers, carrying bows and arrows and blowguns, packs on their backs stuffed with blankets and rock salt and cooking utensils and little pots of green body-paint. Ten tens of women marched behind Nurm, and another five tens besides. Those who were staying behind sat on the housetops and waved and whistled.

But the longer they traveled without finding men, the more dispirited they grew. Linnie was very tired of walking. Two months had passed since she twisted her leg climbing down an embankment, and she was beginning to think it was never going to heal right. It hurt when she tried to go fast, and at night it throbbed so badly she couldn't sleep. The other women must be tired too, but they were too stubborn to say so.

"I been thinkin'," she said one afternoon. She was walking with Terana and Big Awa, a little apart from the main group. They were headed northwest, down the center of a wide green valley. The valley was dotted with clumps of trees, but mostly it was open grassland. Herds of cattle and horse grazed. When the women skirted the edge of a herd, it moved away from them reluctantly, parting like water before the prow of a canoe.

"Thinkin' what?" Big Awa shifted the wicker bag to her other shoulder. Big Awa had shoulders and a jaw like a man's, and a roll of fat around her middle that the walking had hardened but failed to burn off.

"All this country," Linnie said. "We come all this way, and we ain't seen nobody."

"Yeah? So?"

"So maybe there's nobody to see. Maybe not anywhere."

Big Awa growled and raised a fist as if to strike her, but Big Awa was encumbered with the bag, and Linnie easily hopped out of reach. She ignored the stabbing pain in her knee. "I don't want to hear that kind of crap," Big Awa said. "It's hard enough keepin' on all this time, and carryin' *your* share—" She patted the bag with her free hand. "—without you make it harder by whinin' about it." The bag held the cups and bowls from which the men would be fed, when they found men.

"You was thinkin' the same thing," Linnie said.

"I was not."

"We'll find us some men," Terana said softly. "I just know we will." Her eyes narrowed to slits in the smooth roundness of her face, and her fingers brushed her lips.

"Be too late for you," Linnie said. Then she was sorry she had said it. "If we found 'em tomorrow," she went on, "and ran 'em all the way home, it'd be too late for half the women here. Maybe not for you." Terana's husband had still been alive last spring, when the women set out. Uncle Fire Spider had already started stealing his dreams, though.

Linnie liked walking with Terana. Terana was sweet and serious, and she always looked for the good in things. Ever since Makelvy died, Linnie had had trouble seeing the good in things. After Linnie twisted her leg, when it hurt so bad she could hardly walk, Terana helped her keep up. And now she was repaying Terana by being cruel. It was true, though, about it being too late. Tears were leaking out between Terana's long feathery lashes and streaking her cheeks, so Linnie put her arm around her and they walked on side by side, hips bumping. "I didn't mean it," Linnie said. She wondered whether they would all go on like this for the rest of their lives, getting further and further from home, or whether even Terana would one day give up hope.

"I just know there's some men out here," Big Awa said. "I can smell 'em. What I want to know is where they are. You tell me where they're hidin', and I'll walk there on my eyebrows." She glared at Linnie, as if challenging Linnie to doubt her determination.

The valley narrowed at its northern end, and they struck off to the west through a series of hilly passes. Three days later, the last of these opened out on what must have been the largest ancestor place in the world, mile upon endless mile of grassy hummocks and treacherous hollows in irregular but obviously unnatural patterns. In the distance a broad, flat, featureless plain gleamed green and gray. It was an ocean. Gulls wheeled, and the breeze was salty.

They all walked a little quieter among the mounds and ridges, feeling that the ancestors were very near. Nobody wanted to make camp in the midst of the ancestor place, for fear the ancestors would trouble their dreams, but night fell and they still hadn't reached the far edge, so they built a roaring fire and sat close around it, singing songs until very late under a cold clear moon.

When no unquiet spirits disturbed them that night, Nurm decreed that they would rest here for a day or two. A hunting party set out and easily brought down three deer and tens of fat quail, on which they feasted. Sapvod and Garvod, who were twins and often urged one another on to feats of daring, boldly dug into the hummock nearest the camp in search of talismans left by the ancestors. They found no talismans, but they did tug free a big, thin sheet of shiny stuff. The sun shone through it, but dim and confused, as if it were agate or cloudy water. The sheet sprang back with a shuddery floppy noise when they bent it and let go, until the fifth or sixth time, when it snapped in half. Little Awa made a story about how the ancestors had sat on sheets of shiny stuff and flown through the air, and everybody laughed except Big Awa, who chased Little Awa and tried to cuff her.

The ancestor places around Ranoima had mostly been washed away over the years by the River of Missopy, but here only a thin layer of dirt had accumulated. Linnie wondered why Night Sky Mother had chosen to send the ancestors so many powerful dreams. The dreams that came to her own people were vague and jumbled. On the other hand, the ancestors' dreams had dried up. The ways of the Great Ones were perplexing.

Linnie waited until she saw Nurm sitting alone, and went and sat beside her. Nurm pretended to be busy tightening the wrapping on an arrowhead. Nurm was a small woman, with black curly hair and a broad flat nose. Her hands were quick, and her eyes flashed often with eagerness or anger.

Linnie scuffed her toes idly in the dirt. "How much further you reckon we gonna go?"

Nurm looked at her coldly. "Awa said you was wantin' to turn back. That kinda talk don't do nobody no good."

"Can you think of anything that *is* gonna do any good? I'd like to hear about it. And I'm sure I ain't the only one."

"Night Sky Mother *promised* us we was gonna find some men. You tellin' me you think She breaks her promises?"

What Linnie thought was that maybe Night Sky Mother had never come to Nurm in a dream at all. But she couldn't say that without starting a fight. "Maybe it's us," she said. "Maybe She was tryin' to help us, but we gone off the wrong way. Maybe we oughta ask Her what direction to go now. And if She says go back the way we come, I don't reckon there's any shame in it. We can't go no further that way." Linnie waved her hand at the ocean. "I think we oughta ask Her. And I think whoever gets the dream, and whatever the dream says, we ought to mind it real close.''

"Even if it's you that gets the dream?''

"I think Night Sky Mother knows us,'' Linnie said carefully. "I think She knows it'd only cause trouble if She sent the dream to me. I expect probably She'll send it to somebody that everybody will listen to. Or most everybody.''

"And if the dream says to keep on, you won't talk no more about turnin' back?''

"Let's wait and see what the dream says.''

At nightfall Nurm brought out her sacred whistle and painted sticks, and summoned Night Sky Mother. In a long, rambling invocation she reminded Night Sky Mother how far they had travelled, and why. She begged Night Sky Mother to come to them in their dreams and tell them which way to go, now that they had reached a new ocean. She asked Night Sky Mother to visit the women who remained in Ranoima and assure them that their sisters had not abandoned the quest. She asked Night Sky Mother to call on Uncle Fire Spider, who could surely use more strong warriors. Nurm grasped her hair in both hands and tilted back her head and shouted at the stars, and all the women shouted along with her.

In the morning, five women reported dreams in which Night Sky Mother stood before them in the north, beckoning them. The five were all Nurm's close friends, but Linnie judged it best to say nothing.

The mountains in the north were not as high or steep as the ones they had crossed during the summer. The northward pass was marked out by a series of broad, smooth ramps cut into the sides of the mountains. Following these saved them the trouble of climbing up and down the steep places. The presence of the ramps was encouraging, because the ancestors must have gone to the enormous trouble of building them for some good reason. It seemed likely that the ramps must lead somewhere, not just into a blind canyon. The mountains were thickly cloaked in stands of ancient pine, so the walking was easy except where berry thickets clogged the slopes.

On the second day they were halted before nightfall by a kind of rain they had never seen before. Instead of pouring down it drifted, white and powdery and very cold. It turned the distant tree trunks ghostly, and swiftly carpeted the forest floor. Linnie thought it was the most beautiful thing she had ever seen. The women built fires, but crowding close to these was not enough to keep them warm. Linnie and Terana shared their blankets and bundled together, and most of the others found partners too. Terana snuggled down to sleep, but Linnie propped her head up on one elbow, wrapped in the warm cocoon, and watched in the failing light as the white rain whispered gracefully down in the somber gloom among the trees.

Chapter ‖ 4

DAWN revealed a forest transformed to blue-white crystal. The boughs of the trees drooped with their burden of powder, and it crunched ankle-deep underfoot. The women's breath steamed. They blew on their hands and rubbed them together, and swung their arms and hugged themselves. As soon as the blankets were rolled and the fires put out, the whole party set off briskly through the trees. Linnie was thirsty, so she bent to scoop up a handful of the rain powder. It stung her lips and tongue with cold, but it tasted crisp and wonderful, like solid air. They came across fresh tracks of fox and deer pressed delicately into the white carpet. The carpet melted to mud in the places where the sun reached, but lingered all day beneath the trees.

The next afternoon they arrived at the crest of a ridge that overlooked the southern end of a wide valley. The valley stretched north to the horizon, as flat as a lake. Though the air at this height was clear, the valley was swathed in a low veil of haze. Through the haze a pattern of markings swam up, dark lines and indistinct blocks of color. Another ancestor place, Linnie thought. But the pattern was on the surface, not buried. The women looked at one another. They shuffled their feet and licked their lips, shaded their eyes with their hands, and squinted down into the valley. Big Awa lifted her nose and sniffed. "Smoke," she announced. She sniffed some more. "Could be cooking smoke."

The weight of the months of isolation fell from them like a lump of frozen rain dropping from a tree. The women squealed and whooped, startling a flock of gray-brown birds, which boiled up in a cloud from a nearby copse. Nurm stormed among the women, grabbing and shaking elbows. "Shut up, damn you. Shut up! You want they should see us?"

"Who cares?" Tears were running down Terana's face. "If they see us, they'll send out warriors!"

"So you think you can get the best of a warrior," Nurm rasped. "Maybe two or three, all by yourself. Just strip off your pants, and while they're busy you hit 'em on the head with a rock." Terana blushed. Nurm turned her head and spat. "It ain't that easy. We gotta do this right."

Linnie stood a little apart, smiling and fighting tears. She was ashamed that she had doubted Nurm, and frightened of what might happen when they tried to steal some men, and most of all she wanted to cry. She remembered how she had sung to Makelvy, cradling his head beneath her breasts and stroking his hair as if he were a child, how she had promised him that one day, when he was stronger, they would run away together, that she wouldn't care if they had so little they had to eat from the same bowl. But he never got stronger. Even if Uncle Fire Spider defeated Uncle Gnaws-at-Rock with the new warriors, so that he never had to come to Ranoima to gather any more, nothing was going to bring Makelvy back.

Nurm herded the women back beneath the shelter of the trees. They descended into the valley in single file, ignoring the last long straight ramp of the ancestors in favor of a steeper route that offered better cover. They spoke in signs and whispers, and nudged one another and stifled giggles, and fingered their bows and blowguns.

The valley looked like nothing so much as a single huge garden planted with a very, very sharp stick and tended by somebody who could keep at it night and day without ever stopping to cook or clean or run after the children. Linnie was avid for a closer look, but Nurm insisted that they stay hidden until they learned more. Expecting to see villages of thatched huts on stilts, like those in the swamps at home, they were perplexed by the orderly array of fields dotted with sparse clusters of low buildings, and by the stone wall, too tall to leap over but easy enough to climb, that separated the fields from the wild land. They stayed on the wild side of the wall and followed it east and north, hiding among the trees and gullies but keeping the wall in view. A small party crept right up to the wall one afternoon and peered over, but they came back shrugging and scratching their heads. They couldn't even agree about what they had seen.

In the distance, on the other side of the wall, small groups of people moved about in the fields. Some of them were tending animals, but others tended huge, impossible things, like houses that moved. None of the locals ever came over to this side of the wall, which was odd, because the hunting certainly didn't look good on the other side. The women debated in low voices as they marched. One faction was of the opinion that the people in this land were such great shamans that they could charm animals to go to them and lie down to be slaughtered. Another faction held that the party had stumbled upon the Land of Always Spring Blossoms itself, that the figures beyond the wall were not living people but the spirits of the dead, who were nourished entirely on frogs and honey. Either way, it wouldn't do to rush into a raid without working out a plan.

"I say we pick ourselves a village, one of them small ones off by itself, and sneak up on it at night." Sandu paced up and down by the campfire, fingering the handle of her knife. Sandu had conducted two husband-raids out of Ranoima, and was a skilled hunter. She kept her hair hacked off short, claiming it would give anybody who fought her less to grab. "We can round up all the men we need, easy, and move 'em out before dawn."

"That won't work." Nurm poked at the fire with a stick, and sparks spiraled upward to mingle with the stars. "Them small villages don't even have a hundred men, probably, and plenty of them too old or sick, or so mean we'd have to kill 'em."

"So if there ain't enough, we hit another village."

"You're not thinkin'. If we hit 'em in the dark, we can't spot everybody that tries to run off. If we do spot 'em, we can't see good enough to shoot 'em down. So somebody's bound to get away to the next village, and then they'll be watchin' out for us."

"Then let's hit 'em in the daytime." Big Awa pounded her fist into her other palm. "Nobody gets away."

Linnie didn't like the murmur of approval that greeted Big Awa's proposal. As it died away, she said quietly but firmly, "You think Grampa Houn-Dog is gonna like lappin' up all that blood?"

"You hush up about Grampa Houn-Dog," Big Awa said, scowling.

"You two want to fight," Nurm said, "you fight later. Right now I'm thinkin', why get 'em on our scent? Why not fix it so every village thinks we come from the next village?" The women nodded at one another, eyes glinting, faces red and yellow in the firelight. "You've seen how they go out in little bunches, how they root around in the dirt all day like sows. Say we watch until we spot a bunch like that up close to the wall. We move in and take 'em.'' Somebody in the crowd blew three quick puffs into her fist, the sound of a blowgun. There was scattered laughter. ''Then we move on, find another bunch, and do the same thing. They'll never know where we come from, or where we gone.''

''But they'll be huntin' us,'' Sandu said. ''You bet they'll be huntin'. We better not double back on our own trail, not after we start pickin' 'em off. I say we move up north a ways and take the first bunch there. Then we can come back this way, take another bunch, then maybe a third bunch if we need to. After every raid we can leave just a few of us to guard the blinded ones while the rest go in for more.''

''As many of us as there are,'' Agrom said, taking in the crowd with a broad wave of her arm, ''comin' down out of the hills all at once, they don't have to be great shamans to see us comin'. They don't even have to be awake. And we'll beat a trail through the brush that a baby could follow. I reckon we're gonna have to split up. Maybe three tens of us to run down every ten or twelve of them. Then we arrange where we'll meet afterward.''

''We'll have to build a pen to hold 'em,'' Nurm said. ''Like a hog run, but with a taller fence around it.''

A chorus of groans. ''What for?''

''Some of us are goin' to have to travel further than others. Maybe days further, 'til we find the right ambush. Them that gets back to the meeting place first will have to stand guard night and day while they wait for the rest to come back. It'll be a sight easier if the men are penned up.''

''I don't like what I'm hearin','' Sandu said. ''I'd rather go out in one big raid. I want somebody watchin' my back. But even if we do split up, we don't need a pen. We just blind 'em as quick as we catch 'em, and a little hobble'll hold 'em fine.''

''No,'' Nurm said firmly.

''Why not?'' Sandu looked exasperated.

''You're forgettin'. They have to be able to see when they're joined in the blood of Uncle Fire Spider. And I'm the only one can do that.'' Due to the extraordinary circumstances, Nurm had been initiated as a male, so that she could initiate other men. ''You think Uncle wants blinded warriors? Once they been through the ceremony, *then* we can poke their eyes out. Not before.''

''They'll still be blind when they get down underground,'' Linnie said under her breath. She and Terana were sitting shoulder to shoulder in the row nearest the fire.

Terana looked at her disapprovingly. "How else are we supposed to get 'em home?"

"I don't know. All I know is, I don't like it." Linnie figured it was better to let Ranoima be swallowed by the swamp than to put men's eyes out, but she knew Terana wouldn't understand. "What if we get 'em home and Uncle Fire Spider don't want 'em?" she persisted. "Then we got a bunch of blinded men on our hands. They sure won't be no good as husbands."

Linnie stopped abruptly. Sandu was standing over her, fists on hips. "You sayin' we shouldn't oughta blind 'em?"

"I ain't sayin' we shouldn't do it. I'm just sayin' I don't like it."

"You want to be the one to stand guard over a bunch of 'em, maybe you and Agrom and Little Awa all by yourselves, and them not blinded, while the rest of us go back for more?"

"Nah." Linnie could see that Sandu was spoiling for a fight. She didn't much care. "Let's blind 'em right away," she said, "before they get a good look at you. Later on we might want they should still be able to get their peckers up."

The color drained from Sandu's face. "Best you hope you don't hurt your other leg," she said. "Take you a long time to *crawl* home." She turned to the crowd. "Is there anybody else thinks like this gator belly here—thinks we shouldn't blind 'em? You best say so now. We don't need no trouble later on."

The women stirred restlessly. Nobody said anything.

"All right, then." Sandu turned to Nurm. "I still don't like it. You pen a man up, you make him crazy. But if we want Uncle to take 'em, I reckon we got to do it right."

The women travelled north for another half a moon with the wall on their left hand and the mountains at their right. A layer of white, most likely more of the cold rain powder, cloaked the mountains. Sometimes they could see a low line of hills way off in the west: Evidently the valley ran north and south without ever widening out into a plain. They started calling it the Land of Moving Houses, because of the big things that slid across the land, like covered boats. Linnie wished she could slide across the land in a covered boat, preferably one with a cozy fire inside and maybe a big bowl of fresh fruit and a husband to rub her feet.

When Nurm judged that they were far enough north, they left the wall and went deeper into the hills, to find a place that was well hidden. After some searching they found a narrow, boulder-strewn canyon in which a pen could easily be built using the rocks themselves for much of the enclosure. The mouth of the canyon was screened by trees, and the slopes on both sides were steep. At the inner end of the canyon a deep grotto yawned beneath a ledge. This would serve to shield the men's initiation from the eyes of Night Sky Mother, who of course was ignorant of men's mysteries.

They cut wood for the pen at a distance, not close by, because of the danger that trackers would be able to find their hideaway by spotting the felled trees. The hardest part was fastening the logs together. The grasses in this land made only the most inferior sort of rope; even a thick braid parted easily under a bit of tugging. They had to wrap the joints with green saplings and vine.

When the pen was finished, two of the women went inside and tried to batter down the fence. It creaked and swayed, but held firm. "I could get out," Big Awa boasted. Probably she was right. But the men would be weak from the lek-tapru, and bound hand and foot, and guarded. The pen would hold them for a day or two.

Agrom mixed the lek-tapru, pounding a pestle into a bowl between her spread legs, old breasts swaying low above the brown mash. Each of the blowgun hunters dipped three darts in the bowl, laid them side by side on a broad leaf, and blew on them while they dried. Several of the others mixed body-paint, and they all worked far into the night decorating one another's faces and arms and bodies with fanciful swirls and twined vines of green. Linnie drew a single curving line from the sole of one foot up and around her legs and torso, up her neck, across her forehead, and back down to the sole of the other foot. Terana helped where the line crossed her back and face.

Nurm divided them into five raiding parties. Linnie was assigned to the group led by Sandu and Big Awa; with them went Agrom and Terana and Little Awa, and more than twenty others. For two days they walked west, up and down slopes slick with mud. Rain, the ordinary kind but almost as cold as the white kind, whipped down intermittently, leaving them chilled and miserable.

On the third morning only a few drops were still spattering down. They reapplied their body-paint before setting out. By the time they saw the wall ahead, the cloud cover had begun to break up, letting great gouts of sunlight pour down. The fields on the other side of the wall looked so smooth and peaceful that Linnie yearned to run as fast as she could and clamber over the wall before the others could stop her, and go down into the Land of Moving Houses. Surely the people there would make her welcome. I will carry wood, she said to herself. I will eat scraps from

a man's bowl. But with her bad leg she could barely outrun
Agrom, let alone Sandu. They would kill her rather than let her
raise an alarm. So she unlimbered her bow, and stayed among
them, and said nothing.

They ranged along the wall, reluctant to go beyond it because of
the scarcity of cover on the other side. Toward midday they
spotted a group of men in a field, a dozen of them working less
than a stone's throw from the wall. The women crouched and crept
forward with great stealth, and reached the wall without being
noticed. Standing on tiptoe and using hand-signs, the blowgun
hunters began selecting who would shoot at which of the men.
Little Awa had no blowgun, but she peeked over anyway. "No,
no, no," she whispered. Sandu glared at her, but she shook her
head furiously and would not be quieted. "Not enough skin!"

Big Awa risked a long look, after which she nodded heavily.
Linnie looked too. Little Awa was right. The men were clothed
from head to toe. Whether the garments were thin enough for the
darts to penetrate was impossible to tell. Sandu outlined a strategy
using whispers and hand-signals. They would fire once and wait to
see how well the lek-tapru worked. If the men started to move
away, the women would go over the wall in a rush. Bedrolls were
shucked off and gathered in a tidy heap, along with the bows and
the food bowls. Linnie and Agrom and a couple of others kept
their bows. They would stand to one side and shoot anybody who
tried to run.

At a signal, the blowgun hunters raised their heads above the
wall, fitted blowguns to lips, and fired. No cries of alarm went up.
The hunters ducked down. "They'll think it's bee stings," Terana
whispered to Linnie, beaming a broad grin through the green
spirals on her cheek.

The lek-tapru would work quickly, if it worked. Most of the
hunters cast aside their blowguns, but each of them drew out two
more darts, holding the tiny feathered things with great care so as
not to prick themselves.

When Sandu poked her head up, she rolled her eyes in disgust,
and jerked a thumb. Then it was up and over the wall, down the
other side, and forward in a mad rush. Only two of the men had
fallen, and these were not lying still but moving groggily on their
hands and knees. The women ran silently and in dead earnest;
Linnie followed along as best she could, an arrow nocked.

The men had gathered around those who had fallen, and looked
up only when the women were nearly upon them. Big Awa let out

a whoop and slapped a dart into the nearest man's neck. He grappled with her. Little Awa went in lower and jerked at another man's shirt to get at his belly. It was easier than they had feared; these men did not seem to be warriors. They were not armed even with knives, only with long-handled digging sticks. Several swung the digging sticks at the women, but half-heartedly. Others only held the sticks before them to push the women away. The women dodged easily, or knocked the sticks aside. As the men pushed and kicked, they cried out words that did not sound like any words Linnie knew.

The lek-tapru needed time to act. The women outnumbered the men by two to one, but they were not as large or strong. The hunters had to strike with their darts and twist away again without being caught or hit. Linnie tried to tally which of the men had been stuck with the darts and which hadn't. Three darts of the lek-tapru were enough to kill. But she quickly lost track: The men all looked alike to her, and they were milling around. One man tried to run, and Linnie drew her bow, but Sapvod and Garvod ran after him and leaped on him and bore him on the ground.

One of the moving houses slowed and stopped at the foot of the slope. Five more men popped out of it, one after another, and ran toward the melee. The one in front looked so much like a great ungainly bird, with his long legs and the dark cape flapping behind him, that Linnie laughed aloud. The newcomers did not seem to be armed, so she held her arrow. The hunters met them with hand-held darts and then wriggled free before the men could grab or injure them. The man with the bird cape pounced on Terana, twisted her around to face him, and shouted something in her face. She punched him expertly in the stomach, and he collapsed in a heap. Some things worked quicker than lek-tapru.

The men were becoming clumsier, and weaving and rubbing their eyes. Four more had fallen. One of these was reacting peculiarly to the lek-tapru. Rather than passing out quietly, he had begun to twitch and jerk. Big Awa stood over him. "Lie still, damn you." She knelt and tried to soothe his writhing limbs. Linnie could see why Big Awa wanted to take good care of this one; his red robe must mean he was more of a man than any of the others. His body arched, and he cried out. Blood was smeared around his mouth; perhaps he had bitten his tongue. After a second spasm he went limp. Big Awa felt the side of his neck, and then patted his shoulder. "Somebody got you good, didn't they?"

The field grew quiet. Warm sun and cool air and the scent of turned earth mingled. The women stood looking at one another, grins spreading slowly. Linnie grinned too, letting her bow slack. She was glad she hadn't had to kill anybody. One woman was rubbing her wrist, another had a swelling purple bump on her forehead, but they were all standing, all whole. The men lay like sacks at their feet.

The field was too open. They could be seen for miles. Working hurriedly in pairs, they half-carried, half-dragged the men out to the stone wall. Linnie squinted down the hill at the unmoving moving house. She thought she had seen faces inside it, faces that peered out pale and frightened. The faces were gone now. Sandu would probably want to kill whoever was down there, to keep them from carrying word back to their village. Linnie decided not to say anything.

They used a noose under the arms to hoist each man up to the top of the wall and lower him on the other side. There they began binding the men's wrists behind their backs. After inspecting Little Awa's knots and telling her to tighten them, Linnie found a foothold and climbed up to take a last longing look at the neatly tended field. Two more of the moving houses had joined the first one, and people were standing beside them and pointing up the hill. A welter of muddy tracks led straight across the field toward her. "We'll have to do better than that," she muttered. "If we don't, they'll hunt us down for sure."

Chapter ‖ 5

THIRST. Burning thirst and a pounding headache, and nausea and the sharp grinding of gravel against his cheek. Danlo groaned and tried weakly to roll over. He had been dreaming about large puffy orange things, lumpy balls with moist eyes and lips whose tiny arms waved feeble and helpless as they jumped up and down and squealed at him—not a dream he wanted to slide back into. After drawing a stiff, shaky breath, he tried to roll again, and again got no result. Peculiar. His left arm was numb, that was part of it. And both hands. He couldn't feel his hands! He gasped, his heart lurched, and his eyes flew open.

He was lying on his side in the dirt. Somebody else was lying a couple of feet away, blocking his field of view. The other figure was dressed in coveralls, and its arms were bound behind its back with rope. Danlo lifted his head and twisted his neck to see if his arms were in the same position. When he found that he couldn't turn far enough, he reached out in the ktess to borrow whatever pair of eyes might be turned in his direction. The ktess was as murky as mud. He tried again to roll onto his back, and this time succeeded. An agony of pinpricks informed him that his arms were still attached to his shoulders. He flexed his shoulders to help the circulation. His head throbbed with every pulse, and his mouth felt stuffed with cotton. Overhead the clouds were joined in unbroken gray.

Footsteps crunched nearby, and low voices murmured. Women's voices. He strained, but could make out no words.

He closed his eyes again and dozed. Something hard shoved his thigh, and he blinked awake. A person was standing over him, grinning at him. The person's appearance was so bizarre, so far beyond anything in his experience, that Danlo had to assemble his impression piecemeal. Legs and arms and a head and a face: therefore, a person. Female; one of her breasts hung free within her open shirt, and only a faint feathery down graced her upper lip. Her face was painted in a crude pattern of green streaks and sworls, as were her shoulders and arms. From waist to mid-calf she wore a rough-stitched, ill-fitting, soiled pair of trousers. But if her clothing was disreputable, her hair was actively offensive—no curl, no shape, only a greasy braid wrapped in a thong, from which limp strands straggled at random. She carried a long curved stick that had a grip in the middle and a piece of string stretched between the ends. Black dirt was caked under her ragged fingernails.

She said something. It sounded like, "Ee-yohkfai dalala muinb." Which was ridiculous. Had something happened to his hearing? He opened his ktess to her, and felt nothing. A flash of dizziness hit him, as if the earth had opened and he was falling. "Thirsty," he said thickly. "Wah—can you—water?"

"Yohkfai ned puri*aahh*nam." She grinned and nudged his thigh with her toe.

Another woman, just as exotically dressed but larger, strode up, and the two engaged in an extended colloquy accompanied by arm-waving and spitting. Again, Danlo understood not a syllable. The obdurate opacity of the words was more alarming, somehow, than being assaulted and tied up by strangers. The latter was merely impossible, and therefore would prove before long to be part of an elaborate game. Not to be able to understand the game, though, not to be able to explain the mistake—his nausea returned in a rush. He rolled sideways and gagged, and a thin stream of bitter stomach juices dribbled onto the ground.

The large woman cradled his head in the crook of her elbow and put an earthenware cup to his lips. Her odor was powerfully earthy, but he was so grateful for the water that he barely noticed. The cup was lined with bright red glaze, and the water tasted bitter. He drank it all, and asked weakly for more, but the large woman had gone away.

By twisting and wriggling, he was able to sit upright. He flexed his shoulders until his arms stopped tingling and prickling. Other men were moving now, groaning and trying to sit up. The coach driver lay on his back, cursing softly; his purple beard quivered at the sky. Danlo counted nineteen men, all of them trussed as he was—from the coach, himself, Oxar, Walf the driver, Taud Makar the young father, and the duplet of waterworks inspectors, whose name he had already forgotten; and twelve in the field crew, plus a joddie. He did the count twice to be certain. More of the frighteningly attired women moved back and forth among the men. His mind was still scattered, but he thought there were twenty-six of them, perhaps twenty-seven. Three of the women moved from one man to another with cups of water. Five or six others crouched at the top of the ridge, looking off toward the horizon. Most were carrying the curved sticks. These must be some sort of tool, but what use they might be intended for was not obvious. Other implements, equally mysterious, hung from straps across the women's shoulders.

What time was it? And what day? Had he left Woolich only this morning? A whole day might easily have passed since—since what? He had seen some people in a field. The coach had stopped, and he and Oxar and the others had run across the field to help them. That was all he remembered. From the temperature of the air, which was cold and damp but not frigid, it must be close to noon. The bushes rustled in a breeze, leaf scraping leaf. Dead branches straggled unkempt among the green, and a thick bed of black, rotting leaves had been allowed to gather. His surroundings pressed close with an oppressive, cloying strangeness. We're outside the Wall, he realized. But why? Why are we outside the Wall?

Not far away, Oxar got to his knees. Two of the women shouted at him and waved their arms. He glared at them. They strode up to him and shoved him back onto the ground. One waved a knife. He shied away from it, radiating sudden fear. They shouted some more and strode away. He glared at their backs, and then scooted over toward Danlo.

"You're right," Oxar said. "Got to be. We're outside the Wall."

Agreed. Identity of these?

Oxar shrugged. "Care more about what they're planning."
Ken them?

They both tried and met no response. They exchanged worried glances. "Nulls?" Oxar's lips formed the words silently. He answered his own question with a stubborn shake of the head.
Denial. Impossibility.

"Could be they're shutting us out somehow."

Impossibility. "Unless you know a way for somebody to do that," Oxar added.

Danlo realized his suggestion had been careless; he shut his mind tight around the core that Oxar was probing for. "Maybe we can figure out what they're saying," he said. "Almost think I can get a word or two." Familiar-sounding syllables glinted like flecks of quartz in a granite aggregate of jabber, but always the rough chunk spun away before he could puzzle out its contours.

"That one just said something that sounded like 'they follow,'" Oxar said.

"Didn't hear it."

"I can run the sounds through in my head," Oxar said. "No trouble remembering. Can't say them, though. Like she's rolling words around in her mouth. 'Fualluoh.' And 'ruyp.' Could be 'rope.' Don't like this. Don't like it at all. Why should they talk funny?"

"The White Book says that in the time before the Great Cleansing, the peoples of the world spoke many—what's the word? Languages."

Oxar nodded, and quoted: "'There was no understanding among them, for it was the Time of Confusion, when the world was engulfed in suffering and madness.' But that was a thousand years ago! Since the Great Cleansing, the Body has spoken as one."

"If that's true," Danlo said, "then they're not of the Body."

This absurd conclusion chilled him to the bone. He was almost grateful to be interrupted before he could think it through. Two of the women pounced on Oxar, jerked his head back roughly, and threw a loop of rope around his neck. They adjusted the knot under his ear so that the loop left no slack, made a new loop three feet further on, and slapped this down around Danlo's head. It was not tight enough to constrict his breathing, but it was neither comfortable nor reassuring. "Ow!" the man behind Danlo protested. "Hey, what're you doin'?" He got no response. "Lemme go," another man was saying. He said it over and over, in a dull stubborn way. "Hey, lemme go! Lemme go, I said." Taud Makar was sobbing quietly. Danlo kenned a vivid picture of Goody Makar and little Keven, wide-eyed faces pressed against the window of the coach.

The women arranged the neck-tether so that all the men, even those who were still unconscious, were joined in two long lines. Fear rippled from one man to another, making it hard to think.

When the rope was deployed to the women's satisfaction, the one who seemed to be their leader clapped her hands and shouted to get the men's attention. Danlo eyed her closely. As frightened as he was, he was hoping to glean some clue about what was going on. She had a sharp nose and a wide mouth, and her hair was hacked off short in ragged clumps. She clapped her hands again, and frowned in exasperation, and rattled off a long string of gibberish. Most of the men were still gazing around stupidly at one another, sharing words and feelings. "Where's Garpish?" somebody said plaintively.

"Over here. Hasn't woke up. Hey, Garpish!" Ignoring the woman's chatter, the others took up the cry. "Wake up, Garpish! Wake up!" Danlo kenned their affectionate picture of the joddie, a spindly old fellow who laughed often. Just now Garpish looked very ill. His blue-gray skin was deathly against the red of his robe, and dried blood was caked around the corners of his mouth. By concentrating, Danlo was able to shut out the men's mental noise and ken the joddie directly. Garpish was not dead; his mind moved sluggishly, unresponsively, like a slow underground river.

One man tried to stand up, evidently to get closer to Garpish. The rope between him and his neighbors snapped taut, and he fell back with a stricken look. He made rattling, choking noises, and his face got red. After expostulating to the sky, the short-haired woman waved a couple of other women forward. They strode to the man's side and made some adjustment to the loop, and he drew in panicky gasps of air. The man next in line behind Danlo, a short swarthy fellow with yellow sideburns and a drooping black forelock, twisted his neck from side to side in alarm. "What's the rope for?" yellow-sideburns whined. "Hey! Let us loose!"

Silence "Yelling won't do any good," Danlo snapped. But commanding a stranger was impolite. To atone, Danlo spoke of himself as 'he' in the formal mode: "He thinks we ought to pay close attention to what she's trying to tell us."

"Who are you?" yellow-sideburns asked.

"Danlo Ree. Counter from Serameno. This is Oxar Blennish, rememberer."

The man's mouth fell open, and he squinted at Danlo. Evidently, sitting on the ground next to a counter and a rememberer was as strange as anything else that had happened to him today.

The short-haired woman shouted again, and the men fell silent, though not without more grumbling. The woman chattered at them briefly—Danlo was able to identify "ruyp" this time, and "wouk," which he supposed could be "walk"—and then said something that was evidently a question. When the men failed to respond, she repeated it in more shrill tones. They looked at one another and shrugged. She strode up to the nearest man and cuffed him on the ear, so hard his head jerked to one side. The pain shot through the ktess, and Danlo's ear stung in sympathy.

"Ow! What's the matter, are you crazy? Get away from me!" He tried to scuttle away from her, but the rope halted him. She railed at him in a low, tight voice. His eyes were wide, and his jaw trembled. "What's the matter with her? What's she sayin'?"

"Watch out, she's got a knife!"

One of the other women called something to the leader. The leader darted a sharp, distrustful look at her, but straightened up and worked her mouth silently, evidently ruminating on a suggestion. Reluctantly she nodded, and scratched her head and took a deep breath and tried again, this time accompanying her meaningless babble with a clumsy but detailed pantomime. By a combination of pointing, signs, and body movements, she explained the purpose of the neck-rope. Shortly the men would get up and walk. As long as they walked together, they would be comfortable. The woman signed this by pushing up the corners of her mouth with her fingers and bouncing her head happily from side to side. But if any of them stumbled, or tried to run away—she pushed her tongue out between her teeth, rolled her eyes, grasped her own throat with both hands, and grimaced theatrically.

Danlo relayed the gist of this to the other men, who were still too worried about the joddie to pay attention. "How d'you know what she's sayin'?" yellow-sideburns grumbled.

"Watched, goodman."

"You lot come up from the road, didn't you? What'd you say your name was?"

"Danlo Ree."

"Danlo. Hullo. I'm Ved Nirts." Ved was a handsome young man with a high round forehead and rather vacant blue eyes. His curly yellow sideburns reached from well above his ears nearly down to the point of his chin. "This here's Jirry, and Birl."

"Pleasure, goodmen."

"How long you reckon," Ved said, "before they let us loose?" Danlo said, "What makes you think they're going to?"

"Well, I mean, they have to, don't they?"

"Wanna go home," Jirry said plaintively. He was pale, a nervous-looking man with pop eyes and a receding chin. His mustache and forelock were bright green, and sadly bedraggled. "Don't like this at *all*."

Jirry's ktess was awash in chill and distress, which only made Danlo feel worse. "Stop that," he said. "He thinks we should stay calm." But the man had lost all control. The waves of discomfort surged and rolled. Danlo wondered whether he ought to join the man and plant an impulse that would calm him. With the joddie unconscious, there was not much chance that a little joining would be noticed—and anyway, he would only be doing what the joddie would do for them if he were awake. But Oxar was looking directly at Danlo. Not a good moment for meddling.

Ved rubbed his shoulder stiffly against Jirry's. "Got a sore on my arm," he said. "Itches like blazes."

"Feels like I got one on my neck," Jirry said. "Can you see? Right there?" He pointed with his chin.

"Yeah. All swole up, and purple in the center. Looks like a bee stung you."

Danlo became aware of a spot, low on his right side, that felt hot and tender. By twisting his shoulders he was able to bring his wrists around far enough to rub the spot with the side of his thumb. It was as big around as a sand dollar, and his touch set off a wave of itching. Another mystery.

The women urged them to their feet and got them strung out single file in a long line pointing straight at the Sernada. A couple of the women slapped and shouted at the joddie and the two others who were still unconscious. When they failed to respond, the women removed them from the neck-tether, leaving empty loops dangling at three points in the line. The bodies were hoisted like sacks, two women at the shoulders and one carrying the legs. The sharp-faced woman shouted something, and the men jerked and stumbled into motion. Danlo was behind Oxar. He couldn't see who was behind him, but he kenned it was Ved. Ved kicked him several times in the ankles before getting accustomed to the gait, which was faster than a walk but uncomfortably slower than a trot. The women kept them to it, up hill and down, for a very long time, long after Danlo's sides ached and his knees wobbled with every step. One of the women had a bad leg, but even she kept the pace better than he did, her lips pressed together grimly as she moved along in a crooked shambling lope.

"We're gone from the world," Ved said mournfully.

"Been thinkin' about that," the man behind him huffed. "What happens, we die out here with no joddie? We die, we don't get gathered!" The stark terror of this thought surged up and down the line. Nightmare images lashed through the ktess—slimed horrors with fangs and talons that would slash and devour them all before they could get organized to run. Every mind added its own details to the fearful vision, until its force overwhelmed them. The party's orderly progress up the slope dissolved. Men stumbled, gibbered, twisted and writhed uselessly as they tried to free their wrists, and started to run off in various directions only to be jerked back by the neck-tether. When they fell, they dragged others down. In the gasping, choking heap, men crawled over one another and tied the rope in knots trying to reach Garpish, to touch him, to shake him awake. They needed to be reassured that he wasn't dead. He lay blue-pale where the women had dropped him, breath rattling faintly in his chest.

It took the women ten minutes to untangle the mess, and they would have needed longer if they had been less eager to slap and kick. Those who were not helping stood leaning on their curving sticks and looking at the men warily, as if wondering what sort of bizarre conspiracy could blossom into such a useless outburst.

The hallucination passed, but the danger that had triggered it was real. In the normal course of events, when people died their essence was absorbed by the Body. They slid into an interior state, communing with others who had been gathered before them and watching through living eyes as their loved ones went on with the daily business of the world. To die ungathered was to die the way nulls died, ceasing irretrievably, lost to the Body and to oneself.

The danger was a potent reason not to go wandering beyond the edge of the world.

Dying ungathered was rare, a fate that most people had no reason to be concerned about. But Danlo had watched it happen to Julan. He had never been sure, since her death, that he wanted to be absorbed into the Body. He would have to give up the defiance that he kept locked tight in his inner mind. But he had always assumed that, when the time came, his resistance would vanish. Not to have that option. . . . As he sat waiting for the tether to be straightened out, his gut trembled and buzzed uncomfortably.

Another discomfort had been nagging at him unnoticed for some time: He needed to urinate. With his hands bound behind him, he had no way to unbutton his trousers.

Several other men had the same thought. "Hey," Walf cried. "Hey, sister! Gotta pee."

"Have to untie us now," Jirry mumbled hopefully.

"Doubt it," Danlo said.

The women were uncertain what to make of the new commotion. Danlo waited for a lull, and jerked his head in a come-hither motion at a cluster of women standing nearby. They eyed him. He repeated the motion, and pasted on what he hoped was a disarming smile. At last one of them stepped forward and wove a crooked path among the seated men to his side. Because she had to change direction repeatedly and step over sections of the rope, she had nearly reached him before he realized it was the woman with the limp. She stood looking down at him expressionlessly. She had long, dreadfully untidy black hair, dark eyes that flickered like smoldering coals beneath the heavy brows, and a pock-marked complexion that failed to mask the finely molded lines of her cheekbones and jaw.

He dipped his nose several times in the direction of his crotch, and made a pissing noise. The men snickered. The woman said something, then knelt in front of Danlo, grabbed his belt, and wrestled his trousers down around his knees. The ground scraped his buttocks, and the cold air gave him gooseflesh. The men hooted with laughter, and he felt his face burning. She said something else, and pointed at his penis. But now that the opportunity had presented itself, his embarrassment had struck him dry. She gave him a pitying look, and shrugged and moved away.

A warm hand rested on his shoulder. The short-haired woman was bending over him. Her breath stank of bad teeth. She reached down and cupped his shriveled penis and testicles in her hand. Her thumb moved up and down, and she murmured some endearment—not at Danlo, but at his organ.

What happened next was, if possible, even more mortifying. He began to become erect. The woman rubbed and stroked his penis, and squeezed his shoulder with her other hand. She was breathing through her mouth.

Several of the women laughed and called comments. The woman with the bad leg said something in a low, scornful tone, and the woman with the short hair stood up and leaped at her. The two shoved at one another, and the woman with the bad leg fell. After some more shouting, she scrambled to her feet and the two grappled again, grunting. The short-haired woman slapped the side of her opponent's face, and the woman with the bad leg retaliated with a backhanded swing that sent the other woman sprawling in the dirt.

The men watched, wide-eyed with shock and disbelief. Danlo's heart was thudding. He had seen children scuffle, and of course wrestling was a popular sport, but two adults seriously trying to injure each other? Such a thing could not possibly happen. The woman with the chopped-off hair sprang from a crouch and caught the woman with the bad leg in a flying tackle. They rolled on the hard ground, screaming and pummeling each other.

Now that the center of attention had shifted elsewhere, Danlo found that he was able to make a puddle in the dead leaves. He breathed a sigh of relief.

The large woman and the old woman and some of the others gathered around, grabbing at the limbs of the combatants and babbling. Eventually they succeeded in separating the two. Both were suffering from scrapes that oozed blood. Another bout of arm-waving and spitting ensued, but the old woman's soothing voice kept interrupting, and at last the turbulence died down. The old woman got something from one of the pouches that she wore around her waist, and mixed it with her own spit, augmented by a little water from a leather skin, and daubed the paste on the women's wounds. Danlo was sorry that the woman with the bad leg had been hurt trying to defend him. He caught her looking over at him while the old woman worked on her shoulder. He met her gaze for long seconds, until she said something, perhaps to herself, and looked away.

A small, wiry young woman crept up to him, darting shy looks from beneath the hideous tangle of greasy hair that tumbled down

into her face. At first he thought she wanted to fondle him too, but
then he saw she was only trying to get his trousers up. He rolled
left and then right, trying without much success to avoid the
puddle, while she hoisted one side, then the other. Having tucked
his shirt in, she fingered his belt in wonder. It was finely tooled,
with a silver buckle, a Receiving Day present from his maternal
uncle. "Do you like it?" he asked. She started away from him
fearfully. "Nice, isn't it?" he went on in as friendly a tone as he
could muster. "Belt. Called a belt. What's your name?"

She took several slow, lithe steps backward, eyeing him fixedly,
then turned and scampered away.

"Pretty little thing," Oxar said. "Could be if she was cleaned
up, anyhow." *Hair care urgent.* "What floors me is why they
should want to behave like this."

"Maybe they can't help themselves," Danlo said. "Like
hoarders." Being a counter, Danlo had brought several hoarders to
light. They accumulated things, quite useless things sometimes, a
hundred items for every one that they could use.

"Hoarders are harmless," Oxar said. "More like corkers,
these."

The leader of the women shouted and made agitated lifting
motions with her arms. The men struggled to their feet, and the
line shuffled forward.

Agree. "Ever seen a corker?"

"Once. Felt him before I saw him." Oxar shared a sense of
pressure, like the oppressive heaviness before a thunderstorm,
mingled with a thick, disgusting odor, as if the storm clouds were
about to rain garbage. "Then, not fifty feet away, there he was,
screaming and tearing at his face with his fingers. People running
from him. Tore his own eyes out. Then ripped out his windpipe,
that was how he died."

"That's it," Jirry said in a high, tremulous voice. "That's it.
They're corkers, all of them."

"Better hope it's not catching," Oxar told him.

Nobody knew who might turn corker, or when. It was whispered that even the corker didn't know, that the pressure felt no
different to him than to anybody else. Possibly the disorder sprang
from the ktess itself, condensing invisibly like dew until it was
thick enough to fasten upon whoever was most vulnerable.

"Hoarders and corkers," Danlo said. "Something like that.
Explain the way they look, and the way they attack one another.
Not the way they talk, though. Not what they're doing, either."

"Treating us like sheep," Ved said indignantly. "Like pigs."

"Maybe they're going to eat us," Oxar said.

"They've got something in mind," Danlo said. "Wouldn't go to all this trouble, otherwise."

Once again the men were urged to stand. Two of the three whom the women had been carrying were now awake and took their places, ropes looped tight around their necks. Only the joddie remained unconscious. The lines were set stumbling into motion, and the weary trek went on.

Late in the afternoon they halted. The men collapsed on the ground, exhausted. While one group of women trotted away into the brush, another group bustled about gathering wood, which they piled in a small circle from which they had cleared the grass. One of the wood-gatherers knelt before the pile and did something that Danlo couldn't see, and smoke curled upward. In minutes flames were leaping and crackling in an open fire. An open fire! Danlo had not seen a fire since he and a couple of friends daringly kindled one when he was eleven years old. He had visions of it leaping to the nearest tree and setting the whole forest ablaze, but the women seemed unconcerned.

The party that had gone off returned carrying several large brown birds that Danlo assumed must be chickens, a fat, black-haired animal that looked like a pig, and half a dozen rabbits. All of the animals were summarily gutted, skinned, and roasted over the fire. Though he was aching and shivering in every bone, Danlo found that his mouth watered at the smell. When a chunk of meat was held in front of his face, he lunged at it and chewed. Juice dribbled down his chin. The meat was charred black on the outside and still raw on the inside. He didn't care; he ate it anyway, and sucked his teeth, and wished he had more.

Afterward, a little revived, he started to wonder: If there was a farm nearby where chickens and rabbits and pigs were being bred for the table, why not simply take the men to the farm, where everybody could sit down indoors and be comfortable? The more he considered this, the more vexing the thought became. There couldn't be any farm out here, not miles past the edge of the world. So where had the women acquired the meat? It came, perhaps, from wherever the women themselves came from. Mystery upon mystery.

"Beginning to suspect," he said to Oxar, "that there may be a few things we don't know."

"At the moment."

"Beyond that."

Query meaning.

"Everything we're taught in school. Not just the facts. Attitude behind them. 'This is how the world is.' You see?"

"Can't say I do." Oxar turned away.

No, of course. Oxar wouldn't. Dull, conventional Oxar. Danlo wasn't sure what direction his own thoughts were drifting, but there was little to be gained by sharing them.

The women conversed in low voices, and licked their fingers, and ignored the men. The men lay like fallen logs. Then one of the women began singing. Her song was as crude and awkward as her costume, burdened with a nasal gasping lilt. The intonation was beyond belief. Surprisingly, some of the other women took up the tune. They were, if possible, worse than the soloist. Not even a mocking imitation of singing could ever have sounded so awful. The tune went through seven or eight verses, and there was little to distinguish one from another but the incomprehensible changes in wording. Everybody sang the melody together, more or less, with no harmony or antiphony, only a great deal of stammering and bad intonation. As they listened, the men rolled up on their elbows, and those who were sitting sat a little straighter. Ved lifted his bony head off of Danlo's calf and blinked in the firelight.

When the women's song stumbled to a halt, the men launched together into "The Flower Fields Rolling." They did it in five parts, with Jirry singing a shockingly clear countertenor descant from "Sheila Lay." There was a lump in Danlo's throat, and tears in his eyes. "Flower Fields" had always been one of his favorite songs. The men improvised a modulation and a double-time chorus, while Jirry's descant leaped and trilled around them. They hummed the last verse, and when they fell silent the women licked their lips and darted shamefaced, distrustful looks at them. For a singing contest, it had been a short one. The men felt no joy in such an easy victory.

The fire snapped and hissed. Something large flapped noisily across the camp, only a few feet above the fire, startling them all. An owl? A bat? Or something more dangerous, that lived only in the wild? Danlo stared off into the darkness where the last gray remnant of sunset had been swallowed up. He wondered whether anybody in the Body of Harmony would look out their window tonight and see a fire burning in the hills, where no fire ought to be. Almost certainly not. The party had crossed two high ridges during the afternoon, either of which would obscure the blaze. But the land was rising steadily, and perhaps by now they were above the ridge line.

If the joddie had been awake, the fire's visibility would have been irrelevant. A joddie's ktess extended to another joddie's across many miles. The Body of Harmony would have flowed over the Wall like water into a rice paddy, heedless of the dark and the distance, and rescued the men before morning. But until—unless—Garpish regained consciousness, they were cut off. They could not be joined in the ktess of the Body, and neither could the Body ken their distress.

The ground was wet and cold. As the fire died down, the men huddled together for warmth. The last thing Danlo saw before he tumbled into sleep was the lame woman crouched in front of the fire, staring fixedly into it. She was leaning on her curved stick, and her skin, where it was not caked with flaking streaks of green paint, was bathed in red and gold. The way the firelight stroked her cheeks and forehead, the placid curves of her mouth in repose, called forth a memory. He had been five or six years old, and he had used to creep back downstairs at night after his mother had tucked him into bed and peek into the front room, where she sat in the high-backed chair under the lamp. She never looked in his direction, only went on placidly with her sewing, but sometimes she smiled an inner, secret smile, as if some warm thought had brushed her, or as if the whole time she knew he was there, kneeling in the dark, watching.

Chapter ‖ 6

THE men were roused at dawn, and not given any food, and prodded with toes and the ends of sticks until they struggled to their feet. Their breath steamed in the cold air. They stamped numb feet and grumbled while eyeing the women warily. The sky had cleared during the night, and Danlo was enchanted by the crisp fringe of reddish gold, herald of the rising sun, that rimmed the trees along the tops of the nearest peaks.

The women scuffed out the fires and moved down the lines tightening the ropes. By now, all of the men except Garpish had recovered from the effects of the darts. Garpish lay where the women had set him the night before. The women made no move to pick him up. When they urged the lines into motion and the men saw that Garpish was to be left behind, another revolt, more orderly than the panic of the day before, erupted. The men halted in unison and began shuffling backward, ignoring the women's cuffs and shouts. When they reached Garpish, the whole line knelt, in order not to stretch the neck-rope too far, and the two men nearest him tried to pick him up. As their hands were tied behind them, this was not easy.

The women muttered to one another. More men circled Garpish, facing away from him, and tried to assist in hoisting him. With a few watching to provide the eyes, they managed to get him off the ground, and the whole group stood up. Garpish sagged in the middle, but he was off the ground.

The woman with the hacked-off hair regarded this performance with a sour expression. She pushed her way between the men and reached out toward Garpish's neck. Several men were afraid she meant to strangle the joddie, and sidled away from her, but they couldn't get far. She only pressed her fingers against the side of his neck, beneath the corner of his jaw. After a few seconds she said something, and more women approached. One drew a knife and pressed it against Oxar's neck. He flinched, and she pressed harder. Two more women seized his arms, one at each side, while a third worked at the rope that bound his hands. When he was freed, he had only moments to flex his fingers before his arms were roughly moved to the front and the wrists tied again.

When the neck-rope and bodies were sorted out, Oxar and the man in front of him were carrying Garpish between them. Once again the lines moved forward.

Danlo's muscles had stiffened during the night, and he found himself lurching and stumbling. After only a few minutes he missed his footing on a rock and fell outright. The line had to be halted while he and his companions were untangled. Afterward, the rope burn chafed with every step.

Planning, he shared. *Work together as in picking up Garpish. Untie rope.* But his prodding sank like a stone into the general mess of revulsion and fear that smoldered in the ktess. Spoken words might snap them out of their mood. "We've got to figure out some way to untie these ropes so we can get away," he said experimentally, keeping his voice casual. The woman jogging beside him glanced in his direction and scowled, but that was all. "I don't think they understand us any better than we understand them. It's all right to talk."

Behind him Jirry said, "It's hopeless. There's nothing we can do."

"There's plenty we can do. If one of us can crawl over to one of them while they're sleeping, and get a knife. . . ."

"They'll kill us."

"No, they won't. They want us alive."

Oxar glanced back over his shoulder. "What makes you so sure of that?"

"If they were going to kill us, they'd have done it by now. The fact that they want us alive gives us some leverage. We have to find out how far we can push. We've already pushed to keep Garpish, and it worked. There's another thing we could try. If we all join our minds and share the same thought, our ktess is bound to reach farther than any of us can reach alone. Together, we might be able to reach the Body, even from this distance."

This proposal rippled up the line. It interested everybody, but the pace at which they were being driven was not conducive to collected thought. After two attempts were scattered by the necessity of negotiating rough terrain, they deferred the plan until later.

They labored up a hill and down the other side, heading southeast. The bushes and trees looked terribly dirty and disorganized. It was hard to see how plants and animals could survive without the hand of man to tend them; plainly they were suffering. Things died and were left to rot, not picked up and disposed of properly. But even so, Danlo thought, the wildness had a crude beauty. Ahead and below them, a stream sparkled among the trees. The party startled a family of deer, who put up their heads and loped away. Though the air was still crisp, the sun's warmth on Danlo's skin was delicious. He kept his eyes open for the farm that the rabbits and chickens had come from; he had never heard that the Body kept farms in the wilderness, and as a counter he certainly ought to have—but then he had never heard of insane women covered with green paint either, until yesterday. He saw no sign of buildings or roads, only the vast, chaotic, unpeopled land.

They heard the second group before they saw them. At first Danlo thought some enormous monster was crashing through the trees. The thought was not entirely his—several of his companions were imagining the same thing. His pulse beat faster. Tales of monsters in the mountains, he had always supposed, were meant only to frighten children, but they might after all turn out to be true. Then the women shouted, and other shouts answered them. A moment later the men confronted a shorter line much like themselves. The two groups stared at one another and shuffled their feet while the women hugged and jabbered.

"What village are you from?"

"Culler. You?"

"Woolich."

"Do any of your women understand," Danlo asked, "when you talk?" The other line only looked at one another and back at him and shrugged. "It could be important. Do they understand what you're saying?"

"Why shouldn't they?" a big curly-haired man said.

"Anyway, what's the difference?" Ved frowned at Danlo in perplexity. "They don't have to listen to us. If we try to get away, they'll know in the ktess. If we do manage to get away somehow, they'll follow in the ktess." Ved, Danlo kenned, was a thicker. Many people's ktess would be opaque to him, so he had no reason to be surprised that he could not ken the women.

"I don't think they're in the ktess," Danlo said. "I think they're all nulls. Have any of you shared the ktess with any of them?" Several men shook their heads.

"They can't be nulls," the curly-haired man protested. "It's not possible."

"I reckon they could be," the man next to him hazarded. "If their parents hid them or something, so they grew up." It was a bold and shameful thing to say, and the wave of condemnation was quick and strong. The man blushed and hung his head.

Danlo tried again. *Tales ever hear of strange-speaking women?* The eyes that turned in his direction were bleak. Nobody had ever heard such a tale. Not surprising; neither had he.

The lines of men were set in motion, the women ranging around them in the underbrush. The sun was higher now, but each slope seemed steeper than the one before, and they toiled along at a slower pace. Danlo's sides and legs ached, but he saw no sign that the women meant to let them rest. He began working his wrists back and forth to see if he could stretch some slack, but the knots held firm, and the rope cut painfully into his skin, so he desisted.

They reached the bottom of a hill and began working their way along the bank of a stream. Bramble bushes tore at their clothing, and the footing was uneven. Snow lingered in the crevices between the boulders. The stream was deep and swift-moving, and Danlo was glad the women didn't try to force their captives to ford it. If one man lost his footing, a dozen might drown. A mile or so upstream, a halt was called, and the men were allowed to drink. Doing this with their hands bound behind them was awkward. Two of them overbalanced and got dunked.

Danlo drank his fill, and then sat back on the river bank and watched how the sunlight dappled the rocks and ripples. Musing vaguely, he was struck by a thought that set his scalp prickling. One group of violently insane women, clothed in filth, speaking gibberish, might be terrifying and inexplicable, but what they were doing to the men was a personal calamity, of little real consequence to the Body. Two groups, on the other hand—why not a dozen? A hundred? Could it be that this bizarre scene was being duplicated from one end of the Serral Valley to the other? And where could so many wild nulls have come from? They might have stepped right out of the terrible days before the Great Cleansing. He trembled at the conclusion, but it was inescapable: These were members of one of the null races against whom Frank and Olivia had battled so fiercely. The White Book declared again and again, in no uncertain terms, that the Great Cleansing was perfect, that none had survived it save the Body of Harmony. But now it seemed that the White Book must be wrong.

The thought had come upon him so suddenly that he had not considered whether he ought to conceal it. Oxar snorted. "White Book wrong?" *Garbage thinking.* "Shows how stable you are, friend counter. Something like this happens, it feeds all your worst tendencies. I'm not saying it's easy to understand, mind you. But you jump right to condemning the White Book." Oxar shook his head in sad disgust.

"When has it been said I'm unstable?"

Oxar had no way to hide the thought. Danlo kenned the memory of a conversation, months before, between Oxar and white-haired Arbin Tong, their senior at the Central Counting Office. "Worried about him," Arbin creaked in his paper-thin voice. "Cracking up. Watch him. See what he does, what he thinks. He's a valuable man. If he goes off the deep end, get a joddie to haul him back."

Danlo flushed with anger. "You ought to be grateful," Oxar told him. "We're concerned for your well-being."

Danlo arranged the outer layer of his mind into a semblance of contrition. "Olivia's love flows through us all, friend rememberer. You have my gratitude." Oxar smiled a polite, meaningless smile and turned his thoughts elsewhere.

Inwardly Danlo still seethed. He'd think what he liked, about the White Book or anything else, and not be bound by Oxar's chiding. Yes, the White Book was the guiding light of life. Its moral precepts were unarguable. Yet if these women were real—and there was no arguing that, either—then their ancestors had somehow escaped the Great Cleansing. At the very least, the historical account in the White Book was incomplete. Facts had been omitted. Possibly, though the thought was painful to contemplate, some of what purported to be facts were outright errors.

As well argue that two plus two made five. How could a counter count, if numbers might twist and turn so? The whole edifice of mathematics would crumble if only a single instance of such impossible behavior were discovered. Likewise, if the White Book was wrong about one thing, how could it be trusted about anything?

The tangle of the wilderness, which a moment before had seemed safely outside Danlo, invaded his mind in a rush. His head spun. The orderly picture of the world in which he had always lived stood revealed as flimsy and temporary, no better than a stage set made of canvas and sticks. He remembered a night at summer camp when he was twelve or thirteen: The stage had been set outdoors, between lights strung on poles, to represent the famous farmhouse north of Williss, and a gawky Olivia was delivering the ''what we have is infinitely precious'' speech to a Frank who spoke in an inaudible monotone and came up maybe to her shoulder, when a little wind came along and blew the set down. Suddenly dark trees were peering through crazy gaps in the walls of the house, and the Olivia faltered and forgot her lines. The trees had been there all along; it was the house that flew apart. Or, no, there was nothing to fly apart. There had never been a house, only a bunch of children pretending to see a house.

''You feeling unwell, goodman?'' Ved eyed Danlo solicitously.

''I'm fine,'' he managed. ''It must have been something in the food.''

''Must have been. Beastly cooking.''

He turned the revelation over in his mind, searching for some flaw. But no other conclusion was possible: The White Book was not reliable. Even if it were right about most things, what measure could be used to tell which of the precepts were good and which were defective? Danlo knew about weights and measures: To calibrate a grain scale, you used a mass that weighed a known number of pounds. But the only way to know that your test weight was accurate was to balance it against the true weight, which was kept in a temperature-controlled room in Serameno. The White

Book was the true weight for human affairs. If unknown portions of it were false, then the values that the Body lived by might be no better than wisps of cotton fluff. He ached for somebody to share the thought with, somebody who might be sensible enough to point out a line of reasoning that he had missed. Oxar was sensible, of course—too sensible. Oxar would reject the whole morass without even acknowledging that it was there. And voicing such inharmonious ideas to farm workers was unlikely to be helpful. Possibly the teacher, or the waterworks inspectors. But they were far down the line.

Before he could quite collect himself, the group was urged up and driven on. As he walked, Danlo tried to recall everything the White Book said about the Great Cleansing. Even if portions of it were wrong, there might be something that would help him understand the women.

In the beginning, according to the Book, the Body was far smaller. It had lived secretly among a much greater number of violently insane people called Americans. Americans were only one of the kinds of people in the world then, but they were all much alike: War and sickness and starvation were everywhere. When the people of the Body came upon one another, they shared the ktess, and rejoiced, but they knew nothing of their numbers or their destiny.

Frank Rettig was the first joddie. In his ktess, the Body was united, and knew itself. Fifty thousand scattered minds were joined, and the song of the ktess was raised.

The Body made plans to retire to a remote community where the new thing that had been born among them could be nurtured. But Frank and his wife Olivia saw that this course was foolishly shortsighted. The Body could live forever; thus it must learn to think in longer terms. This was the great weakness of the nulls: Each null thought only of its own immediate advantage. It might be able to predict the long-term consequences of its actions, but it was incapable of acting prudently on the basis of such a prediction. Thus the nulls were rapidly destroying the world. They were ravaging the forests and poisoning the rivers, and they had built terrible weapons called H-bombs that might be unleashed at any moment. The weapons could fly everywhere and destroy the whole world at once. There was nowhere that the Body could go and be assured of safety.

Frank saw that if the nulls were allowed to go on in their vicious way, they would surely destroy the world, and the Body of

Harmony along with it. But they were many, and the Body were few.

To make provision for the future of the Body, the plan for the Great Cleansing was born. Instead of forming their own isolated community, the Body sought out work within the industries of death. Some of the Body learned to fly the great winged machines that were built to rain down fiery death; others went into the laboratories where poisons and diseases were developed.

One of the diseases that the Americans had invented was so potent that it was kept buried in a deep vault guarded night and day by men with weapons. But the Body learned of it, and arranged that those who were of the Body should share in the guard duty. The disease was called AMLP-B. It spread easily from one person to another through touching, or even in the air. It had no visible symptoms for a month after the infection began, yet it killed within days after the first fever appeared. It affected only humans and some animals, now extinct, called monkeys, leaving other animals untouched. And most important, the disease organism could not survive for long without a living host. Within a few weeks after the nulls had died, the world would be free of it again, and safe.

Now the Body arranged a retreat, to a remote region in the far north. An advance party built shelters that could not be seen from the air, and flying machines stocked the shelters with supplies. A dozen volunteers said goodbye to their loved ones. As soon as the rest of the Body was safely isolated, the volunteers infected themselves with AMLP-B and set out to travel, spreading the disease to great cities and tiny villages in a well-considered pattern.

A great silence fell across the world. The first stage of the Great Cleansing had been accomplished.

The Body returned to their homes in the place called California and set about making it a fit place to live. The wreckage left by the nulls was immense. As many as one null in a thousand had survived the disease, and the survivors had to be driven out of the ruins and dealt with. For the first time, the blood of the Body was spilled. The nulls fought with great savagery, and had to be hunted down in the streets and fields. This was the second stage of the Great Cleansing.

In the third stage, machines called satellites hovered high in the sky. Satellite telescopes sent back pictures that showed all the places in the world where the surviving nulls had banded together.

Flying machines set out from the great flying field at Soyvill. On the largest enclaves of nulls they dropped H-bombs. The smaller settlements were more trouble: The planes had to drop bombs on single buildings, and then fly low and drop fiery stuff called napalm on the nulls who tried to run away. The third stage went on for many years. Each time the machines flew out, a smaller number of nulls survived. At last the satellite pictures showed no survivors at all. The Great Cleansing was complete: The world had been saved.

But now it appeared that a few nulls had escaped. Perhaps they had hidden in caves or mine shafts, so that the satellites failed to spot them. The Body, after seeing no danger for years, gave up the vigil. Too soon: The nulls had emerged from their caves and bred unchecked. Millions of them might be spread across the land by now, poised to sweep down on the Body. Danlo shuddered, imagining nulls behind every tree. But the only thing behind the trees was more trees. He was extrapolating from a very small number of nulls. And all female, which left a mystery the question of how they had multiplied. These couldn't all be a thousand years old, could they?

Toward the middle of the afternoon the party emerged into a little bowl-shaped valley between frowning bluffs, and the women called a halt. They built a large fire, and again some of them disappeared into the woods. An hour later this group came back with freshly killed animals, which were efficiently skinned and spitted. Another rabbit farm? It hardly seemed possible. But then a truly amazing thing happened, one that explained everything and yet raised more questions than it answered. Four of the women began digging with sharp sticks. Soon they had amassed a pile of roots, which they proceeded to wash, wrap in leaves, and bury again at the edge of the fire. Danlo shook his head, astonished at his own naïveté. There was no farmhouse anywhere in sight, no sign of tilled land, and it surpassed belief that the women had planted this crop themselves months before and left it untended, only to return to it now. The conclusion was inescapable: Food could be procured in the wilderness beyond the edge of the world, without growing or herding it in any way!

He had never known food that didn't come from farms—but after all, the farms raised plants and animals. Many of the plants and animals around him now must be edible. The question was, how did the women know which ones were edible? How could they avoid poisoning themselves?

He watched the process intently. Two women came back from a nearby tree carrying an outstretched skin laden with nuts of some sort. They sat on the ground with wooden bowls and pounding-sticks between their knees and pounded the nuts into a paste. A bed of coals was raked out and banked, and six large, shallow bowls were set in the soil above the coals and filled with water and half-cooked meat and roots and nut paste. Shortly the bowls were bubbling and steaming in the cold air, and the old woman bustled back and forth from the stream to the fire, pouring more water into the bowls from the skin under her arm.

In spite of his weariness, Danlo was fascinated, not only by the existence of the uncultivated food and the women's knowledge of how to harvest it but by the neat organization and purposefulness of their activity. He was beginning to suspect that they were not insane at all, but simply different. People were much the same, in his experience, from one end of the world to the other. Which was as it must be, since all were joined in the Body of Harmony. Mechanics were different from counters, and counters different from dreamers. Young people were different from old people, men from women. Yet these differences never masked a deeper similarity. Perhaps these women were so different because they were all nulls. Perhaps in a village peopled entirely by nulls, such differences would flourish.

Surely nulls could not work effectively together. The White Book was very clear about this. A village of nulls would tear itself apart. Yet the women were working together—quarreling, yes, but working. Could they have some mode of understanding that the White Book said nothing about? The White Book talked about the tokens that nulls exchanged during many of their activities. What was the word? Money. They used money because they could never trust one another. He had not seen them passing any money back and forth, but he resolved to keep an eye out to see when and how they did it.

The afternoon was waning, and the sun's meager warmth was being sucked into the cold ground. He shivered, and hunched his shoulders, and wished he could hug himself for warmth. Instead, he scooted closer to the fire. The savory steam rising from the half-buried bowls made his mouth water and his stomach rumble.

He was glad the joddie was still unconscious; the thoughts rising in him were dangerous. A village of nulls, beyond the edge of the world, getting its food directly from the wilderness. . . . Possibly the women had come from such a village. If he had known where to look for it, he could have taken Julan there before she was Cleansed! They could have slipped away from the Serral Valley under cover of night. Of course, if the Body learned of such a village, it would be Cleansed. A pang of despair twisted in his throat: How could he have known of the village, in order to save Julan, without its existence also becoming known to the Body? Impossible. In any event, the women's existence was no longer a secret. Even though the Body could not ken the men's where-abouts directly, a massive search was doubtless being mounted. The village, wherever it might lie, would be found.

A third group arrived before nightfall—twelve women, one with her arm in a sling, and only seven men. The men slumped to the ground, leaden and dispirited. In the ktess, Danlo saw why. Two of the new group had been killed that morning, their bodies left to rot along the trail. They had freed themselves somehow and jumped one of the women. After the women swarmed over them and brought them to their knees, one held their heads back by the hair and slit their throats with a knife. "Slit their throats," Ved whispered, horrified. Danlo shuddered. Maybe Julan was better off Cleansed than living in a village where women did such things.

At dusk the bowls were retrieved from the fire. Three were set among the men, and the other three among the women. Two of the men were unbound, knives pressed against their necks the while, and their wrists tied again in front. They were instructed with gestures that it was their job to feed their fellows. Danlo found himself envying them; he longed to move his arms with even that much freedom. Bits of this and that were fished up from the bowls on big flat wooden spoons, and the spoons went from mouth to mouth around the circle. The stew lacked salt and spice, and it had a bitter metallic aftertaste, but there was plenty of it. Danlo lay back and belched, and yawned, and watched the stars come out.

"Anybody care to guess where they might be taking us?" he said. "Or why?"

"Heard one time how some folks ate some bad mushrooms," Ved said, "and they all started dancin' around and talkin' to animals what wasn't there. Maybe these women is all from a village up north, and they all ate some mushrooms. If only Garpish would wake up, we could find out for sure."

"When these people ate the mushrooms, did they stay crazy, or did they get over it?"

"I disremember."

Mushrooms. It was an intriguing theory, but not a very good

one. Musing on mushrooms and madness and villages of nulls, Danlo fell asleep.

The women were no less crazy the next morning than they had been at nightfall. For an hour the whole party waded upstream in the icy water; when one of the men set a foot on the bank, he was cuffed so hard on the ear that he howled. Then they left the water, climbed a brush-choked embankment, and proceeded in single file along a bare rock face that canted at a steep angle. Footholds were scarce, and Danlo was in terror of slipping and strangling. He pressed his lips together and crept forward grimly. It seemed to be a very long time before they descended again into the trees.

At midday, the women led the way into a close-packed stand of trees that pressed against a steep hillside. Danlo groaned, anticipating a climb, but instead the line snaked down a canyon so narrow that it was little more than a crack between two opposing hills, and emerged in a wider, boulder-strewn valley patchy with old snow. More women, perched atop the boulders, waved to the newcomers.

Between two of the boulders was a grotesquely misshapen but obviously artificial lattice of tree limbs. Withered, drooping greenery still clung to them. The women untied a rope that was woven into the lattice, and one section swung outward; it was a gate. The men were marched through. The structure proved to be the front of a very efficient stockade, perhaps sixty feet on a side, with walls to a height of about twelve feet. Altogether, five gaps between boulders were sewn up with the crude log fencing. The sweet smell of pine resin was strong. A group of about a dozen men was in the stockade already. Sitting in the dirt, they eyed the newcomers without curiosity or hope. Seven or eight women looked down from the boulders into the compound. The women were all holding the curved sticks. The gate swung shut.

Not long afterward, the women came back in and stripped off the men's trousers and shoes—the trousers for sanitary purposes, Danlo guessed, since they still were allowed no use of their hands. And being both naked and barefoot would make it harder for them to travel, if they should escape. The women removed the neck tethers as well, but not until they had tied a short length of rope between each man's ankles. The men could hobble about the enclosure freely. Not that there was much to see. The latticework offered plenty of handholds and footholds for climbing, but unless they could regain the use of their hands and feet, they were not going anywhere.

Walf the coach driver scuttled angrily from one group of men to another. "We've gotta do something," he said. "Gotta do it. Can't just stay here like this." At his urging, two of the men managed to get one another free of the ropes by working together behind their backs. But the women perched on the rocks saw, and before any more could be freed, the two were brought down—and in a terrifying and remarkable manner. The women used the curved sticks to throw shorter, straight sticks with blades on the front end and feathers at the back. To Danlo, the technique looked preposterously ineffective, yet they were able to throw the blade-sticks with amazing strength and accuracy. This must be how they had brought down wild animals for food. One of the men was pierced through the chest, and died shortly afterward. The other was pierced through the thigh, so that the blade-stick went in one side and came out the other. After letting him scream for a while, the women came in and carried him off. They brought him back pale and sweating, but bandaged. They one who died they left lying in the stockade. They only pulled the blade-stick out of him and took it away. After this incident, nobody tried to get free of the ropes.

Garpish was still unconscious, but his breathing was stronger, and he began to mumble and twitch. The whole group focused at once on pouring into him what feeble powers of healing they could muster. But still he failed to wake. At sunset the women brought food, but the men, busy concentrating on Garpish, ignored them, which led to more shouting and shoving. In the end, the food was left to grow cold. The silent vigil went on far into the night.

For a while Danlo lent support to the effort, but then he stood up and walked off by himself. Privately, he wasn't sure he wanted Garpish to wake up. While frightened and miserably uncomfortable, he was avid to learn more about the women. How did they know what plants and animals were edible? What skills did they use to gather them? He withdrew into his inner mind, leaving his surface as smooth as glass. He remembered, vividly, the nulls being Cleansed in the square in Woolich. Julan was dead, yes; nothing would change that. But more nulls appeared among the children every year. Did they all have to die? To think that Cleansings were a tragedy was permitted, even encouraged. It aided in the purging of grief. But to think that the tragedy was unnecessary—no. Cleansing was an imperative beyond questioning. No other option could ever be considered, if the Body was to sustain itself. But suppose a few nulls, here and there, simply vanished from proctor stations before they could be Cleansed. Suppose they were able to find their way, somehow, to a safe place in the wilderness. Suppose they had the skills to *survive* there? The Body would search, certainly, but for how long? The wilderness was large.

It was a startling idea, and filled with difficulties. How would nulls learn that the place existed, or how to find it? Somebody would have to tell them. And it would have to be somebody who knew a secret way to hide his thoughts from the Body. Somebody like Danlo Ree.

I? Could I do such a thing? he thought. Impossible. How in Frank's name would I manage it?

The moon, nearly full, sailed cold and white among the clouds. The enclosure was silent; men sat ringed around the supine form of the joddie. Danlo leaned back against a boulder at the edge of one of the log fences and chewed his lip. As ludicrous as the idea seemed, it sent a thrill through him. Yet the difficulties were insurmountable. He knew nothing about surviving in the mountains. If he were to have any serious hope of helping nulls escape, he would need weeks—months—to learn from the women. He would have to learn their language and win their trust.

But if the joddie woke, he would not have weeks, or even days. Was there some way he could distract the others, so as to prevent them from healing Garpish? Dangerous—if they saw what an appalling thing he was trying to do, their anger might spill over into violence against him. The Body fighting itself? Impossible to think such a thing, yet suddenly not impossible at all. Everything was changed now.

"Ni—volyanam boreh."

A face was framed by a gap in the lattice. After a moment he recognized the woman with the bad leg. She wrapped her fingers around one of the narrower limbs and peered through at him. He wondered if there were some way he could use her to create a distraction. If he could trick her into climbing into the stockade, maybe the men would surge forward to attack her, and the women rush to her defense. In the confusion maybe he could do something to the joddie. Kill him? He could never kill a man. He didn't even know how.

He edged closer, until he was looking through the gap into her eyes. "What are you?" he asked softly. "Where did your people come from?"

She said something. She looked sad.

''How do you survive? I wish there was some way you could explain.''

She pointed at the cooling bowls of food, then at Danlo, then at her own mouth. She said something insistent. Perhaps it was a question. After a moment her eyes softened, and she said something else in a lower, more liquid tone.

''Why don't we eat?'' He gestured at the men with his head. ''What they're doing is more important than food.''

An animal howled not far off. The woman looked away, out into the darkness, her profile a moonlit line at the edge of a mass of black hair. Her hand was still wrapped around the branch. He thought of creating a distraction by biting her. He could lock his teeth into a finger and hold on until she screamed. But the idea was as useless as it was ignoble. Instead, moved by some obscure impulse, he leaned forward and brushed his cheek, now bristling with three days' beard, gently across her knuckles.

The hand was jerked away; his cheek scraped rough bark. When he looked up, she was gone. He heard the soft crunch of feet as she moved away. He leaned his head against the poles and closed his eyes.

Chapter ‖ 7

IN the frost-rimed chill before dawn, Garpish coughed weakly and opened his eyes.

The change in the ktess was electric. All thought of cold, hunger, fear, fled before an outpouring of love and comfort. Compared to their clumsy groping, the joddie's mind was as sharp as a slap. It infused them, and they fed strength into it. Garpish reached out across the dark hills, and his call was answered. Through him the ktess of the Body flowed back into the men. Suddenly they were no longer at the mercy of the chaos beyond the edge of the world. They were One.

Danlo had grown careless with his stray thoughts, letting them come and go without worrying whether they were harmonious. Though still logy with sleep, he forced himself to become rigidly two-minded. And none too soon. For in upon the tide of the ktess, into the enclosure with a raw intensity that crackled in the men's hair like ball lightning, rode Frank Rettig. The men whispered,

"Frank." "Frank is come." They looked at one another in wonder. Frank's awareness drifted like smoke throughout the Body; he woke most often from the slumber of centuries on the great Feast days, when his praises were sung from dawn to dusk. To have even a remote chance of becoming Frank for a few minutes, one had to travel to Serameno and sit in the great amphitheater before the Triple Gate. Yet here he was in the wilderness, among common laborers, looking through their eyes, moving their arms and legs.

Frank saw the men lying half-naked on the ground, and the women perched on the boulders, and he was enraged. *Stand up,* he commanded. *Show that we are One.*

The men rose to their feet. A few whispered comments, but there was no outcry. Even so, the guards tensed and fingered their stick-throwing sticks. *What have we here?* Frank asked. *I want a closer look.* Half a dozen men moved smoothly over to stare up at the nearest woman, who bared her teeth and brandished her weapon at them. *They're nulls, aren't they? Wild nulls! Impossible!* Alarmingly for an Immortal, who ought to have been above such things, Frank seemed to be having a fit. He lapsed into an extended tirade in words that none of the men understood. Ancient English, Danlo suspected. Many among them were mouthing Frank's speech, and several of the weaker-minded fell to the ground and lay twitching.

The women on the boulders shouted down to those outside, and many faces appeared at gaps in the fence. They shouted at the men, but even if the men had been able to understand the women's words, they were beyond replying.

After a while Frank withdrew, and the men sat or lay down again. Danlo found that he was trembling. He was grateful that the Immortal had been distracted. A force so powerful could have stripped a mere counter's mind to the bottom, could have rooted out the inharmoniousness and left a babbling wreck. A few days ago he might have welcomed such a fate, but now he had a powerful reason to want to remain himself. If he could learn the secrets by which the women survived in the wilderness, he might be able to free nulls—if only a few here and there—and guide them away to safety. In the secret chambers of his mind, he wondered again whether it would be possible to kill the joddie. But the thought troubled him. If he meant to save lives, how could he begin by killing?

The day dawned bright and cold. The gate swung open, and

women brought in fresh bowls of food and took last night's uneaten bowls away. Garpish was able to sit up. He was fed first, and everybody watched silently until he shook his head and turned away from the spoon. Then the rest took their turns.

Even though Frank was gone, the Body was with them. Garpish assured them wordlessly that their rescuers, who for two days had prowled aimlessly across the foothills, were organizing a direct thrust. By tomorrow night, perhaps sooner, they would be re-united.

About midmorning the gate opened and half a dozen women entered. They carried curved sticks and blade-sticks at the ready. The men shrank away from them, surrounding the joddie with their own bodies. Having cloaked his mind again, Danlo was slow to react, so he was in the front rank of the crowd. The women surveyed them coldly. The biggest of the women marched forward, clapped her hand on one man's shoulder, and dragged him out. He stood shivering on the open ground while she selected another.

Danlo was the third of the four she picked. They were hustled out through the gate and up a path to where a bonfire crackled merrily at the mouth of a grotto. The grotto yawned beneath an overhanging ledge from which a tangle of naked tree roots groped at the air. The inner recesses beneath were cloaked in shadow even in full daylight; perhaps it was a cave.

Fifty or sixty of the savage creatures squatted in the dirt, nudging one another and voicing comments. One of them stood before the men and held up a food bowl. "Kets," she said. "Kets." She pointed at the man next to Danlo, but he only stared at her. "Kets!" she said again.

"Kets," Danlo repeated. "'Kets' is bowl. Or maybe 'food bowl.'"

"What do you mean?"

"It's how they talk. They're trying to teach us how they talk."

"So what? We'll be home again tomorrow. This bunch of nulls will be dead meat. Who cares how they talk?"

The wind shifted, and the smoke of the fire stung Danlo's eyes.

The woman shook the bowl in the first man's face and said "kets" again. When he failed to repeat the syllable, she back-handed him hard across the mouth. "All right," he whined. "Kets. Kets." The other men did not have to be convinced.

Then she held up another food bowl and said, "Griff." This bowl would have been indistinguishable from the first except that it was lined with green glaze rather than red. So maybe "kets" meant "red" rather than "bowl." "Griff," Danlo repeated. She held up the bowls alternately, and they all said dutifully, "Griff. Kets. Griff."

Next the woman pointed to herself and said, "Nurm." She pointed to the big woman and said, "Awa," and to the old woman who had mixed the medicine paste and said, "Agrom." Indicating all three with a circular motion of her finger, Nurm said, "Nififol." Each woman by herself was "nifol," and all together they were "nififol." The men, collectively, were "drafifol," and each of them was a "drafol."

The other men cooperated sullenly, but Danlo paid close attention. After an hour, his mind was buzzing with new words. He couldn't remember what the food bowls were called anymore, though, and they hadn't been taught how to ask questions. Having tagged most of the nearby objects with words, Nurm started in on commands. She untied one of the men and barked a word at him. Then Awa and another woman seized his limbs and saw to it that he carried out the action that was required. The command was repeated, and he was allowed to perform the movements himself. In this way the men learned how to walk, sit, eat, pick things up, carry them, clean them, and put them inside other things.

An urge to sing welled up in the ktess. From the stockade floated the exquisite opening notes of "We Are One in the Body." The men by the campfire looked at one another; to sing, in the circumstances, seemed imprudent, but to remain silent was painful.

The lush harmonies and lilting rhythms of the hymn, hanging like layered wisps of lace among the trees, inflamed the women. They rose from around the fire and thronged toward the stockade. Awa and Nurm and a couple of others clamped hands on Danlo and his fellows and urged them roughly in the same direction. Women were scrambling like squirrels up the cross-poles of the fence. Those at the top hooted and screeched and waved their arms at the men, but they failed to disrupt the song. In the confusion Danlo was passed from hand to hand, and scarcely noticed. He was bathed in the elation that the joddie was sharing. A rescue party three thousand strong was crossing the Wall at the edge of the world and streaming in their direction. He could see hands and feet climbing the Wall, and more hands and more feet.

Something cold slid between his wrists. His arms, abruptly, were free. He looked around in confusion. He had been led off behind a bush. The woman with the bad leg was squatting beside him, hacking with a knife at the rope that hobbled his ankles. They were alone.

She stood up and pressed some trousers into his hands. Her eyes were filled with tears. She said something and urged him with her hands to go, run, flee. He could only stand and look at her in perplexity. There was no need to escape. He would be far safer here for a few more hours than wandering alone in the forest. But of course she didn't know that.

He handed the trousers back to her, or tried to. She let them fall to the ground. He put a hand gently on her cheek, wishing he could soothe away the hurt in her eyes. She pressed his hand tight against her face with both of hers, and squeezed her eyes shut. "I'm sorry," he said. "I hope it will be easy for you," he said. "I hope you won't suffer much." The Cleansing to come would not be orderly, like the one in Woolich. It would be messy.

Three women came around the bush. Two of them pounced on Danlo; one pressed a knife against his throat. The third knocked the lame woman to the ground and stood over her, shouting. The lame woman pushed herself up on one elbow and said something in a low, even voice. The standing woman pushed on the lame woman's shoulder with her foot and sent her sprawling in the brambles. As Danlo was led away, he heard the lame woman cry out in pain.

Back in the stockade, wrists and ankles bound firmly again, he had nothing to do but wonder. What obscure impulse had led her to try to free him? What was she trying to save him from? Speaking lessons?

"They'll be here by dawn," one of the men said confidently. "By dawn." The words echoed around the enclosure. But Garpish dozed off after supper, and when he awoke under the fat and frosty moon, they saw that the Body had halted for the night, still many miles away, in order to rest and tend to numerous minor injuries. Supplies and weapons were being brought up from the rear, and those whose courage was greater than their fleetness of foot trickled into the resting place far into the night. Coaches and carts lay canted in gulleys, axles broken.

The next morning the joddie was fully occupied channeling messages to and from the men's loved ones. One man learned that his father was dying, and became hysterical. He rushed toward the fence, meaning to climb it even though he had no use of his hands. The women on the rocks pointed feathered sticks at him, but before they could let fly the joddie reached out gently with his mind, and the man slumped to the ground and lay snoring.

The same four men were removed from the compound and given more speaking lessons. Danlo looked for the woman with the bad leg in the throng around the campfire, but didn't see her. He observed the women's tools and utensils closely. How were they made? The pottery had been thrown by hand, not on a wheel—but what sort of clay was used? How did they build ovens to fire it? The knives were of finely worked stone—but how were the blades mounted in the handles? What sort of stone was it? How was it worked? He learned nothing of value.

At sunset, no food was brought. The men grumbled, but not much. What matter if they missed a meal? With every passing hour, the Body flowed closer.

Danlo's heart was heavy. In spite of the harsh treatment the women had dealt out, he didn't want to see them killed. Also, his half-formed idea was about to be ground into the dirt. To know that survival was possible was one thing; to know *how* to survive was another. It had been an absurd idea anyway. His grief had festered until it erupted in discord.

Oxar appeared at his shoulder. "Been worried about you. Glad to see you're taking stock."

Danlo very nearly dropped his barrier and let the whole scheme flow out, but habitual caution stopped him. "Quite a lot to think about, all at once."

"Back to normal soon. Forget this ever happened."

"You're a rememberer."

"All the same. Think I'll get a joddie to block it. You should too."

"One of them showed me a kindness. Or tried to." Danlo shared the memory of how the lame woman had freed him. "Don't know that I want to forget that."

Resurgence of stubbornness. "That's what you need *most* to forget. Couldn't have been kindness, anyway. They're animals. She was—who knows what? You get confused about these things. You know why." In Oxar's mind Danlo saw more of himself mirrored than he had realized Oxar was aware of. A stagnant canal, and Julan's face, her hair scattered on the floor. "Somehow you've got the idea that these animals are like her." Oxar shook his head. "Get it blocked, for Frank's sake. Get it all blocked good and hard."

Danlo stiffened. "They are like her. They're nulls."

"And if you could, I suppose, you'd stop the Body from Cleansing any nulls at all, because they remind you of her."

The flash of shame spurted out; Danlo had no time to conceal it.

Oxar's eyes widened. "Been thinking along those lines, have you? You're farther gone than I suspected. You've got a way of seeming simple on the surface. What's going on underneath? What's going on?"

"Don't know what you're talking about."

"No? Well, it's not for me to worry about." Oxar chuckled, indulgent on the surface but with an angry smugness underneath. "Brother Garpish and his friends will see to you."

The moon rose full and cold and white over the mountains, and the stars glittered in the frigid air. The gate swung open, and an armed party, larger this time than before, entered. Instead of curved sticks, several women were laden with coils of rope. As the others watched, alert for trouble, these fastened one of the long neck ropes carefully among a dozen men, another rope among another nine, and so on. In short order the men were trussed together as firmly as when they arrived. The women selected one of the groups of men—it happened to be the group that included Oxar—and led them out. The gate swung shut.

"Don't like this," the man next to Danlo muttered. "They're up to something."

"It will come to nothing," Danlo said. But he felt less confident than he tried to sound. The nearness of the Body was palpable, but in the ktess distances were difficult to judge. Their rescuers might be as close as the next hill, or they might not arrive until morning.

From the direction of the campfire, chanting started, a crude call-and-response. After a while it stopped, and one voice, high and clear, rang out in a long invocation.

Searing pain stabbed Danlo's eyes, and he recoiled. Those around him were blinking too, and shaking their heads. The pain had come through the ktess. From the men by the fire they received a jumbled visual image: a man stumbling out of the cave, crying out in agony, hands pressed over his eyes. Between his fingers and down his cheeks, dark blood leaked.

Belatedly, Danlo understood what the lame woman had been trying to save him from.

The crowd inside the enclosure swayed back and forth like water sloshing against the sides of a bucket. Danlo's neck was jerked. "Stop it," he shouted. "If we don't stay still, we'll strangle!'' Several voices were making the same point; the mass halted and stood quivering.

The pain in their eyes came again. And again. Danlo counted. He had counted the men being led out, too. There had been eleven of them. He was ready when the pain abated and the gate swung open again.

''Rush them!'' ''No! No!'' The men milled, confused.

This time the women were doubly wary. They could see that the men were on the edge of panic. The big woman named Awa strode forward and jerked on a man's arm, and he stumbled into motion. The man behind him was forced to follow, and the next after him.

Danlo's neck was tugged. It was his line that was being led out of the stockade. He broke into a trot, silently cursing the oaf behind him.

They were quick-marched up the canyon and into the open area before the overhang. A great bonfire was roaring, and sparks spiraled skyward. To one side, Agrom was administering something from a bowl to the eyes of a man who lay sprawled in the dirt.

The first man in Danlo's group was unhitched from the tether and dragged screaming into the cave. Through his eyes Danlo got glimpses of the interior. The woman named Nurm was wearing a headdress with tall curving horns, and something long and red dangled obscenely between her legs. She held a knife poised high in both hands. Through other eyes he was back in the stockade, where order had broken down. Some of the men were squirming in the dirt, choking, as others knelt and fumbled, wrists still bound behind them, at their comrades' necks. Through still other eyes he was rushing at top speed among dark trees, scraps of moonlight flickering. He felt the scrape of briars on skin, the rasp of breath in a dry throat. There—just ahead—a column of smoke, glowing fiery at its base. The nearest of the rescuers were spilling into the canyon!

His neck was jerked. He snapped back into his own body. The man just in front of him was being led toward the cave. The man looked back at the other end of the canyon, his face twisted into a mask of terrified yearning. The men in the enclosure were raising a wordless, keening cry. The women who had been squatting or sitting were standing now, clutching their knives and curved sticks nervously. They could hear the approaching horde, though they had no way of knowing what it was. Danlo strained his eyes against the night, and saw nothing. *Hurry!* he beseeched the Body silently. *Hurry!*

The cave disgorged another gore-spattered victim, who whimpered piteously as he clutched at his ruined eyes. He staggered into Danlo, lost his footing, and fell in a heap. By the smell, he had beshitten himself. Big Awa, her jaw set grimly, jerked on Danlo's arm. When he failed to respond, she twisted his elbow in a painful grip, grabbed his hair, and propelled him swiftly into the mouth of darkness.

Chapter ‖ 8

THE interior of the grotto was bathed in thick red light. Four spitting, sputtering torches flanked Nurm, two on each side. She was naked to the waist, the swirls of paint on her breasts and arms smudged by rivulets of sweat and spatters of blood. Her eyes glared wide, showing the whites. The imitation penis swung below her knees. It was made of cloth; in other circumstances, Danlo would have laughed.

He found that he had floated past the edge of fear, out onto a calm gray sea. She would put out his eyes, and then the Body would come and Cleanse the women and lead him home, and he would be cared for. The dream that had flickered awake during these past days was swept away. He had time to notice the little things—the way Nurm's horned headgear had slipped crooked, the fragrance of crushed flowers mingling with the complicated stink of terror. Nurm was shorter than Danlo; she looked like a bloodthirsty child.

She began intoning a savage litany in a ragged voice, drawing loops with the point of the knife in the air above her head. But she was interrupted. Outside the cave, a woman screamed. For a moment the voice hovered on a note of fear, but this was transmuted into a raging battle-cry. Other women took it up.

Nurm's knife wavered. She lowered it and said something sharp. The women in the cave looked at one another uncertainly. Now those outside were shouting words. In the ktess, Danlo could see that the Body had reached the stockade. Twenty hands were tearing at the log fence. A blade-stick thudded into a bole inches from a hand, but the hand never faltered.

He was knocked to the floor of the cave. The fall drove the wind out of him, and sent a shock of pain from shoulder to wrist. He twisted around cautiously and saw that he was alone. He got to his knees and crawled toward the mouth of the cave. Would it be safe for him to wait here? What if the women drove off the advance party and returned to finish their ritual? The calm vanished; suddenly he was quaking violently. Urgencies that had passed out of his life forever returned in a jarring rush.

He needed a knife. He looked around the cave floor, but of course Nurm had taken hers. Could he burn the rope in one of the torches without burning his wrists? Impossible.

He broadcast the strongest call he could for somebody to come release him. He sank back on the floor of the cave and tried to ken whether anybody was responding, but the ktess was too confused. He tried a second time. Still nothing. Through other eyes he got a tangle of images—women running, blade-sticks flying, the cold gleam of hand-held spotlights arcing crazily among the trees. He concentrated, searching for somebody who was close enough to see the mouth of the cave.

There! He boldly entered the man's mind and rode him, guiding his feet past the bonfire toward the overhanging ledge. The man tugged at his own limbs, trying to free them, but Danlo held firm. Into the cave. He saw himself lying helpless, eyes closed, face screwed up with effort. He knelt and fumbled at the knots at his own wrist.

"I understand the need, goodman." The man forced the words out through balky lips. "This will go faster if you let me do it." Danlo relaxed, sliding back into his own mind, and in seconds his wrists were free. When he opened his eyes, his benefactor was already plunging out the mouth of the cave. Danlo had never seen his face.

He brought his hands around and flexed them, staring at them in fascination, old friends that he had not seen for a long time. His fingers were thick and stupid; the hobble binding his ankles fought them. He tore and poked at the knots until at last they came loose. He kicked the rope away and scrambled to the mouth of the cave, where he crouched apprehensively, peering out at bedlam.

A group of women had gained the brow of the nearest ridge, and rained down feathered blade-sticks with deadly efficiency. Members of the Body were scaling the slope on both of their flanks and falling back, terribly wounded. On all sides people lay bleeding and dying. The women were better fighters, and better armed, but they were far outnumbered, and those still in the canyon were ringed by implacable attackers swinging sticks, kitchen knives, farm implements, or heaving stones two-handed overhead. Blinded men wandered, groping and stumbling. Somebody—it was no longer possible to tell from which party—had fallen into the fire, and now lay facedown, flames licking at the charred hair.

The urge to strike, to kill, boiled through the ktess. But Danlo had become two-minded again. He stood paralyzed. *Kill nulls. Kill all nulls.* His ktess-self moved mindlessly to obey. His arms burned to hit and strangle. But his secret self wrestled for control. He stood shuddering for some seconds before he dared move, and then his limbs were great heavy things that had to be instructed how to make the simplest motions. *Strike them down now. Come back later and finish the kill.*

A pile of trousers had been gathered outside the cave, to clothe the men after they were blinded. He rooted among these until he found a pair—they were not his—whose legs looked long enough. By the design of the silver buckles he recognized his own shoes, and donned them gratefully. The act of covering himself restored some of his self-assurance. He prowled through the devastation, moving in a zigzag path that he hoped would fool the raining blade-sticks.

He was looking for the woman with the bad leg. He wondered whether any of the others might do just as well, or better. But she was the only one he was sure he could trust: She had showed she understood about freeing the condemned. Where was she? A woman of the right build was backed against a tree, snarling and swinging a knife to keep three of the Body at bay. Danlo moved toward them. What could he do? How could he pull off the attackers without betraying himself? But then he saw it wasn't the right woman. He moved on.

He circled down toward the ruined pen and then back to the fire. More of the women lay dead than before, throats ripped open, skulls brutally smashed. One was sprawled facedown with no visible wounds. He set his foot under her shoulder and flipped her over. White bone gleamed in the red mass where an eye had been.

Shouts echoed from the ridge. He looked up. The blade-sticks were no longer falling.

In the center of the area where the bodies lay thickest, he saw a naked, green-painted arm protruding from a tangle of fallen flesh. He knelt swiftly and wrestled the dead aside. Joy welled in him. The lame woman was unconscious, but she had no obvious injuries. He put a hand to the corner of her jaw and felt a pulse.

He scooped her up in his arms. She was heavy, but he didn't care. He staggered away from the fire toward the shelter of the trees, carrying her limp form.

From the trees burst three of his own people, disheveled but madly vigorous. One of them, a boy of sixteen or so, was swinging a sickle viciously at the tall grass and chanting, "Die, die!" Just behind the boy, looking no less inflamed, was a joddie.

Danlo felt the joddie's mind enter his. He became two-minded as swiftly as he could. He knew he had not been quick enough: His intent had been lying open. But perhaps the joddie was distracted by the amount of activity on all sides, or by its intensity. He frowned uncertainly at Danlo and probed again. In his outer mind, Danlo painted pictures of the dark things he meant to do to the helpless body. Rip the throat open. Pulverize the skull with a rock. "Do with her as she deserves," he added aloud.

The joddie smiled and nodded, satisfied, and he and the others filed past. Maybe Danlo was not the only man intent on such revenge. Shuddering at the thought, he plunged into the forest. The climb was steep, the footing bad, the darkness nearly impenetrable. Branches raked his face, and he had to disentangle the woman's legs from a bush in order to force his way through. A few paces further on, he stumbled and fell. He forced himself grimly to rise and go on. Gradually the ktess of the Body ebbed, the visual images less intrusive, the compulsion to kill more easily ignored. His arms and sides ached and burned. Using the moon as a guide, when he could see it, he tried to keep to a straight line down one hill and up the next.

He fell again, to both knees, at the edge of a broad meadow, and this time he was too weary to get up. The ktess was tenuous, only a dim impression of some painful activity far off. He lowered the woman to the ground and sat beside her, cradling her against him—more for warmth than for protection. The meadow lay blue-white under a film of frost, and he shivered as his sweat chilled. The woman's breathing was scarcely perceptible, but it was regular. He pressed his fingers gently here and there against her skull, and found the swollen, blood-encrusted place just above the hairline. He had no way to tend the injury. If she died, she died.

Exhausted, he dozed. He woke in the gray light before dawn, so stiff with cold and fatigue that every movement was torture. Stubbornly he flexed his sore limbs where he sat, not standing up because he needed the woman's body for warmth. High overhead a couple of large dark birds were gliding. By twisting his neck, he could see more of them off to the north. They were circling thickly near the base of an irregular column of smoke. At its top the column was smeared into a plume, and the plume was touched with red gold. After a while the gold made its way down to the treetops, and the sun came up. The thin, delicate warmth was like honey on his skin.

The woman stirred and mumbled. His heart leaped and his breath quickened. But as seconds passed and her eyes stayed shut, his joy was swallowed by a new pit of worry: How was he to explain what had happened? How convince her to join in what he hoped to do? His mind flew back to the speech lessons, but the fury of the night had driven every word out of his mind. Think! Nurm had taught them to say "carry," and "I," and "you." I carry you. En dohl ahga. But he wasn't sure, when he had managed to reconstruct it, that the sentence didn't mean, "I wash you." Or even, "you wash me." Better to say nothing than say something idiotic.

The woman lay inert, her open mouth pressed slack against his arm. The sun lifted clear of the snowy peaks. He shifted his weight, hoping the movement would rouse her, but she failed to stir. He would have to wake her soon, if he could: The men had been given no meal at sunset, and he was hungry. There must be plenty of food nearby, but she would have to show him how to find it.

No longer enmeshed in the ktess of the Body, he was free to look openly at the idea that had been growing, submerged, for days. Food was only the first necessity, but it was the crucial one. If one band of nulls could live beyond the edge of the world, as plainly the women had lived, then so could another. He meant to learn how it was done.

He had wanted to carry Julan off somewhere, anywhere, rather than let her be Cleansed. He had wanted it until every bone ached. But the certainty that they would starve or be eaten by wild animals paralyzed him. It was too late for Julan, and for the girl he had seen beheaded in Woolich, but a few nulls were Cleansed every month. Somehow—he still had no clear idea how—he would penetrate the heart of the Body without alerting the joddies, and help the nulls run away to the mountains. The lame woman could show them how to live. By twos and threes he would steal nulls out of the proctor stations before they could be Cleansed.

Someday a whole village of nulls might prosper in this very meadow! He saw Julan's gentle smile, and knew she would have liked to walk the streets of such a village. But until he could learn how to find food in the wilderness, and how to avoid the hidden dangers, the plan could grow no further. "Don't die," he whispered to the woman. "You must not die."

Or did it matter? Wasn't the whole scheme crazy? For nulls to live together in harmony was unthinkable. He reached out to touch and be comforted by the ktess, and met, like a blind eye seeking light, nothing. In all the hollow space beneath the sky, he was alone. The tracery of connectedness, the web of fellow feeling that had upheld him from the day of his Receiving, had been torn into tatters and blown away. I am Danlo Ree, he said to himself, counter, son of Carl Ree, a weaver of Lirmorr, ortho-cousin of the Melitts and the Furds of Plezton, levo-cousin of. . . . I am Danlo Ree, levo-cousin of. . . . I am. . . . Who am I? His skin crawled. What am I? His fingers itched to dig in the dirt, so he could burrow in a hole and hide from the naked sky. The alien world beat upon him until he clanged. He shut his eyes tight and shuddered.

In a welter of images—happy nulls, dark birds, bloody eye sockets, a sickle slicing through grass—he nodded off again. When he woke, the fear had passed. He felt only a dull numbness. It was different from the numbness he had felt when Julan died. That had been the numbness of a closed and shuttered room. In this room the windows were open, and a wind was blowing through. It might not be safe to look out the windows, though. Not yet.

The sun was high in the south, and in the north the smoke was gone, all but a whitish smudge up high. The woman was breathing more strongly now, making a noise in her throat with every exhalation. He shifted her weight to get the blood back into his leg, and felt her stiffen. Moving with care, he tried to bring his arm around behind her shoulders, to comfort and restrain her, but with sudden energy she pushed him away and scrambled to her feet, already backing up. Fear brimmed in her eyes. He tried to stand up too, not very successfully. "It's all right," he said, holding out a hand. "I won't hurt you." She jabbered an incomprehensible stream at him—and caught her heel and pitched backward into the weeds. He hobbled forward, cursing the stiffness in his joints. She glared at him from the ground, and raised herself slowly on one elbow, still glowering, and took a long look past him at the trees,

and around in all directions at the empty meadow. Slowly the
ferocity went out of her. She touched the wound on her head, and
winced, and touched it again more gingerly. Then she sat for a
minute gazing at the ground, gazing at nothing. He guessed she
was remembering the battle. She blinked back tears and talked
some more, to herself, with little hand-motions.

With exaggerated gestures he showed her how he had found her
in the battle and carried her away. She nodded to show she
understood, though her eyes were still troubled. She asked him
something. He shrugged. "We have no words," he said. He sat
beside her on the ground. "We must learn. Learn. Look—I'm
Danlo." He put his hand on his own chest.

She pointed at him: "Ahmdanlo."

"No, no." This time he tapped his chest. "Danlo." She
repeated it correctly, so he pointed at her: "You?"

She pointed at herself. "Linnie."

"Linnie. Linnie."

She nodded happily.

"Danlo carry Linnie," he explained. "Carry." He held his
arms out, hefting an imaginary weight.

"Danlo carry Linnie." She laughed. "Dusslah Linnie carry
Danlo." She mimed sawing apart the rope between his wrists.

He sighed. "I think we haven't quite got it yet. Listen, we can
talk all we want, tonight and tomorrow. Right now we need food.
Food." He put a morsel of nothing into his mouth, and then
gestured empty-handed at the surrounding forest. "Food. And a
fire. Definitely a fire."

She gazed around at the trees, the distant peaks. Her attention
was caught by the birds still circling in the north: She stared
intently at them. With a cry, she sprang to her feet.

"What's the matter?"

Looking down at him, she said something, but it broke off in a
sob. She covered her face in her hands. A moment later she had set
her jaw and was striding away, first walking and then, in her
unfortunate lopsided gait, breaking into a lope.

Danlo scrambled to his feet. "Where are you going? Come
back!" But she paid no attention. In a few steps she had
disappeared among the trees.

Why should she be so concerned about the birds? If he lost her,
he'd never learn. He dashed after her.

Somewhere ahead, she was crashing through the dimness
between the trees. As his eyes adjusted, he caught glimpses—her

back, her flying hair—in the sunshafts that slanted between the majestic boles. He was too stiff to catch her, but she was still weak from her head injury and hindered by her bad leg, and the ground was uneven. For a while she was mere paces ahead, and he croaked, "Stop," a couple of times, but he had breath for no more, and of course the word meant nothing to her. Eventually he had to slow, gasping, to a dull trot, and she outpaced him.

He would not have been able to find the way back to the campsite, so he was surprised to come out of the trees at the top of a steep slope and see its ruin spread out below. Except for the pulled-down wreckage of the stockade and a broad, irregular circle of ash, black and gray and thickly strewn with flecks of white, little remained to show that last night the canyon had been filled with people. A few sticks, trampled brush, scattered clothing. The dead were no longer to be seen, nor the survivors. The burned area seemed to be larger than the fire he remembered, though he had not seen it from this angle. More than a dozen large, ugly birds were hopping and flapping and quarreling with one another between the still-smoldering hot spots. The rich, bitter smell of burned meat enfolded him.

Linnie was walking aimlessly through the camp, wailing in a loud voice. She was using words; it was a chant, or a lament. The tone chilled him. He hung back under the trees, frightened that stragglers from the Body of Harmony might still be about. But when he saw that she was not set upon, he picked his way down the slope to join her.

Not wanting to disturb her in her grief, he went and looked first in the cave, which was empty except for the burned-out torches and the scraps of rope he had left, and not awe-inspiring at all in the daylight, merely an ordinary recess of weathered stone. As he approached the remains of the fire, the birds flapped heavily away, but they quickly settled back, ignoring him. The white bits scattered through the ash were bone. Human bone.

The smell was thicker here, and repellent, yet it renewed his hunger. He went and planted himself in front of Linnie. She had picked up a knife somewhere, and was fingering it in a vague way, holding the blade close to her breast. Her eyes were bleak and stricken. "Forgive me," he said, "but we need food. We need to eat. Food. Eat." He made putting-morsels-into-mouth motions. "You." He touched her shoulder. "Find food."

She looked at him without comprehension, and returned her gaze to the knife. This wasn't getting him anywhere. He remembered the women bringing fat rabbits into camp already spitted on the blade-sticks, so he roamed through the grass until he found one of the weapons where it had fallen, and returned to her and waved it in her face. "Food! Food!" He made eating motions again.

She lowered the knife slowly, and looked from him to the blade-stick and hesitantly back again. "Vood," she said. This was followed by a stream of gibberish. Then her mouth curled open, and a laugh, low and hoarse, forced its way out. The laugh grew. It split her face into a broad grin, and her body jerked with it, and she shook her head while tears squeezed out down her cheeks, and all he could do was stand there, holding the feathered blade-stick and watching her and understanding nothing. "Vood," she hooted. "Dlu mas ogogn' mureh *vooood* brnesh!"

Chapter ‖ 9

WHEN she had finished laughing, Linnie felt better. Her friends were singing their walking song on the path to the Land of Always Spring Blossoms, but as much as she might wish she were among them, Night Sky Mother had dreamt otherwise. After wiping her eyes, she set about prowling through the grass, searching for what she would need to go on living. The attackers had been thorough in their killing but careless in their scavenging; she had no trouble finding knives, boots, even bracelets and combs.

The food man stood watching her with a fixed, mournful air. She ignored him. First she located several bows that were still strung. One she kept; from the others she unhitched the bow-strings, which she coiled around her fist and put in the bottom of a quiver. She filled this and another quiver with unbroken arrows, and strapped them both on her back. Next a fire-starting bow, two blankets, a water-skin, a spool of twine, and an axe. She pressed the blankets into the man's arms. He had sense enough to fold them into a neat packet. She uncoiled twine and showed him how to tie the packet. With this slung over his shoulder, he began following wherever she meandered, looking as she was looking in the dirt. When he spotted something, he would pounce on it with a little cry and hold it up for her to inspect. But most of the things he found weren't useful. She had spotted them already and not bothered to stoop for them. She had to take them from him and pitch them away. He looked so sad that she let him carry the axe. She worried that he might attack her with it, but if he meant to kill her, he had had plenty of chance during the night.

She kept an eye out for Agrom's medicine pouches, but not with much hope. They would still have been tied to Agrom's belt, so unless the old woman had escaped the massacre somehow, the pouches had been burned. It seemed unlikely to Linnie that anybody had escaped except for herself; she had seen the ferocity of the attackers in their first rush across the camp. Two had set upon her. One seized her in a grip of stone and the other flung himself at her face. She remembered no more.

There was no shortage of sacred blowguns. Linnie picked one up, chuckled sadly, and threw it as hard as she could. It spiraled end over end into the trees. Nurm's spear, however, was worth keeping. It needed no lek-tapru to do its work. Linnie found a third blanket and tied its corners together to make a pouch, which she let the man carry. Into the pouch she tucked a little bag of paint-sticks, and unbroken bowls and mugs of red and green. He accepted it all gravely, without complaining. Maybe he was good for something after all. Carrying, anyhow. What had he said his name was? Danlo. If he had been blinded, Danlo would have been no use at all except for carrying. Whole, he might be good for other things too—but he might be dangerous. She would have to keep a close eye on him.

The canyon stank of death. She was glad to climb out of it onto higher ground. The land to the east was mountainous, and capped in cold whiteness. To the west lay easier travel, but the avengers had come out of the west, and might still be lurking. The route home lay to the south, but the thought of returning across all those empty miles filled her with such despair that she turned instead to the north, just to avoid the feeling. After a while they forded a stream, and she washed off some of the stink. She nocked an arrow as they went on, keeping an eye out for supper, but the game was hiding today. Maybe the animals were spooked by the lingering smell, which had drifted a long way in the cold clear air, but more likely they were given ample warning by the ridiculous amount of noise the man made when he walked. She hissed at him over her shoulder, but either he was the clumsiest creature ever born or he didn't understand what she was trying to tell him. When she found deer droppings so fresh they were still steaming, she tried to impress upon him that he must sit on a log and wait while she followed the trail, but when she turned away he popped up and came after her, babbling about food. She grimaced and stamped her feet in exasperation. "I hope Grampa Gator chomps a bite out of your ass," she told him. He smiled at her hopefully. "A big bite."

In the end, she decided to put off hunting until the next day. She found a sheltered spot between the exposed roots of a gnarled walnut tree and gathered kindling. Danlo watched intently as she arranged the tinder in the rubbing-hole, so she gave him a pinch of grass and showed him how to feed it in. He kept dropping the grass and fumbling for it, and when she got a spark he fed it so quickly that the spark flipped out onto the ground and went out. She got the fire started, finally, but it took twice as long with him helping as it would if she had done it by herself.

They scrabbled for last year's nuts in the dirt until it was too dark to find any more, and then cracked them between a pair of stones. Danlo was an enthusiastic walnut cracker, but he mixed rotten nutmeats among the good ones. She was too tired and too disgusted to try to explain to him what he was doing wrong; she only snarled at him and hoarded as many of the good ones for herself as she could. That would teach him quick enough. When the nuts were gone she was still hungry.

He untied the blankets, handed one to her, and wrapped the other across his shoulders. He sat cross-legged, huddled close to the fire. She did likewise. She wondered whether he would want to talk again, to teach her more words, but he had withdrawn into himself. Wishing he were home, probably, not off in the cold with a lame woman. His people would be used to his clumsiness and stupidity. He seemed a nice enough man; she had fought Sandu over him twice, she might as well admit she liked him. But could she afford to be saddled with such a bungler? On the other hand, if she drove him off, she would be entirely alone. She was afraid, suddenly, of being alone. She looked at Danlo out of the corner of her eye. If she moved to share the blankets, would he think she wanted sex? Probably. Well, how *did* she feel about sex? She had not been with a man for a very long time, not since Makelvy got too weak. Yielding to this new man would feel very nice. But the long walk back to Ranoima, if she decided to attempt it, would be arduous enough for a woman in prime condition—probably impossible for one who had to travel the last leg through the swamps with a swollen belly. And what if the trip took more than nine months? Could she give birth unaided?

She was sure she could fight him off if he got ideas, but in the end, as much as she wanted the comfort of his closeness, she felt it would be better not to tempt him, or herself. She curled up under her blanket and watched her friends' faces flicker in the flames. After a while she slept.

During the night the cold rain powder came again and spread its white blanket across the world. Danlo told her the stuff was called snow. Snow would be good for hunting. It would make tracking easy. But still he refused to let her hunt alone. So she explained, by arching her legs to walk on tiptoe and pointing, one by one, to every twig that poked up through the snow, that he must move without stepping on them. When he had got the idea, she took him up and down the side of a hill five or six times, stopping silently and pointing a rigid accusing finger every time he made the slightest noise. Only when she was satisfied that he was at least making progress did she set off on a trail she had spotted. She deliberately didn't let him know that the training was finished and the hunt begun. He thought they were merely following a new route, and was still sweating with effort when she put out a hand to halt him, drew the bow, and knocked a fat raccoon out of a tree with one arrow. It skittered away, but she pounced on it, dug her fingers into the fur of its back, and dodged its teeth and claws long enough to slit its throat.

Danlo stood wide-eyed, his mouth hanging open. He looked again and again from the limb where the animal had perched to Linnie and to the carcass at her feet.

She made him carry it back to camp. She was glad game was not scarce. They might have starved before he learned to keep quiet enough. She was encouraged that he wanted to learn about hunting. Clumsy he might be, but not completely impractical.

She was less encouraged by his reaction to the skinning. She knelt beside the raccoon, splayed it on its back, and slit its belly-skin. When she grasped the edge of the skin and pulled it apart, it made a soft ripping, sucking noise. Danlo's face turned greenish. He lurched away to the other side of the tree and was loudly sick.

But even before the raccoon was cooked, he was recovered enough to make signs that he wanted her to teach him to shoot. She put a protective hand on the bow and scowled at him until he desisted. The idea of scouring the forest floor for the arrows he would send flying astray did not appeal to her. First, she thought, she would find a source of flint and teach him to make arrow-heads. And a bow of his own. After that he could learn to shoot.

If he never learned to shoot, at least he could keep her supplied with arrows.

The next morning, as soon as he woke up, Danlo began jumping up and down and waving his arms energetically. She worried that he was having a fit, but the activity was too well-coordinated to be a fit, and it went on too long. Next he lay on his face, put his hands under his shoulders, and began pushing himself up from the ground and letting himself back down. From the solemn expression on his face, he was doing something that he considered important. Maybe it was his way of dancing the praises of the Great Ones. She tried not to laugh.

She found some wild onions and made raccoon stew. He ate out of his bowl, she out of hers. She set her bowl down without finishing it, and when he picked it up she cuffed him and grabbed it away from him. She scraped what was left of the stew into his bowl. Afterward she felt bad. As strange as it seemed, he must be ignorant about the difference between men's and women's things. She was hurt by the apprehensive way he looked at her when he thought she wasn't watching. But it was no use to coddle a husband, or somebody who might, if no better prospects came along, become a husband. If he got into bad habits, he would only be unmanageable later.

They stayed by the walnut tree for three nights. At night he tossed and turned under his blanket, and sometimes she woke in the dark to find him sitting bent forward over the embers, shivering. He was terrified by noises and large animals. When a family of bears sauntered by one afternoon, he actually whimpered as he tried to hide behind her.

He insisted on teaching her more of his words. Sometimes she pretended to understand less than she did, or deliberately mispronounced things just to watch his face get red. But she knew she was a long way from home. She could try to convince Danlo to make the journey back to Ranoima with her, but she would need to be able to talk with him to do that, and even then he might not agree to go. It would be easier just to walk downhill until she got to the great valley. If she settled among his people, learning their speech would be useful. And it was nice to be able to communicate, however haltingly, to understand when he said, "Good," between bites of stew, and afterward patted his belly and said, "Full." She taught him a few of her words too, including "bow" and "arrow."

She wondered why he didn't go home himself. It was an easy

three days' walk to the wall. At first she thought maybe he had no sense of direction, and was teaching her his speech so he could ask her to show him the way. But he was not too stupid to see where the sun set. More likely, he had been driven out from his clan, and couldn't go back. That would explain why he hadn't escaped from the stockade when she gave him the chance. He had no place else to go. If he had committed an offense against Night Sky Mother, even feeding him could invite dire retribution. But the Great Ones, it was known, made allowances for husbands. As long as she was careful to correct him at once if he did anything sacrilegious, she would be safe.

On the fourth morning, Linnie went hunting alone. Danlo stirred himself to build up the fire, but he didn't do his ridiculous jumping and waving, only sat silent and unresponsive. She wondered whether he was getting sick, the way men did. Could Uncle Fire Spider have followed her so far from home, and begun recruiting a new warrior so quickly? Worrying about this, she wandered farther afield than usual. So it happened that she emerged at the crest of a hill and saw three people. She dropped to a crouch and peered down at them warily. They had not seen her. By the elaborately piled-up hair and the stiff way they carried themselves, they could only be Danlo's people. They were walking around a shiny thing the size of a house. It looked quite a lot like the moving houses in the great valley, so she was not surprised when one of them opened a door in its side and they climbed in.

The house began to hum like a hive of giant bees, and after a minute it lurched forward across the uneven ground, crushing the bushes in its path. She watched until it disappeared over a ridge. For a while after it was gone, she could still hear the hum and the crashing noises.

On the way back to camp she surprised five does and a four-point stag, who bounded away in alarm. She didn't bother to let fly. The plume of smoke from the fire could be seen for miles. How could the people in the moving house miss it? She cursed her leg, wishing she could run faster. She was frightened that he would be gone when she got there, or lying murdered. Her heart lifted when she saw him perched mournful and still on the root of the big tree. She raged past him, grabbed a heavy stick to stir the fire apart, and scuffed dirt over the coals. "See man," she told him. "Hill, valley, hill, hill," indicating how far away, and in what direction. Then she counted on her fingers: "Man, man, man." He had taught her numbers, but in her excitement she couldn't remember them.

"Three."

She nodded vigorously. "Three man. Three man—" Both hands made up-and-down motions in imitation of the way the house rocked across the uneven places in the ground. He looked confused. He babbled some words at her. She broke off the useless conversation with a wordless growl, and wadded up the blankets and threw them at him.

He understood. Without any more urging, he gathered up their meager belongings, and they set off.

In the days that followed, she thought about the moving house that sounded like bees, but she said nothing to Danlo. Communicating any but the simplest ideas took too much effort. He seemed to be as concerned as she was about encountering such patrols. When they came to the edge of a stretch of open ground, he would halt her with his arm and look this way and that, shielding his eyes with his hand and squinting at anything that moved, before nodding that it was all right to proceed. She thought this mix of pompousness and nervousness was extremely funny, but at least he was learning to be observant, so she bit her knuckle to keep from laughing.

They had no way of knowing how far they would have to go to be safe, so they continued north for two weeks, pausing at night to eat and sleep and pressing on the next morning. Sometimes Linnie wished they were going south instead of north; every step took her further from Ranoima. But she thought probably it was silly to worry about going home. If Makelvy had still been alive, she would have felt very differently. Without him, any place was as good as any other. This land, though drier and colder than she liked, was not a bad place to make a home. Soon they must pass beyond where word of the raids and massacre had spread. If they didn't find a settlement in the mountains—and it seemed strange to her that Danlo's people all lived in a clump behind the wall, leaving the eastern forest uninhabited—they could move west and find a village.

They came to a little valley where an icy river chuckled over stones, and fruit trees and berry bushes promised full bellies come summer. A hollow house-shaped chunk of crumble-stone, obviously left from the time of the ancestors, offered shelter. It lay half-buried on a shallow slope, as if it had tumbled down when the river cut under the bluff behind it. Since then, the river had shifted away by a stone's throw, digging a new channel that left the talus slope dry. The ancestor thing had three walls and no roof, but one of the walls overhung far enough to provide some protection from rain.

Unfortunately, it already had occupants. When they approached, a spotted yellow cat sprang to the top of the wall, hissed, and bared its fangs and talons. Linnie killed it with an arrow, but when it fell back into the structure a great screeching erupted, and several more cats darted out, ears flattened. She killed one more with an arrow and two by jabbing them with the spear. Several more ran off. When they crept forward to look inside, a furry ball the size of a human baby jumped at Danlo, fangs bristling. His knife was already in his hand, and he stabbed the animal again and again, clumsily but energetically, until it fell dead at his feet. Afterward, she was pleased to see, he looked more surprised than shaken. He scraped the thick bed of offal out of the shelter with a stick, and afterward spread a layer of fresh grass on the floor. The cats were good eating, and useful too. Linnie saved a little pile of claws to make needles. They built a large fire that night in the open side of the shelter. She had learned to say, "More wood," and Danlo grumbled but obeyed. She knew they would need the fire to warn the rest of the cats not to come back. Long after midnight she lay awake, one hand resting on the spear, her neck prickling every time an enraged yowl scraped across the darkness.

Over the next few days she began to notice that a change was coming over Danlo. Instead of twitching restlessly under his blanket, he began to sleep until well past dawn. He smiled more, and sang scraps of songs. He was willing to let her hunt alone. And he began staring wistfully at her when she went down to the river to bathe. That was a nice change; she had been worrying that perhaps he was one of those men who liked boys. The chilly water puckered her nipples and gave her gooseflesh, but it was good to be clean. She washed her clothes and spread them out on a rock to dry, and then made him undress so she could do the same with his. He was embarrassed to be naked, but not so embarrassed that he didn't watch closely to see how she was doing the cleaning. She learned his words for "wash" and "clean" and "dirty."

While the clothes were drying he sat beside her in the sun, and she thought he was going to put his arm around her, but after a minute he stood up abruptly and plunged into the river to wash himself. She laughed: The cold water made short work of his erection. His beard was coming in more gray than brown, and the last weeks had burned the fat from his muscles. He was a fine-looking man, even though he was older than Makelvy. If he wanted to put his arm around her, she decided, she would let him. Of course, she still had to worry about how she would give birth without a midwife. Linnie had never had a baby. In the first few months that she and Makelvy were married, he had made love with her, but after that he grew too weak. When they saw she wasn't getting pregnant, his friends offered to help, but she loved Makelvy too much to let anybody else touch her, and after he died she lost interest in sex and babies both.

She wondered why Danlo had saved her from the massacre. At first she assumed that he wanted a wife. Maybe all the women in his village had rejected him. But if so, why was he so diffident about approaching her? "People kills," she said. "More kill. You carry me. And? And?"

His explanation left her thoroughly confused. He started by teaching her the words for "baby" and "child" and "grow." Also the words for "think" and "open" and "closed," and what looked like "steal" and "protect," though the last two were so abstract that she wasn't sure. An altogether useless jumble of words, taken together, but by now she was finding it easier to learn, and there was plenty of cooked meat from yesterday's hunt, so they had nothing better to do than talk. He talked about stealing children who think closed instead of think open. Which made no sense. He seemed to be saying that he had saved her so that she could help him steal some children, but she couldn't make out why that was important, or why he needed her help. Most of their conversations were full of arm-waving and head-scratching, and broke off in frustrated silences. She would think she had understood what he was getting at, and nod enthusiastically, but then he would say something else that showed she hadn't understood at all. This conversation was no different.

The weather grew milder. Concerned that she might run short of arrows, she made a snare out of green saplings, baited it with fish scraps, and caught a young raccoon. But the second animal she caught—probably a larger raccoon—tore the snare apart escaping from it, and building another was hard work. When she found a deposit of good flint, she went back to hunting, and taught Danlo how to break the flint into three-sided pieces and press flakes from the edges. His first efforts were suitable only for scraping meat off of bones, and he grew discouraged. She had to nag him to keep at it.

A pack of dogs came down out of the east—huge, gaunt, brindle-haired beasts. They prowled along the river, snuffling and barking. Frightened, Linnie and Danlo stayed in the shelter for two days except when they went out together to gather wood. On the third day they had to hunt, so she gave Danlo the spear and made him follow along behind. They had travelled less than a mile when three of the dogs jumped them. One sank its teeth into Danlo's hand before they could kill it. She washed the wound in the river, and they went back to the shelter, still hungry. They stayed hungry for three more days, only going out for water and wood, until at last the dogs moved on.

He asked her what she and the others had meant to do with the men, so she tried to explain how Uncle Fire Spider needed warriors, and how the women had hoped that Uncle would take the men from other villages and leave the men of Ranoima alone. She could see that he didn't understand. She tried to find out what his word was for "husband," but she felt it would be more discreet to do this without pointing to him as the husband and her as the wife, so getting the idea across took time. Once the word was established, she showed him how husbands got lazy and sleepy and finally died. He ask her to describe the details again and again. He didn't seem to care about the war between Uncle Fire Spider and Uncle Gnaws-at-Rock. What Danlo wanted to know was whether some men got sick while others didn't, whether their limbs swelled, whether they died only at some special time of year. She thought most of the questions were silly, but he seemed to take the answers seriously. He frowned at the ground while he digested them, and got up and paced back and forth beside the river.

Once she started remembering the lazy, useless men of Ranoima, she couldn't figure out why she was being shy with this one. He was strange, but he was kind, and handsome too. She had just about made up her mind to crawl under his blanket in the night, when he did something that shocked her. For no reason at all he pounced on his food bowl, stared into it as if it contained a dead rat, and threw it as hard as he could. The bowl smashed to shards at the edge of the river. He hurled his cup after it.

The cups and bowls were precious; they had no oven for firing clay—no clay, in fact. She waited for an explanation, but he said nothing, and avoided her eyes. "Danlo eats uses fingers," she said.

"You have bowl. We use this bowl together."

She snorted in disgust. "This woman bowl." He nodded. He

looked sad. After that he ate with his fingers, and went down to the river and scooped up water with his hands. She waited for some explanation of the outburst, but he said nothing.

He kept right on doing things she didn't understand. One afternoon when she came back from spear-fishing, he had cleared a wide, level area and was heaping large rocks there. As she watched, amused and skeptical, he began piling the rocks in a line. The line became a low wall. By sunset a second wall angled out from the first.

He was building, she deduced, a stone house. Linnie had never seen a house built of stone, and wasn't sure why anybody would want to live in one. What if you were sleeping beside a stone wall when a wind came and blew the house down? A light wooden frame with slats of bark, that was how to build a house. After a hurricane, it was no trouble to pick up the pieces and build the house again. Besides, he hadn't started by calling on Uncle Thunder-Belcher to keep the land underneath the house solid, so nobody would ever be foolish enough to set foot inside.

While the fish were baking by the edge of the fire, she considered whether to make him tear the stone house down and build a proper house. But building a ridiculous impractical house wasn't an offense against the Great Ones. And why should she care what sort of house he built, unless she meant to live in it? Did she mean to? This valley wasn't a bad place—plenty of game, and no really nasty predators, now that the dogs were gone. What she missed, and desperately, was the company of other women. Sometimes when she was off alone, Terana and Little Awa would come into her heart with such a fierce pang that she had to sit on a log and weep. The hurt would not be healed until she had new friends to laugh and gossip with. Danlo by himself wasn't enough, wouldn't have been enough even if they shared as much speech as brother and sister. He never laughed. He was stiff, and the things he did were incomprehensible. Stone houses, and breaking his bowl, and lately he had started sneaking up beside her not to put his arm around her but to try to fuss with her hair! Being friends with a man was impossible in any case, but friends with a man like that? No, she would have to move on.

She said nothing. Let him build a stone house, if it pleased him. There was no harm in waiting here for a month. She would have to know more of his people's words before she headed down into the great valley. When she had nothing better to do, she sat and watched as he carried rocks from the riverbed and piled them up, and then took them one by one from the pile and placed them on the wall. Once, one of the walls teetered and fell over with a great clatter and crash, and she had to press her hand over her mouth to keep from laughing. After glaring at her, he stooped in the rubble with great dignity and stubbornly started building the wall again.

He kept talking about stealing children. She still couldn't understand this weird obsession, but it did become clear that he meant to bring the children back to this valley and start a new village, a village with lots of stone houses.

"Many villages in west," she pointed out, trying to inject a note of reason into his madness. She was stitching up the arm of his coat with a piece of twine. The afternoon sun slanted across his bare shoulder, catching the arc of skin in a sheen of dull gold. "We goes there."

Danlo's hand twitched in agitation. "No, no, no. They kill you."

He had said this before. It made no sense. True, she could expect hostility from the villages where they had taken the men. But those villages were far away to the south. "Linnie good woman. People not kills Linnie."

"They kill you (with?) children."

There he went about the children again. "Linnie not child."

"Linnie thinks closed, children think closed. In village, people think words and (talk?) head with head." He grabbed the twine away from her and gripped it so it thrummed between his clenched fists. "Head," he said of the left fist, "head" of the right. "Think." He pointed at the twine with his nose.

Linnie hoped that everybody in the great valley wasn't as crazy as Danlo. Probably they weren't. Probably that was why he was afraid to go back. By now she was sure they had driven him out. She might have considered starting a new village with an ordinary man, if she liked him enough, but not with a crazy one. She took the twine away from him, none too gently, and went on with her work. "I goes." She nodded firmly. "You goes?" She shrugged. "House. Linnie holds good house. Not steals children. Maybe makes children." She had not meant to be so bold. Her face grew hot, and she peeked at him out of the side of her eyes to see whether he had noticed.

He met her eyes with a look of longing and suppressed adoration. She felt her face grow hotter. "Linnie finds good man," she said defiantly. "Makes strong children."

Danlo put out his hand, very slowly, and pressed the palm

against her cheek. She felt very small suddenly, and a loosening started in her belly. She felt angry too. She wanted a strong man, not a crazy, clumsy one. But her need was stronger than her anger. She let him draw her close, into the warm sweaty circle of his arm, and arched her back to press tighter against him and opened her mouth greedily to his kiss.

The months of closeness and separateness, of glances and averted glances, of hunger and being full, of sticky animal blood and icy river water, of sudden dangers and the nightlong wheeling of the star-besotted heavens, would not let them remain apart. His hands explored her. She bit and licked his neck, his ears. Their limbs found ways to intertwine. She discovered, to her delight, that in some things he was not clumsy at all.

They slept in each other's arms. The next day Linnie was bursting with affection. She giggled and chattered like a girl. But Danlo, for no reason that she could fathom, was sunk in dark melancholy. When she touched his shoulder, he shrugged her hand away.

She wished she knew more words. "You feels bad? Linnie bad?"

"No." A long pause. "No. Linnie is good." At last he roused himself, but not to come close to her. He got up and went back, lethargically, to building the accursed stone house. She felt miserable—cheated, and lonely, and frightened of his mania. She had hoped that loving might cure him of it. Maybe she couldn't cure him, but the people in the valley might know how. If he was going to be her man, she wanted him to be sensible. "We goes," she said, fists planted firmly on her hips. "We goes west, find village." She stretched out her arm to point. "You builds house in village."

He put his head in his hands and rocked it up and down, as if it hurt. "In village Linnie dies," he said. "Here Linnie eats, hunts. Grows children."

"You not likes Linnie. People in village likes Linnie."

"People in village kill Linnie."

"People in village *not* kills Linnie. Linnie good woman." She struck her breastbone with her fist. "Linnie hunts good, makes strong babies."

"Linnie is a good woman, yes. Linnie is a good woman." He tried to come close and hold her, but she wriggled out of his grip and stamped away. He looked so sad, standing with his shoulders slumped, not looking at her, that she wanted to go and pull him

down and sit beside him and put his head in her lap, the way she
had used to hold Makelvy. But what was the use of that? He would
only do something else crazy. Unable to bear watching him, she
went off to hunt, and lost two arrows.

Chapter ‖ 10

AS they moved north, Danlo mused about the three men Linnie
had seen. Why were they prowling beyond the Wall? Possibly the
Body of Harmony wanted to be certain that none of the women
had survived. Or the proctors might have taken a nose count and
found one man missing. They might be trying to save him. That
effort would end soon enough: There was too much empty
country, and one travelling counter wasn't that important. Or what
if other men were missing as well? Some of the women might
have escaped, and taken men with them. In that case, the search
parties might not stop for some time.

Certainly the Body would want to learn where the women had
come from. Danlo was curious about that himself. Linnie's
answers were vague—not surprising, since she had no names for
the places along the route she had travelled. They had come
from the southeast, and they had been walking for most of a year.
So if the Body found any signs, the signs should lead them in the
other direction. Even so, he pushed her to go further north each
day. Nearly two weeks passed before he felt sure they were safe.

He soon gave up his program of exercises. He had considered at
first that being in good condition would help him cope with the
rigors of the wilderness, but he found that the coping itself left him
no energy for gymnastics. In their place, he began a makeshift set
of mental exercises. He knew he would never have the powers of
a joddie, but he would need whatever feeble abilities he could
muster. He dwelt as never before on the delicate process of being
two-minded, of keeping his outer mind empty while the inner
remained fully alert. He catalogued the handful of times when he
had ridden others, analyzing every remembered detail. What had
he done well? What must he do better? He thought, too, about the
various things that joddies did. Garpish putting the hysterical man
to sleep—that was a new one. Danlo sought within himself for the

place where sleep could be summoned, and for other keys that would allow a trained mind to guide an untrained one.

As the days passed, a mysterious heaviness descended on him, weighing every limb. He thought he must be ill. But he remembered a strange word from *Tales of the Elder Days*, a word for the melancholy caused by separation from other people: The condition was called loneliness. The word was no longer used among the Body; what would it describe? As little value as Linnie's company offered, he was miserable when they were apart. He was wary of her moody outbursts and revolted by her uncivilized habits. She scratched, often and quite unself-consciously, and blew her nose onto the ground by leaning sideways and pressing one nostril with a finger. Yet as he waited for her to come back from a hunt, he trembled inwardly at every rustle in the bushes. His heart lifted when he saw her grinning, striding through the high grass, holding aloft a fresh kill.

She was a null, so there was no sharing with her. But her physical presence, a body across the campfire, a body whose little movements he could rely on to be there each day as they had been the day before, eased, if only a little, the ache of loneliness. He had never known an adult whose inner life was a blank—except for Julan, and he had already known her, almost as well as he knew himself, when she vanished from his ken. The minds of children were shrouded in mystery, and he was tempted to think of Linnie as a child. A strong-willed, ill-mannered child. What would it be like, he wondered, to live in a world where everybody was so tightly shuttered from one another? Terrifying, even if their habits weren't so gross.

Eventually his fear of her subsided. He began to appreciate the economical resilience with which she lived. Once her immediate needs were met, she seemed quite content to do very little for hours at a time. Danlo had always lived in a complicated world, so he admired simplicity. She wasn't beautiful—far from it. Her hands were callused and scarred, her complexion rough, her teeth uneven. But he found himself waiting for her quick mischievous grin, admiring the curves of her body. He began imagining ways that they could both be less lonely. He recoiled at first from his own desire. The contrast between Julan—gentle, refined Julan— and this coarse creature could not have been more glaring. He didn't intend to develop an emotional attachment to a woman who grunted when she ate.

The little river valley, garlanded when they came upon it with the first flowers of spring, offered a perfect place to settle and make a start on the future. Any settlement, he knew, had to have a supply of fresh water. The crumbling concrete relic in which they found shelter suggested how much more could be done here. He envisioned whole rows, not of crude makeshifts but of real houses, a street with shops and a little amphitheater at the end where in the evenings the villagers could sing and put on plays and pageants. It was a lovely vision. Even so, the strange heaviness never entirely left him.

The closer attention he paid to the process of living in the wild, the more he was overwhelmed by the extravagant disorder into which he had plunged. From the distance, a field of yellow flowers seemed a solid entity. Closer, the flowers nodding and trembling in a scrap of breeze, the field had no clear borders, and no consistency within. An isolated clump of yellow might stand well away from the main area, or a darker mass of some other growth intrude among the flower stalks. He wanted to fence and weed it all, but there was too much of it.

As simple a task as getting kindling forced him to wrestle with tangles of dead branches, which might spring apart without warning, a sharp end poke directly at his eye. Wood-gathering, unlike counting, was never the same twice. Every foray presented new challenges. There was no stability, no constancy anywhere. Meat rotted. How had he lived for so long without seeing the ubiquity of rot?

He admired Linnie's ability to calmly plot a course through the chaos. He had intended to learn from her how to survive so that he could teach others, but he soon revised this idea. Far better to enlist her help, let her do what she was so expert at. This would free him to do the things that she could not do—plan, build, learn.

She found some of the stone that her arrow blades were made from, and tried to show him how to press flakes from the edges to make new points. His fingers were soon dotted with nicks and scrapes. Still, making points was preferable to hunting. The long walks uphill and down in pursuit of game tired him. He thought he must be getting old.

The pack of dogs, when they appeared one morning, frightened him. The dogs cast about on the far bank of the stream, trotting and snuffling and yapping. He hoped they would stay on the other side, but they soon crossed, scrambling and splashing among the rocks, heads high as they paddled across the deepest part. When they got to the near bank they shook themselves, and drops of water sprayed glittering.

He didn't want to leave the shelter, but he was frightened of what might happen to Linnie if she went hunting alone. They waited until the dogs had vanished upstream, and set out in the other direction, moving more warily than usual. Tension buzzed up and down through him, and his legs twitched so that he couldn't quite get firm footing. Even so, his reactions were lethargic. He turned, but too slowly. The dogs were nearly upon them. When one of the beasts lunged at him, he should have been able to get the spear between them, but his arms felt puffy and distant, and the dog knocked the shaft of the spear aside with its shoulder. Its teeth sank into his hand and it hung on, trying to drag him down. Linnie grabbed the spear and killed the dog with three deep thrusts. The pain in his hand didn't start until after they pried its jaws apart.

For the next few nights his hand throbbed so badly that he couldn't sleep. As he gazed up at the stars he found himself wondering, for the first time, what the women had meant to do with the men after they put their eyes out. Their actions had been so utterly incomprehensible that he hadn't bothered looking for an explanation, but now he knew Linnie well enough to know that she did nothing without a reason, and she knew enough words that he could frame the question and hope to understand a reply.

Her story made little sense. Somebody named Fire Insect had been stealing the men of her village. Fire Insect was a "huge thing." She talked of the huge things with awe. At first he thought she meant large animals, but it developed that the huge things were invisible. Fire Insect was an invisible person who took an active part in the lives of her people. And yet, as far as Danlo could tell, none of her people had any direct contact with Fire Insect; they knew of his intentions only by reasoning backward from visible events, which couldn't be a very reliable method. Fire Insect had an insatiable appetite for men, and the band of women had been intent on satisfying him. Their idea was that if they gave him enough men from elsewhere he would leave the men of their village alone. He was hungry for men's dreams, she said; he took their dreams. Afterward, when they had no dreams, they died.

The White Book mentioned somewhere that in the Time of Chaos men and women had practiced absurd adorations of nonexistent beings. The practice was called religion. Fire Insect must be a religious obsession. Since she understood Fire Insect's

intentions by observing visible events, Danlo saw that if he wanted
to get at the truth, he would have to learn what the visible events
were. Here her description was more concrete, and he found
himself on firmer, if no less disturbing, ground. The men of
Linnie's village were dying of an epidemic. But what sort of
contagion would strike men and spare women? He asked more
questions.

Danlo had no medical training, but he had read a great deal
about obscure diseases during Julan's illness. Much of what he
had learned then was long gone, but enough remained. He realized
at last that the cause of the epidemic was quite literally under his
nose. The men of Ranoima were dying of lead poisoning—and the
lead was coming from the red glaze used in the men's pottery. The
worse the epidemic grew, the more rigidly Linnie's people would
adhere to the code of behavior supposedly laid down by the huge
things. But it was precisely the huge things' insistence that men's
utensils be red and women's green that caused the epidemic. From
her description, not just one village but her entire race was on the
edge of dying.

Breaking the bowl and cup solved his immediate, physical
problem, but it left a deeper dilemma, which he wrestled with,
unhappily certain that whatever he did, it would be the wrong
thing. He knew he ought to tell her, but he couldn't bring himself
to do it. After all, lead poisoning was only conjecture on his part.
If he told her, she would want to go home, to tell her people how
to save themselves. He knew her well enough to guess that the
thousands of miles of trackless wilderness, the unguessable
dangers, would not deter her. And he simply couldn't afford for
her to leave. He needed her to help with his own mission of mercy.
She hadn't even consented to teach him to shoot the bow yet! And
what if he were wrong about the pottery? What if the men were
dying of something else? Or if she were killed before she reached
her village? In either case, he would lose everything by telling her,
and she would gain nothing. If he kept silent, at least one group
had a chance. Not a good chance, but a real one.

The other reason was harder to admit to himself. He was
starting to care for her. He wanted to be close to her, to touch her.
He daydreamed about what she might look like if she were nicely
dressed and had her hair done up. But his desire raised new
questions. Probably she wondered why he hadn't approached her
before now. What would she think if he tried suddenly to change
the unspoken rules by which they lived? Would she welcome a

sexual overture, or be offended? What if she reacted with fear or revulsion? What if she ran off, and didn't come back? He needed her—for the sake of the nulls, not to fulfill his own needs. Could he afford to take the chance?

Within days after he stopped eating out of the red bowl and drinking from the red cup, he felt stronger. The idea of rescuing nulls, which had begun to seem massively daunting, assumed somewhat more manageable proportions. He would simply slip across the Wall and fade into the daily life of the Serral Valley. Nobody would think twice to see a travelling counter going about his business. Once he learned of a town where nulls were being kept for Cleansing, he would release them from the proctor station under cover of night. He considered trying to locate suspected nulls before they were locked up, and rejected the idea. He would have to inquire too broadly; his mission would quickly become known. It was better to let the proctors and the joddies do the finding for him.

A search would be mounted when the proctors discovered that nulls had escaped, but nobody would expect an adult to be helping them. He would find a coach to drive, and they could be across the Wall almost before their absence was noted. He and Linnie would have to stay with the first few until they learned to live in the wilderness. Once they were self-sufficient, they could teach others, and he could spend all his time locating and freeing more.

How long could one man expect to evade detection? Sooner or later, he would be caught. What then? Could he make some arrangement to insure that the process would go on without him? He needed allies among the Body who could carry on the work. There might be a few who felt as he did—but how was he to find them, and how approach them?

Other nagging problems remained: How would the Body respond to the ongoing disappearance of nulls from proctor stations? Would the nulls be better guarded, or Cleansed without delay as soon as they were certified? And what if the nulls themselves didn't trust Danlo, or proved incapable of surviving? He worked at these questions doggedly for a while, and then put them aside. The enterprise was not, he told himself, one whose success could be assured. He could only do the things that were within his power to do.

The ethical loneliness, he discovered, was as burdensome as the social loneliness. He was setting out to violate the deepest values by which he had lived. When the wind stirred among the leaves, he thought he heard Olivia whispering to him, *Set aside this waywardness. Be One in unending oneness.* He had to put his fingers in his ears to stop the voice. Sometimes at night his own mind screamed that he was sick, vicious, contemptible. He had visions of everyone he had ever known running after him throwing rocks. But then he thought about what they had done to Julan, and he knew he was doing the right thing.

If he meant to build a village in this valley, he might as well get started. He considered building houses of wood, but he thought wood would probably rot unless it was painted or varnished, and he didn't know how to make paint or varnish. Besides, he already spent more time gathering wood than he wanted to. Round stones abounded in the riverbed. He started making a pile, and when he had enough he laid out the foundation of a house.

The house made Linnie uneasy. She wanted to live in the Serral Valley. He tried again and again to explain to her that she was irrevocably different from the people of the Body, that this valley was the only home she could hope for. She refused to understand. She wanted, she said, to find a man who would give her babies. In a flash Danlo understood how dense he had been: She thought he didn't care for her, so naturally she wanted to move on. She wanted to find a husband.

A long time had passed since he had been with a woman—and in those distant days the woman's ktess had always shone brightly to guide him. Feeling as if he were groping in the dark, he reached out and gently touched the side of Linnie's face.

He was shocked at the power of his need for her. Every touch of skin to skin sent fiery ripples leaping through his body. He fell back, spent and winded, and was ready again faster than he would have thought possible. But as she snuggled down to sleep against his chest, the hollow pit of loneliness opened again. He understood, in a way that he had not before, what it was like to be a null. With Linnie, he would always be a null. And the making of love between nulls was a feeble thing, awkward and soon concluded, an imperious itch culminating in a spasm. When he and Julan had lain together, they had been one person for hours at a time, touch and tenderness flowing in an unbroken circle. How could he have thought that this new love might supplant the old?

At least he had solved the problem of Linnie's restlessness. She would be content now to live in the house he was building. In time, he might even learn to enjoy the small comfort of this null lovemaking.

His contentment was short-lived. The next morning Linnie was more adamant than ever about going west. Nothing he could say convinced her of the danger his people posed to her. Evidently she had decided that he was lying or mistaken. After shouting at him in her own language, a string of syllables that sounded venomously like a curse, she grabbed the bow and strode away into the forest.

When she returned, after sunset, she was calm. She slung a dead rabbit down by the fire, shucked off the quiver, and began skinning the rabbit without saying a word. After spitting it and fixing the spit over the flames, she leaned back and regarded him speculatively. "Linnie makes baby. Danlo and Linnie makes baby, or not." She shrugged.

"Maybe make a baby, yes."

"What word, what word, woman helps makes baby?"

"A woman who helps make a baby?"

"Takes head of baby, arms, pulls out. Washes baby, cuts—cuts *asveolh*. Two woman. One makes baby in stomach, one helps."

"Oh, you mean a nurse." Of course! She was worried about how to deal with a pregnancy. Danlo cursed himself for his obtuseness. "We'll have to do something about that. I suppose I could get some books. I don't see what else to do. Look, if you start to make a baby—" He expanded his palms away from his abdomen. "—I'll go down to a village and get a couple of books on delivery, and potential complications and things. We can study them together."

Her eyebrows furrowed. "What this word, 'books'?"

"Books, um, small, hold in hand, open, close. Inside paper, writing, pictures and writing. You know what writing is. Writing is words on paper. On paper in book." He held an imaginary pen and scribbled on an imaginary piece of paper. "Words."

Her head tilted slowly over to one side. She looked at him with the skewed expression that he had learned presaged an outbreak of utter disbelief. She wriggled a thumb and two fingers in a loose imitation of his mime of writing. "Words?"

"Yes. Words that you can see. Here, I'll show you." He lifted one of the arrows from the quiver, and in the dirt beside the fire he scratched her name. "There. Writing. Words in writing. It says 'Linnie.'" He sounded the letters out phonetically, pointing with the arrowhead. "Ll-ih-nn-ee. You see? 'Linnie.' This is writing. Much writing—" He spread his arms and brought them together. "—is gathered into book."

She looked from Danlo to the letters in the dirt and back again. "Words on dirt." The juices from the rabbit sizzled in the fire. "Linnie on dirt."

"No, not Linnie on dirt. It's just a way of writing your name. The dirt's not important. If we had paper, I'd show you. You must know about writing. Your people have writing, don't they?"

" 'Writing'?"

"Yes. How do you keep records? How do you—oh, never mind." Was it possible that she didn't understand the idea of writing? Surely not.

Linnie reached up and rotated the rabbit. She sat back and sighed quietly. She seemed to have lost interest in the conversation. She didn't look at him.

"I'm not making it up," he said. "Writing is how words are—are captured. So you see, we don't need a nurse. I can get a book, and I'll read the book, and then when the baby comes, the words in the book will tell us what to do."

"Linnie wants woman helps makes baby."

"But that's not practical! I can't just go find a nurse and say, 'Look here, I've got a wild null stashed away in the hills, and she's pregnant. Would you mind helping us out?' We'll have to do it some other way."

She repeated the statement in a dull, tired voice. "Linnie wants woman helps makes baby."

When he came back from carrying the rabbit bones down to the trash heap, she was curled up on her side under her blanket, eyes closed, breathing evenly. He wondered if he should crawl in beside her. He wanted to. Maybe he could explain without words what he couldn't explain with them. He sat down beside her and rested his hand on her shoulder. She twitched it off, casually, as if her shoulder were a horse's flank and the hand a fly.

He wrapped himself in his blanket and lay down on the other side of the fire. For a long time he lay awake, hurting, rehashing the conversation, wondering what he could say that she would understand. At last he drifted into an uneasy sleep.

He woke at daybreak to find her standing over him, nudging him with her toe. Sunrise glowed in her face. He blinked up at her, still thick with sleep. She seemed to be carrying too much gear for a hunt. Both quivers were strapped across her back, along with the bow, and she was carrying the spear. Pouches dangled from her belt.

"Linnie goes. Goes west. Finds village."

In a panic, he scrambled to his feet. "No, you can't. Look, we've been through all this. I explained it. If only you'd—"

She wasn't listening. She turned her back and stepped out of the shelter. The morning sun, nearly horizontal, shone off the river and bathed her in milky light. "Danlo good man," she said, swallowing back tears. "Danlo carries Linnie."

"Listen to me. I won't let you—"

He seized her arm. She twisted away, but his grip was firm. Swinging in toward him abruptly, she drove her fist into his gut. He doubled over. When he could draw a gasping breath, she was striding away down the river bank, not looking back. "Linnie! Linnie, wait!" He started after her. He broke into a trot. So did she. He sprinted. She dodged away into the trees. He plunged doggedly after her, up the slope toward the western ridge. It was a long, steep climb. He scrambled in gravel on his hands and knees, and cut himself, and kept climbing. He could hear her ahead, and a rain of gravel rattled down on him.

When he emerged, exhausted, at the top, she was already across the crest, running downhill. He knew he would never catch her. She looked back just once, a flashing glimpse of her face like a startled fawn's. He fell to his knees and beat his fists against the ground and wept.

Chapter ‖ 11

THE music of flutes and bells danced merrily across the afternoon. Down the lane toward the amphitheater the young men and women strolled, laughing, waving to one another, wearing their brightest colors and most radiant smiles. Sleeves bellied like balloons in crimson and citron and silver, tight stockings flashed in azure and ocher and jade. The hair of girls and boys alike bounced and swirled in elaborate curls or fanned stiff from the teeth of jewelled combs.

Mooly sat in the shade, cross-legged on a low, sawed-off tree stump, and watched them pass, and wished he was among them. His copy of the White Book rested in his lap. It lay open, but he was only pretending to read. One of the girls waved at him as she passed. He lifted his hand and acknowledged her greeting with a halfhearted sign, then dropped his eyes to the book to hide the flush of embarrassment. Her name was Glinva. She lived down the street from him. She was fifteen, nearly a year younger than Mooly. She was going to the Receiving. Mooly was not going to the Receiving.

"Look at 'em, carryin' on like that."

Mooly looked up, surprised. He had thought he was alone. Another boy was standing beside the stump, a short, wiry red-haired boy whose hands were jammed deep into his pockets.

"You know what I think?" From his small frame, the red-haired boy might only have been eleven or twelve, but the long trace of a shaved sideburn roughened his pale, freckled skin, tapering to a point well below the bottom of his ear. "I think they're fakin'. I think if we got dressed up nice and went out there and started laughin' and stuff, they'd never know the difference."

"What are you talking about?"

"The all-fire ktess, what do you think? The way I figure it, there isn't any such thing. It's all a game, only they're fakin' us into thinkin' it's real."

Mooly scrunched up his mouth. He decided the red-haired boy was kidding him. "Who are you, anyhow?"

"Name's Gairth. Gairth Espollivan. You're Mooly Farn. I heard about you."

"What did you hear?"

"Heard you're a null."

"Am not!"

Mooly set the White Book on the stump and scrambled to his feet, fists clenched. He was taller than Gairth, and heavier, but the smaller boy seemed unconcerned. "How old are you?"

"Fifteen," Mooly said.

"Heard you was sixteen. Heard your mom started sayin' she can't remember what year you was born."

"You leave my mother out of this." Mooly shoved Gairth's shoulder, but not hard. He didn't really want to fight.

Gairth looked disgusted. "Lay off. If you want to beat on somebody, beat on them." He jerked his head at a couple of peacock-splendid stragglers skipping down the path. "They deserve it."

"How old are you?"

"Old enough. They're gonna come for both of us before long. Lock us up and take us out and—" Gairth brought the edge of one hand down on the other wrist, and made a noise with his mouth like an axe plunging into a watermelon.

Mooly shut his eyes hard. *Please Frank please Olivia please Frank.* . . . "You're crazy. Some of us just blossom a little slower than others. That's what my mom says."

"Yeah, sure. You ever been with a girl?"

Mooly felt his face burning. "Have you?"

"Lotsa times." Gairth hitched up his trousers and swelled his narrow chest. "But not—you know, the whole way. I been thinkin' about it. Thinkin', there oughta be some way to manage to do it, at least once, before—you know. I know a girl I was gonna ask. I think maybe she might say yes."

"You're talkin' like you think you're gonna be Cleansed for sure. It's not like that! Lots of kids come into the ktess a little later, and then it's all fine."

"Ah, grow up."

"It's true," Mooly said stoutly. He wished he felt as confident as he tried to sound.

"So anyhow, this girl likes me," Gairth said. "So I was thinkin' maybe I'd go out there this afternoon and see her, but I saw you sittin' here, and I thought I'd give you the chance, if you're interested. I'd rather do you a favor than them, any day, even though I don't know you. So if you want to come along, I'm not promising anything, but she might do it with you, if you're nice to her. I don't know. Maybe she won't."

Gairth looked at Mooly kind of sideways, and Mooly got the idea that Gairth was scared to ask the girl. He must be hoping that if Mooly came along, Mooly would take the initiative, or that if there were two of them to egg one another on, neither would be able to back down. All the same. . . . Mooly shook his head. "I don't think we should. Making love is for those who can share it fully. That's what it says in the Book. It's not for kids."

Gairth snorted. "You're not a kid. You're never gonna live to grow up, but you're not a kid anymore either. And what do you care what it says in the Book? It's their book."

"I just don't think we should." Mooly kind of wanted to go with Gairth, but his guts quaked at the thought.

Gairth shrugged. "Okay. Suit yourself. See you around." He stuck his hands back in his pockets and sauntered away.

"No, wait! I—"

Gairth turned and looked back. "Yeah?"

Mooly shook his head. "Nothing. Never mind."

He watched the red-haired boy cross the lawn and sink out of sight over a shallow knoll. In the amphitheater the singing had started. Tears stung Mooly's eyes. The singing was so beautiful! He sank down on the stump and picked up the White Book. Somewhere in the Book, he was convinced, was hidden the key. He had read it through from cover to cover three times now, but there were still places that he just didn't understand. He was doing something wrong, that was obvious. But he didn't know what it was. His mother was no help. When he pestered her about it, she patted his cheek in that sweet, sad way and told him he was perfect just the way he was.

He opened the book to the place he had marked, and read slowly, tracing each word with his finger and moving his lips: "They raised, then, a Triple Gate in the center of Sacramento, where all could come and pass beneath to receive the blessing of Frank and Olivia. And around the Gate, in spreading waves, the work of Renewal began. The buildings and machines they dismantled, part by part, to set aside that which was useful and carry the rest away. From the libraries also, they kept the books that told how to grow food, and heal the sick, and how to build machines, and all useful things. The other books, those filled with the hatred and bad thinking of those days, they gathered together and burned, in a great fire that burned for many days. In that fire all human knowledge was purified and made new. Uncounted errors were scoured away, like specks of filth clinging to the bottom of a skillet, so that only the pure shining metal of the ktess remained." The secret certainly didn't seem to be in this part, but Mooly was determined not to skip a word, for fear he might miss it.

The part about human knowledge being purified and made new, maybe that was a clue. Maybe he had somehow learned something that was wrong. If only he could figure out what it was! What he had learned in school was the same stuff all the other kids learned, so if he had learned a wrong thing there, they would have learned it too. What had he learned that he hadn't learned in school? Lots of stuff from his mom, how to brush his teeth and comb his hair and stuff. But his mom wouldn't teach him something wrong, not on purpose. She might have if it was something that she didn't know was wrong, but in that case she must think it was right, and if she thought it was right she'd be doing it too, so if it was what was causing the problem then she wouldn't be in the ktess either. But she was in the ktess. So whatever it was, it wasn't anything that she had taught him. What did that leave? Stuff from the other kids, sometimes, about how to trick grownups, about the rules of games. Mooly shook his head despondently. He'd never have time to examine everything he had learned— and most likely a piece of wrong learning wasn't the source of the problem anyhow. That was only a hint, or possibly a hint, from one sentence in the White Book, and there must be thousands of sentences. He shut the Book and stood up. He didn't want to hear the singing anymore. It made him mad. He wanted to rush down into the middle of the amphitheater and scream at them to tell him what he was doing wrong. But that wouldn't be a harmonious thing to do. Besides, it would call attention to the fact that he was a year, or even two, older than the kids being Received today. Instead, he tucked the Book under his arm and trudged across the park toward the street, scowling at butterflies and kicking an occasional dandelion.

He took the long way home, stopping to get an ice cream cone and stare in the window of the big hardware store on the corner by his house. Mooly thought maybe he wanted to build and repair machines if—when, when!—he grew up. Either that, or be a gardener. Gardeners got to work outdoors, and you didn't have to be good at math, but plants didn't look like as much fun as machines. A couple of the people that he passed on the sidewalk looked at him strangely and hurried on. He knew why. It was because of how big he was. He didn't look like a kid anymore.

The bright yellow cottage where he lived with his mother was not much bigger than a dollhouse. They had lived in it ever since Mooly's father died. Mooly barely remembered his father. The cottage was just the right size for a woman raising one small child by herself, but by now Mooly was constantly running into the corners of cabinets.

His mother was humming and clanking silverware in the kitchen, and the smell of broccoli soup and frying egg-bread made his mouth water. He put his tattered copy of the White Book in his room, ignoring the rumpled bed and the underwear on the floor. He felt like lying down for a minute, but his bed was so short he couldn't stretch out in it anymore. Usually, when he woke up in the morning, either his head and one arm would be hanging down over the side or his feet would be sticking out. He went into the kitchen and slumped into one of the spindly little chairs at the table. His mother smiled at him brightly from the stove. "Did my little Mooly have a nice morning?" She was a tiny woman, proportioned to fit the cottage, though in the last few years she had grown thicker through the middle. Her thinning hair stood up in a wavy purple halo, and her hands twitched in a perpetual haze of fidgets. The spatula in her hand quivered and made small shining circles in the air. She blinked watery eyes at him expectantly.

"You're gonna burn the bread," he said. She always burned the bread.

"Are you catching a cold, dear? You look pale." She fluttered around behind him and stroked his shoulders, his hair.

The edge of the spatula brushed his neck, and he flinched. "I'm fine, Ma. I was out in the park, reading."

"Studying for the math test, I'll bet. You wanted to surprise your mother by getting a good grade."

"The bread's burning, Ma."

"The bread. Oh, the bread!" She spun across the kitchen, dug into the skillet with the spatula, and flipped a pair of blackened, torn pieces of egg-bread onto a plate. "I'm sorry, dear. I got distracted. Well, they'll taste just as good, won't they?" She always said that. She set the plate in front of him, set the bottle of tomato sauce beside the plate, poured him a big glass of milk, and finally ladled soup into two bowls, one of which she set at her own place. "There, now." She sat, and spread her napkin, and picked up a spoon.

"Ma, can I get a new bed?"

"Don't talk with your mouth full, dear."

"I need one."

"What? A bed? I can't think why. You've got a perfectly nice bed."

"It's too short, Ma. I'm almost six feet tall."

"Nonsense. I'm sure you're not an inch over five foot six. You were always big for your age. Anyway, your room is so tiny, and the hall is just impossibly narrow. I don't know how we'd get a bigger bed in there."

"Then let's move to a bigger house."

She laughed nervously. Her hand shook, and soup dripped on the table. "Look what you made me do." She dabbed at the soup with her napkin. "Now, Mooly, you know your mother wants what's best for you. This just is not the time to go asking for a bigger—oh. Oh, no. Oh no, no, no." The spoon clattered into the bowl, splattering soup. Her eyes were wide and stricken. She shook her head distractedly, and her hands fluttered in the air.

"Are you all right, Ma? What's wrong?"

"No, you can't. I won't let you. He's just a baby. Just a baby!"

She pushed back from the table. Her head jerked from side to side, as if she were looking for something that wasn't there.

The front door of the cottage opened, and quiet footsteps came down the hall. Mooly turned to look over his shoulder. The two broad-shouldered men nearly filled the kitchen. Their stiff blue proctor shirts had metal buttons. Behind them, serene in his red robe, stood a joddie.

The first proctor inclined his head formally to Mooly's mother. "Goodwoman Farn. I am called Sten Larsen."

"G-Goodman Larsen. Welcome in our home." Her voice broke on the last word. She was wringing her hands. The veins on the backs stood out like blue claws.

"This is Goodman Cottis, and Brother Meldino. It is our sad duty to inform you that the One wishes to examine the harmoniousness of your son."

"No, look." Mooly pushed back his chair and got to his feet. "This is a mistake. You gotta give me a chance." Nobody looked at him. He licked his lips. "I've been studying the White Book. A lot. I'll bet I know more what's in it than any of you."

Proctor Larsen said, "Goodwoman, will you consent to the examination?"

"He's just a little boy." Her voice was bloodless, lost.

"I'm sorry." The proctor turned to Mooly. "You'll have to come with us now."

"I can't," he said. "I've got a math test next week."

The second proctor touched Mooly's arm. "Please don't make this difficult. You will only hurt those who care for you."

"Ma?"

She snuffled and wiped her eyes. "You'd better go with them, Mooly. It'll be all right, you'll see. You're just a late bloomer. Maybe in another week, maybe two. They're just too eager. They don't know how to be patient."

"We've been patient, goodwoman," said the first proctor. "As you know. None of us likes to face these necessities. There was—an incident today. We realized we could delay no longer."

"Yes. I see."

"What incident?" Mooly saw that they were all sharing a vision, and he felt terribly cheated not to know what it was.

"Come along, son."

His mother, still wearing her apron, followed them into the street. "I'll come visit you," she said. "I'll bring whatever you'd like to eat.'' The proctors had come in a sleek little six-passenger coach. One of them opened the passenger door. ''What would you like me to bring?''

''Don't worry about it, Ma. Don't worry about me.'' He put one foot up into the coach, and bent to kiss her cheek. ''I'll be okay.''

She clutched at his arm and patted him. ''I'll make sure they take good care of you. You're a good boy, Mooly. A good boy.''

One of the proctors slipped behind the wheel of the coach, and the doors thudded shut. Mooly sank back in the soft seat between the other proctor and the joddie. His mother's anguished face pressed against the window. He couldn't bear to look at her. After what seemed a long time, the coach hummed into motion.

''What was the incident?'' he asked again.

''Another boy. He became angry for some reason, and tried to commit injury.''

''What's that got to do with me?''

''We thought it safest not to chance it happening again. Especially after the events earlier this year, the One wishes to minimize disruptive influences.''

''The events—oh, you mean the wild women.'' Mooly didn't understand what that had to do with him. He guessed it didn't matter whether he understood or not.

The ride to the proctor station was not long. The coach pulled up before the wide front door, but for several minutes none of the men moved. Mooly stared out the window. The Receiving must have ended by now, and the procession passed this way, because the street was strewn with flower petals, red and pink and white. The petals chased one another in little corkscrews of wind.

At last the proctors opened the doors and ushered him out. Two more came out the door of the station and joined the first two. The joddie nodded formally at them, accepting their bows in return, and walked away. He had not spoken a word.

''Any trouble?'' one of the proctors asked.

''No, this one's well-behaved. Not like the other.''

They escorted Mooly toward the rear of the building and down a flight of stairs. The basement was dim, and crowded with large, dusty objects. One of the proctors produced a ring of metal keys and inserted one in a little hole in the door. ''In here, son.''

''When will the examination be?''

''It's already been.''

''What do you mean? Don't I even get a chance—''

"That's why Brother Meldino was with us," the proctor explained gently. "He conducted the examination. You—" The proctor shook his head. "You didn't pass."

"But that's not fair! You didn't tell me! Maybe I could have tried something different." Hands urged him through the door, and it clicked shut.

Two bunks lay parallel on opposite sides of the little room. The only window, set high in the outside wall, was barred. Lying on one of the bunks, fingers laced behind his head, was Gairth Espollivan. Gairth grinned at Mooly with wry bitterness. "Didn't expect to see me again so soon, did you?"

"You! You were the one. They said somebody tried to commit injury."

Gairth shrugged. "I got a little mad. The girl I told you about—she laughed at me. So I yelled at her."

"Is that all?"

"I threw a chair. Through a window."

"That's great. That's just great." Mooly sat down on the vacant bunk. "If it hadn't been for you, I'd still be eating lunch with my mom."

"So I'm supposed to stay a virgin so you can have a nice quiet lunch with your mom? That's terrific."

"That's not what I meant. You know what I meant."

"They would have come and got you before long, anyhow. What's the difference?"

Mooly got up and went over to look out the window. Afternoon sun warmed his face, and the fresh, moist scent of new-mown lawn swept away some of the dark anger. The main floor of the proctor station was above ground level, so the basement was not entirely underground. The window of this room looked out on the garden at the rear of the building, and the soil of the nearest flower bed was nearly flush with the windowsill. On the other side of the black iron bars rosebuds were opening. Mooly hung his fists on the bars and squinted out at the roses. What was it the White Book said? Something about flower petals falling but the bush remaining.

A copy of the White Book, bound in white leather with a tooled, gold-embossed cover, lay on the table between the two bunks. He opened it and flipped through. The vivid colors and three-dimensional depth of the pictures captivated him far more powerfully than the simple line-drawings in his dog-eared paperback copy. But the words were always the same. When he held the

Book in his hands, it seemed more real than his own life. He found the passage he was looking for, and sat on the bunk and began to read aloud. " 'Have compassion for them, as you would for the beasts of the field. For like the lamb that goes willingly to slaughter, in their sacris—safice—sacrifice they renew the vitality of the Body.' "

"What a load of crap."

"Don't say that!"

"Why not? Crap is what it is."

"Is not!" Mooly scowled at Gairth, who smirked back at him. "That's why you're a null, I bet," Mooly said. "You don't have any respect. Frank and Olivia looked down at you and they said, 'No, sir, we don't want that one, no way.' "

"Oh, is that so? Then what about you? How did you get so screwed up?"

"I don't know," Mooly said miserably. "I don't know what I did. I been tryin' to figure it out. I hooked a pie one time, and told my mom I never."

"That's nothin'. I know guys hooked lots of pies, and they're not nulls."

"Did they have to do something after, to make it right? Like tell what they did? Maybe I should of told my mom about the pie."

"Grow up."

"I know the answer is in here somewhere. I just know it." Mooly looked down at the place in the Book where his pudgy finger still rested. " 'Take them, at dawn, to the Triple Gate, and present them there to us, so that—' "

With sudden lithe energy, Gairth sprang from his bunk. He wrenched the White Book out of Mooly's hands and flung it into the corner. Paper flapped, and dust billowed and swirled. "I don't want to hear any more of that crap," he said hoarsely.

"You sure are touchy. If I learn anything from reading, it might help you too. Besides, reading is supposed to comfort us. That's what my mom says."

"Does it comfort you?" Gairth kicked the White Book savagely, and wheeled to glare at Mooly. "Does it?"

"No." Mooly hung his head. "I guess not."

Chapter 12

STILL gasping from the steep climb, Danlo shouted hoarsely, brokenly, for Linnie to come back. The only answer was the mocking screech of bluejays. Choked by tears, he had to stop to cough. A great silence descended on the forest. The sun sailed warm among the boughs. A squirrel paused on a low branch to study him before darting away with an impudent flick of its tail.

So stubborn. So ignorant and so stubborn. If it were only her life, he wouldn't have cared so much. Let her lay her head willingly on the block, if it pleased her. (No, not that, not ever!) It was for the sake of the children that he needed her. Without her mastery of the ways of the wild, he had no hope at all. He might as well follow her back to the Wall. He would probably have to watch while she was Cleansed, but afterward he could accept the healing of the joddies and be rid of these fever dreams of freedom.

He wandered listlessly down the hill, taking a longer but less precipitous route back toward the crumbling shelter and the unfinished stone house. He had thought himself alone in the first days after the massacre, when the ktess lay cold and still. But he had been with Linnie then. For all her crudeness, she had been a comfort. He had dared imagine that she might be more. Now he had no comfort, not even a weapon, only the fire to warm him in the dark hours.

The fire! His eyes leaped toward the campsite. The trail of smoke spiraling skyward was thin at the base, very thin. Shocked into motion, he galloped along the gravel bed beside the river, pebbles flying from his heels, and fell to his knees before the hearth. Embers still glowed there, and heat pressed against his face. Trying to still the shaking of his hands, he fed twigs and blew on the embers gently, as she had taught him, until a flame, pale in the daylight, danced and swayed. Only when the blaze was crackling did he search the shelter to see whether she had left him the fire-starting bow. It was gone. She had taken both knives too. She had left him only a blanket and the axe.

The woodpile was low. Best replenish it first. He had long since scoured the area near the camp for fallen branches, but dead wood still jutted, starved of sun, from the pines further back from the river. He set to work with the axe, and piled up an armload. On the way back to camp he thought to take a look at the axe itself. The lashings that held the head to the shaft were badly frayed. He tucked it into his belt, resolving to use it only in dire need. A hand-held stone would do as well, if it had an edge.

After piling the wood in the shelter, he found such a stone and carried it back into the shade beneath the canopy of pines. It proved too large to hold comfortably, and his shoulder soon ached. Now and again he paused, breathing hard, to wipe hair out of his eyes and stare around at the trees. He had begun to get used to the forest, but now everything was strange again. Could he eat these seed-pods, or were they poisonous? Were those the shoots whose roots she had dug up last week? He couldn't remember.

He began imagining that she might change her mind, that she might turn around and come back. Maybe she would be waiting for him by the shelter. Twice he stopped working and walked back far enough to see it in the distance, a crooked gray box perched above the river. She wasn't there. He forced himself to go back to the wood-chopping.

When he had amassed enough wood for several days, he went down to the river to splash cold water in his face and drink. The face that stared back at him from the glassy surface of the pool was that of a stranger, bearded and gaunt. Though the day was bright, the eyes were deeply shadowed. Obscurely frightened, he looked away.

His eyes fell on the unfinished walls of the stone house. Yesterday he had been proud of it, but today he felt only bleak contempt. How could he have been so foolish? When he should have been going out with her every day to learn the ways of the forest, he had lulled himself into believing that she would always be there, that he had a more important task.

Fire was the first necessity, but not the only one. His mouth watered at the thought of the pheasant and rabbit she had so casually tossed at his feet. He would have to make a bow for himself, and some arrows. He rooted around the shelter, hoping she had left a few arrows at least, and found only the broken chips he had sheared from the chunk of arrow-point stone. Useless, useless. He put his head in his hands and rocked on his buttocks in the dirt. What could he have said or done differently? He had tried so hard to make her understand. . . .

If it had been only his own life he was trying to save, he would have lain down and let the dogs come for him. But he refused to abandon the children. They were not "the nulls" anymore; he had ceased to think of them that way. They were children. His children, his and Julan's.

By noon he had found three sticks that were the right length and thickness to be bows, and several lighter, straighter ones that might serve as arrows. He would have to make points for them. Attaching the points to the arrows, and the feathers to the other end, would be harder. Only after he had gathered the bow-sticks and tested their strength by flexing them across his thigh, which broke two of them, did he begin to puzzle about what he would string them with. And this question defeated him utterly. Plaits of wild grass? He gathered some, and twisted it until it shredded. Vine? Leather? He had a vague idea that animal skins could be treated so as to stay supple instead of rotting, but learning by trial and error how to treat them could take the rest of his life. Besides, without the bow, how could he catch an animal to skin?

Next he gathered some green, springy sticks and tried to fashion a snare. He wrestled with the sticks until it was too dark to see, and at daybreak set his jaw grimly and went back to work, but every time he had a crude cage assembled, it fell into a heap as soon as he let go of it, or sat seeming solid but flew to pieces when he picked it up again. Probably it didn't matter; he had nothing to bait a snare with.

The next day he tried eating some small, hard, bitter berries. An hour later he vomited them up. The only thing he was sure he could eat was meat. So he found some rabbit-holes, and spent most of a day sitting on a sunny cliff a quarter-mile away watching the area to see which paths the rabbits took. At sunset, weak from hunger, he drank copious amounts of river water and tried for an hour to catch a fish with his hands. The next morning he chose a well-hidden spot by one of the rabbit paths and lay down, axe-hand drawn back, to wait. He waited all day, not even scratching when insects walked on his back, but no rabbits came.

Not knowing what else to do, he went back to the same spot the next morning and lay down again. This time, before noon, a rabbit blundered by. He swung and smashed its hind leg, and it shrieked in pain. He had to swing again to kill it. He shredded and lost as much meat as he saved, skinning it unhandily by hacking and tearing, but every morsel tasted wonderful. From that day forward he found that he could stalk and kill. He had learned to be silent physically as well as mentally.

Spring burst into full flower, and the nights were no longer frosty. He thought of Linnie often—sometimes wondering how she would approach a task, sometimes simply wishing she were there by the fire at night, scowling at him, scratching herself, making unintelligible comments. By day he strode along the ridges beneath the trees, axe swinging loose in one hand. The peaks and the clouds and the sky lay spread around him, mile upon open mile in brilliant and always-changing perfection. He no longer shrank from a confrontation with a bear, only stood and stared at it, making no threatening motions, until it dropped down on all fours and waddled away. He wondered whether Linnie had been Cleansed by now. If not already, then soon. It was better to turn his thoughts to the children. Every month a few were Cleansed, but more always appeared. Before long he would be ready. He debated whether this valley was far enough from the world to be a safe haven, but he had no reason to suppose that it wasn't.

He discovered that the rabbits avoided places where he had made a kill. They must scent the blood. So he went further afield every day, searching for a fresh place to lie in wait. He stoked and banked his fire before departing, and the thin column of smoke coiled high in the still air, providing a beacon that called him home.

Sitting patiently one day cross-legged in the grass, he heard what he thought at first was a rock slide or a distant swarm of bees. He quickly realized it was an engine. A dull roar throbbed, shifting as it echoed against the peaks, but growing louder. He looked around in alarm, and saw nothing.

He clambered up onto a little promontory that overlooked the valley, and shaded his eyes with his hand. He was in time to see a flying coach settle vertically toward the campsite, a white machine with wings whose streamlined contours were half-obscured by billowing clouds of dust. A flying coach! He had not thought such conveyances were still built. And what was it doing here? Had the One persuaded Linnie to talk about him? Or were they imagining that the mountains were full of wild women?

It didn't matter. If the Body had flying coaches, they didn't need an informant. They could find any permanent settlement he tried to establish, simply by flying over it. He would never be able to build a village. And how could the children survive without houses? Perpetually wandering, soaked by every storm? No, it was impossible.

But he wasn't quite ready to give up yet. He strode downhill through the trees. The roar of the machine had fallen silent. He could touch, distantly, the ktess of those in the coach. They were surprised at the smoke. He made his outer mind as empty as the sky. They would know from the fire that somebody was nearby, but unless they saw him, he should be safe. If they did see him, he could still escape: They didn't know the trails.

He could hear them now. They had descended from the coach and were calling to one another, laughing and exclaiming. Three of them, perhaps four. His best course was to stay clear of the camp until they had flown away. He would have plenty of time afterward to consider how to deal with this unwelcome development. Knowing he was taking a risk, he moved closer. He was not sure why he wanted to catch a glimpse of them—maybe to be close to his own kind, after all this time, to see well-trimmed hair and hear words spoken in the accents of home.

A hissing, spitting noise erupted, accompanied by more laughter, and a cloud of steam topped the trees where the smoke had been. Danlo's anger flared. He hadn't considered that they might put out the fire. Should he try to drive them off before the embers died? Useless; armed he might be, but he was not a young man, and he was outnumbered.

What, then? He had to do something. Without the fire, he was doomed. Approach them in a friendly way, perhaps. Claim to have become lost in the battle with the women, to have wandered alone this far north. But of course they would wonder how he had built the fire. More important, they would insist on taking him home, and the joddies who came to learn his tidings would ken the truth.

They must have matches. They would not have ventured so far into the mountains without the means to survive if the coach broke down. Could he sneak into it and take some matches while they were off prowling on foot? Worth trying, but he wanted to know more about them first. He was surprised how easy it was to ken them deeply without alerting them to his presence. He had thought his ktess might be blunted by disuse, but it was stronger than ever. They were frightened at being so far from the safety of the Body, but determined to serve the common good. They had not come here by accident. They were assigned to investigate whatever traces of human habitation they might find, and elated that after weeks of fruitless search they had stumbled onto his camp. He delved beneath the surface of their thoughts and found names— Virn Taubgren and his son Lonss, and Clae Forvuna.

He crouched among the bushes along the river bank and crept

close enough to get a clear view. The three were poking around in
the shelter, a good twenty meters from where the coach had set
down, but they had chosen the most open ground on which to land.
Danlo had no hope of getting to the door of the vehicle without
being spotted. He would have to distract them somehow, lure them
away into the trees.

So much trouble, just for a handful of matches. What else might
they have in the coach that he could use? They might be equipped
for an extended stay in the wilderness; they might have food, more
weapons, a sharp knife, waterproof bedding, even soap. Soap!
Every pore itched at the thought. If he could get into the coach, he
would search first for a carrying case, and then fill it. No, first
matches, then the carrying case.

He opened his outer mind no wider than a crack, and shared,
briefly, a vague feeling of weakness, and delirium, and pain. The
men straightened up and looked around. He waited a few seconds,
then repeated the sharing.

The men came out of the shelter, but not to go toward the forest.
They headed straight back toward the coach. He could see their
thought—a circling search pattern to spot from the air the lost,
injured person that Danlo had conjured up. This wouldn't do at all.
If they took to the air, they might not come down again.

The first man opened the door of the coach and stepped in. The
second was on his heels. In desperation, Danlo shared a more vivid
vision: the deeply shadowed view from beneath a thick canopy of
trees, a place where sunlight never penetrated. The second of the
three paused indecisively with one foot in the door of the coach.
Their minds were questing outward for the source of the sharing,
but Danlo cloaked his outer mind tight. He considered, fleetingly,
joining the man who was still on the ground, encouraging him to
run toward the trees, to think he had kenned exactly where the
injured person lay. But if the man became aware that he was being
joined, they would grow suspicious. Better to wait. If the coach
did become airborne, he could force it down by riding the driver.
Or he could simply walk out into the open and wave.

The three conferred among themselves. From inside the coach,
Forvuna handed down tools of some sort—no, weapons. He
stepped down and they set off on foot, at an angle to where Danlo
lay concealed. A flying coach, and now weapons. Rifles, that was
what they were called. Long metal barrels that threw lead slugs at
high velocity. Danlo had never seen a rifle, but he knew they were
used sometimes against wild animals. The Body had decided that

the women represented a real threat. That would make Danlo's task far harder.

He waited, scarcely daring to breathe, until the men vanished among the trees. He would know in the ktess if they turned back; for the moment, his path was clear. He sprinted across the open space. The coach had a rounded body with windows at the front and an enclosed area behind. In the center of each wing was a cylinder as fat as a wine cask, each cylinder capped by a trefoil of almond-shaped metal blades. Danlo was no mechanic, but he guessed that the cylinders contained the engines, and that the blades were designed to push the air the way a boat propeller pushed water. They were aligned vertically, so that the coach could take off as it had landed, rising straight up into the air.

He fumbled at the door handle. The smooth cool metal was exotic in his hand after so much wood and stone. As he stepped up into dimness and the clean odors of cloth and plastic, a new and exhilarating thought came to him: Why search for a case to carry away a few miserable scavenged items, when he could just as easily fly away in the coach? He scanned the bank of buttons and switches, and instantly abandoned the idea. Driving an air coach, evidently, was more complicated than driving one designed for the road.

"Amazing," said a soft voice. "You're not a null, are you? Rather alarmed when I heard your footsteps. Kenned you only when you got quite close."

As Danlo's eyes adjusted, the silhouette of a little round bald head resolved itself into a bright-eyed, bespectacled joddie. The joddie, perched in one of the rear seats, blinked and smiled at him amiably. "Was it you who shared that distress? Of course." *Deliberate falsehood.* "Remarkable. Why should you do something like that? And how are you able to? Still not kenning you well. The One must know of this at once." The joddie closed his eyes, and his chin sank toward his chest.

Without pausing to think, Danlo slipped the axe free of his belt, pulled his arm back, and brought the axe around in a wide swing that connected solidly with the joddie's skull. Bone crunched sickeningly. The wash of pain in the ktess was brief but blindingly bright. Danlo reeled back, gasping. Spots swam before his eyes. When his vision cleared, the joddie had sagged to one side. Blood ran down his face from the hideous wound, in which the axe was still embedded.

Danlo sank nervelessly into a seat, appalled by his own

violence. Time seemed to hang suspended. The air inside the coach was warm and stale, and all sound was muffled. Through a wordless numbness, one idea swam to the surface: To kill, even for what seemed the most powerful of reasons—I'm no better than they are, he thought. How can I go on believing that they're wrong to kill the children, when I'm just as wrong?

Running footsteps came closer, and shouts. The three men burst into the coach. Lonss shoved Danlo aside and knelt beside the joddie. The elder Taubgren crowded in next to him, while Forvuna fingered his rifle and glared at Danlo with something between bewilderment and rage. Danlo barely looked at them. He breathed shallowly through his mouth and examined his hands, the backs, the callused palms.

Lonss gently pried the axe blade out of the joddie's skull. He turned and held the axe out toward Danlo. Lonss was young and blond and broad-shouldered, with a square jaw and gray eyes that even now radiated a childlike innocence. His hair was drawn into a braided knot above one ear, and the knot was interwoven with gold ribbons. "Is this yours?" he asked. "What happened?"

"Who are you?" the elder Taubgren demanded. He was just as blond and big-boned as his son, but lines were etched around his eyes and mouth. Forvuna was smaller and dark, with a heavy, unbroken line of eyebrow and long brown hair that fell in rhythmic waves to his shoulders. His rifle was pointed at Danlo.

"Was it you we kenned in need of help?" Taubgren went on. "Can you even speak?"

"I'm not kenning him," Forvuna said. "I think he's a null."

"I'm not a null," Danlo said hoarsely.

"He speaks!"

"Did you strike Brother Acadian?"

"Why are we not kenning you? Answer!" Taubgren shoved Danlo's shoulder roughly.

"I'm sorry. I'm very sorry." Danlo stood up. They backed away from him a little, as if they were afraid of what he might do. Or perhaps it was the way he smelled. The dark man's weapon dipped uncertainly. Danlo stepped around him. Hands grasped at him, but he shook them off. He stepped down out of the coach onto the ground. He wanted only to go lie down under the trees and go to sleep.

A body struck him from behind, and he sprawled headlong in the dirt. He turned his head as he fell, but gravel scraped his cheek and jaw. The body was a weight on his rib cage. He twisted to try to shake it off. After a moment the weight lifted, and he rolled onto his back to look up at his attacker.

Again in the ktess, sharp pain, this time in the right shoulder. Young Lonss staggered backward, clutching at his shoulder. Blood oozed around his fingers.

The feathered shaft of an arrow was buried in him.

An arrow! Lonss fell against the side of the coach and slid to the ground, his face gone deathly pale. Forvuna put the rifle against his shoulder and sighted down its barrel at the surrounding forest. He discharged the weapon, two deafening crashes in quick succession. Taubgren knelt beside his son and plucked at the arrow. Danlo got to his hands and knees. A second arrow hit the side of the coach with a hollow thud, and bounced harmlessly.

Forvuna fired the rifle again. Danlo threw himself at the man and bowled him backward onto the ground. The rifle clattered free. Danlo scrambled after it, but something hit him on the back of the head, a roaring red pain that swallowed everything. After a few seconds he was dimly aware of rough hands grasping him. He was being dragged across the ground and up the steps into the coach. The coach door banged shut, and the engines rumbled to life.

With a heavy lurch the coach sprang into the air. Danlo could see through Forvuna's eyes now. The dark man was guiding the coach expertly, nearly scraping the treetops. Through some special visual apparatus he was tracking a figure that fled before them on foot. Danlo could make out no details, but he recognized instantly the crooked gait with which the figure ran.

Forvuna fingered a lever that would fire a weapon built into the air coach. Without opening his own eyes, Danlo gripped the man's mind fiercely and fought him for control of the hand on the lever.

At first Forvuna seemed unaware of what was being done to him. He looked down at his arm as it jerked and flopped. Then he let out a wordless cry and slapped at that arm with the other hand.

The air coach bucked and dipped toward the trees. Taubgren left off nursing his son and dove toward the controls. Danlo opened his eyes and watched the two men at the front of the coach. He lay on the floor, still riding Forvuna, whose forehead was beaded with sweat. Taubgren wrestled with the controls, and the coach wheeled and angled upward in a stomach-turning spiral.

"He's doing it!" Forvuna cried, trying to point to Danlo. "Stop him!" Taubgren stepped away from the controls and swung a heavy fist at Danlo. As Danlo dodged, his mind pulled on

Forvuna's hand, which grabbed a lever of some sort. The wrong lever. With a scream of metal on metal, the coach reared back and flipped clean over. Bodies flew and collided in a jumble. Jammed beneath a seat, Danlo caught a blurred glimpse of pine boughs whipping past the window. A loud scraping, ripping noise terminated abruptly in a bone-jarring thump.

The engines whined and shuddered and died. Danlo opened his eyes. His face was inches from the joddie's. The joddie's sightless eyes were open, and his mouth gaped. The round, rimless spectacles were still perched on his nose, but crookedly, in a kind of obscenely jaunty abandon.

Cautiously Danlo reached out in the ktess, and met no other minds. He levered himself carefully out from under the seat, which had kept him from being bounced off of the ceiling during the crash, and slid down the slanting floor to the door. An arm protruded from behind another seat. He felt for a pulse, and couldn't find one. The arm belonged to Forvuna, whose neck was bent sideways at an impossible angle. Taubgren lay crumpled against the shattered front window of the coach, shards of glass glinting in the raw meat of his face. A sharp edge had sheared through one side of his neck, and blood was still welling sluggishly. Swallowing back nausea, Danlo averted his eyes.

He dropped out the door onto a carpet of pine needles, rolled out from under the coach, and stood up and brushed himself off. His right leg was tender from hip to knee. It would bruise. But nothing seemed to be broken.

Linnie sprinted toward him between the trees. He opened his arms, and she slammed into him with such force that they both fell. Her body was warm against him from neck to knee. He had to free one arm to move the point of her bow, which was threatening his eyes. She mumbled tearfully into his chest. After a minute she translated, laughing: "Big bird eats Danlo. Danlo bad eats. Big bird dies." She gulped happily. "Dies then spits out Danlo."

"Yes." He stroked her hair. "I thought you were dead too. I missed you terribly." He kissed her mouth, tentatively at first, then hungrily. She wrapped herself more firmly around him and returned the kiss. "I didn't know how much you meant to me," he said, "until you were gone." He lifted her shoulders far enough to wave an admonishing finger under her nose. "Don't do that again. You understand? Don't go away. Stay with me."

She lowered her eyes. "I not goes this next."

"You make Danlo very happy."

She blushed, and said prettily, "Danlo makes Linnie very happy."

They sat up. He kept an arm draped across her shoulder, and massaged gently. "What happened to you? You go west. Many days. Next come here. Many days."

"Goes west. Over—" She held out her hands and arms to make a flat barrier.

"Over wall."

"Wall." She nodded. "Over wall. Finds village. Big village. Animals, children, all very fat. Watches village." Her fingers pulled apart an invisible curtain of bushes. "Woman comes on path. Linnie stands, speaks with woman. Linnie says, 'Not danger. Friend.' Woman runs fast away. Sun—" An angle of an hour. "People in village comes. Many people comes very fast." Linnie looked at Danlo shamefaced, and said, indignantly but reluctantly, as if she still could not quite believe it, "People in village wants *kills* Linnie."

Chapter ‖ 13

THE coach had plowed a hole in the forest canopy, laying bare a swath of sky. Danlo squinted at the sky apprehensively. If the Body had one flying coach, they might have several. To stay in the vicinity could be dangerous. All the same. . . . "Let's see what supplies they've got in there," he said, jerking his head at the smashed craft.

"'Supplies'? What this word?"

"Food, knives, blankets, anything."

They walked toward the coach. Its body was crumpled in the middle, and a tree branch had punched a hole in the side. Linnie stopped short, eyeing the aircraft and clutching her spear tighter. "It won't hurt you," Danlo said. "It's dead." He pushed against the side with both hands, to test the craft's stability. When it failed to tilt or rock, he got down on his hands and knees and ducked through the doorway. Linnie followed.

A couple of flies were already buzzing around the bloody thing that lay against the front window. Danlo stepped over it and reached back to give Linnie a hand. "There are sure to be things we can use," he said. "We'll have to find something to carry them in."

"Carry in thing. Yes."

"Wonder if they brought any extra clothing. I don't think I could stand to wear what any of them is wearing now." A stench of released bowels was thickening the air.

At the sharp click of metal on metal, Danlo froze. Careless, careless! Lonss Taubgren's ktess blazed like an arc lamp. Though dazed by pain, the young man was awake—and enraged. Danlo peered around in the dim green light, his heart hammering.

Lonss stood wedged between a seat and a wall locker. The rifle tucked under his good arm pointed at Danlo and Linnie. "You killed my father," he said. Before Danlo could reach out to take control of his hands, the rifle discharged. In the enclosed space the detonation was painfully, deafeningly loud.

Danlo seized Linnie's spear and flung it. It yawed crooked, and the shaft caught Lonss across the forehead. He seemed not to notice. The rifle had recoiled so strongly that he had nearly dropped it. He was leaning over and fumbling one-handed to get a better grip so as to bring the barrel up for another shot.

Struggling to keep his footing on the steeply canted deck, Danlo reached the fallen spear, brought the point up, and pushed it with all his weight through the middle of the young man's abdomen. The rifle clattered free. Lonss's eyes opened wider. Danlo let go of the spear, and Lonss toppled over onto the joddie. His ktess expanded outward like a many-colored balloon, pain mingling with filaments of memory. Danlo reeled, dazed by the flow, but he let the young man's essence dissipate ungathered. To have made welcome even a portion of somebody who hated him with such intensity could only have made him very ill.

The death passed quickly. He looked back toward the doorway. Linnie had drawn her bow. She lowered it slowly. "Are you all right?" he asked. His voice sounded muffled, as if his ears were stuffed with cotton. "Are you hurt?"

"Not hurt. Ears hurt."

"Mine, too." He wiped his hands on his thighs. He wanted to step outside for a breath of air, but he suspected that if he did, he would not have the stomach to come back in.

Twice within a few minutes he had failed to ken someone whom he ought to have kenned. He had been relying on his eyes and ears for too long, and had grown lax. Both times he had had to kill. He resolved not to be careless again. He felt less remorse this time than the first. Probably that was why the Body of Harmony had been able to keep doing it for so long: After a while, there would be no feeling at all. He hoped he would never reach that point. Next time, he hoped, he would have the courage *not* to kill.

He had to lever two bodies out of the way to get at the storage locker. He found two sheath knives, and a box of metal cylinders that must be rifle projectiles, and bottles with straps for carrying water, and a great many other things. They carried it all outside and made a pile. The pile grew to include a portable stove and a packet of fabric that, by the diagram on the cover, must unfold to become a tent. Having lived in plenty all his life, Danlo had never appreciated the value of such simple things. Now he had an almost physical craving to keep them. There was far more than two people could carry—but how could he bear to leave any of it behind? With such equipment, maybe a life of perpetual wandering would be feasible after all. He found no spare clothing, but overcame his revulsion far enough to remove Forvuna's boots, which fit him tolerably well. Linnie had no use for most of the treasure, but she examined one of the steel knives with great wonder, turning it over and over before her face and repeatedly testing the edge with a thumb. In the end, they left the tent and the stove and the rifles, but took a pair of waterproof blankets, a first-aid kit, some packages of food, a box of matches, the water bottles, a pair of binoculars, and two bars of soap.

They travelled until dusk, and made camp in dense forest, where their fire would be less visible from the air. Linnie was entranced by the matches, and would have used them all if he had let her, just for the wonder of seeing how easily a stick could burst into flame. The dried rations, on the other hand, repelled her. He chewed on a sweet, fibrous bar that the label said was well fortified with nutrients, and unwrapped another and held it out, but she pushed it away. Only after she had watched him hungrily for several minutes did she consent to bite off a small piece.

She grunted, and made a face. "Tree bark." But she finished the bar, and took another. They passed a water bottle back and forth, and Danlo took off his new boots and stretched his toes.

Though the night was not cold, he unfolded one of the blankets. He spread it and made a place for her to sit next to him. She pretended not to notice. Now that the first flush of their reunion had passed, the awkwardness that had driven them apart had returned. He realized that nothing had actually changed. She still wanted a nurse to help her give birth. It was up to him to demonstrate how he meant to provide one. Well, how *did* he mean to do it? Maybe now, having seen the air coach and the matches, she would believe him when he talked about learning to tend at a birth by reading a book.

While he was still considering the problem, she scooted across and sat beside him on the blanket, hip touching hip. Her mouth worked silently for a minute while she stared into the fire. "What word," she said at last, "what word two people—" She clasped her hands together. "Man man, man woman, woman woman, any. Man hunts with man, woman hunts with woman, two like one. What word this?"

"The two people are friends. 'Friend.' "

"Friend." She looked at him shyly. "Danlo friend Linnie friend. Yes?"

"Yes. Oh, yes." He put his arm around her, and she snuggled against him, and they kissed.

In the night he jerked awake, crying out, drenched in sweat. In a dream the dead men in the air coach had been stalking him. Linnie smoothed his brow.

He didn't feel like going back to sleep, so he asked her to tell him how she had fared while they had been apart. After eluding the villagers in the Serral Valley by lying submerged all night and all the next day in an irrigation ditch, she had made her way cautiously back to the wall, travelling under cover of darkness. Disgusted by the impossibility of establishing any settled way of life in this land, she had made up her mind to make the trek back to her own village, and had worked her way south through the foothills for a week before the nagging tug of her concern for Danlo became too strong to resist. Once she admitted to herself that he had been right about the danger posed by his people, she began to suspect that he might be right about other things too, that he might not be quite as crazy as she had thought. Convinced that she had done him an injustice, she retraced her steps, determined to find him if he were still alive, and to help with his bizarre scheme.

"Danlo builds house, Linnie kills food," she finished. "Children eats, children—what word?—in house."

"Live in house. Eat, sleep, walk, talk, any, is 'live.' " He fed another twig into the fire. He would have to tell her that there wouldn't be any houses. The mountains were vast, but the Body could build hundreds of air coaches as easily as one. In fact, now that wild nulls had appeared, the Body would undoubtedly prowl the sky again until it found where they came from. He owed it to Linnie to explain that to her, so that she could return to her people and warn them. He had no right to condemn them to death through his silence. And it would be absurd, he saw, to tell her about one mortal threat and keep another concealed. He would have to tell her about the lead poisoning in the pottery as well.

She listened very quietly while he did his best to explain. When he finished, she sat silent for so long that he wondered whether she had understood. She hugged her knees and stared into the fire. "Eats from red bowl makes man die," she said at last.

"That's right."

"Many big bird flies to Ranoima. Throws fire from sky."

"You can warn them. I know it's a long way to walk. But if you go home and tell them, they can find places to hide." Evading the new Cleansing would be nearly impossible, he knew, but maybe the Body had forgotten how to make some of the weapons that were used in the first Great Cleansing. Maybe Linnie's people, being forewarned, could make an effective defense.

She lay down on her side on the blanket so that her head rested on his thigh, and curled up into a ball. Her eyes were still open. He stroked her temple and ear. After a while he lay down behind her and wrapped his arms around her. "I'm glad you came back," he said.

In the morning, she was up before him. She had built up the fire, and a small animal of some sort was roasting. She squatted with the bow between her legs, attaching a fresh string to it. He went off behind a tree to urinate. When he came back, she stopped working and looked sidewise at him. "Linnie goes Ranoima, many danger."

He thought she was announcing what she meant to do. His heart sank. But she went on: "Linnie goes with friend Danlo, many danger." She made a two-handed gesture as if hefting two pieces of invisible fruit to see which was heavier. "In Ranoima, many woman, not many men. Danlo for Linnie man."

He didn't quite understand. "And? And?"

"What this word, sees with sleep? Sleep, sees, eye closed." She lifted the roasting animal off of the fire, inspected it, put it back.

"You mean 'dream'? You sleep, and in sleep see inside of head? Dream. This word is 'dream.'"

"Linnie sees dream. Old Many Tooth comes in dream. Old Many Tooth says, 'Old Many Tooth breaks red bowl. Old Many Tooth tells in Ranoima big bird throws fire from sky.'"

"And? And?"

Instead of answering, she got the green food bowl out of her pack, set it beside the fire, and unspitted the cooked meat into it. Next she unsheathed one of the metal knives and carved several small pieces. She picked one of these up daintily with the tips of her fingers, put it in her mouth, and then solemnly handed the bowl to Danlo. "Eat. One bowl."

The meat scorched his fingers. He didn't care.

After packing up their new belongings, they put out the fire and headed down through the foothills, moving still further north in order to avoid approaching the world at a point too close to where the air coach had disappeared. Linnie was so thrilled when he showed her what the binoculars did that she tried to walk along while looking through them. When that proved impossible she agreed, reluctantly, to put them back into the case, but she was constantly snatching them out again to get a closer look at things. She stalked and killed a deer, and they feasted. The next day, in a pool at the edge of a mountain stream, he showed her how to use the soap. She giggled at the lather, and splashed, and tickled him. They made love on the bank of the stream. Afterward, leaning on one elbow and watching her strong, still profile as she lay napping on her back in the sun, Danlo decided that perhaps love between nulls was not as pitiful a business as he had felt at first. His heart swelled with tenderness for her. He brushed her eyebrow with a fingertip, and she caught at his hand and kissed it.

Before they dressed, he asked her to help him trim his hair. She grumbled as she fussed around his head. He hoped she was doing what he requested; having no mirror, he couldn't inspect the results. It would be a mistake to expect too much, since she was haggling off hanks with a knife. Lacking curl and color, he settled on a decent trim all the way across the top, with a loose fringe hanging down in back. It would look odd, but not, he hoped, so odd as to brand him instantly. Getting the beard closer than a week's stubble without drawing blood proved impossible. Linnie wanted to pluck the hairs out, but when he protested, she desisted.

Two days later, they lay in a little hollow beneath some bushes, looking down at the Wall. Linnie reluctantly passed the binoculars to him so he could inspect it better. He had half-expected to see sentries, but of course the Wall was far too long for the Body to watch every mile of it night and day.

"I goes with you," Linnie said firmly.

"No." This was the third time they had had this argument. "You cannot speak words the right way. It would be like before. They would chase you."

"I speaks words. You teaches more words speaks. I speaks good."

"You speak very good, yes. With me, or with nulls—the children—you speak good enough. But to speak is only the left hand. The right hand is the mind-speak."

"You teaches me mind-speak." Her jaw was set.

He shook his head sadly. "I wish I could. Teaching to mind-speak is impossible.

"What this word, 'impossible'?"

"Like jumping over the moon. Nobody can do it." If only they could! "This travel into the valley will be hard enough if I'm by myself. With you along, it would be ten times harder."

She seized his arm forcefully. "I hides behind trees. I hides, watches, shoots. Like when men comes in big bird. I shoots."

"No, you mustn't shoot. I don't want any more shooting."

"I comes with you."

"There won't be any trees in some of the places I'm going. No place for Linnie to hide. People will see Linnie. People kill Linnie and Danlo."

She turned her head away, and spat. "Danlo not Linnie friend. Danlo leaves Linnie, not comes back."

"Don't be ridiculous."

"What this word, 'ridiclus'?"

"Never mind. Look—I'll have to go into towns. Big places, lots of people. Maybe be there for days. Even if you hide outside of town, the land is all farms. No place to hunt. Do you understand? No big animals, only birds and squirrels. Nothing for Linnie to eat."

"Danlo not eats?"

"I can get food at any hostel. You can't."

"What this word?"

"A hostel is—well, it's a place where they have food."

"Danlo carries food to Linnie."

Not, he was forced to admit, an unreasonable idea. If he could find a good-sized coach, she could hide in the rear seat, and he could get carry-out meals. She would be an encumbrance, worse than useless—but what choice did he have? If he simply ordered her to stay here, she would likely follow him and cause worse trouble. If he agreed to let her come, he could at least exact an agreement from her to put up with the indignities of concealment. "All right. Yes. Danlo carries food for Linnie. You can come."

She squealed and hugged him, and kissed his cheek noisily a dozen times.

"But nobody must see or hear you," he said sternly. "Everybody will know how you and the other women took the men. When anybody sees you, they will know you are not like them. They will chase you. You understand?" She seemed to, but her blind spots were not always evident. Even if she did understand this one thing, they would encounter much in the Serral Valley that would mystify her. And she was impulsive. She might easily ruin the whole undertaking. Was he making a mistake? Too late now to reconsider. "When I say hide, you hide. Sometimes hide in a little, tight, uncomfortable place." He mimed the idea by curling up and bending his neck over. "Hard to breathe. Not much air." He panted. "Linnie waits, and waits, and waits, and waits for Danlo, and makes not a sound. No sound. Like when hunting."

"Linnie waits, makes not sound. We gets more b'noclars?"

"All the binoculars you want. Books, too. I'll get you a picture-book. Maybe even teach you to read." He sighed. The plan was not developing in the direction that he would have chosen. But what of this had he chosen? His grief? To be kidnapped? Perhaps he had no real choices to make at all; perhaps he had never had any, only the choice to follow willingly where the path led, or to drag his heels.

They scaled the Wall. Footing was plentiful in the rough stone, but treacherous. At the top, they peered over cautiously. Orchards alternated with parcels of pastureland. Sheep were grazing in the distance, but of the shepherds there was no sign. After observing quietly for a few minutes, they slithered over and dropped down among almond trees.

From this point on, they would be in constant danger. They might easily be apprehended before they had gone a mile, and taken to a proctor station and locked away while the One decided what to do with them. Danlo had no illusions about his ability to protect Linnie from the wrath of the Body. He wasn't even sure he would be able to prevent others from kenning that he had lately killed four men. One way or another, the enterprise was almost certain to fail. Not to try, though, to give up and slink away into the mountains, would be a far worse failure.

''Nobody must see you,'' he instructed. ''When we see any-body in the distance, we'll have to hide.'' She nodded soberly. He gave her the spear, but kept a knife.

They proceeded down one hill and up the next, slipping among the trees. When they came upon a path, he debated whether to follow it. It didn't look well-travelled, and there was good cover on both sides, so he judged it was an acceptable risk. The farther they went, the more paths they would cross; he could not avoid them all. It might be no more than a sheep-trail, but as it twisted among the trees he felt that he was once again in the civilized world. His legs tingled, and sparks danced before his eyes.

They crossed two roads; at the second one they had to hide and wait while a twelve-seat coach passed. When it was gone, they dashed across. Shortly the chimneys and grain elevators of a farm hamlet appeared, nestled among the trees. The travellers skirted wide around it. Danlo was searching for an isolated farmhouse. The fewer who saw him looking so shabby, the better. He marveled at how well-kept the land was, even in this outlying sector. Low stone walls protected the path from erosion, and a mossy footbridge crossed a gulley.

Musing about the differences between this country and the mountains, he failed to notice a party of field workers. Linnie hissed, and he looked around and saw her disappear into a ravine. He stood stupidly in plain view as the workers tramped along a hedge that paralleled his own path, rakes and hoes over their shoulders. He had to quell a moment of blind panic. Two minds, two minds. What would his ktess be like if he were exactly who he was pretending to be? He shared a friendly greeting, and waved. A couple of the workers waved back, and the group passed on. He kenned them carefully; his ktess felt as wobbly as an arm just emerged from a cast. Several of them had noticed that he was unshaven, his clothes ragged, but while they disapproved, they attached no special importance to the fact.

Linnie clambered out of the ravine and they went on. The path joined a dirt lane rutted with the tracks of cycles. Rather than be surprised by a vehicle, they struck out across a hill. At the top they halted in the shade of a broad tree and looked down cautiously at a large farmstead. The three-story peak-roofed dwelling, sur-rounded by barns and outbuildings, was profusely gabled. It seemed no more real to him than a dollhouse. Two clotheslines fluttered with gaily colored clothing, and chickens wandered in the yard. Nobody was in view, but he kenned a young man kneading bread in the kitchen, an older man shoeing a horse in the big barn, a man and woman working together on a tractor engine, and two women sewing.

Danlo's stomach twisted at the thought of marching boldly in, but he had no choice. He needed presentable clothing, and a shave. He turned to Linnie. "I'm going to have to go down there."

"Danlo takes children?"

"No, not the children here." Apparently she had the idea that every household harbored nulls. "The children we want are only a few, scattered widely. Many days' walk. Maybe down there they will tell me where to find the children we're looking for."

"Linnie wants Danlo children."

"Yes. Well—thank you. People there want to kill you, yes? You wait here."

She frowned worriedly. "I waits until sun—" Her arm traced the arc to mid-afternoon. "—there. Then comes carries Danlo."

"No. You wait until tomorrow morning. Sleep here." He made a pillow of his hands. "Maybe I come back today. Maybe tomorrow."

Her hand tightened on the spear. "Comes back fast."

"I will come back fast, as fast as I can. But the people there will want to be hospitable. Friendly. I will have to speak with them, and mind-speak." He touched his forehead, out and back in.

"In mind-speak they sees me? Me in your mind?"

"You are very much in my mind." He touched her cheek, and she trapped his hand and kissed it, her eyes squeezed shut. "But they won't see you, not if I'm careful. You understand careful? Like with fire. Careful not to get burned. I will be careful in mind-speak."

"Like with fire. Good." In one of her abrupt mood shifts, she squatted without further ado in the high grass, unstrapped the quivers, and settled down to wait.

He hovered indecisively, then knelt beside her and pulled her close. The bow got between them and made the embrace awkward. "Linnie, thank you. Thank you for being my friend, for opening my eyes, for helping me. . . ."

She avoided his eyes. "You good man, Danlo. Good friend. Man like Makelvy." She swallowed hard, and pressed her lips together.

"I will come back. I promise."

"What this word, 'promise'?"

"Promise is—oh, never mind." He stood up. What was the point of explaining, when he couldn't promise any such thing?

"Linnie waits," she said, not looking at him. "Danlo comes back fast."

Chapter ‖ 14

HE trudged down the slope toward the farm, his feet oddly heavy and awkward. The buildings grew larger, old but freshly painted, with scallops of brilliant blue around the doors and windows. The fences were well tended, the flower beds raked, and machinery stood gleaming on a concrete slab beside the barn. Danlo felt inexpressibly shabby and filthy. Also, the story he had concocted to explain his appearance seemed absurdly thin. Surely they would see the truth at once. The outer layer of his ktess was still transparent; none of those in the buildings had kenned him. And suddenly he didn't want them to. He was ashamed, and frightened. He ducked behind a tree and stared covetously at the clothesline. Why not slip into the yard, take some clothes, and slip out again? Properly clad, he would be less repulsive. He could go on to another farm to have his hair and beard seen to, and nobody need ever know that a wild-looking man had been seen in the foothills.

He was accustomed by now to walking silently, but not to watching his footing while keeping his ktess transparent. So he went forward slowly, nerves balanced on a knife-edge. At the fence around the yard he paused to ken the area, then unlatched the gate and left it ajar.

Between the parallel lines of washing he was invisible from the knees up. He selected a well-worn pair of black trousers whose legs might just be long enough, and a cream-colored shirt with puffed-out sleeves. Underwear too—he hoped it would fit. Again he cast his mind across the farm, and was reassured to find that none of the inhabitants was even looking out a window. He began to relax.

When he emerged at the end of the clothesline, both arms wrapped around the little bale of garments, he came face to face with a small boy. Danlo started violently, and nearly dropped the clothes. The boy, no more than five, stared at him wide-eyed, thumb jammed firmly into his mouth. Danlo smiled what he hoped was a reassuring smile, though it felt brittle. "Hi," he whispered. "Ssh. Don't tell anybody."

The boy took his thumb out of his mouth, tilted his head back, and hollered, "Mom! Mom!"

Four of the adults heard the cry. The man in the barn set down his hammer and nails and came toward the barn door. Danlo froze. He couldn't even reach the gate before the man saw him, much less get up the slope. Back to his original plan, then. He opened his ktess, and felt the man's surprise that somebody should appear out of nowhere. He made the feeling of friendliness as deep and honest as he could. These people *were* his people, after all. He meant them no harm. *Greetings.*

The man came out of the barn, wiping his hands on a large red kerchief. He was about Danlo's age, and dressed in dusty brown coveralls. He had long arms, a long graying fringe of hair around a bald crown, and a gold tooth that flashed in the sun. The little boy ran to him and clung to his leg, and he ruffled the boy's hair. As the two adults bowed, they greeted one another with formal warmth in the ktess, but Danlo kenned the man's caution. Anyone who lived near the Wall would be cautious now, and his visitor certainly didn't look prepossessing, especially clutching a bundle of surreptitiously appropriated clothing.

"Your forgiveness, goodman. He hopes he may explain."

"Fine idea, yes."

A face peered out one of the windows of the farmhouse. A woman came out the door of the barn, but kept her distance. Danlo took a shaky breath, and said formally, "He fears his appearance is extremely disreputable. He had hoped to avoid frightening anybody unnecessarily by changing his clothes—" He held up the bundle. "—before he was seen."

"How become so disarrayed?"

"Wandering beyond the Wall." Alarm flickered in the man's ktess. "Taken by a band of strange people. Nulls, all of them, and insane. I only lately escaped."

The farmer nodded gravely. "We have heard much about these happenings."

"Have there been others?" Danlo showed amazement. "I know nothing of what has transpired since I was taken."

"A large group, some months ago. All were rescued, but with much bloodshed."

"Terrible, terrible. I was taken alone, and knew nothing of this. I should like to learn of these matters, and share my own tale. But first, would it trouble you if I were to ask for food, and a bath, and perhaps something decent to wear? I have suffered grievously, and not only from being alone.''

"Yes, of course." *Food/care need.* And from within the house, *Come.* "I am called Hald Chiniss."

"My name is Dappa Snee. I am a counter from Lirmorr."

"Welcome to the Chiniss farm, Goodman Snee. It is your farm."

"You are kind."

"This is my wife's sister," Chiniss said, beckoning to the woman at the barn door. "Auppel Dalgiver."

"Goodman." Auppel nodded. Her round, plain face was smudged with grease.

"You will meet my wife, Thessie," Chiniss went on, "and Furmin Dalgiver, and my wife's mother, Melia Kett—and the children too, I should think. They will not want to miss seeing one whose name is sure to be sung." Chiniss led Danlo toward the house.

"Name sung?" Danlo concealed his alarm. The last thing he wanted was notoriety.

"New verses will doubtless be added to 'Vengeance for the Blinded' so that your tale can be included."

A thin, pale boy of sixteen or seventeen stepped from the door of the farmhouse and fixed Danlo with a dark, uncertain stare. He kenned the boy's revulsion at his appearance, and did not trouble to hide the flash of shame. Chiniss chided his son silently. Radiating comfort, he put an arm across Danlo's shoulder. "Let Teumas take the clothing," he said. "We will provide better."

Danlo handed over the bundle. "My actions must seem peculiar. But to be seen in such a state—"

"No need to blame yourself. You have been infected by the discord of warpers. Cleanse yourself of wayward thoughts while we attend your bodily needs." He ushered Danlo up three wide wooden steps and into the farmhouse. The kitchen smelled of mingled spices. A smiling gray-haired woman came out of an inner doorway holding folded bath towels, fat and white and fluffy, before her large bosom. "This is my wife Thessie," Chiniss said. Children tumbled into the kitchen, chattering; Danlo quickly forgot their names.

Thessie Chiniss led him into the bathroom, all yellow tile and gleaming fixtures wreathed in steam. He let his stiff, tattered garments fall away and sank gratefully into the tub. He leaned back and closed his eyes. When he opened them a moment later, the clothing was gone, and a plate of sweet pastries rested at his elbow.

The hot water was marvelous, the scented lather exquisite, the pastries delectable. But these paled beside the closeness of the Body. He opened himself very nearly too much, letting the farmer's happy family salve away the roughness of the long months of cold and pain. How could he bear to be without this? He couldn't. Why should he want anything more? There was no reason. Nulls had died. More nulls would die. Who was Danlo Ree to think he knew a better way? He wanted to sink down into the warm, fragrant water, let it close over his head.

After he had toweled himself pink, he pulled on a pair of Chiniss's trousers, which were almost long enough, and a shirt as smooth as cream. The socks were fresh and thick; he wiggled his toes delightedly. A razor had been set by the basin. After using it, he felt the strange smoothness of his jaw. The face in the mirror was drawn, weathered, the eyes troubled.

He sat in the kitchen and ate eggs with ham while the family related their distorted version of the kidnapping of the farm workers. He professed astonishment, and unfolded the tale he had rehearsed. A second, smaller band of women had seized him, he explained, as he was walking alone on a road in the far north. They had set off through the mountains and taken him to a city built entirely of mud, from which he had escaped by spilling each day a little water onto the wall in a corner of his cell, until the wall had melted enough for him to burrow through. If the Body was going to search the mountains, at least he could set them searching for a city that wasn't there. He wondered what the family would think if they knew one of the wild women was lying in wait within a stone's throw of their house.

Two girls of ten or twelve years saw to his hair, instructed with much clucking by a very old woman whose gnarled hands seemed frozen around the top of a heavy cane. He emptied mug after mug of crisp cinnamon tea. Two boys nudged and tripped and glared at one another vying for the honor of refilling the visitor's mug. His audience soaked up every word uncritically. Their eyes glowed with admiration, which reassured but saddened him. "I must be on my way to Serameno without delay," he ended. "My affairs will be in fearful disarray, and I long to be reunited with my dear ones."

"At the next farm is often a joddie," Chiniss's eldest son said.

"I will drive you." The joddie would, of course, begin by sending the joyful news to those nearest Danlo's heart. There were not so many who fitted that description as in his younger years. His fellow counters at the Central Counting Office would celebrate, of course. How joyfully simple, to be absorbed back into the Body! The nightmare of the past months began to dissolve. No more danger from wild animals, plenty of food, a soft bed. . . . But the joddie at the next farm would probe for details. He would learn of the men Danlo had killed, would learn that, far from being a simple wandering counter, Danlo had entered into a terrifying pact with a wild null.

The adults had drawn back a little, sensing his alarm, and the children had seen the change and fallen still. "You must forgive me," Danlo said hastily. "The ordeal I have been through—sometimes I remember more than I would like." What would they do to him when they learned he was a killer? Could he rejoin the Body and yet prevent them somehow from finding out? If he did, would he ever be truly joined? His head spun. He took a sip of tea, and saw that his hand was shaking. "Let us talk of happier things," he said with an effort. He asked how much acreage Chiniss had under cultivation, and they chatted about crop yield, labor distribution, and the planning of surpluses. Seeing that Furmin Dalgiver, like his wife, had grease under his fingernails, Danlo brought the conversation around to a subject that interested him. "Do you repair the farm machines yourselves?" he asked.

The young man inspected the backs of his hands with modest pride. "We take care of most things, yes. There's a shop in town for the big jobs."

"On my way down through the hills yesterday—or was it the day before?—I saw a marvelous thing. You must have heard of it. A flying coach."

The young man nodded brightly. "They call them airplanes. That's the old word, from the time before the Great Cleansing, when they were last made. One's coming to Oburn in just a couple of days! They're bringing it around for all to see how the Body plans to comb the wilderness, and you bet Auppel and I are going down to see it! Maybe they'll even let some of us go up in it. Do you think?"

Marvelous hope. "I only saw this one in the distance. Oburn, you say? Do you know how many have been made?"

"Oh, a dozen at least."

"I don't suppose you know how far they can fly without refueling."

"You kidding? I found out all that stuff. Five hundred miles is what I heard. But that's air miles, see?" *Wind pressing backward.* "They can't always cover so much ground."

The young man was avid to explain about airplanes. Danlo would have been happy to oblige, but it might be dangerous to appear too interested. Another question wanted asking—partly for its own sake, and partly so he could see how they responded. "Have there been, in these parts, any nulls this past spring? Not wild ones. The ordinary kind. I am perhaps excessively concerned with nulls, now. They frighten me. I hope you'll indulge my curiosity. I'd like to avoid travelling near where any are held."

"Better not to talk of such things," Thessie Chiniss said.

Danlo kenned their reactions as closely as he could. A great deal happened in a few seconds, but if there was a flash of rebelliousness, he did not catch it. Some sadness, yes, and the quick diversion of thought into other channels—flowering fields, festivals of song. It was what he had expected.

If he lingered much longer, the family might think of questions that he would find awkward to answer. Also, Linnie might grow restive and take it upon herself to rescue him. "I must be on my way," he said. "If you would show me the road to the farm where the joddie may be found. . . ."

"Teumas will drive you in the two-seater," Chiniss said.

"There is no need."

"It is our pleasure. To speed on his way one who has fresh knowledge of these terrible goings-on—how could we do less?"

"I have walked a long way," Danlo said, forcing a friendly laugh. "I can walk a little further."

"If you will not be driven, then take the vehicle yourself. I can send somebody for it tomorrow."

"I have certainly troubled you enough," Danlo said. "The coat especially—it's too fine. I shall send it back at once when I reach home." He stood up and struggled into the coat. The sleeves were a bit short, but the shoulders were wide enough. The tailoring was conservative, and the soft plum-colored fabric was nicely set off by an embroidered gray vine dotted with tiny gold flowers. "Still, the use of a two-seater would speed me. I should not like to strand you."

"We seldom have use for it."

"One thing more you could do," Danlo added. "I have

subsisted for so many weeks on such poor fare, your wife's good cooking is a gift from the One. I am too full now to touch another bite, but if the goodwoman could prepare a little pack of bread and apples that I could take with me. . . ."

"The Itkunin farm is but ten minutes' drive. They will have plenty."

Danlo chuckled and shrugged lightly, doing his best to make the request seem a mere whim. "Of course. Silly of me. I have been hungry for so long, I had nearly forgotten that the getting of food was such a simple thing."

"You are too thin," Thessie Chiniss said. "Perhaps I will prepare a little something, so Clenna Itkunin will not have to bother."

Great kindness. Deep gratitude.

The whole family trooped outside. The two-seater was an unusual model, a three-wheeler whose front and top lifted to provide a door. Danlo got himself settled into the seat, and Chiniss pointed past the barn toward the narrow road. "In about two miles you'll see three big oaks close together on the left, one with a lightning burn. The Itkunin drive is just around the bend from there."

"My thanks, Goodman Chiniss. You have been very kind, you and all your family." Danlo paused. "One thing more. Perhaps it would be best if word of my coming were not spread among your neighbors. As you said, the Body is perturbed with tales of outlandish happenings. If my report reaches the One most directly, with the fewest grand imaginings swept along with it, all will be best served. Don't you agree?"

The farmer radiated disappointment, but he nodded soberly. "I had already, in my mind, been making up verses. I am not a bad songwriter, if I do say so. But there is wisdom in what you say."

The request would do little good, Danlo knew. The first joddie who happened upon a member of the family would have the whole tale in short order. But days might pass before that happened, and the days would serve him well. "Again, my thanks." He pulled the door of the two-seater down, thumbed the starter button, and pressed down on the pedal, and the little vehicle jounced across the farmyard. He waved, and the family returned the wave.

Coach travel was another seduction; he savored sitting in comfort while the land rolled by, and opened the window to enjoy the breeze. He kept on in the same direction for some minutes, not sure whether a vagrant hairpin turn in the road might bring him back into the view of the Chinnisses, but the road ran down into a vale, and presently he found a place where he could drive off into some bushes. He left the two-seater, slung the parcel of food over his shoulder, and struck off across a field to circle back toward Linnie.

He was not sure what to do next. The warmth of the Body, even as he held himself apart, was like the tug of a riptide carrying him away from a rocky shore. He wanted to float on his back in the sun. Still, if he allowed himself to be absorbed, the One would not be content to let the joddies do their usual job of Guidance on him. Deeper powers would be brought to bear. He had spent years rebuilding the memory of Julan in a place free of their ministrations, but now he would have to give up both Julan and far more—Linnie, and his hopes for the nulls, and the raw joy of walking the mountain trails, axe swinging free in his hand. He would be a counter again, no more than that. But he would be comforted.

The sun was well down in the west by the time he worked his way back to where he had left Linnie. At first he didn't see her, and his mind cast outward automatically to locate her in the ktess—foolish, but the reflex had reawakened. Then she stood up among the bushes, gripping her bow, and he felt as awkward in his new clothes as he had approaching the farm in his old ones. "I brought food." He held up the parcel.

She took it from him, and opened it, and sniffed at the contents. "You looks *ararathusa*," she said. "Bird with colors."

"Does it bother you?"

"What this word, 'bother'?"

"Never mind." She was a bottomless mystery to him, and he to her. Tenderness welled in him. How could he have thought of abandoning her? In the absence of the bond of the ktess, his obligation to her, to all of the nulls, was stronger, not weaker. No more of this wavering. No more yearning for comfort. He had chosen a hard road, knowing it was hard. Now he had only to walk it. But he wondered whether his resolve would be strong enough.

He wanted to reach Oburn in time to see the flying coach—the airplane, Dalgiver had called it. Also, his search for allies would go faster in a town, since he could comb more minds with less travel. He reached out delicately in the ktess, found Hald Chiniss's mind, and led the man's thoughts gently around to musing on the roads of the region, the distances and branchings and guideposts.

Shortly Danlo had the information he needed. He led Linnie back across the fields toward the two-seater.

"House moves," she said when she saw it. "This word my friends calls it. Danlo word?"

"Coach. Coach."

"Coach," she repeated. "This coach flies?"

"No. Only goes on paths. Big paths called roads."

Linnie was enchanted by riding in a coach. She sat forward on the seat, exclaiming, her head swiveling from side to side as the trees and fields slid past. When an oncoming vehicle topped the next hill, she gripped her spear, and Danlo projected calm while considering wildly. The front of the two-seater was a clear plastic bubble, and there was no room behind the seat for Linnie to hide. Let them think she was a child, then. A young couple were in the other coach; Danlo greeted them casually in the ktess, and held the thought that he was driving his daughter to Oburn. He pictured Linnie smaller and neatly dressed, and held the image as firm as he could. The other coach passed. The man said to his wife, "Big girl." Danlo slowed the two-seater and concentrated on stilling their ripple of suspicion.

He managed to get them off on another subject, and dulled their memories, but another vehicle might come along at any moment. "This isn't going to work," he said. "Have to wait for dark." He pulled the two-seater off the road, and he and Linnie shared the fruit and fresh bread in the parcel while night settled around them.

Late in the evening, they sat at the crest of another hill and looked down on the lights of Oburn. It was a small enough town compared to the vastness of Serameno, but it was a bigger concentration of humanity than he had seen since that morning, so long ago, in Woolich. The golden haze of ten thousand minds wafted outward. He could go among them unnoticed, like a cinder folded into a soufflé. But Linnie couldn't. "I shouldn't have let you come," he said. "There's no place for you down there. Even out here. . . ." For miles, the houses they passed had been growing closer-packed. They might, if they searched, find a place where a small fire would go unnoticed, but he couldn't leave her safely. What he needed was a building, preferably in the town, that was unused. Such buildings were not uncommon; with luck, he could find one before dawn.

Linnie had not taken her eyes from the lights of the town. Yellow and green and pink and blue, they wavered in the updrafts of dissipating heat and dusted her cheeks with moonglow. "Sparks. Pretty."

"Yes. They are." What would it be like to live in a town like this with a woman like Linnie? To drive out at night with a loved one and look down upon one's own home? He would never know. That was what had been taken from him. He hardened himself, and released the brake, and the coach rolled down the hill into Oburn.

Chapter ‖ 15

THE airplane sat before the Triple Gate in the town square, its hard, sleek lines dwarfing the weathered wooden structure. It had arrived, with a roar heard from one end of Oburn to the other, just after daybreak. Within minutes a crowd had gathered, but no presentation was scheduled until mid-afternoon, so all morning the crowd milled, people leaving and being replaced by others. A bold few went up to touch the flanks of the mechanical marvel.

Danlo spent half an hour in the square, circled among the nearby streets, and came back, trying to seem interested but not too interested. The crowd was festive: A pair of jugglers practiced their intricate art, a trio of flutists strolled, and two waking dreamers shared streams of exotic images.

The plane itself looked identical to the one that had found him in the mountains—a smooth wraparound window in front, and tapering wings mounted with engines on which were set large three-bladed fans. He was less interested in the construction than in how the craft was piloted. Such a vehicle, if he could lay hands on one, would provide a quick way in and out of the Serral Valley. To learn piloting, he needed to ken the pilot, and the pilot had gone off to a hostel with the rest of the touring party to rest and eat. Nobody seemed to know which hostel, and Danlo judged it would be imprudent to show too keen an interest. So he passed the time trawling the crowd.

He had begun to call it trawling, because he was casting a wide net, but perhaps, with so little catch to show for the effort, it was closer to angling. He was a fisher of people. He wandered the streets, seeming purposeful but unhurried, turning corners often so as not to remain in anybody's view for too long, noting where the joddies gathered and staying away from them. As he went, he sifted through the ktess. It was a tedious business. For one thing, he was not sure what he was looking for, or how he would recognize it if he found it. Sadness? Anger? Restlessness? Recklessness? He came upon all these. Unobtrusively he followed the individuals who felt them, probing deeper to see whether a seed might be sprouting into the sort of waywardness that he could use. Each time he was disappointed. The sad were sad for ordinary reasons, the angry firmly Guided, except for one bull-necked man whose seething made him a danger to any enterprise more subtle than driving nails into boards, that being the task at which he was employed. The restless and the reckless were few, and their exploits, which might once have seemed daring to Danlo, were paltry. Beneath the spiky surface lurked placid conformity. A dozen times, over the course of two days, he came upon people whose siblings or children had proven nulls. Their grief was muted by Guidance, as his had been, and none of them had had the strength to throw the Guidance aside. They were useless to him.

Even if he *had* found a kindred purpose, the one who harbored it would have been useless to him. The minds of the people of Oburn lay as open as books—to him, and surely to the joddies. There would be no conspirators; they could not conspire.

When the lecture started, Danlo was near the rear of the crowd. He snagged a toffee-apple from the tray of a passing vendor and drifted closer to the plane, munching. Two men stood on one wing of the plane, where they could be seen across the square. A joddie sat unobtrusively on the ground below, amplifying their thoughts so that all could ken clearly. One of the two, chubby and well-scrubbed, had a beautiful mane of golden curls. The other was taller and leaner, with piercing eyes and black hair that trickled down his forehead in glistening ringlets.

"Life is good," the golden-haired man began, clasping his hands together. "Praise be to the One." His voice boomed out through a mechanical amplifier.

"Praise to the one," many voices echoed.

"The One provides all that we need, and protects us from all harm."

"Praise to the One."

"Beyond the borders of our fair land lies chaos. Yet we are safe."

"Praise to the One."

"Today—today, goodmen and goodwomen of Oburn, the One faces a new challenge. A thing that nobody had thought could

happen, has happened. From beyond the Bound Wall, a foul
disruption has appeared.'' A compressed image of the women's
raid and its aftermath flashed through the ktess. Danlo pressed
closer. Which one was the pilot? Ah, the black-haired one, who
had not yet spoken. ''But the One has moved swiftly to meet the
challenge,'' the golden-haired man went on. ''Moved swiftly on
many fronts. My friends and I have come to—to Oburn today, as
we were in Grawly yesterday and Yubasty the day before, to share
with you what has been accomplished, and to enlist your good will
for the labor that remains to be done. While the source of the
disruption has yet to be rooted out, I can say to you today with
complete assurance that thanks to the vigorous efforts of our
crafters in Soyvill, the Body of Harmony is entirely free from
danger. Praise be to the One!''

Every voice in the square was raised: ''Praise to the One!''
Danlo said it fervently, and kept his reservations to himself.

''You want to know more—how this marvelous vessel has been
constructed so swiftly from plans so ancient that scholars had to be
called to read the script. How it will be armed with explosives and
other, deadlier weapons for the Second Cleansing. I should be
honored to share of these things, but am a person of no importance. I but sweep the leaves from the road. I stand aside now for
a young man of singular courage, a young man whose calling is to
guide the vessel in its flight. When songs come to be sung of the
Second Cleansing, his name will ring loud in every ear. Your
affection and respect, goodfolk, for Goodman Pilot Luth Vardiki.''

The outpouring of affection went on for many seconds. Luth
Vardiki smiled and lowered his head in acknowledgment. ''Your
pleasure, goodfolk,'' he said. Again, the amplification carried his
words. By now Danlo was close enough to hear them direct. ''To
fly this machine is a great honor. Only nine are yet completed, and
one of those has been lost in the mountains.'' A collective sigh of
dismay washed across the crowd. ''The circumstances will not be
clear until we have found where it came to earth. Perhaps a
mechanical failure. There is much we do not yet know about
flying, much that has been forgotten. A larger fleet, of forty
planes, is under construction in Soyvill, where the old records of
flying were kept. What we learn from flying the first group will
aid us greatly in making the second airworthy.

''Our purpose is twofold. First, to search out where the wild
nulls came from. We fliers will be aided in this by information

gleaned from the three captured alive, whom the One has appointed scholars to study.''

Danlo's face turned cold, and his breath caught in his throat. Women captured? He kenned the shared vision of three wild women in a room, improbably dirty and fierce-looking. Don't react—two minds, two minds. He kept tight rein on his thoughts until his pulse had slowed. He had assumed, somehow, that the Body would have killed all of the women that first night. He wanted badly to think through what this news might mean, but this was not the place to do it.

The pilot was going on about the design of the plane. Danlo dipped beneath the surface of his mind, looking for the tendrils of association that would tell him how the machine could actually be flown. He found a morass of jargon—flaps and stabilizers and ailerons and r.p.m.'s—and a bank of unfamiliar buttons, levers, and indicators like the ones he had seen on the first plane. Also in Luth's mind, not being shared with the crowd but not concealed either, were several terrifying experiences during the first test flights. The craft had veered out of control, and Luth had narrowly avoided smashing into the ground at high speed. Piloting, Danlo concluded reluctantly, was not something to be learned second-hand in a casual encounter.

Luth Vardiki's personality, however, caught his attention. Reckless, yes—he had actually enjoyed his brushes with death. Stubborn, too. He had insisted on mechanical changes that the crafters thought were impossible, and gotten his way. And underlying all, the fierce joy of an eagle, which came upon him when he soared alone high above the world, where the ktess attenuated and fell away. Exactly the sort of man Danlo had been seeking—and a pilot! How long did Luth mean to stay in Oburn? If Danlo was to seek him out privately in order to learn more, it would have to be here. He had no desire to chase the plane hop by hop across the Serral Valley.

Luth talked about the plane's weaponry. ''A door beneath the plane can be opened in flight, and explosives dropped that detonate on impact. In the First Cleansing far larger planes were used. They carried huge loads of explosives, as well as poison gas weapons. If we need to build such aircraft, we will. Great effort would be required, and sacrifices on the part of all, to mine metal and provide for the redirected workers. Until we know the extent of the null threat, and until the design of the explosive devices themselves is perfected, smaller planes will suffice.

"They're highly maneuverable. The engines on the wings tilt upward, as you see them now, for vertical rising and controlled descent. This is of great advantage in the wilderness; a plane designed for horizontal ascent is capable of greater forward speed, but it requires a smooth, level area of considerable length to rise and descend. Once the plane is in the air, the engines are rotated forward so as to propel the plane. This rotation, while the engine is spinning, presents the greatest mechanical challenge. In horizontal flight, lift is provided not by the engines but by the passage of air across the wings, which creates a pressure differential."

Questions were shouted from the crowd: Were the airplanes equipped with special sensing and imaging devices? Yes. Did the One mean to bring back more prisoners, once the source of the disruption was found? Only enough to be studied, so that the Cleansing of all who remained at large could be assured. Had maps of the wilderness been found? No—the archives of the ancients were extensive, and in poor condition, and not well catalogued. But the old maps might not be needed, since the planes could see everything from the air and record it all so that new maps could be drawn.

Danlo waited patiently. He was learning a great deal, none of it encouraging. Before the lecture ended he had another surprise, more distressing than the first. The golden-haired man, whom Luth addressed as Goodman Pilcher, took over the presentation again for a few final words. "Before we part," he said, "I should like to remind you, or tell you if you had not heard of it earlier, that we flew here with one other, one whose sharing will make most vivid, if it is not compelling enough already, the reason for our industry. This evening, in the Sharing House, our companion will lay before you his own experiences during the terrible trek into the wilderness. Dozens died so that he might be brought back among us. You will learn of his sacrifice—enough that you will not want to learn more. This man's misfortune is our good fortune, for it strengthens our resolve. Yes, you will have the opportunity to ken the sharing of one of the Blinded." Which one, Danlo wondered. He barely remembered their names. "Compounding our good fortune, among those who were seized and mutilated was a rememberer! Every detail that could be wished, goodmen and goodwomen, you will have from Goodman Rememberer Oxar Blennish."

Danlo started violently. He managed to disguise it as a coughing fit, and got several friendly pats on the back. *Fine, fine,* he shared. *Need to sit down.* Hands guided him toward a bench. Oxar here? Being blinded, Oxar couldn't recognize him visually, but that offered no safety. The blind freely used others' eyes. And Oxar knew him well enough to recognize his ktess, though perhaps not in a crowd. Danlo sank down on the bench. While clearing his throat, he scanned the crowd visually. No sign of Oxar. Which meant, knowing Oxar, that he was comfortably ensconced at the hostel. Approaching the pilot at the hostel would be doubly difficult. The best course would be to wait for evening, go to the Sharing House, and hope for an opportunity to strike up a conversation with the pilot while Oxar was busy sharing.

But to what end? Anything Danlo shared with Luth, Oxar would ken. A stray wisp of thought, a hint that the average joddie would attach no importance to, might be enough to set Oxar thinking. He was a dull man, but tenacious, and he liked puzzles. Forget the pilot, then? No; he would have to find a way.

The coughing fit had attracted attention. He got up and sauntered peacefully away. The edges of the crowd were thinning, though behind him Goodman Pilcher's closing exhortations still rang across the town square.

It was still early for supper, but he needed to think more than he needed to trawl the streets. He ordered takeout at a restaurant and walked ten long blocks to the side street off of which he had parked the two-seater. His only assurance that it would still be hidden in the deserted shed was that no alarm had gone up. He had, of course, shut the doors of the shed and cautioned Linnie to stay inside. To make the doors balky and difficult to open, he had removed a hinge pin from each side. He had emphasized to Linnie that if anybody came she was to stay hidden, not to attack them, but there was no place in the shed to hide except behind the coach.

He kenned no disturbance in the area of the shed, and nobody watching. Inside, the air was warm and stuffy. Linnie moved forward soundlessly out of the darkness. "Good smell," she said. They sat in the front seats of the coach and ate the cooling steamed vegetables and spiced chicken dumplings. After so many weeks of scorched meat, Danlo relished the variety. Linnie's appetite was voracious; if she were consigned to a life of leisure, she would undoubtedly grow fat, but the prospect seemed remote.

"I heard some news today," he said.

"What this word, 'news'?"

"I heard words. I learned a new thing. When—when my people attacked your people, and killed them—you remember this?"

Her face clouded. She took a bite of dumpling and chewed obstinately.

"In that place, with the big fire, I thought your people all died. You thought this too, yes?"

"Bones in fire—speaks on this thing not good."

"I'm sorry. We must. I heard today that three of your people were taken alive. Three women. Not killed."

"Three women. Not kills three women." She fussed over a concept for which she had not learned words. "Kills Linnie—want kills Linnie. Not kills three women. And? And?"

"They'll kill them soon enough. They're studying them. Umm, they keep them in a house, and talk to them, and watch them. The women are captives, just as we were captives, the men, when your people took us. Men captive, women captive." He twisted his wrists behind his back, as if they were tied.

"Women names?"

"I didn't learn. I don't know."

"Where this house, captives house?"

"I don't know that either. Serameno, I suppose. A long way from here, south and west. In a big, big, big village. Many people."

"Your people kills women tomorrow-morrow?"

"Yes, they will."

"How many days?"

He could only shrug.

"Big, big village."

"That's right."

"Danlo helps children."

He knew what she meant, though he wished he didn't. "I'm not sure there's anything we can do. They'll be heavily guarded. Many strong men with weapons—weapons like the ones you saw in the plane—the flying house that fell, the big bird. Strong weapons to hurt anybody that comes near."

"Danlo helps children."

"It's not the same thing! The children didn't come here and attack our people. The children didn't put anybody's eyes out."

"Linnie helps Danlo helps children."

At present she was as much a hindrance as a help, but he couldn't argue the justice of her claim. "All right. Look, we don't know yet what's practical. I'll learn more. I'll find out where they are, and what plans my people have for them. If we can help them, we will. But there's no sense getting ourselves killed if it's not going to help free them. We need to consider larger issues.''

"What this word, 'issues'?''

"Issues are—oh, never mind. I'll learn what I can, and we'll talk about it again tomorrow. Yes?''

She nodded, but the tilted, watchful look in her eyes said she didn't entirely trust him. He felt the weight of lives on his shoulders, and sank deeper into the seat and stared out the front window at the bright T-shaped crack around the doors of the shed.

If the Body had finished its revenge that first night, he would not be faced with this problem. The revenge had been deferred, that was all. It wasn't his most pressing problem, either. The pressing problem was how to approach the pilot. Caution was vital—but with the touring party likely to depart in the morning, he had no time for caution. And what if, when he probed the pilot, he *did* find the sort of person who might be willing to take part in such a mad venture? The pilot was no ordinary citizen, brushing the odd joddie on the street. He was travelling with one. How could a seed be planted that would stay beneath the earth until the day when the fruit was needed?

The joddies were capable of controlling others in such ways. Danlo had heard tales of a few who made sport of it—to Guide a man with hidden Guidance, so that at the ringing of a bell he would think himself a dog, or be incapable of speech from dawn to sundown and not know why. Could an ordinary man force such a compulsion on another, and keep it hidden? Danlo lay back in the seat and closed his eyes. For a long time he lay not moving while he passed like a whisper along the shrouded pathways of the ktess.

When he opened his eyes, the narrow bar of sun had slid well across the floor of the shed. He thought perhaps he understood the process. Well enough to succeed? A good question, but by now he was used to doing things that he didn't know how to do. He kissed Linnie's cheek, and she snuggled against him. "Danlo strong, does many things,'' she murmured into his neck. "Linnie thinks Danlo throws mountains, catches stars in mouth. Linnie has air inside head.''

"Well—maybe we'll be able to help them. We'll see.'' He kissed her forehead, and her mouth. Again he was surprised by the intensity of his feeling for her. His inability to ken her seemed, if anything, to add poignancy to their closeness.

After a while he drew back. "I have to go. There's a meeting tonight. Many people come together in a big house. One man will be there that I must speak to.'' And another that he must avoid at all cost.

The Sharing House in Oburn, unlike those in small villages, could hold only a fraction of the population. By the time Danlo arrived, the crowd was spilling out the door into the street. He kenned that Oxar's presentation had not yet begun. The sun had set behind the hills, but the sky was still streaked by silver strands of cloud. The air was fragrant with clematis and honeysuckle; spring was bursting into summer like bread rising in an oven. Danlo crossed the wide porch purposefully. He gave the townsfolk the vague impression that he was part of the official party, and they made way for him.

Inside, amid the buzz of conversation, an impromptu singing match had begun. A hundred voices paced through the halting half-cadences of ''Deeper Within.'' Bodies pressed close, but Danlo was tall enough to see over heads. Across the lobby, half a dozen doors were flung open on the interior of the hall. At each side of the lobby, a broad staircase led up to the balcony seats. Beside the stairs were narrow arches that opened, if this was the commonly used floor plan, onto halls that led along the sides of the building. He forged toward the nearer side hall, steering around a knot of people who were avidly exclaiming over a woman's towering hairdo, a confection interwoven with white feathers.

At the arch, bidden by an obscure impulse, he turned to look back across the crowded lobby. His eyes were caught by the eyes of a young woman—no, a girl, sixteen or seventeen, but wrapped in a calm self-possession that made her seem older. Not wanting to attract attention, he broke off his gaze and strode away down the side hall. But her image stayed with him, long blond hair that framed a classic oval face, small fine-boned hands clasped soberly at her waist. Perhaps she had been looking at someone standing near him, someone on the stair. But he thought not.

The side hall carried him down a short flight of stairs and on to a large, low-ceilinged room beside the stage. Those who had, or could pretend to have, business here were milling about as thickly as in the lobby. Finding the pilot was easier than he had feared, but getting a chance to be alone with him did not look as if it was going to be easy at all; Luth Vardiki was surrounded by a knot of the curious, mostly young men eager to know more about the airplane. He was sharing, in words underscored by breathtaking visions, both the mechanical details and the startling sensations of flight.

Danlo stood back against the wall and scanned the crowd for Oxar Blennish. No sign of him. But there was little assurance in that. Oxar might be standing just beyond the door that led to the stage, and might ken somebody in the room who was looking in Danlo's direction. He might, for that matter, have been in the lobby and using that blond girl's coolly appraising eyes.

Danlo planted himself at the edge of the group that surrounded Luth. He was less interested in what Luth was sharing with his admirers than with teasing out a thread from elsewhere in the man's mind. But which thread? With a little effort, Danlo was able to shut away the distractions of the others' minds and peer into Luth's. Childhood memories, the faces of lovers, the undigested residue of forgotten angers and hurts—the usual assortment. What was not so usual, as he had kenned earlier in the day, was the joy the man felt at soaring free. He relished the way the clinging warmth of the ktess dropped away, like vines that stretched until they snapped. Though he would have been loath to admit it, Luth did not like sharing; he felt soiled by it, as if it left a thin layer of grease on his skin.

Luth had fallen silent, confused by the random chains of thought sparking across his mind. But he couldn't ken where the disruption was coming from. He assumed a joddie was responsible. Danlo looked studiously at a spot on the floor. Luth's eyes swept the room. No red robes. Danlo caught a glimpse, no more, of himself through Luth's eyes, standing at the edge of the circle, looking distracted. He wondered whether his clothing and demeanor were appropriate to the occasion, but it wouldn't do to steer Luth's eyes back to him in order to check.

Luth looked to the door. Another throng was spilling into the room, among them Oxar, Goodman Pilcher, and a joddie. Danlo slipped away from Luth to monitor his own ktess. Outwardly, he hoped, he was as clear as glass. He kept his face averted from those around Oxar, and breathed evenly, and slumped a little to disguise his height. The trio swept toward the stage door, but they slowed, and Oxar's braying voice rang out: "Luth! You coming?"

"A moment."

Danlo rode in swiftly and goaded Luth's dislike of sharing. He amplified it—swimming, floundering in the soup of a thousand minds.

"Go on without me," Luth called. "Need fresh air."

They went on toward the door, but Oxar hesitated again. From the ears of half a dozen people close to him, Danlo heard him mutter, "Now, that's odd. Hmm. Well—well, later." Then he was through the door and gone.

The circle around Luth had thinned as everybody rushed to find seats in the Sharing Hall. Luth turned away toward a side door, and Danlo drifted after him, letting him stay well ahead.

Dusk was falling in the narrow strip of park beside the Sharing Hall. Danlo didn't see which way the pilot had gone, but he kenned him easily, leaning against a tree, unwrapping the paper from a piece of candy. Luth's black jacket gleamed with snaps and zippers.

"Pleasant evening, goodman," Danlo said.

"It is. Licorice?"

"Thanks."

Luth passed a piece of candy. "Not interested in Goodman Blennish's sharing?"

"Kenned him before." Danlo popped the licorice ball into his mouth, and tucked the wadded wrapper in his pocket. "Flying calls for an unusual sort of man."

"Every calling calls for its own sort of man. You?"

"Counter."

Luth shuddered. "I could never do that. Sitting indoors, staring at books and papers week on week. I'd go corker."

"As it happens, I've been outdoors quite a lot lately. Not counting. Walking, mostly. Sleeping under the stars, even."

"Sounds pleasant."

"At times." How to proceed? "You ever flown beyond the Wall?"

"Last week. Searching. You heard we lost a plane? Still haven't found it. They're installing transmitters now on all the planes, so even if they're down they can be located."

Danlo picked up Luth's distaste at the idea of always being locatable. "Lot of land out there," Danlo said. "If a plane went down, a man could walk away from it, walk for quite a long time and not be found."

"Starve."

"Not necessarily. There's plenty to eat. Just have to learn to catch it before it runs away. That's where the wild women came from, yes? Somewhere out there. They didn't starve. You don't know where they're being kept, do you? The ones that were taken alive, I mean."

"In the Jewel, I heard."

The Jewel of the One—an enormous maze of a building, forever thick with joddies and proctors. Danlo's heart sank.

"This saddens you," Luth said.

"I have—some compassion for them. Degraded though they must be, they're human, like ourselves."

"Not like us. Nulls."

Danlo smiled wryly. "You don't think we're like nulls?"

"Not in the way that matters."

"And yet—your pardon, goodman, but I kenned your sharing earlier. You're most happy when you're furthest from the Body. When you're most like a null. If, Olivia forbid, you were a null, would you not be happier still?"

Luth turned his face away, so that Danlo saw his strong profile. "I'm happier having my head on my shoulders."

"There is that." Danlo took a breath. "A shame, that with so much untenanted land beyond the Wall, we can't simply let the nulls go, let them live out there."

"I hadn't thought of it that way."

"Nobody thinks of it. I think sometimes the One sees to it that nobody does."

Luth looked at Danlo sharply. "You're spinning out a very strange line of talk. What did you say your name was?"

"I didn't. My name is not important. What's important is the question I touched on. This question: With so much empty land, why not let the nulls go rather than kill them?"

"Madness. They'd breed. That would lead us straight back to the Time of Chaos."

"That's not you talking," Danlo said gently. "It's the Guidance. I'll ask the question again. Don't answer by reflex; think how you feel, and answer slowly."

"I don't want to hear this sort of question."

But Danlo could see that he had struck a nerve. "Then I'll ask it a different way. You like being off by yourself. If it were in your power to take nulls—perhaps only a few, perhaps more than a few—to a place where they could live by themselves, not among us but in some land of their own, would you do it? Rather than permit them to be Cleansed?"

Luth wet his lips. "I'm only one man. There's nothing I could do."

"If you weren't alone—if others were working toward the same end—would you be willing to help?"

"You're talking crazy talk!"

"Answer slowly. Think. If you could help, would you?"

"It wouldn't do any good. What if I were to say yes? An hour from now I'll be sitting across from Brother Neander at the hostel. He'll have this whole conversation from me, if he wants it."

"That's a problem, of course. But what if I were to—rearrange your ktess just slightly, so that he wouldn't have access to it? What then?"

Luth snorted contemptuously. "Can you make eggs disappear from under hats, too? Joddies aren't children. You can't play parlor tricks on them."

"Perhaps not. I can tell you this, though. I've been wandering the streets of Oburn for two full days now, thinking the most scandalous thoughts. Everything I've just shared with you, and a dozen times more. Nobody has taken the slightest notice."

"Impossible. Blennish put you up to this, didn't he? He's hoping to cast a shadow of waywardness over me. He'd like to see me booted out of the pilot corps."

"I'm no friend of Oxar Blennish. Look, I can understand your skepticism. A few months ago I would have responded just as you have, though I had greater reason than you to feel otherwise. Let me show you what I can do to keep a part of you hidden from Brother Neander. Then give me your answer again."

Luth raised a fist. "If you're not a joddie, I'll not have you rummaging in my mind."

Danlo had already prepared the way. He acted swiftly.

Luth's hand dropped to his side. "Evening, goodman," he said. "Care for some licorice?" He patted his pockets. "I know I brought some away from dinner."

"You already gave me a piece." Danlo bubbled with glee. It worked!

"Did I? Do I know you?"

"We've been talking for five minutes now."

Luth chuckled. "Now, I'd remember that, wouldn't I? Do I look ancient to you, or simple-minded?"

"You've never seen me before this moment?"

"I've seen a great many people in the past month. I can't remember that we've ever spoken."

"You're certain of that?"

"Why wouldn't I be?"

Now for the unlocking cue. Danlo fished the licorice wrapper out of his pocket and held the wadded-up paper before Luth's eyes. "What is this?"

"It's—" Luth swayed, and put his hand to his head. "Oh. We've been talking about— Oh." After a nervous moment, he started laughing, a nearly soundless but heartfelt laugh.

"I don't know," Danlo said, "that a block of that sort will prevent a joddie from kenning beneath it if he wants to. But why should he want to, when he has no reason for suspicion?"

"So you *can* hide an egg under a hat. But you can't make an omelet out of it as long as it's under the hat. What if I were to agree—and I haven't said that I have—with this absurd idea about nulls roaming free? What then? Once you've protected me from Brother Neander, I won't remember that I agreed to anything."

"I haven't yet dug to the bottom of my sack," Danlo said.

"No, I don't suppose you have."

"The question is, does the proposition interest you? If it were in your power to snatch nulls from beneath the axe and carry them away to a place where they could live out their lives, would you do it?"

"Not because I care for them especially, no. But because I'm like them, yes. Because I would hope somebody would do the same for me—and because I know nobody would."

"It means terrible danger, and the chance of success—" *A spark. A grain of sand.*

"Danger doesn't concern me," Luth said. "But I do like to know who's building the plane, if I'm going to fly it. Who are you? How do you come to have such a farfetched notion?"

"I'm nobody special. My wife fell ill. This was many years ago. She fell away from the ktess." He did not need to add what had happened after that.

"Yes, I see. And somehow the coming of the wild women put this idea in your head."

"You might say that."

"You spoke about catching food as if you'd tried it."

"You might say that as well."

"You're remarkably reticent. I can't ken you at all."

Danlo smiled. "I'm not letting you."

"Why should I offer any aid to a man about whom I know so little?"

"The more you know, the more danger I'm in. Even to speak to you like this is foolhardy. To reveal my resources, or my plans—no. I'll tell you why you should offer your aid: because you love freedom the way most men love comfort. So little of your life is your own; most of it belongs to others. Take that little piece that's your own—'' Danlo cupped an imaginary ball of clay in his hand. ''—and make it count for something. This is the best opportunity you'll ever have. Perhaps the only one. I can't compel you to help, the way the joddies can. I can only ask you to help because you want to. And if you say yes, you might, just conceivably, live long enough to find freedom for yourself as well.'' He shared, as powerfully as he could, what that would feel like—walking a rocky ridge, the stone axe swinging in his hand, an eagle overhead against the sun.

''You've been out there. Were you with the wild women?''

''I've been on a tangled trail. The impression I just gave you was of a time when I was entirely alone.''

Luth looked back at the Sharing Hall, from which snatches of song drifted toward them. He grimaced in distaste. ''What do you want me to do?''

''For the moment, nothing. Go about your business. I will go about mine, and the less you know of it the better. If the time should come—and I think it will—when I need to get away from the Serral Valley quickly, I will send you a cue, not unlike this bit of paper, which will free you to remember this night, and this conversation.''

''Send a cue?''

Within. ''Also, I'll let you know where I am, so you can fly your airplane to meet me.''

''How?''

''I'm not sure yet.''

''And after I pick you up?''

Danlo shrugged. ''We'll go where we can and do what we have to. I promise nothing. As a friend of mine lately pointed out, I can't throw mountains or catch stars in my mouth. But perhaps, between your airplane and my skill at hiding eggs under hats, we can build a bridge that a few children can walk across.''

''I'd like that,'' Luth said. ''I'd like that very much.''

''Good. Now I'm going to do more thoroughly what I did a moment ago. Sit down against the tree here. You'll think you've been napping. And in case I don't get a chance to say it later, many thanks.''

The pilot sat on the grass. ''You realize this is absurd. We've got no chance whatever of accomplishing anything.''

''I find that I work more effectively when I worry less, and I worry less when I don't think about what's possible and what isn't. Remember that, when you remember.'' He found the river of memory in Luth's mind, and turned it aside, and built a little wall against the flow. On the wall he sealed an image. When the image next came to Luth in the ktess, the wall would crumble. Danlo hoped the image was odd enough that nobody around Luth would prompt him with it accidentally. On the wall was imprinted a blue rose lying in a drift of crimson snow.

He touched Luth's sleep center as well, so that the man's nap would be genuine, and stepped softly away.

Inside, Oxar's sharing was still in progress. Danlo could ken without trouble the gruesome images of the days in the stockade. He headed down the path toward the street; his work here was finished. As he passed the door through which he had exited, he saw that it was standing ajar. Which was odd. He remembered closing it. A chill of apprehension washed across him. He cast his eyes around at the dimly lit strip of park, and scanned the ktess for nearby minds. Nobody.

Then, seemingly out of nowhere, the blond girl stood before him, blocking the path. His body jerked in surprise.

''It'll never work,'' she said. She seemed less calm than in the lobby; her body vibrated with suppressed energy. How much had she kenned? He probed swiftly, but his mind slid off a slick impenetrable blankness that was unlike anything he had ever encountered. Some new variety of null? ''Of course not. And it's a good thing for you I'm not. My mother dragged me into town to hear the rememberer. What an awful man. So smug and petty. Anyhow, he noticed you on the way in. He hasn't quite noticed that he noticed, but it brought you to the front of his mind. For the last fifteen minutes he's kept coming back to images of you in that place with all the logs. He's shared your face with half the people in Oburn. I just came out to tell you you'd better get out of town quick, before the assembly lets out.'' She turned to go.

''Wait! I don't even know your name. How did you—''

''He doesn't know yours,'' she said, nodding to where Luth dozed beneath a tree. ''It's better that way.''

''Why are you willing to warn me?''

Her face wrinkled in a *moue* of distaste. ''I don't know. Maybe what you're doing is just impossible enough to be interesting. Oh, there's another thing I was going to tell you. Three days from now, there's to be a Cleansing.''

''Here?''

"In Yubasty. Two boys." With a hint of mischievous false optimism, she added, "I'm curious to see whether you can do anything to stop it."

She turned again to go. He reached out to grab her arm, and found himself plunged into a frozen place where time hung suspended. When he could move again, the wedge of light was being cut off as the door closed behind her.

Chapter || 16

HE hesitated with his hand hovering above the door handle. As badly as he wanted to follow her, he could not ignore her warning. To go back into the Sharing Hall, even to linger at the front waiting for her to emerge, would be suicidal. But as he strode back through the dark streets toward Linnie and the hidden coach, he found himself turning the unsatisfying encounter over in his mind. The pilot could prove a treasured find, yes, but the girl was something else. Her mental powers were more than remarkable. To ken Oxar's subconscious processes in the midst of several thousand people—Danlo could not have done it. He doubted most joddies could do it. So why was she languishing in a little town like Oburn, when she should be in Serameno training for some important post? Most likely she was able to conceal her powers as easily as she had concealed her thoughts. Yet she had revealed them to him. And she was willing to help him! At least to the extent of warning him. He would have to find her, convince her to do more.

When he got back to the shed, Linnie was already asleep on the mattress they had put on the floor beside the coach. He lay down beside her, and she murmured and snuggled close. After months sleeping on hard ground, he relished the luxurious softness, and slept deeply.

When he woke to gray daylight, Linnie was gone. Irritated and then a little alarmed, he set out to find her. The ktess assured him she had not been spotted—so where had she gotten to? She wasn't in any of the nearby yards. He finally resorted to putting people to sleep while he prowled through their houses, alert for children. In the seventh or eighth house, he put to sleep a woman who was painting a model carousel while her babies played on the floor, and then tiptoed down the hall and up the stairs. A closet door was open a crack, and Linnie was crouched among the shoes, knife drawn. When she saw him, she opened her mouth to speak, and he shushed her. Then he broke into barely contained silent laughter. She had shed her leather leggings and vest in favor of a white blouse and a bright yellow skirt. She glared back at him, sheepish but defiant. "Linnie wants—"

"Ssh." He stooped to scoop up her old clothes. She gave him a stubborn, surly look, but he tucked them under his arm and beckoned her out of the closet. Carefully they made their way down the stairs and out the door.

"What did you think you were doing?" he demanded softly but urgently. "You could have—"

"Linnie wants Danlo looks, sees Linnie in women of village clothes. Linnie sees village houses, big, goes into house, all bright, clothes, flower smells, not knows what many things. Linnie thinks, this house like Danlo lives in, thinks, Linnie lives and Danlo in house. Linnie—what this word? Water from eyes."

"Cry. Linnie cries." He touched her cheek.

"Linnie cries, not listens good. People comes under. Linnie hides, waits. People not goes long time."

She had wanted to find out what it was like to live in a place like this. She had wanted to imagine what it would be like to live here with him. He hugged her, and tried to keep from crying himself. Well, let her keep the clothes. If she were seen at a distance, they might help. There was no help for her hair, of course. He imagined her touching the bedspread, looking at herself in the mirror— things he had taken for granted all his life. As reckless as she had been, he couldn't blame her. "If you want to do something like that again, tell me first. We'll find a way."

The morning was slipping away. He wanted to be out of Oburn, now that Oxar had made it a dangerous place. No—a more dangerous place. All places were dangerous, now. But he still had one vital mission to perform. When Linnie was hidden beneath a blanket on the floor behind the coach seat, he swung the doors of the shed wide and started the engine.

His destination was the Office of Public Records. This worthy edifice stood just opposite the local proctor station. He cruised past it slowly. Proctors in their blue shirts were coming and going, and a large coach disgorged passengers at the corner. He pulled up to the curb on a side street and closed his eyes. Only a few clerks were inside the records office, poring over dusty files. Two of them had shared Oxar's visions at last night's lecture, but they were both working upstairs. The woman at the front desk had stayed home and gone to bed early.

"I've got to go into this building for a few minutes," he said over the back of the seat. "Wait here, for Frank's sake."

"Linnie waits."

He flipped down the blue "immediate need" tag in the front window of the coach. Such tags were generally, though not invariably, respected. He wished, again, that the child-locks on coach doors could be fixed to lock the doors from the outside as well as the inside.

The best cover, he had already learned, was to act as if he had no reason for concern. He marched boldly up the wide steps and into the shaded entrance. The desk clerk, a pale woman of advancing years, was poring over a large volume, licking her thumb to turn the pages. She was wearing a green eyeshade. He greeted her with formal warmth, and she returned the courtesy. Through wide windows, warm sun made dusty slanting bars and laid gold rectangles on the much-scarred, often-polished hardwood floor. Behind the clerk an irregular bank of drawers teetered to the ceiling. "Receivings," Danlo said. "Last five or six years."

"Third floor, aisle L. What sort of data are you trying to retrieve?"

"I had a cousin, remarried and moved up this way. Years ago. Don't remember the name of the man she married. She had a daughter. By now, about that age."

"Well, of course there are hundreds of children Received every year. You might better look through the marriage records. The mother's name would be listed there."

"They weren't married here. I was hoping one of the children's names would jog my memory."

"A joddie would be happy to jog your—"

"No need. Happier prowling on my own. The mother—my cousin—was quite fair."

"Let me think. Fair women who moved to this area—how long ago did you say?"

"Fifteen, twenty years. I was thinking, portraits taken at the Receivings, yes? The daughter should look like the mother, you see."

"Well, of course. Seems a roundabout way to go about it, but if it pleases you. . . . The portraits aren't on the third floor. They're in hanging folders in the basement. Aisle R, I think. Yes.

We only keep the last hundred years. After that we give them to any family that wants them.''

''Aisle R. Many thanks.'' Danlo descended the creaking stairs. In the basement, metal racks extended to the ceiling in the dim light, and the musty smell of antiquity was thick. Aisle R was narrow and receded almost endlessly. Drawers of all sizes and shapes were labeled with faded, yellowing tags. He prowled slowly, squinting, stooping, standing on tiptoe, moving on a few steps and doing the same thing again. As a counter, he had often generated information to be stored in Public Records, but he had never tried to retrieve any of it himself. There ought, he thought, to be better ways to organize things.

Ten minutes later, he found the right drawer. Group portraits, three feet wide and two high, in plastic covers, each with more than a hundred smiling adolescent faces. He extracted the five most recent sheets, carried them to a table, and switched on the study lamp.

Voices murmured in a nearby aisle. He shut them out in order to concentrate. Nothing in the most recent year. A couple of blond girls the year before who looked possible but not quite right; he noted them and went on. The third year back, he found her. Unmistakably. She was standing with her arms around two beaming classmates, smiling but with a kind of wistful detachment. He counted the faces and the names in the caption twice to make sure he had a match: Ainne Murrinder.

The voices were moving closer. As he picked up the portraits, he scanned the ktess automatically, and froze. The woman from upstairs was escorting two visitors—Luth Vardiki and Goodman Pilcher, who had introduced him in the square the afternoon before. Danlo switched off the study light. What in Frank's name were they doing here? Ah. In quest of ancient maps. Luth wouldn't recognize Danlo, not if the block were working properly, but Pilcher had undoubtedly partaken of what Oxar shared. ''You're sure there are none that show the eastern wastes?'' Luth said.

''Why ever would we have kept them?''

''Archives, then. Useless items left by the ancients.''

''We've two whole rooms, packed to the ceiling, but none of it is arranged or catalogued, you see. In the earthquake of 781, I'm told, everything on the shelves was dumped in a mess on the floor, and rather than sort it all out they just stacked what they could salvage and started over. If we had needed the rooms, it would have been thrown out long ago.''

"We've got to be in Orvill tomorrow. Could you assign a couple of people to have a look through it?"

Moving carefully, Danlo slipped down another aisle and made his way back toward the stairs. Behind him the clerk called, "Oh, goodman!" He could see his own retreating back through her eyes; it was no use pretending he thought she was calling somebody else. He turned. "Did you find what you were looking for?" she asked.

"Yes, thanks."

"Oh, I'm so glad. What was the husband's name?"

"Palm," he said. It was the commonest name in the captions.

"Some help, but not much. Hmm. A blond woman marrying one of the Palms fifteen years ago. No, I can't—" She glanced at the study table. "Oh, you've forgotten to put the materials away. Tsk-tsk-tsk. 'A place for everything.' "

"Sorry." Obediently he scooped up the portraits and carried them back to their proper drawer.

"Do you know who those goodmen in the next aisle are?" she whispered. "They're with the airplane! I'm sure they wouldn't mind touching your hand."

"They must be on important business. I wouldn't dream of bothering them."

"I've been wondering," she said, "if they ever take people up. Just for the thrill, you know, and so we could share it with others afterward. They couldn't take everybody, naturally, but perhaps one or two, if they were asked in just the right way. What do you think?"

"Grand idea. Why don't you ask them?"

"Oh, I *couldn't*. What would they think of me? Now, if someone like yourself were to bring the conversation around tactfully. . . ."

"I do wish I could help, dear lady." Danlo patted the clerk's frail shoulder affectionately. "Unfortunately, I have an ungovernable fear of heights."

"Oh." She looked terribly crestfallen.

"If it's Olivia's will, you'll have your airplane ride." Olivia's will for this woman, he thought, had never encompassed anything beyond dusty stacks of moldering records. Yearn she might; she would never fly. "Again, thanks for your assistance." Before she could rally her forces for another plea, he escaped to the stairs.

His next stop was to look for Murrinders in a public directory. Most directories were kept in tea-shops, and at this hour of the morning most tea-shops were crowded. He cruised until he found a tiny one where only two patrons were munching pastries. They paid no attention to the tall stranger. He found three listings for Murrinders, and noted the streets in the map in the front of the directory.

Nobody was home at the first Murrinder house, a small, steep-roofed shack perched precariously on a river bank. He parked, waited a few minutes, and then went on to the second. Here again, no Murrinders were in evidence, but he was able to ken from the neighbors that none of the children in the household was named Ainne. The third house was across town. Here a woman was at home. She was a spinster, with no children. Both of the other local Murrinders were her brothers, and she had no nieces named Ainne.

The day was advancing, and Danlo was becoming uneasy. He wanted to be away from Oburn, but more than that he wanted to find Ainne Murrinder. His memory teased him with something she had said: "My mother dragged me into town." Could the rural listings be in a separate section of the directory? Not wanting to be seen twice in the same tea-shop, he braved another. A man wielding a mop stared hard at him until he made the man lose interest. In the back of the directory he found a Glin and Sarra Murrinder. Their address was in the hills south of town.

He tucked several sweet-rolls into a paper sack and went back to the coach. When at last they were rolling through open country, he started to relax. He slid the window down and guided the coach around the curves lightly with one hand. Linnie threw back the blanket and poked her head up beside him, and he handed her a sweet-roll. She exclaimed loudly over the sugary confection, tucked an enormous bite into her mouth, and mumbled crumbily, "Where we goes this path?"

"To see the girl I told you about."

Linnie licked her fingers. "Girl not mind-speaks? We takes girl to mountains?"

"No, she's—she's more like me, I think. I hope." It was a fanciful wish based on a brief, enigmatic encounter. He cautioned himself not to assume too much, to be circumspect, to stand clear of the clutches of disappointment. But he wanted badly to believe that he might have found an ally.

They passed farmsteads surrounded by outbuildings, flocks of sheep, orchards, and wilder stretches where ferns luxuriated beneath stands of pine. As the miles unrolled, he wondered what he could say to Ainne. Just as urgent was how he would explain his presence to her family. Presumably she lived on a farm; he wouldn't likely find her at home alone. Why should a man in his late forties pay a visit to a teenage girl who was, as far as they knew, a complete stranger? Social pretexts among the Body of Harmony were an art both transparent and many-layered, but none of the usual graces applied in this case.

He was still mulling over the possibilities when he spotted a wooden sign, weathered to gray, standing between two posts at a T-shaped intersection; carved in it were the words "Four Moons Road." He turned. The road narrowed and the pavement grew rough. A hundred yards past the turnoff, a creek tumbled beneath a bridge. He pulled the coach off on the shoulder and stopped. Birdsong and the tinkle of water enfolded them. "I'll have to drive right up to the house," he said. "You stay here. It looks isolated enough, but don't go far. There are probably other houses close by."

Linnie needed no urging. She clambered out of the coach, clutching her bow and other gear. She was still wearing the white blouse and yellow skirt, with which the leather belt and shoulder straps made an odd ensemble, and she fussed for a minute to get everything adjusted. "Danlo comes back fast." She leaned in the window and gave him a quick, hard kiss.

"As fast as I can. But I don't know how long I'll be. If it starts to get dark, see if you can't catch something for dinner. But don't let anybody see you. And build the fire away from the road. You understand? Fire back there in the trees. People come along here. If they see fire, they'll know you're hiding."

"People not sees fire."

As he was starting the coach, a voice spoke clearly in his head: *Not yet.* And a moment later, *Get the coach off the road, quick.* The voice was Ainne's.

He maneuvered the coach down the slope beside the tiny bridge. There was no really effective cover, but he got it half-concealed behind a stand of scrubby trees and shut off the engine. Linnie crouched behind the vehicle and they waited in silence. He kenned a coach approaching from up the road, and a moment later heard it. Two men, one a joddie. Danlo stilled his mind to what he hoped was perfect transparency. In a quiet whoosh of tires, the other vehicle passed. It rumbled hollowly over the bridge and disappeared around the next bend. Even then he stayed still. Long seconds passed.

All right. Come on.

"I go," he told Linnie again. "You wait."

"Linnie waits."

The Murrinder farm lay only half a mile up the road, a scatter of wooden buildings painted sunny yellow, among them several older stone structures covered with vines. He kenned seven adults in the vicinity, none of them in view. Ainne might be one of them, or she might be making herself invisible in the ktess. In any event, she wasn't making this any easier for him. She knew he was here; why not come out to meet him? Fear of her parents' disapproval? Or was she trying to put obstacles in his path?

As he pulled the coach into the yard, a wiry little man came out of the house and strode forward. Though he walked with a buoyant, youthful stride, his ktess had the broad spaciousness of late middle age. As he approached, Danlo could see that the hair he had taken for blond was mostly gray, the smiling furrows at the corners of the eyes deep and branching. Danlo got out of the coach and bowed formally. "Goodman Murrinder. Dappa Snee, a youth counselor from Seramemo."

"An honor, Goodman Snee. Glin Murrinder."

Around the corner of the house, barking excitedly, streaked a brown-and-white dog, on its heels a blond boy of eight or nine. The memory of the attack by the wild dogs surged up, and Danlo shrank back.

Murrinder laughed in uneasy surprise. "Ho, Sparky! Quiet, boy!" He put out a restraining hand, and the dog stopped short, still yapping, its tail wagging.

Danlo collected himself. "Your pardon, goodman. I suffer, occasionally, sudden attacks of baseless, morbid fantasy." *Inconsequential.* He forced himself to stroke the dog's head, and allowed the dog to lick the puckered triangular scars on the back of his hand.

"My son Arrie. Goodman Snee."

"Pleasure, goodman," the boy mumbled. He straddled the dog's back and wrestled its neck and ears playfully. "C'mon, Sparky, let's go chase rabbits." But the dog was more interested in sniffing the cuffs of Danlo's trousers.

"What brings you to our farm?" Murrinder asked.

"An unusual errand. Of high importance to the Body." *Directly from the One.* "New needs call forth new efforts." Danlo shared an image of the wild women.

"Heard all about them last night. In fact—"

"Doubtless you're wondering," Danlo said, hurrying to head off Murrinder's surfacing memory of Oxar's lecture, "why I should come to you."

Readiness to receive.

In addition to Murrinder himself, Danlo kenned, three other adults were listening in, though not all with full attention. He chose his words with care. "Picked your name out of the register in Oburn. Might have picked anybody's, but farm children seem the easiest place to start. You have more than one child."

"Three. The eldest—a girl—has been Received. Arrie here, eight, and his brother Nohl, who's eleven."

"Nohl the pole," said Arrie.

"Arrie," said his father. "The grownups would like to share."

"Okay. Come *on*, Sparky." This time the dog was ready to be persuaded. The two of them ran off.

"Seems a bright lad," Danlo observed. "More in this area? Your neighbors' children?"

Fuzzy. "'Area.' Ten or fifteen in walking distance."

"We'll want to include them all. May as well start here, go on to the others tomorrow. Glad you sent him off. Delicate question, how to nurture their enthusiasm. Don't want to frighten them."

"Assuredly not." *Reason for fear?*

Negligible. "I've worked with youth groups for years," Danlo said, smoothly sharing a fabricated vision of happy faces singing and dancing in a gaily decorated room. "Also had some experience in the North when I was younger, fighting forest fires in rugged terrain. Thus the honor of initiating—or anyhow looking into initiating—a new type of youth program. Well, not new exactly. Told the ancients had something similar. Uncivilized, of course. Abandoned centuries ago. But in these new circumstances. . . ." *Uncomfortable necessities.* "The second Great Cleansing could be a more drawn-out affair than we hope. Might take years. These children grow up, some of them are sure to be involved. Maybe directly. Long forays in airplanes—and who knows how prone such machines will be to fall out of the sky? Ground marches far into the mountains, skirmishes along the Wall. Point is, children grow accustomed to living in comfort. As you and I did. They don't get the kind of experiences that would aid them if they were in rough surroundings for a day or two. You see?"

"Nobody wants to subject children to unnecessary hardship."

Truth-speaking. "Or any of the Body. Point is to make a

game of it. Start while they're young, show them a bit about the skills they might need. Give them ribbons and badges like the ones they get in school, but for dirty-hands skills like gathering wood for a fire and keeping it lit. Like finding food in the wilderness, knowing how to follow animal tracks. Take a group of them out on an overnight trip, like summer camp but with no cabins. Sleep under the stars.''

Murrinder shuddered, and shared revulsion.

Natural feeling. All share. ''That's the point. Train them out of it. Once they're comfortable with the idea, what comes later—or what might come later, if matters run against us—won't seem such a hardship.''

Murrinder nodded slowly. ''Some value in that. The schools would be best equipped to put it in motion.''

''As we proceed, doubtless it will become part of the regular curriculum. What we're conducting now is only a preliminary study. Find out how the children respond. Then we'll know what resources to provide for the schools.''

''And my children are the first you've selected?''

''First in this area. Got a good group started now in Grawly. Ran into some resistance at first. Children can be very stubborn. Parents too, you'll forgive my saying, but where the child's heart goes, the mother follows, as the Book puts it. That's why I was hoping—your eldest has been Received. She could form a link with the youngsters, and since she's more tractable. . . .''

Murrinder laughed. ''That one? Let you judge for yourself.'' *Ainne. Come.*

The air before them wavered like a column of heat haze, and Ainne Murrinder coalesced. She was as beautiful as Danlo remembered—no, more so. The sunlight poured through her long, straight white-blond hair in a nimbus of rainbow hues. Her head cocked sideways as she regarded her father, and her mouth pursed judiciously. *You wanted?*

''Not like that,'' Murrinder said. ''Not polite. You can walk down a flight of stairs.'' The apparition burst like a soap bubble. Murrinder shrugged apologetically to Danlo. ''She's like this sometimes. Her mother and I don't know what to do. Even her uncle. My wife's brother is a joddie. He left just before you arrived, in fact.''

''Must have been his coach I passed on the road.''

''He can't manage her either. So you're welcome to try to

interest her in your woods-tramping club, but I doubt you'll get anywhere.''

''As the One wills.''

The door of the farmhouse opened and Ainne appeared in the normal way. She walked toward them casually, negligently, not quite looking away from Danlo but not looking at him either, as if daring him to say or think something. Her hair was no longer framed by the impossible rainbow, but still it glowed so bright in the sun that it hurt his eyes. It hung long and straight, framing her delicately molded features. He thought at first that it hung loose, but then he saw it was caught at the small of her back in a ball that twinkled with tiny gold beads. Knowing that his mental defenses were useless against her, he kept them raised anyway against the rest of the family.

''Goodman Snee. My daughter Ainne.''

''Goodwoman.'' Danlo inclined his head.

''I'm curious,'' Ainne said. ''You say the One wants us all to learn to grub for food like animals. To me, that sounds as if the One fears the wild women a great deal—fears that they'll descend on us again, so many and so bloodthirsty that they'll tear the Body apart.''

''We're acting solely out of concern for the children—children who might, when they grow older, find themselves in difficult circumstances. As you know.''

She said a little sharply, ''Nobody knows what I know.''

''I can see that. You're a very remarkable young lady.''

''There are lots of farm kids you could enlist in your silly club. But you came here.'' She said again, in a lower tone, ''You came here.''

''That's right.''

''Daddy, I think I'd like to find out more—a little more, anyway—about this fire-making club, or whatever it is.'' Murrinder looked at his daughter in surprise. She said to Danlo: ''You didn't bring any matches, did you? Of course not.''

''Some in the barn, I think,'' Murrinder said. ''In a drawer above the workbench.''

''I think I want Goodman—Snee, was it?—to show me how to make a fire out of sticks. If he knows anything at all about it, which I doubt.'' She scampered off in the direction of the barn.

''Don't know what you said,'' Murrinder said. ''She hasn't taken an interest in anything in months. Anything.''

''Probably she only wants to prove to me that I don't know what I'm doing.''

''Do you? Not, you understand, that I'm doubting the wisdom of the One in choosing you—or in choosing this project. But it does seem an odd thing to force such barbarous activities on children. Childhood should be a carefree time.''

''On that we're agreed.''

Ainne appeared at the barn door. ''Found 'em!'' She beckoned to Danlo. ''Come on!''

''Until later, Goodman Murrinder.''

Olivia be with you.

Ainne led the way across a field waist-high in fragrant grass toward a wooded hillside. She kept her hands jammed into the pockets of her long blue skirt, and the breeze picked at the escaping strands of her hair. Beneath the trees she stooped and scrabbled at the ground, picking up twigs.

''You really want to learn to make a fire,'' Danlo said.

''I've made fires before. Daddy will be happier if he sees smoke. Well, are you going to help?''

''I'm supposed to ask you that. Here—show me what you've got.'' She held out the handful of twigs, and he sorted through them. ''Green. Green. This one's dry. See the difference? Don't waste time collecting material you can't use.''

''Mmm. That's why you're here. You think you can use me.''

''No. Not the way I might use the pilot. I think I might persuade you. But I can't do that until I understand you. Why are you so angry?''

She cast the twigs away violently. ''Let's just walk.'' She strolled among the shafts of sun. He walked beside her, and waited. ''What's it like out there?'' She waved her hand in the direction of the Wall.

''Beautiful. Terrifying. Mysterious. Quiet. Difficult. We're so used to having things defined—the hours of the day, relationships, streets and sidewalks. Out there nothing is defined. It took me a while to appreciate that.''

''Were you ever attacked by wild beasts?''

He held up his hand so she could see the scars, and shared his memories of the attack of the dogs; also of the fever afterward, the weakness and the knowledge that there was nowhere he could turn for help. Ainne took his hand and ran her thumb across the scars, as if to anchor them in her mind. ''We were going to do that,'' she said. ''I guess I may as well tell you. It's not like it's a secret. My mother knows—most of it, anyhow. I never kenned her to find out if she knows the part at the end. I don't want to know.''

Lost in fog.

''I had a friend,'' she said. ''A special friend. He was—they took him and—I won't call it what they call it. I won't. There was nothing clean about it.'' She pressed her lips together and blinked back tears.

''Yes.''

''I couldn't do anything. I tried to keep the Hand from swinging.'' Her voice twisted with anguish. ''All I could do was make him swing crooked, and he cut off Borry's arm, and he had to swing again, and he missed again, and he kept hacking and hacking—''

She sobbed. Danlo put his arm across her shoulders and drew her to him and held her close while she wept, and stroked her amazing soft hair, where the sun glistened in filaments of fire. ''I'm sorry,'' he said softly.

She pulled away, and wiped her face and snuffled. ''I'm all right. We talked about it. We talked about it a lot, when we started knowing that he was—that he wasn't—you know. We were going to sneak away. That was when we tried making a fire. We took some pork chops off into the woods and cooked them. They got burned, but we ate them anyhow. We knew that was what we'd have to do. Only we kept thinking of more things we'd need, until there were so many things we knew we could never carry them all. And we were scared. All the stories about wild animals, and falling off the edge of the world.''

''I don't think the world has an edge. It just goes on and on forever. I wish I could have helped your friend.''

Ainne shrugged, a stiff jerk of bitter worldliness. ''There's nothing you could have done, even if you'd been here. There's only one of you, and thousands of them. Millions. And you're not good enough. You try to keep things covered up, but you're real bad at it.''

''Can you show me how to be better?''

''Why should I? There's nothing anybody can do. They'll catch you and stop you, and it'll all go on the way it always has.''

''If you believe that, why did you come out here to talk to me?''

''I'm not sure. I guess maybe I wanted to talk about Borry. I thought maybe you'd understand.''

''I do understand. But I think there's more to it than that. You'd like me to convince you that I can make it work. But you see, I can't do that. I don't know that it will work. Probably you're right. Probably I'll be caught and stopped. I'm not doing it because I have any assurance that I'll succeed. I'm doing it because it's the right thing to do. How would you have felt if you'd simply stood by and let them do what they did to your friend, and not tried to stop it?''

She shuddered. ''I would have hated myself. I would always have wondered.''

''Yes. And that's why you warned me last night, and that's why you were willing to talk with me today, and that's why you should help me. You're far more powerful than I. Together—''

''You're more powerful than you know. Parts of you are still asleep.''

''Wake them. Show me. If you do nothing else!''

''Maybe I could try something.'' She pressed her lips together and closed her eyes. A small sun burst inside his head. *Take hold of it,* she shared. *Follow the patterns.*

This inner sun, he saw, was covered with a network of dark lines. As he traced the patterns with his mind's eye, they stabilized. There was no heat, only light. He wasn't sure whether he was looking at the fiery ball from the outside, or inside it looking out. He saw how his memories were connected to his emotions, how his ears were connected to his eyes. He saw the small, dark, unraveling knot of Guidance that remained buried in him, and dissolved it. He saw the tendrils that linked him to Ainne, and tugged at them playfully. Distantly he heard her chuckle. Gradually the sphere of light faded, leaving a feeling of immense clarity. He opened his eyes. He couldn't tell whether seconds had passed, or half an hour, but the afternoon had deepened. The sun had sunk behind a hill.

''That might help,'' Ainne said.

Great thanks.

''You're going to Yubasty, the way I told you last night? What are you going to do when you get there?''

''I don't know,'' he admitted.

''I still don't think there's anything you can do,'' she said. ''It was probably a mistake even talking to you. When they go into you to fix you, they'll find out who I am. They know I'm here somewhere, but they don't know who I am, or how to find me. I'm good. The trouble is, the next time I do anything like what I did with Borry, they'll be able to trace it back to me.''

''How long can you go on like this?''

"Does it matter? A while."

"Why not come with me now? To Yubasty. It might make a big difference."

"You're forgetting. I'm not old enough." She was right: Dazzled by the force of her ktess, he had stopped noticing that she was only a teenage girl. "If I'm not back by supper, it'll look like that stranger who was so interested in kids went corker and grabbed me. My parents will have the whole Body out hunting. I would like to come with you now, though, just for a minute. I can see this Linnie person in your mind, but she's all—the way you think about her is complicated. I'd like to see her for myself."

"I shouldn't leave the coach."

"You can come back for it."

"No. I've learned to husband my resources. That's another lesson, like fire-making."

"Well, it would be hard to explain to my parents why I want to ride off with you. You drive off and wait, and I'll come down the road in a little while."

They walked back to the farmhouse. As they passed the barn, Arrie came out through the wide doors. "Hey, sis, did you see Sparky anywhere? He ran off."

She riffled the boy's hair. "No. Sorry."

"Dang. Well, he's gotta be around here somewhere. Sparky, Sparky!" Arrie dashed away.

"I think the whole thing is disgusting," Ainne said. She shared scorn forcefully, without troubling to conceal it. Beneath it, in a place that Danlo assumed only he could ken, she shared, *For their benefit. I'll be down in a little while.* "There's lots of kids around here that might like to get involved, but *I'm* certainly not going to."

"Very sorry to hear it, goodwoman." Danlo bowed courteously. "Thank you for your time."

From the house, a wordless apology. Danlo watched Ainne walk stiffly away. When the door had swung shut behind her, he climbed into the coach and made his way back down the road.

He stopped by the little stone bridge and drew the coach into the same thicket he had used before. The afternoon was fading from the treetops. He looked around, didn't see Linnie, and decided that was probably good. When Ainne hadn't come ten minutes later, he got out of the coach to stretch and waited some more.

Ainne arrived, as she had the previous night, without his kenning her. He had been staring up into a tree, calculating which branches would take his weight if he were to climb for eggs, and when he turned around she was standing there. She peered around. "Is she here? Does she hide?"

"I don't know where she is," Danlo said. "Probably back along the creek somewhere." They started walking.

"How can you tell what she's going to do?" Ainne asked. "I'd think that would be the hard part."

"I can't tell. Even aside from her being a null, she's—different. The way she sees things. In the days before the Great Cleansing, people everywhere must have been different the way she is. But I'm beginning to think that's not such a bad thing."

He bent over and looked for signs on the ground. Ainne stood and watched. He wondered whether Linnie could have been captured without his hearing or kenning the fight, but Ainne cast about mentally for a moment and then shook her head. "Nobody's found her."

A fresh notch cut into a tree flared white in the failing light. He went in that direction, Ainne at his heels. A second notch, and a third, led them up over a hill and down the far side. Here, traces of wood smoke turned the dusk fragrant. A tiny fire flickered beneath the overhanging bank of a dry gully.

The fire was untended, but an animal, skinned and spitted, was roasting.

Ainne wrinkled her nose. "This is how you eat?"

"We had some bowls for a while. I broke mine."

A cry caught in Ainne's throat. He kenned her alarm, and looked up from the fire. Linnie was squatting on the slope above them, leaning on her spear. "This woman," Linnie said softly. "What this woman?"

"She's a friend. Her name is Ainne."

"Ainne friend." Linnie stood up and hobbled toward them. She bent forward to inspect Ainne up and down. Danlo was struck powerfully by the contrast between them, the dark, dirty, crippled woman and the blond girl so clean she glowed. Linnie looked sharply at Danlo. "Ainne helps makes baby?"

"What's she talking about?"

"She thinks you're a nurse."

"Oh, you mean a midwife. I can do that. At least—maybe not with a null. I don't know."

Linnie took Danlo's arm possessively. To Ainne she said, "Danlo good man."

"Yes," Ainne said. "I believe that. I believe you're a good

person too. Not like us, not at all like us, but good.'' To Danlo she said, ''Now I see why you're different. Even though she's not in the ktess, something of her has gotten into you. It's changed you. I can see why you think you've got a chance. I don't know. Maybe. . . .'' She let the thought trail off.

''Ainne wants eats?'' Linnie waved her hand at the animal. ''Good food.'' She knelt and turned the spit.

''No, thank you. I couldn't.'' Ainne licked her lips uncertainly. ''Well, maybe just a bite.'' She hugged herself, and shivered a little, and sank down neatly cross-legged and wrapped her skirt around her knees. Linnie unsheathed one of the knives that they had scavenged from the airplane, and expertly sliced a chunk of meat out of the carcass. She offered it to Ainne on the point of the knife. Ainne looked at the knife speculatively, and at the little pile that contained the water bottles and the binoculars, but she said nothing. She took a dainty bite of meat, and chewed, and swallowed.

''Mmm. That's good. A lot better than when Borry and I tried it.'' She took another bite, more enthusiastically. ''We didn't know how we'd ever catch anything, or how to kill it. Is this what you kill animals with?'' She put out tentative fingers and brushed the shaft of the spear.

''Kills uses arrow.'' Linnie pulled one out of the quiver. She drew the bow, and pointed off into the darkness.

''Is that how you killed this? What sort of animal is it?''

Linnie shrugged.

''Probably a sheep,'' Danlo said. ''Sheep? White, curly hair, baah-baah?''

''Not white,'' Linnie said. ''White and brown.'' She made, softly, the noise of a dog barking. ''What word this animal?''

Danlo remembered the Murrinders' dog, and how little Arrie had been looking for it.

Ainne began trembling visibly. In a small, choked voice she said, ''You killed a *dog?* Brown and white? This is Sp—Spah—ah—'' With an anguished cry she leaped to her feet.

Before Danlo could stop her, she rushed away into the gathering darkness. He stood up and ran a few steps after her, then faltered and stopped. ''Ainne! Wait!'' Linnie was at his elbow, the bow half-drawn. He put a hand on her arm. ''Let her go.'' Possibly trusting the girl had been a mistake. She might run straight to her mother and reveal everything. But Danlo had had enough of killing.

He turned back toward the fire. For a long time after Ainne's high, gasping wail had merged with the small noises of the twilight, he could still ken, as palpably as if he held it between his fingers, her revulsion and despair.

"What word this animal?" Linnie asked again.

"What? Oh. It's called a dog. Dog."

She smacked her lips. "Dog good eats."

He sat back down on the ground beside her and pulled his jacket tighter. After a minute, not sure whether he was being defiant or merely practical, he sawed off another piece of dog meat. He put his arm around Linnie, and chewed and swallowed the flesh without tasting it, and stared into the fire while the dull red embers crumbled and died. He felt very tired, and very alone.

Chapter ‖ 17

THE soft, incessant thrumming of the rain enfolded the tree house. Eppy sat with one leg dangling between the planks of the floor, his back against the rough bark of the trunk. He was wearing a heavy sweater, but it wasn't really cold. It never snowed in Sancruz, not even in the middle of winter. Eppy was surprised at how steadily it was raining, though. The rain had started soon after Pumpkin Day, and had continued without letup, it seemed, for months. Every day when he sneaked off to the tree house to read, he was enveloped in the hiss and patter, the damp musk of rotting wood, the directionless gray-green light. Time seemed suspended. When it started to get dark, he would climb down and go home for supper, but the afternoon stretched on and on.

The heavy, leather-bound *Lives of the Great Joddies*, braced against his stomach, was hundreds of pages long, and he turned the pages lingeringly, stopping often to pretend that he was directly involved in the quiet dramas that had unfolded over the centuries in far-off Serameno. Just now he was reading the chapter about a joddie who happened to have the same name he did, a joddie named Epigrass. The chapter about Epigrass was very long and detailed, though in Eppy's opinion most of the things Epigrass did were not the sort that qualified a joddie for greatness.

This picture, for instance, of Epigrass walking along a corridor in the Jewel of the One. It was a dull picture. Eppy had seen many just like it. The Jewel was large, and shot through with long, echoing corridors, and Epigrass, who lived in the Jewel, seemed forever to be striding down one corridor or another.

Eppy had never been to the Jewel, he had only seen pictures. Actually it was called the New Jewel, because it had been erected on the site of the original Jewel after the Great Quake of 781. The Jewel was six stories tall, and shaped like a hollow hexagon. Six rays radiated from the center. Between the rays were six court-yards, each with its own name and style of landscaping. Three of the courtyards were entirely enclosed by the Jewel, but the alternate three opened outward through great arches set into the hexagonal rim. Beyond the arches were the elaborate formal gardens and parkland of the Hub of Roads.

Hundreds of joddies lived in the Jewel, and hundreds more were always coming and going. Proctors and servers and cleaners and gardeners worked in the Jewel, but they lived elsewhere in Serameno, with their families. In spite of all the activity, the Jewel was so large that it seemed nearly empty. Once in a while, in the hall, Epigrass passed another joddie, and nodded in greeting. Once in a while he saw a server hurrying on some errand.

Lives of the Great Joddies was filled with brightly colored illustrations, and the illustrations moved. Many of them were as dull as the corridor picture. Epigrass in the refectory. Epigrass lying on his side in bed. Epigrass in the Courtyard of Repose, sitting on a bench beneath a plum tree. In this part of the book Epigrass was starting to get old. He was fifty-five, older than Eppy's father, and had no hair at all on top of his head, only a gray fringe around the sides. He had blue veins on his legs, and in the spring he was short of breath from hay fever.

Eppy wasn't just looking at the pictures. He was twelve years old, and had no trouble reading even the biggest words in the text. He had always been a happy, noisy boy, bright but not especially bookish or solitary. He knew, though, that next spring or summer he would come into the ktess. This rainy winter was the last time in his life when he could get away from everybody else in the world and think what he liked.

Eppy had decided that when he grew up he would like to be a joddie like the Epigrass in the book. He would find ways to make the life of a joddie more fun, though. Give people sneezing fits, or make them think snakes were crawling in their trousers. Not all the time, certainly. Joddies had more important things to do. But once in a while, to relieve the monotony. Eppy figured he could do a better job, too, of some of the important things that the other Epigrass did. The business about the wild women, for instance. In this part of the story Epigrass was studying the three who had been captured, which was by far the most interesting thing he had ever been involved in, and probably explained why his story was in the book.

Epigrass had been given an assistant, an energetic young joddie named Smaun. Eppy didn't like Smaun. He thought Smaun was cruel and sneaky. Once, Smaun ordered that the women be given raw meat and the bark of trees to eat. Two days passed before Epigrass found out and had their normal meals restored. Smaun claimed he was only trying to find out whether their eating habits were as disgusting as their other habits. Even then, Epigrass didn't chastise Smaun, or ask that he be given a different assistant. His reluctance to confront Smaun made Eppy mad.

The Joddirate was deeply divided about the proper course to take in dealing with the threat of the wild women. Certainly a renewed Cleansing would be needed, but how exactly to go about this was unclear. Smaun was a member of an extreme faction that supported an immediate and massive buildup of long-distance weaponry. Epigrass wasn't sure which faction to support. He wanted, as the One had charged him, to learn more about the women, in order to make an informed judgment. The task was vague and open-ended, and the One was patient, but the learning went slowly. Sometimes Eppy had an urge to flip forward a few pages, to find out whether Epigrass had discovered where the women came from, or how their ancestors had survived the Great Cleansing. Eppy was curious, too, whether the captured wild women were going to be put to death in a ceremony, as nulls, or simply strangled and thrown onto a compost heap. (Smaun favored the latter course. Smaun wanted to do the strangling himself. He had shared how afterward he would go out to the compost heap every day to watch them rot, so he could share what he saw and felt among the whole Body.) But skipping over anything in the book didn't seem right, so Eppy read one page at a time, even when it was boring or painful.

Epigrass had a hard time learning the wild women's speech. At first they shrieked gibberish at him, and spat. Then they retreated into sullen silence, and wouldn't talk when he was in the room. They were kept on an upper floor on the rim of the hexagon, in a room whose window looked in on the Courtyard of Repose. The women talked to each other when they were alone, so he ordered a recording device set up, and tried to transcribe what they had said. After only a couple of hours he saw that the task was beyond him, so he sent to the University of Higher Harmony for a linguist.

The woman who arrived was dour and abrupt—Epigrass kenned that she had an ulcer—and nervous at first to be in the Jewel. Her name was Thonia Vaddis.

"Is this where I'm to stay?" Thonia was a vacuist. Her hair, brown going gray, was drawn back in a bun, and she wore no jewelry. Her slightly bulging eyes blinked often as she looked around the airy room, at the plain bed in the corner, out the window at the Courtyard, at the recording apparatus, anywhere but at Epigrass.

"Yes." The word sprang from his throat with unexpected rawness. It was the first word he had spoken aloud in days. Perhaps weeks.

Two servers entered with Thonia's case of books, which they thumped down against the wall. From the recording apparatus, without warning, came a stream of jabber. This was interrupted by a barked exclamation, and the jabber subsided. Thonia looked directly at him then. "They're here?"

"In the next room."

Thonia hunched her shoulders. "They're not—" She shared a vision of savages leaping through a door and attacking her.

Safety deep reassurance. "Door kept locked. Two proctors posted outside at all times."

Thonia shared a vision of the women as viciously bloodthirsty and maniacally strong. It was the common impression. Smaun and others like him had been reinforcing it throughout the Body. Epigrass did not suggest that Smaun was wrong, he only shrugged and repeated his calming and reassurance.

"May as well get started. You'll join me in running this thing until I get the hang of it?"

Leading-by-the-hand/clarity. Epigrass placed himself on a chair in a corner and sat quietly for several hours while the linguist replayed the recordings, made notes, made sounds with her lips and tongue, and leafed through text after text. Servers brought them supper, and afterward took away the dishes.

The next afternoon he kenned her sense of excitement as the strange language unfolded. Rather than stir around in her thought processes, he waited patiently for her to announce the results. At last she put down her pencil. "Fascinating," she said. "About half of it's pre-Cleansing English. Olivia be praised; this would have taken months otherwise. There's a strong consonant shift toward palatal and labial stops in place of fricatives, falling diphthongs and double syllables separated by a soft 'j' in place of the old long vowels, and a lot of reduplication, which I suspect has supplanted the old forms for both plural and past tense. The other half I don't recognize. New words.''

Communicate two-way flowingly?

Groping/clumsy. "Just got a grip on the sounds. Need more lexicon. Grammar's another matter too. Infixes? Word order? Very slippery.''

Epigrass wanted to interrogate the women immediately, but Thonia insisted that she would need weeks, and far more material to work from. "If we could stimulate them somehow. Feed them subjects that we can use as points of reference.''

"They won't talk when we're present.''

"Give them something to talk about, then. Picture-books.''

So he took picture-books into the room and left them. The women leafed through the pages idly, but made only a few monosyllabic comments. Soon they ignored the books.

On the table next to the recorder sat a monitor screen on which all of the women's activities could be observed. The lights were kept on at all times, and the curtain had been removed from the door of their sanitary closet, so that they were never out of sight. They were filthy, and while they took sponge baths they still had not thought of using the bathtub. They had, however, found it useful to tear some of the towels into small rectangles. This gave Thonia another idea. "Whatever they normally use, they can't get it here. Ought to give them pads. Underwear, too. Pants and shirts, even. Those outfits are falling off of them.''

Epigrass lowered his eyes. "Smaun suggests that it's important for all to witness their true repulsiveness. We dare not become sympathetic.''

"They're human beings. Who's in charge?''

"The One has taken a direct interest. Until some conclusion is reached, a central course is being followed.''

"I'm only thinking of ways to get them talking. What would the One do if you threw out their old togs, got them something decent to wear?''

This not think.

Sometimes while Thonia worked, Epigrass would watch the screen and think about what it would be like to be locked up in a room that was always lighted, a room with bars on the windows.

Sometimes he would summon four muscular proctors and go into the next room, where he could sit and watch the women directly while the proctors stood behind him. He would draw phrases from Thonia's mind and try them out on the women. From the way they looked at him, or at one another, he got the idea that he was saying things they could understand, but they refused to reply. It was maddening to be dependent on them to provide him with a vocabulary, because they didn't talk about anything that concerned him. "Food taste good?" he would ask. "Yes?" No response.

Sometimes when the women were alone the big one worked at tearing the bars out of the window. When it appeared she might succeed, the women were removed to another room while workers came in and replaced the bars with a more firmly mounted set. The other two never tried to bend the bars, but sometimes the round-faced one stood for hours looking out the window at the Courtyard of Repose, where the fruit trees were budding. When Epigrass scanned the visual recording, he stopped at this scene, surprised and moved to see that she was weeping. Not in any dramatic way; she stood with one hand resting on one of the bars, looking out levelly, but her cheeks glistened with wetness, and her mouth trembled.

Eppy could imagine how she felt. He reflected vaguely that he seemed to have been in the tree house for far longer than a normal afternoon. His memories of climbing down, of his parents, of the boys and girls at school, were dim and fragmentary. He burned with an itch to run across an open field, to play kickball with his friends—but of course it was raining, so nobody would be out at the field. And the roof of the tree house was sound, so he was quite dry and comfortable. If he climbed down, the rain would soak him. He might just as well stay and read a few more pages.

Eppy didn't much care for the big woman. She growled like an ill-tempered dog. He liked the little one, because she moved in a way that was awkward and graceful at the same time, like a colt. "You ought to let her go," he whispered. "Or maybe let them all go, so they can take care of one another." But he knew Epigrass would never do such a thing—could never even consider doing it. If he thought of it, the One would know what he was thinking and make him think something different. Epigrass replayed several times the recording of the round-faced woman staring out the window, but then he erased it.

One day, for no reason, the little one sprang at Epigrass and scratched his face. Before the proctors could drag her off, she tried to bite him. She said a great deal then, but so quickly that Thonia couldn't follow it. Epigrass was shaken. He had thought their violent phase had passed, that they were absorbing from him the peaceful rhythms of civilized life. He saw how little he understood them.

Eppy could see that Epigrass was handling the women all wrong. They were scared of him. "You ought to bring them presents," Eppy whispered. "If you're afraid of what Smaun will say if you bring them nice clothes, bring some candy." A couple of pages further on, Epigrass had a server bring up a tray of sugar cookies. Eppy was proud of himself for having thought of the idea first. The women only stared at the cookies, so Epigrass showed that they were good by eating one himself. He licked his fingers afterward (Eppy could taste the almondy sweetness), and pushed the tray across the table at them. After a minute the big one reached out and closed her fist around a cookie. She sniffed it, and nibbled a tiny bite with her front teeth, and scowled at Epigrass as if it hurt her to admit that he might be capable of a kindness. Finally she jammed the whole cookie into her mouth and chewed muscularly. The little one looked at the big one wide-eyed, and when the big one didn't spit the cookie out or choke on it, the little one took one for herself. She retreated to a far corner of the room, where she ate it by holding it between the fingers of both hands, like a squirrel, and taking tiny bites until it was gone. The round-faced one didn't take a cookie, but she said something to Epigrass. Her voice was low and intense.

Epigrass dipped into Thonia's mind, looking for a translation. *She's asking—no, offering. Choose this or that of our something for a something. 'Muyp' could be 'wife,' I think. We will something your something. Make ourselves low in front of your big something. Now she's talking about houses. Oh, and she wants to know where you keep the frogs. 'Prraugaug,' that's 'frogs.' Unless it means something else.*

Frogs??

Best I can do. Sorry.

The cookie experiment had one concrete result. "Think I've got their names," Thonia reported the following day, after replaying the recording for the fifth time. "The one standing by the window right now—" She gestured at the monitor screen. "—that's Tewana, or Terana, something like that. The other two—this is the weird part. They're both named Awa. Could be Spanish. *Agua* meant 'water.'''

"Spanish?"

"Another of the old languages. Spoken in the southern areas."

"So they could be from the south."

But it was a tenuous clue. Epigrass felt that he was being left behind by events. The Body was building aircraft to search for the women's point of origin, and testing weapons to use against whatever population might be found. There was even talk of sending up a satellite, though a technical project of that complexity would require years. Sentiment in favor of a public execution was rising rapidly. And he had nothing to offer. Even with Thonia's help, he hadn't managed to establish a bond of communication.

"You have to be nice to them," Eppy whispered. "Forget about Smaun. Bring them fresh clothes, and have Thonia show them how to bathe and stuff."

Eppy had noticed by now that Epigrass seemed almost to be kenning him. Which was worse than absurd: In the first place, Eppy was only twelve, and not in the ktess yet. More to the point, Epigrass had been a real joddie once, but now he was only a character in a book that a boy was reading in a tree house. All the same, the connection seemed very close. Within minutes after Eppy made the suggestion, Epigrass had sought out two clerks from a clothing store in Serameno, and a coach laden with garments was rolling toward the Jewel.

When the coach arrived, servers carried the boxes of clothing up the stairs and piled them outside the women's door. The clerks, two young women dressed in the latest high fashion, with sequined slippers and enormous floppy bows in their hair, giggled and chirped at one another, excited by the honor of being called on to enter the Jewel and by the prospect of seeing the wild women.

Thonia, pale and sweating, tried to beg off. "You understand them," Epigrass told her.

"Not possible to understand them," she said. "Not really. Know a few of their words. Not the same thing."

But he insisted. They all thronged into the women's room together—proctors, servers, clerks, the joddie, and the linguist, who kept well to the rear. Whether she was more interested in staying away from the wild women or away from the contaminating cherishist influence of the fancy young clerks was hard to tell. The clerks made dismayed noises over the women's condition, and flatly refused to go near them until they were bathed. Of course, there was no way to explain this to the women. Epigrass could have the proctors bathe them forcibly; possibly he should have done it weeks ago. But they would make a fuss, and somebody might get hurt. What had begun as a gesture of friendship threatened to turn into an ordeal.

"Curtain," he said. "Or screen." *Bring.* The servers scurried away. *Draw hot water.* Epigrass pointed at the oversize tub in the doorless bathroom. The clerks looked at him in perplexity and then in dismay. "You first. Show them. We'll be behind a curtain." *Safety assurance.*

"Of all the bean-brained—"

"Come on, Ginny. It'll be fun. When's the last time you got to bathe with somebody famous?"

"Oh, I guess."

While the servers were setting up the screen, Epigrass raised an eyebrow at Thonia. She pressed her lips together and shook her head. He nodded pointedly. She sighed. "This was not," she said, "what I aspired to when I took my degree." But she crossed the room behind the clerks, slowly, as if walking on broken glass, and while they folded and smoothed their finery she brusquely stripped off her robe and plunged into the steaming water.

The wild women watched the splashing and sudsing with slightly less than their usual stolid imperturbability. After a couple of minutes, Terana said something. Thonia translated for Epigrass. *She thinks this something water is something for wives.* Big Awa muttered a reply. *Something never something kill something sleep. Kill husband when sleep?*

At Epigrass's urging, the two clerks climbed out of the tub and padded across, dripping, to the wild women. The clerks were terrified, but they put on a bold front. In a friendly, cajoling tone, as if to a balky child, Ginny said, "Come on, you'll like it." Becky said, "You will, honestly. It's ever so nice." They took Terana's hands and drew her gently toward the tub. She allowed herself to be drawn.

The linguist climbed out of the tub hurriedly to make room, toweled herself roughly, and put her clothes back on, averting her eyes from the sybaritic scene. Little Awa crept forward, skinned quickly out of her rags, and plunged into the bubbly water. Once the clerks had illustrated the process, Terana and Little Awa needed no further instruction, which suggested to Epigrass that they were not ignorant of bathing but simply of bathtubs installed inside buildings. Big Awa only sat with her arms crossed and glared at the others.

The clerks got the two wild women out of the tub and dried off. "You ought to have brought somebody to do their hair," Becky said.

"Ours too," Ginny echoed. "This is awful. At least bring us a mirror." So a server was sent for a full-length mirror. After a quick combing session, the clerks began showing the wild women the clothes, starting with the underwear. This required some demonstration, owing to the hooks and snaps, but by this time the two women's hostility had evaporated, and they were actively helping. They asked questions, pointed to things, exclaimed to one another. The mirror arrived. Little Awa started fearfully when she saw it, and hid behind Terana. But it fascinated her as well. After a minute she crept forward cautiously and stretched out her fingers to touch it.

Big Awa, forgotten, grunted suddenly and stood up. Behind the screen, the proctors snapped alert, but they were not needed. With a loud exclamation she strode across the room and jumped into the tub fully clothed. Her considerable backside slapped the water with explosive force and sent soapy waves arcing in all directions. The clerks, doused again, squealed.

The big woman wrestled her clothes off sitting down in the sloshing water and slung them away hard. They splattered against the wall in a clump and slid to the floor. She plunged her head in and emerged spluttering.

Eppy was amazed by the pictures. It had been a long time since Epigrass had troubled to ken naked women.

The door burst open and Smaun strode in. Younger than Epigrass by a dozen years, Smaun wore his black hair long, and kept it plastered back against his skull with oil. His face was lean and pale, with prominent cheekbones and thin, colorless lips. His eyes flashed as he regarded the scene—proctors, servers, folding screens, and the warm steamy air. *Waywardness.*

Gentleness, Epigrass responded.

"You suffer from the illusion," Smaun said aloud, "that they are like us. You contaminate us—" He gestured at Thonia Vaddis. "—with the poison of wayward individuality. Contaminated." Smaun shook his hands once, heavily, as though trying to shake off slime. He turned toward the linguist. *Inquire: New material sufficient?*

More than sufficient.

Reason for activity thus fulfilled.

Epigrass lowered his eyes. *Harmoniousness.* He instructed that the clerks finish dressing. Mops were fetched, and the screens folded. The wild women, arrayed in colorful new blouses and loose-fitting pants, looked far less savage than before, though their hair still hung limp. Becky impulsively hugged Terana and then Little Awa, and Ginny reluctantly did the same. Big Awa scowled and folded her arms, and they stayed away from her. The whole party retired to let the prisoners talk about their strange afternoon. Which they did, at length. For the first time, Thonia had more conversational material recorded than she could absorb. In her excitement she almost forgave Epigrass for the humiliation of making her take a bubble bath with cherishists and savages.

A few days later, Epigrass was summoned before the One. He was walking in the Courtyard, and suddenly it winked out like a candle flame. His senses were commandeered so completely that it seemed to him he stood bodily in the Inner Chamber of the One. The Chamber was dim, the air fragrant with incense. Twelve joddies sat slumped in large soft chairs along a low table. Pitchers of liquid refreshment, some beaded with moisture and some steaming, sat before them, and bowls of delicacies. Servers hovered in the shadows. The joddies seemed to be asleep, but now and then one stirred and murmured indistinctly. Epigrass could feel the solidity of his body—heartbeat, breath, tongue curled behind teeth. He knew that if he held his hand before his face it would block the light. He also knew that his body was still in the garden. His presence here was a cunning illusion. Or perhaps he was physically present after all. The One could as easily steal all his senses, including his sense of the passage of time, and walk his body through the corridors to awaken him here. Physical reality, in the Jewel, faded seamlessly into the more fluid reality of the ktess.

A single soft note rang out from a bowl-shaped brass chime, which hung suspended within a burnished clockwork mechanism in the center of the table. Thirty seconds later, when the note had died away, it sounded again. He waited.

Your progress not inspiring.

Difficulties convoluted. More time require.

Situation altered. In a rapid series of visual scenes, the One told him of the unexplained loss of a search plane in the mountains. How, the One inquired, could poorly armed savages bring down a plane? Epigrass had no answer. Nor could he offer a theory about the fragmentary glimpse of a man who was *not* a null climbing into the plane in the moments before contact was lost. The One received his full report on the months of study, and was not pleased. If he did not produce concrete results, he was told, the study would be terminated. He was given no specific date by which he should produce the results, nor any indication of what the results ought to be. The chime rang again, and the room dissolved, and he found himself back in the garden.

After the disappearance of the plane, the One increased the manufacture of aircraft tenfold. Eppy could see what was coming: The One was going to find where the women came from, no matter how far away it might be. When the place was found, everybody who lived there would be killed. Eppy wished Epigrass could do something to stop it, but he knew that would never happen. Epigrass was too close to the One. Whatever the One wanted, Epigrass wanted.

Anyway, why *should* Epigrass care about wild nulls? The life and welfare of the Body were his only concern. Eppy knew that that was the right way for a joddie to think, but he wasn't convinced. Why should the Body be something special? Why should the Body be allowed to kill anybody it didn't like? Sure, the Body might have a way of life that was better than any other way of life had ever been, or could possibly be. But just because you were smarter and happier, did that make it right to kill people who were stupid and miserable?

For Epigrass, seemingly, the question did not arise. His task was clear. With Thonia's help he was able, haltingly, to interrogate the women. "Where did you live?"

"In houses."

"Where were the houses?"

"In Ranoima."

"Where is Ranoima?"

"By the river."

"Yes, and where is the river?"

"The river flows past Ranoima."

"How far away is Ranoima?"

"Far. Far."

He didn't think they were being deliberately obtuse; they simply didn't understand what sort of information he was seeking. Perhaps they didn't have it, in any terms that he could understand. Or perhaps he was being too charitable. After all, they had seen their people slaughtered. Why should they tell him where Ranoima was?

At last he stumbled onto a useful question. "What is the name of the river?"

"Missopy."

Excited, he had a server bring an ancient map of North America, and unfolded it crinkling and crackling on the table. "Missopy," he said, tracing the faded line of the river called Mississippi.

The women bent over the map, and shrugged and gabbled with one another. His anticipation crumbled. They didn't know what a map was. Or if they did, they certainly didn't know how to read this one. The Mississippi River, even if that was the river they were talking about, was more than 2,000 miles long. But it was a place to start the search.

"In Ranoima it is warm? Yes? No?"

"Warm sometimes. Sometimes not warm."

"Sometimes cold?"

"Sometimes."

How can I ask them if it snows?

No lexical reference. Describe.

"White water in Ranoima? White cold water fall?" With his fingers, Epigrass mimed flakes drifting down.

Terana said, "White falls from sky? Like little white leaves?"

"Yes."

"No. We see this white where we walk, where we walk up high, where land is piled high. Not see this in Ranoima."

It was little enough, but he congratulated himself. On the Mississippi, and toward the southern end.

His elation was short-lived. Early the next morning he was dragged out of bed and summoned—bodily, this time—to the Inner Chamber, where his progress was examined. Only nine of the Council were physically present, and four of these continued eating breakfast while the examination proceeded. He outlined the linguistic findings to date, and explained his conclusion about the southern Mississippi.

Insufficient. Replacement. The Council shared that Epigrass was to step aside, that Smaun would take over the interrogation. Epigrass glimpsed a little of the methods that Smaun planned to employ. They were not gentle.

"Tell them they can't do that!" Eppy cried.

Reason inquire, Epigrass shared.

Developments. During the night, a very disturbing report had arrived from the north, a report so far beyond credibility that the One did not entirely trust the ktess. Joddies had been sent to examine the witnesses firsthand. *Inharmoniousness contagion wider than expected. Even among us.* Not knowing how deeply the contagion might have penetrated into the Body, the One had no wish to harbor a possible source of inharmonious thought so near itself. It had decreed that Smaun was to work swiftly, so that within days the women could be dispensed with. Even as Epigrass stood, head bowed, in the Inner Chamber, Smaun and six proctors were passing through the halls of the Jewel toward the women's cell, to proceed with the new phase of the questioning.

Eppy was outraged. "Tell them to stop," he said firmly. "Tell them—oh, I know! Tell them you'll take the women away somewhere, somewhere far away where they can't cause any trouble. Tell them you're just about to discover something really important, if they'll only give you more time."

Epigrass raised his chin off his chest. *Shame of waste,* he shared. *Tantalizing closeness of fulfillment-yet-invisible. New direction tentative—permit share? Urgent to suspend present action.* With astonishing boldness, he went on to outline exactly the course of action that Eppy had suggested. *Future contact wide,* he finished. *Infection of thought develop into stubbornness. With early knowledge of nature of infection, we have tools to build thicker wall to shut it out.*

"All right!" Eppy's heart was racing. He had been bored by so much of Epigrass's life, but now he felt very close to the joddie. The seconds that stretched out while the One pondered the proposal seemed interminable. The brass chime chimed another stroke. One of the joddies poured milk from a pitcher into his bowl of cereal and fresh fruit. Epigrass could ken the proctors in the Jewel's rim. They had ascended the last flight of stairs and were approaching the women's cell, boots click-thumping on the tile floor. The proctors smelled, to one another, of new leather and after-shave. Epigrass was not surprised or frightened by his own proposal. He awaited the pleasure of the One quite calmly, not thinking anything at all. The proctors reached the door, and one of them pushed the lock button. The brass chime chimed another stroke.

"Tell them you'd happily die ungathered if they think the women are too much of a threat to be left among the Body." Eppy was shouting now. "Tell them you'll take them off into the mountains and study them there. Tell them you're on the verge of a great discovery!"

Grain of sand I. Isolate absolute for study, return only bearing deep gladness of thought.

The joddie slumped at the far end of the table, a fat, pasty-faced man with several days' growth of beard, stirred restlessly. Without opening his eyes, he said, "Already."

"Knowledge," another croaked.

This interchange made no sense to Eppy until he traced the next paragraph with his fingertip to see how the ktess fleshed it out. The first joddie was saying that Epigrass had already caught the contagion of individualism from the wild women, which proved the danger, and the second was countering that in that case they had all the more need for knowledge of how the process worked, which might mean that Epigrass's bizarre proposal was a good one, though not for the rather vague reasons he had suggested.

Two of the proctors seized each of the women, while four others stood at the ready. Smaun's face twisted into a smile. The women looked at one another fearfully. The brass chime chimed, and the fragrant smoke coiled languidly upward from the censers along the walls. One of the joddies shifted in his chair and made a short, abrupt snoring noise at the back of his nose. Thonia Vaddis entered the women's room behind the proctors, her eyes flashing. "Where's Epigrass? What do you think you're doing?"

Procedure efficient make.

The One showed no inclination to consider Epigrass's strange proposal further. Perhaps it was doing so, or would do so in future. Perhaps not. Epigrass turned to go, and was not halted. Eppy was screaming, "Tell them to stop! Make them stop!" But this time Epigrass seemed not to hear. He walked calmly, his mind unruffled. Gradually his pace quickened. He descended two flights of stairs and set out down the long, echoing hall that led from the hub of the Jewel down one of the spokes to the rim. Ahead, the glowing rectangles of the polished floor tile receded into a brilliance of distance. By the time he reached the end of the hall he was almost running. Instead of turning toward his apartment, he went the other way, down another, wider flight of stairs, and emerged in the park that surrounded the Jewel. Looking neither left nor right, he strode rapidly down the wide, shallow steps toward the tree-lined boulevard.

The perpetual sound of the wind and rain no longer soothed. It roared so loud that Eppy thought his head would burst. The book squirmed in his lap like a nest of snakes, and he could not tear his eyes away from it.

Chapter ‖ 18

IT was a sad vigil, sitting up these last three nights—not the sort of duty that all the proctors cared for. Pal Cottis had not volunteered: Brother Meldino and Brother Wex had asked him to shoulder the duty. They had seemed troubled, though they had not shared the reason. Pal was not curious. The Body had been disturbed of late in many small ways. The best contribution that a proctor could make to the restoration of harmony was simply to do whatever might be required, and let the joddies worry about the whys and the what ifs.

The proctor station creaked and popped as the heat of the day bled away, and darkness pressed against the windows in the duty room. While the water for tea was heating on the hot plate in the corner, Pal laid his tool kit out on the table. From a wicker basket he drew out a half a dozen cloth-wrapped bundles. He untied the string so that the cloth fell away into little wrinkled many-colored puddles.

At the center of each puddle stood a wooden animal—a dog, a cat, a mule, a pig, a cow. But Pal Cottis's menagerie were more than animals. The surface of each figure was a swirl of smaller figures, vignettes in relief inlaid with contrasting woods. The vignettes depicted scenes from the White Book, or from *Tales of the Elder Days*. He had no duties tonight except to keep an ear open in case the nulls stirred up a fuss. Plenty of time to do a little carving.

The teakettle whistled. As he was filling his cup, he kenned somebody coming toward the back door. He thought it would be Goodwoman Farn again. A thoroughly unpleasant woman, the sort whom one tolerated out of courtesy and avoided when possible. But no, the visitor was male, and a stranger. *Enter.*

A tall, thin man, middle-aged, wearing an ill-fitting plum-colored coat. The newcomer had a tanned face, dark eyes, and a long straight nose. Though his movements were edgy, he smiled at Pal and projected an aura of composure and good will. "Forgive the intrusion, goodman."

Cottis opened his hand in acceptance. "Don't believe I've had the pleasure," he said. "I am called Pal Cottis."

Pleasure of meeting. "I am called Dappa Snee." The newcomer lowered his head in a slight formal bow.

Pal echoed the nod. "What brings you to the proctor station so late in the day?"

The newcomer licked his lips, as if considering what to say. Pal could sense the branchings of his thought, but the fruit at the ends of the branches hovered in shadow. "Only just arrived from Serameno. I had heard. . . . Is this your work?"

"A hobby, no more," Pal said.

"You are being too modest." *Permission to touch?*

"Certainly."

Dappa Snee picked up the wooden cow and held it to the light. "Exquisite workmanship."

"They're not just carvings," Pal explained. "They're puzzles as well. Each one comes apart. Here, let me show you." He took the cow and twisted one of its horns. In a few deft movements he had separated it into seven pieces, on each of which new decorations came into view.

"Remarkable." Snee was enthralled. "I've never seen anything like them."

"Nor I. I began by doing simple figures for my children, but as the children went on to other things I began to see how much more one could do. A simple idea can bring endless pleasure." Pal felt a joddie's mind slide lightly across his. His eyes returned to Dappa Snee; he noticed the unevenly trimmed hair, the triangular scars on the back of one hand. "Care for tea?"

"Yes, thanks. I've had a long ride."

"From Serameno, you said?" Pal poured a second mug. "I'm sure you haven't come all this way just to see my animals."

"If I had, the trip would have been worth it. But no. I'm a counter. I'm on my way to Oburn to take on some work there."

"Yubasty is the long way around if you're bound for Oburn."

"True, true. I made the detour because I'd heard that nulls were being kept here, to be Cleansed."

"True, goodman. Two boys. One very rebellious. Sometimes he shouts. He says foul things."

Dappa Snee shook his head sadly. "Perhaps I could offer them words of comfort."

"No harm in it." Pal glanced at the ring of keys, which hung on a hook behind the head proctor's desk. "But little good either, I think. The Body will be Cleansed of them soon enough."

"As to that," Snee said, "some friends with positions close to

the Council have asked me to look more closely into the question
of nulls. It's thought that perhaps if we understand them better, we
can learn what makes a child a null, and from there discover ways
to prevent such tragedies.''

"That would be a great blessing," Pal agreed. "Surprised
nobody's thought of it before now.''

"It's not a new idea, but difficult times call forth new
urgencies." Snee sipped his tea. "It's a perplexing problem.
We've studied their blood, and given them perceptual tests. We've
even dissected the brains, afterward, hoping to see what the
missing organ might be, but their tissues appear no different from
anybody else's. Perhaps we'll try dissection again with these
two.''

"Simple enough to arrange." Pal glanced at the wall behind his
visitor, where the broad-bladed ceremonial axe rested on its pegs.
The Hand of Cleansing had already come and worked up a fresh
edge with his whetstone.

"Good. I'll return in the morning and speak to the head
proctor.''

"I had always thought," Pal said, tearing his eyes away from
the sheen of the axe-blade, "that being a null was a birth defect,
like color-blindness. In time, I had hoped, we would be bred free
of it.''

"Genetics are not always so straightforward. I read up on the
problem when I was a young man, because of a family tragedy.
Learned that hundreds of years ago, in the first flush of victory
after the Great Cleansing, the One undertook to codify the genetic
heritage of the Body, so as to locate and eradicate not only the null
gene but others that caused diseases. Turned out to be a more
complex undertaking than anybody had imagined. Eventually it
was abandoned. Nulls do run in families, so you might think those
families could just be asked not to produce children. But over the
long haul, it seems, all families produce nulls occasionally, and
those that produce more than their share also produce more than
their share of joddies. Rid ourselves of one, we lose both.''

"Strange.''

"Yes. Now, because of the new urgency, the One is looking
into the question from fresh angles.''

"Why is the inquiry not being conducted by the joddies
themselves?''

Dappa Snee blinked rapidly, and his ktess rippled, as if many
thoughts were jostling one another. "The joddies have little

insight into the ways of nulls, for obvious reasons. It was thought that a counter or a mechanic, being inclined toward the handling of material things, could delve more readily into matters that are not of the ktess. This is excellent tea, by the way. Should we make a pot and take it to the nulls?''

"Don't see why not." Pal got up and put the kettle back on the hot plate. "Since you've been delving into matters that are not of the ktess, you must have some thoughts about the madwomen." He shared the image of them that he had received—not actually fanged, but maniacally savage, with bloody fingers and wide glaring eyes, grunting and snarling amid the stink of unmentionable filth.

Dappa Snee suffered a coughing fit, and had to wipe his eyes and blow his nose. "Forgive me. I fear I have an allergy." After tucking away his handkerchief and taking a sip of tea, he picked up one of the cow's legs and examined the carvings. "Extraordinary. The dog comes apart like that too."

"They all do. You were going to share your theory about the madwomen."

"Ah, yes. I fear I'm as much in the dark as anybody. Certainly they weren't ordinary nulls. They may not even have been human." A smile flickered across Snee's face. "Have you carved the story of the madwomen into any of your animals?"

"It's too recent. And I'm not certain what animal to put it on. A squirrel, perhaps. Squirrels hoard nuts, and the madwomen were hoarding men. These are mostly ancient stories, and I wasn't sure that such recent happenings belonged among them. But the tale hasn't died down. The Body rings with it like a bell."

"Perhaps when my work in Oburn is done, I'll come back this way and see your squirrel. The water is boiling. Where did you say the nulls were being held?"

"Barred room in the cellar." Pal put two mugs and a teapot on a tray. But before he could take up the tray, they sensed somebody else coming. "One of the mothers," Pal said quickly. "You must forgive her."

The stress of impending bereavement was not proving kind to Goodwoman Farn. Her face, pinched to begin with, had grown pale and blotchy. Her nose was red, her eyes red-rimmed and bracketed by dark circles. Her hair attempted gaiety, and failed. A fashionable blend of purple and silver, it hung down over her forehead in broad loops that might, framing a different face, have been coquettish. Her arms and legs stuck out like sticks from her round little body. She dabbed at her eyes with a handkerchief, and frowned at Dappa Snee, and said, "Who are you?"

"Goodman Snee is visiting from Serameno," Pal said. "He came to see your son."

"My Mooly? Why?" Her voice was querulous and nasal.

"The Body is concerned about the recent appearance of so many nulls."

"Mooly's not a null," Goodwoman Farn declared. "He's just a late bloomer. You'll see. You'll see."

"Sixteen," Pal said to Snee, shaking his head. "Come into his manhood two years since."

"It's not true. He's just a little boy. He's just my little boy." She sat down on a bench, and snuffled, and pressed the handkerchief beneath her eye.

Pal Cottis looked at his carvings with regret. It was not shaping up to be a quiet night.

"Hate to keep you from your work," Snee said. "If you'll show me the way to the cellar, I'd be happy to let myself in and out." He gestured at the keys.

"No trouble." Pal picked up the tea tray, and got the keys down from their hook.

"You're going to let him see Mooly." Goodwoman Farn glared at Pal. She got up and clutched at the front of Snee's coat. "They won't let me see him. Is that fair? I ask you. That's not fair. I'm coming too."

"I shouldn't think—" Snee began. But before he could go on, the woman stiffened, turned abruptly on her heel, and sat back down on the bench.

"I'll wait here," she announced, looking a little dazed.

The two men shrugged at one another. "Follow me," Pal said. He led the way down the hall.

"This is one of the oldest public buildings I've seen," Dappa Snee said. "Nicely kept up." He trailed his fingers along the much-scarred but lovingly polished paneling, and Pal caught the edge of a wistful thought about how warm and dry the building would be in a rainstorm. "Solid, too. Dates back to the Lezarvin period, doesn't it?"

"I'm not much on architecture," Pal said. "Nor on history."

"The proctor station in Lirmorr was built during that period. It had three entrances—the big one in the front, that opens on the square, the one through the back garden, and another little one at the side."

"Well, this one's only got two." Pal opened the cellar door, switched on the light, and led the way down a well-worn flight of stairs. "Front and back."

Most of the rooms along the cellar's central hall lay open. Dim, widely spaced light panels threw huge shadows across the stored property of the community—flags and banners to be brought out at festival-time, cabinets filled with records, and on the walls portraits, their colors grown dull with age, of leading citizens of centuries past. Glass cases housed dusty relics. Danlo stopped at one, brushed off the glass, and peered in. A square board of smaller squares in two different colors (both, by now, shades of brown), and standing on the squares an assortment of markers, some yellowish and some a faded red. Several of the markers were stylized horses' heads, and others resembled miniature stone towers.

At the end of the hall were three closed doors, and on a table at one side a small monitor screen. Pal Cottis set the tray on the table and switched on the monitor. A little room sprang into view, two bunks on opposite sides of a bedside table. Two young men were lying on the bunks. The proctor nodded in satisfaction and fumbled at the key ring. Finding the right key seemed to take a very long time. A faint light was coming from under the center door, so Danlo was surprised when Pal inserted a key in the left-hand door and opened it. *Room empty?*

"I'll bring them to you." Pal stood aside to let Danlo precede him. The room was dark, and Danlo's shadow fell across the floor.

The door swung solidly shut behind him, blocking out the light. He turned, puzzled. *Mistake? Light switch where?* The only reply was the impression of a rapid retreat down the hall and up the stairs. He tried the door, and found it locked. Odd. His heart beat faster, and his breath came quick and shallow. But there was nothing to be frightened of, really. Some sort of mixup, or an emergency that the proctor had to respond to.

Danlo groped along the wall until he found the light switch. The room was just like the one he had seen in the monitor—two bunks, a little table with a copy of the White Book on it, and a small barred window high in the wall opposite the door, through which the night scent of the garden wafted. Peering out through the bars, he could see light streaming from a similar window to his right. "Hello," he called softly. "Hello. Is anybody there?" A low murmur of voices came from the lighted room, but nothing

distinct. He called again, more sharply this time: "Hello! I'm a
friend! I've come to help you."

"There is nothing you could possibly do for them," a woman's
voice said. "Nothing that would truly help them." The voice
seemed to come from everywhere and nowhere. It brushed his
mind like fine sandpaper, yet it was wrapped in the softness of
velvet.

He knew the voice. It was Julan's.

He turned, knowing what he would see, dreading it, unable not
to look.

Julan was sitting on the bunk. Julan as she had been, brown hair
falling in loose curls across her shoulders, the oval face with its
delicate arching brows, the perfect, berry-stained mouth. Golden
light spilled from her in a flood. She was wearing a simple white
dress with a square embroidered neckline; the skirt hung loose
nearly to the floor. He remembered the dress. At first she seemed
no more than a flat image, but with every pulse his desire grew,
and she gained depth.

"You can't help them," she repeated. "You can still help
yourself, if you will. It's not too late."

His head exploded in a rush of dizziness. He tottered to the bunk
and sat beside her. "You're not real," he said. But he said it
weakly, without conviction. He remembered the perfume she was
wearing, the lilacs and musk, remembered how she tipped up the
beveled bottle and touched the hollow at the base of her throat.

"I am as real as you, in the only way that matters. I am
remembered in the Body."

"You died ungathered."

Julan's eyebrows pinched in sorrow. "Why must we dwell on
such sad things? I can see that you're tired. I can see how you've
suffered. I want to comfort you." She touched his shoulder. The
warm softness of her hand was naked on his skin, as if the shirt
and coat were not there. Her fingers slid upward to the place
beneath his ear where she had always massaged him.

"You died ungathered," he repeated doggedly. He could see
and hear her perfectly, but her ktess was no deeper than a puddle
on pavement. "How much of my mind have they dipped into, to
give you this semblance of life? And why?"

"The Body sees that you are gravely confused," Julan said.
"My only wish is to lie with you, and soothe away your hurt."
She moved closer. Her lips parted, and her head tilted a little to
one side.

"A visit from a departed lover is a reward," he said, reasoning aloud so as to keep from being sucked into the bottomless pool of her kiss. "Yet I am not fit to be rewarded. Since you are here, the Body knows that I am here. And if the Body knows that, it has learned enough to know that I am not fit. So you are sent not to reward me but to distract me, to batter down my resistance. The Body fears me. But why would it fear what it could ken? That must be it!" He leaped up from the bunk and backed against the door. Julan's eyes followed him, hurt, beckoning. "The joddies can't ken me completely. They want to know what I'm up to. You're here to weaken me so they can find out."

Julan shrugged lightly. "Enough is known, dearest." Her aura shimmered hypnotically. "Your every thought is a fish in a small pool. If the pool is cloudy, what of it? The fish will still be netted." Julan indicated the locked door with an airy wave. "Where are you going to go? You must see that your effort is doomed. Accept the healing that is offered. In resisting, you only harm yourself."

He pointed a shaking finger at her. "If it were truly doomed, why would the Body be concerned enough to send you? No, not 'send' you. You are not sent. You are reconstructed. You are not Julan. Julan died ungathered."

"We have been watching you for some time," Julan said. "I was among the watchers, in my way. In the One, nothing can be truly lost, or forgotten. I woke, and felt again the love I had known for you. Not only love, but admiration for your strength, and your compassion." She sighed, and shook her head sadly. "Yet you must see how misguided you have been."

"You, of all people, should know what guides me. What was done to you must not be done again, not to anybody, not ever."

"What was done to me was for the best. Did it hurt me?" She gestured at herself, as if to say, 'See? I am whole.'

"It hurt Julan. More than 'hurt.' You are not Julan."

"If I am not Julan, then you are not Danlo. You have become something else—a null yourself, nearly. Danlo was a man who shared freely. I remember the sharing. Do you?" She came toward him. A smile played at her lips. "What did you plan? To steal nulls out of proctor stations like a child stealing sweets? Did you actually think the Body would allow it?"

"I had hoped I wouldn't come to their attention."

"Even if you hadn't been noticed this time, you would have been, soon enough. We need only surround the nulls with armed men. What could you do against us? Nothing.'' She pressed herself against him. His hands, unbidden, sought the familiar curves of her back. His every bone ached with the need to lie with her.

"Since you died ungathered," he said through gritted teeth, "you are sustained only by my memories of you. Somehow they're tapping into those memories, using my own mind against me. If I can only shut them out. . . ."

"I am gathered as I was before I fell ill. I am as real, as alive at this moment as you." She nuzzled his neck.

"You are not sustained by me?"

"No. I assure you."

"Then you will not object," he said. He shut his eyes, slid deep into the caverns within himself, and found the place where Julan still lived. He had been using the memory and the grief since the beginning. It had provided, in some sense, the power with which he closed off portions of his mind. Without that source of power, his ability to hold secrets might collapse. But he was close to collapsing now. They were driving the memory into him like a wedge, to pry open his deepest recesses. Even if he were never to save a single null from the block, he would not let them use Julan against him. With a convulsive shudder he shut the door on that part of his mind, and rolled a boulder in front of the door.

When he opened his eyes, Julan was gone.

He sank onto the bunk and ran his fingers through his hair. To give up Julan again—it was the hardest thing he had ever had to do. Especially when there seemed so little reason. His plan for stealing nulls had been blown into a scatter of matchsticks.

But the proctor station was not made of matchsticks; it was wood and stone. Even if he were strong enough in the ktess to resist the joddies, they didn't need the ktess. They could come for him at their leisure, and do with him what they chose. This was the end of his hopes. Pain flooded through him.

The bare little room repelled him almost physically. He shut his eyes and fled among the minds nearby. There were the two joddies who had created the Julan visitation. They were still casting about for him, confused. Danlo had never tried to ken a joddie while remaining undetected, and a little flame of elation sprang up when he saw how easy it was. Either he had greater powers than he had suspected, or a thousand years of complacency had left the joddies—these two, anyway—unprepared to deal with a renegade. Maybe he still had resources that could be brought to bear.

Leaving them to their fruitless groping, he floated further. A good many people were hurrying down the streets near the proctor station. They were carrying gardening tools and hammers and flashlights, and they were stopping to look under porches and inside rain barrels. In every mind was a clear picture of Linnie.

He thought for a moment that the picture had been taken from his memory, but more facts emerged from the tangle of cross-purposes. A young man had come upon a coach parked in an alley, and seen but not kenned a figure inside, and thought it might be a sick person. He opened the door, and Linnie reached out and tried to grab him, and he ran away. Now the coach stood empty.

Why had she shown herself? No matter. She might be able to elude them for an extended period, or she might not. Unless he could escape from his cell, Danlo could do little to help her. He would have to find a way!

The proctor was gone, probably helping search for Linnie, but Goodwoman Farn sat forgotten upstairs, twisting and untwisting the handkerchief around her fingers. Her self-pity was as rank as rotting cabbage. Danlo steeled himself. By now he was growing used to riding people, but he still found it shameful to bend another's will. He would have preferred ripping a stranger's clothes off.

He got her to look around the duty room without noticing that she was being ridden. The ring of keys was back on its hook behind the desk. He was well into her now, could feel the dampness under her arms, the ache of a tooth going bad. He got her to her feet and aimed her at the keys, and she gasped in alarm. *Reach out, reach out now, that's good.* The bony fingers closed on the cold jagged metal.

She swayed down the hall, rebounding from one wall to the other as her muscles fought one another, and opened the door to the cellar stairs. Below lay darkness; the proctor had turned out the light. Danlo patted one wall and then the other. Where was the light switch? She was trying to send a silent cry for help to the nearest joddie, and he had to keep a damper tight on that as well. Forcing her down the stairs in the dark would be a mistake; she might fall and break a leg, or simply drop the keys and be unable to find them. Her breath was coming in short gasps, and her chest was painfully tight. Where was the shirking switch? He couldn't find it.

There must be a handlight in the duty room somewhere. *Let's

*go back now. Easy, don't run, just put one foot in front of the
other, that's right.*

He rummaged in several drawers without finding a handlight.
Twice she dropped the keys. The second time he stood her up too
quickly, and nearly lost her as the blood rushed away from her
head. What could he do? One of the proctors might come along at
any moment and ken that the woman was being ridden, or simply
take the keys away from her. Holding her motionless, Danlo slid
back into his own body far enough to turn his head and look at the
door. Yes, there was a keyhole on this side. Excellent! He urged
the helpless woman out the back door of the proctor station and
down the half-dozen steps into the night-shrouded garden. To the
left of the steps, two cellar windows glowed.

The first window belonged to the room where her son was being
held. And she knew it. Danlo tried to force her toward the second
window, but she had ideas of her own. He moved toward his
window from the inside, thinking he would reach out and take the
keys from her, but he banged his shin painfully on the corner of
the cot, and she slipped away from him. He regained only enough
contact to watch through her eyes as she knelt in the soft turned
earth of the flower bed and peered between the bars at the two
boys sprawled on their cots. "Mooly," she said softly. "Mooly,
son." She tapped the keys against one of the bars. They jingled.
"See what Mama's brought you? See?" A long arm in a purple
sleeve reached out of the next window and stretched toward her,
fingers groping blindly like pale white worms exposed suddenly to
the air. She saw the arm and hand out of the corner of her eye, and
paid no attention to it at all.

Chapter ‖ 19

IN the warm, bright morning, while birds warbled and chased one
another in the trees, Ainne Murrinder went gathering wildflowers.
She strolled through the tall grass, picking small flowers and
rearranging the bouquet by easing stems out of the bundle and
sliding them back in at different spots. She was not thinking about
flowers. She was thinking about the remarkable man who had
been out beyond the Wall, and about his dreadful companion. She
was trying to puzzle out the difference between killing a dog

because you were hungry and killing a person in order to preserve a world of happiness and order. She was fairly sure there was a difference, but she couldn't figure out what it was.

Last night's vomit still lingered, sour and bitter, at the back of her throat. She had thrown up, kneeling by the side of the road, until she couldn't throw up any more. She felt betrayed and defiled as well as wretched about poor Sparky. When she pulled herself together enough to stagger home, the cheerful lights of the farm-house mocked her feelings—but she didn't much care for the idea of staying out all night. For one thing, the wild woman might be lurking among the trees. So she dragged herself inside. She was too distraught to hide from her mother the fact that something was wrong. Sarra Murrinder put down her needlepoint, her eyes troubled. *Soothing need?* Ainne scowled and turned away, blocking her mother completely. Certainly she needed soothing; it didn't take the ktess to see that. But as much as she longed to break down and cry, she wasn't quite ready to reveal what she knew about Danlo.

"You really must learn not to shut others out," Sarra said aloud. "It's not healthy."

"How would you know?" Ainne pulled a handkerchief out of her pocket and blew her nose.

"I know lots of things, dear. Except about you. You're my little enigma. Come sit over here." Sarra patted the couch. Ainne complied reluctantly, and let her mother stroke her hair. "You have such power," Sarra said. "Someday you'll use it to help others. But first you must get over this terrible stubbornness. You never used to be like this. It all started the summer you spent so much time with that boy. You've never let me work with you to heal those feelings—no wonder they're festering!"

"I'm all right."

"No, you're not. If you were, you wouldn't be hiding from me. You used to hide under the porch when you were little. Do you remember that? And now you're practically grown up, and you're still hiding under the porch. It's not healthy. If you don't show more maturity before long, Uncle Foony will lose patience. And I know you wouldn't want that."

"You really don't care about me, do you?"

Sarra drew back, sincerely puzzled. "Well, of course I do, dear. That's what we're talking about."

"No. I think—I think if you cared, you'd let me be who I am, instead of trying to make me act like everybody else."

Sarra pressed her lips together. "I see. And of course, at the age of sixteen, you know exactly who you are, and how it would be best for you to act."

"I know a lot," Ainne said. "I know more than you think."

"Well, I'm sure that when I was your age I knew a lot too. I kept some dinner warm for you, if you want it."

Ainne swallowed, and swallowed again. "I don't think I could eat anything right now."

The next morning her mother spent an hour sharing with the woman at the next farm about how they might cajole Ainne out of her recalcitrance. Ainne sat on the porch steps and watched a mockingbird strut along the edge of the barn roof. She was filled with an uneasy mixture of resentment and smug satisfaction. The satisfaction was because she could ken them effortlessly without their kenning her. They had guessed that she might, but since they wanted her to share freely, they welcomed the prospect. The resentment was more complicated. They had figured out exactly how her life should be laid out, and they meant to bind her, like a wayward tree branch, to that stake. Sarra was convinced that her daughter was destined for a seat on the Civic Council, the highest authority short of the One. She might even be chosen, as only five other women had been in history, to join the One directly.

Ainne was not surprised that they were thinking of her in those terms, but the prospect of being enmeshed forever in the Body's labyrinthine machinery of rumination didn't appeal to her. All right, smarty, she challenged herself. If you don't want to do that, what *do* you want to do? Her mind drifted back to Danlo. There was somebody who was doing something different, or trying to. Not just different—important. He couldn't possibly succeed, but somehow that made it seem *more* admirable rather than less. She wished she could do something that exciting. She envisioned herself running out to the paddock, throwing a saddle on the white stallion, and galloping after Danlo to help him. If only he weren't embroiled with that disgusting creature! Ainne shook her head sadly, and got up off the porch, not to saddle the stallion but to go pick wildflowers.

She was waylaid by Arrie, who wanted her to help find Sparky. She blinked back tears and tousled his hair. "I'm sure Sparky will come home soon."

"He's had time to catch a whole *bunch* of squirrels!"

"Maybe he got tired, and decided to take a nap in the barn. Did you look in all the stalls?"

"No, I'll bet that's where he is. Sparky, Sparky!" The boy ran off.

When she got tired of picking flowers, she sat down on a log and kicked off her sandals. Down the gentle sun-drenched slope, the farmhouse with its peaked roofs looked like a dollhouse. The bouquet dangled slack from her hand, and she let her mind drift out past the profusion of commonplace pleasures and frustrations scattered among the nearby farms, out into the net of mental connectedness maintained by the joddies. Here too she could observe without being observed. She took a guilty pleasure in it. Not that there was much to overhear; life was placid—dull, really—from one end of the world to the other. But grown men trained for years to do what she was doing quite casually, and it amused her to feel superior to them.

The previous spring, when the memory of Borry was still fresh, her parents had thought to distract her by taking her down to Serameno, to the Founders' Day festivities. She had sat in the great amphitheater before the Triple Gate while Olivia herself filled the entire gathering with boundless love. Because Ainne had cast her thoughts in that direction, she found herself suddenly *in* the amphitheater. Such things happened to her once in a while; she knew the joddies had ways of controlling them, but she was not eager to ask the joddies to teach her. Now, she looked out through a stranger's eyes. By the labored breathing and stiff joints, an old man. He was pushing a broom down an aisle between two banks of seats. The amphitheater was empty except for the carefully hoarded mound of scraps and dead leaves that the old man was pushing ahead of him down the shallow steps toward the Triple Gate.

A year ago the seats had been filled, ten thousand joyous voices raised in song. She tried to recapture the rich sense of peace and joy that had bubbled within her on that day. For a moment, fleetingly, she thought she had it. Being one with the Body— united with the very substance of love, aflame from head to toe, swept away so completely that floating down afterward to inhabit a single two-armed, two-legged human form seemed absurd. Who was it that had drifted into this particular body, when there was only the One, unendingly?

But sooner or later, she thought, I always do come back and discover that I'm still me. You can't stay in a blind ecstasy all the time. Shirts have to be mended, brooms pushed. Who wants to push a broom when you're being one with the Body? She lifted the old man's head and gazed out through rheumy eyes at the Triple Gate, which cast sharp shadows in the sun. I can look out through anybody's eyes, but I always know they're *their* eyes, not mine. I might learn new ideas from them, or feel new feelings, and that changes me, so I'm not exactly the same person I was before. My identity is always changing. But there's a thread that ties it all together. That thread is the most important thing there is. It runs vertically, and the ktess is like another thread that runs horizontally, and you have to have both kinds of threads, the way they showed us on the loom in crafts class. You have to have the warp and the weft. If you just have the weft and not the warp, you don't have a piece of cloth. You have a basket full of loose thread—and that's about what the Body of Harmony would be like if there weren't any individual personalities in it.

And if that was true, wouldn't the strengths of individuals have some value to the Body even if the individuals were nulls?

The most powerful personality she had ever known had been Borry's. The other boys had seemed dull by comparison—dull when they were children, and duller still when they grew into the ktess and she could sample their narrow conceits. Borry was different. He was athletic, and quick at word games, and his dark stare sent shivers up her spine, even before she knew she loved him, or knew what it meant to love a boy. She was selfishly glad at first that he was slow coming into the ktess, because she cherished the mystery of never knowing what he might say or do—propose a fantastical theory about the world, or catch her hand and make her run down to the creek as fast as she could so they could see a new species of water bug he had discovered. Afterward they would fall laughing to the ground beside the rippling stream, and do the sweet things that boys and girls did together.

When they guessed that Borry was a null, he tried to stop seeing her. He shut himself away in his bedroom and wouldn't come out, so she stood outside the door and screamed at him until he let her come in, and they cried together for two hours and then ended up doing it right there in his room, not even caring that his parents were downstairs listening.

Borry wanted to run away to the mountains, and she swore she would come too. But the more they planned, the more obvious it became that they would never be able to survive. If they had been city children, they might have been naïve enough to try it. But they were farm children. They knew about raising crops. Raising a crop involved fifty-pound bags of hybrid seed, and tractors drawing plows, and careful applications of pesticides and fertilizers, and electronically timed irrigation systems. And while the crops were growing, you had to live for months on last year's, which had to be stored in sealed bins so the rats and bugs and mold wouldn't get at them.

Borry and Ainne didn't know much about the mountains, but they guessed that tractors and bags of seed would be in short supply. Three times they made lists of what they would need. Borry tore up the first list when it got too long. Ainne tore up the second. The third one she still had, crumpled and tear-stained, at home in her top dresser drawer. Her mother knew she had it. Her mother was waiting patiently for her to throw it away.

We should have tried it, she told herself bitterly. We should have gone away. Even dying of starvation would have been better than what happened. And now somebody else *was* trying it—and she was afraid to help. She had all but talked herself into going along with her mother's plans. She was going to spend the rest of her life being disgustingly comfortable and doing boring things with boring, boring people. And worst of all, for the rest of her life she would know that she had failed not once but twice.

Back in the amphitheater, the old man straightened his shoulders. "I don't want to be on the Civil Council," he said loudly. He shouted, so that the ten thousand invisible people in the ten thousand empty seats could hear. "I don't want to be on the Council, not ever! Not after what you did." He looked around, embarrassed, to see if anybody had seen him. "Who's there?" he whispered. "Who's there?" He tried to ken who had ridden him, but Ainne was miles beyond his reach.

She withdrew from the contact and drifted back toward herself. Closer to home, an unusual ripple attracted her attention. She pursued it—and gasped. The joddies were sharing about Danlo. They had been observing him, and they knew, in a general way, what he intended to do. Apparently they didn't know where he was at this moment, but they had set people looking.

Her first impulse was to find him in the ktess and warn him. But he would be far away by now. Unless she stumbled into another accidental contact like the one she had just broken off, she might search for hours. In order to establish a link, she would have to be closer to him physically.

She snapped back into her own body. Her unattended hand had let the flowers fall; the jumble of color and crossed stems lay strewn across the ground. She bent to pick them up, thinking, Why should I care? It's not as if he ever had a chance. But she did care. Maybe it was because he was trying to stop the killing—or maybe it was because he was the only person she had ever met who was living his own life, as difficult as that was, instead of just quietly going along with everybody else. If he killed and ate dogs, maybe it was because he had to.

As she was putting the flowers in a vase in the kitchen, her mother came in. "Mama," she said, doing her best to sound casual, "I need to drive into Oburn today in the two-seater."

Sarra Murrinder stood quite still for a moment. "May I ask why?"

"I, uh, I've got to see a doctor. I've got a pain right here." She touched her side.

"You do not. You may be able to hide your conscious thoughts from me, but I can ken your pain receptors perfectly well. This is about that man who stopped by here yesterday, isn't it? First you're out 'til after dark and you come back pale as a sheet, and now you want to go running off by yourself. I want an explanation, young lady."

"Well, you're not going to get one," Ainne said coldly. She set the vase in the center of the table so forcefully that water splashed, and brushed past her mother and out the door.

Behind her Sarra said, "Ainne! You come back here this instant." A heavy impulse rode into her as her mother tried to force her to stop. Sarra's mind was powerful enough to exercise absolute control over most people. Ainne slipped out from under it as easily as if it were an arm draped across her shoulder.

The two-seater was scooting out of the farmyard in the direction of the road. Belatedly she realized that her mother had alerted the harvestman to take it. "Josper!" she shouted. Normally Josper enjoyed doing what would please "the young miss," as he called her, but now his jaw was set grimly. Ainne saw instantly that her mother was tinkering with Josper's feelings. Well, if her mother could do it, she could too. She concentrated on the harvestman, willing him to stop the vehicle and turn it around. But she found herself locked in a contest with her mother, who was urging Josper to speed up. A hundred yards away, he twitched spastically behind the wheel of the two-seater. Together, the three drivers managed to steer it down into a drainage ditch and up the other side, where it banged into a fence post. The vehicle teetered precariously and rolled back into the ditch, where it tipped over on its side.

Sarra hitched up her skirt and ran to see that Josper was all right. Ainne had another idea. If the two-seater was out of commission, she *would* take the horse.

At the door of the tack room, her father barred the way. "Would you kindly explain—" he began.

"Daddy, don't make me—"

"You're not going—"

"Get out of my—"

He put out a hand to catch her wrist. She knew she would never be able to break his grip, and she had never quite dared take control of her father's mind. No saddle or bridle, then. She wheeled and dashed out of the barn.

Champion was a big, gentle horse, a bit past his prime. Ainne had been riding him since she was a little girl. As she unlatched the paddock gate, he snorted softly in greeting. "Want to go for a little run, boy? Bareback today. Daddy's being stubborn. But we'll show him, won't we?" She sprang up to the horse's back and leaned low to clasp her arms around his neck. "Come on, boy, let's show them." She dug in her knees, and Champion started off at a heavy trot. Glin Murrinder stepped in the horse's path. There was no bridle for him to catch, so he caught at Champion's mane. Ainne's knee struck his side. He lost his grip, and then the horse was past him and he had to run. She pressed herself lower and dug in tighter. "Faster! Come on!" Champion broke into a lumbering, reluctant gallop. Ainne clung as tight as she could. The tilted two-seater flashed past, and her mother's startled face. Girl and horse flew down the shoulder of the road.

Champion couldn't keep up the gallop for long, but Ainne knew her father wouldn't bother to chase her in the tractor. A walking horse could outpace it. She let Champion slow to an easy trot. If they righted the two-seater and came after her in that, she would cut across the fields.

She wished that she had taken the time to pack a case; she might easily be gone overnight. In fact, the more she thought about the future, the hazier it became. What would happen if the One intercepted Danlo before he could get to the nulls? Even if he freed them, he would never be able to escape with them to the mountains, not with the One alerted to stop him. Would she be able to help them any better than she had been able to help Borry? And would she be able to do it without being discovered, now that her mother had an idea what she was up to? What would the One do to *her?* Spank her and send her home? Probably something worse than that.

Champion's hooves beat a steady rhythm. Sunlight flashed yellow-green through the trees and dappled the road. Up ahead, the road curved out of sight around a bend. Whatever lay beyond that bend, she would cope with it when she got there. She threw back her head, closed her eyes, and let the wind wash her face.

Chapter || 20

GOODWOMAN Farn was not going to get up from in front of the window; her love for her son was buried too deep for Danlo to neutralize it. After a little groping, however, he found that she wasn't using her mouth. "Listen, boys," she went on in a lower, faster tone. "Listen closely. There's a man in the next room. I'm the man in the next room. I've—borrowed your mother. I'm sorry. Wanted her to give me the keys so I could let you out, but she doesn't want to part with them. Like a chance to explain, but she's fighting me. Take the keys from her, let yourselves out, then let me out."

The two nulls had crowded to the window. Danlo could see them only indistinctly, because Goodwoman Farn's vision was smeared by tears. "Mom? Mom? Are you okay?"

"Take the keys," said her choked voice. "Free the man in the next room."

The keys were wrested from her grip. Danlo slid out of her gratefully, keeping only enough contact to prevent her from spreading distress through the ktess. The voices in the next room were louder now, and sobbing came from outside the window.

A minute ticked by. Another. What were they doing? The woman was no use as eyes or ears; she had fainted. He pressed his ear against the wall, but couldn't make out words. He cast about with his mind, hoping to find nobody near the proctor station. A young plumber and his girlfriend, both rather drunk, were weaving down the street, but that was all. Danlo moved further afield: Had the searchers found Linnie?

Before he could learn, a faint pop and creak told him that the door of the next room had opened. A moment later, metallic scrabblings came from the latch of his own door. At last they found the right key, and the door swung wide. A pair of teenage boys, one large and olive-skinned, his face rounded by baby fat, the other small, with a sharp face and red hair. They stared at him apprehensively. "What did you do to my mom?" the large boy said. He was trying to sound pugnacious, but succeeded only in sounding nervous.

"She'll be all right." Danlo stepped out into the hall. "You're the two they're going to kill."

"You're not supposed to call it that," the large boy protested.

"What are your names?"

"That's Mooly," said the red-haired boy. "I'm Gairth."

"All right, Mooly and Gairth. Listen closely. We don't have much time. If you don't want to be killed, you can come with me." All he had to offer them was the pieces of a shattered dream, but even that might be better than beheading. At least they ought to be given the choice. "I may be able to get you away to a place where—well, it's not a safe place to live, but at least nobody will care if you're a null."

"You're crazy," Gairth said. "There's no such place."

"There is such a place. I've been there. I can't promise we'll be able to get there without being stopped. But if you come with me, at least you've got a chance. That's more than you'll have if you stay here."

"There's no such place," Mooly said, shaking his head. " 'In all the land, one way.' That's what the White Book says."

"The White Book is wrong."

"You're not supposed to say that!"

"Do you want to argue, or do you want to go on living? I can't drag you out of here kicking and screaming. The proctors can. They will."

Mooly wrung his hands and bunched his forehead into a frown. "I don't know. We're supposed to be Cleansed, like it says in the White Book."

"Do you *want* to be Cleansed?"

"Well, no, sure I don't, but people do stuff all the time that they don't want."

"You don't have to let them chop your head off if you don't want them to."

Mooly fingered his neck, lingeringly and with a forlorn expression. "What kind of game is this?" he asked. "I never heard anything like this."

"It's not a game. And you've never heard of anything like it because there's never been anything like it. This is something new. Come on.'' Danlo led the way to the foot of the stairs, and ascended a few steps. They only stood staring up at him, not quite willing to follow. He flicked his mind outward again; still nobody coming, but somebody surely would before long. The pair of joddies who had created the illusion of Julan would wonder how he had slipped away from them. They would come to talk with him directly. Thinking him safely locked away, they had no reason to hurry, but they had no reason to delay either. Would he even ken a joddie as one approached, or could they routinely cloak themselves as the one in the airplane had?

''I like what you said about the White Book,'' Gairth said. ''I've been telling him that. But you're still crazy. Even saying we believe you, which *I* sure don't, where are we going? And what's the Body going to do, just let us walk away? And what happens when we get there? They'll only come after us and bring us back.''

''The Body's not going to know where you are. At least I hope not.''

''The Body knows everything,'' Mooly said.

''Not everything. The Body doesn't know we've gotten out of those rooms. But it will before long.'' He turned his back on them deliberately and started up the stairs. After three steps he looked back over his shoulder and said, ''If you want to die, just go back in that room, shut the door, and toss the keys out the window. I'm not going to wait for you.''

As he had hoped, they swarmed up the stairs after him. ''I'm going to see how my mom is,'' Mooly said. ''That's all. I'm not going anyplace with any crazy old man.''

''We'll find a coach,'' Danlo said. They emerged in the upper hall and headed toward the rear of the building, moving quickly. ''I'll drive, and you can lie on the floor whenever we pass somebody.''

''Right,'' Gairth said. ''And the first joddie we come across will ken that you're thinking about us. What good is hiding? Or are you a null? They'd know. If you're not in the ktess, they'll know that, and they'll grab us and Cleanse us all.''

''Let me deal with the joddies. I can do things that they don't understand.'' He turned to face them, in the room where Pal Cottis's carved animals still marched in a frivolous procession across the table. ''I'm not saying it will be easy. If we get there at all, living there won't be easy either. You won't have nice clothes or a warm house.''

"You're talking about out beyond the Wall," Gairth said.

"There's nothing beyond the Wall," Mooly said. "It's chaos. I want to see how my mom is doing." But he shifted indecisively from foot to foot, his eyes fixed on Danlo in unwilling fascination.

"I want to know how you're going to get away from the joddies," Gairth said.

He hadn't expected them to show such resistance. But then, he had had months to get used to the idea. They had had only minutes. "Sometimes I can make them think they're kenning all of me," he said patiently, "when they're only kenning the part that I want them to. It's a gift I have."

"Tricks are kid stuff. Grownups can't trick one another."

"I can't explain it. All I can tell you is that I know how to do it. The joddies' biggest enemy, I think, is their own complacency. They've known for so long exactly what goes on everywhere in the world that it never occurs to them that somebody might be hiding something right under their noses. And nobody has defied them for so long that they don't know how to organize a response." Danlo opened the door a crack and peered out. Except for a few bugs darting across the cone of light cast by the lamp above the door, the garden lay serene and empty.

"And it'd just be the three of us?"

"Later, maybe others. For now, the three of us and one other. A woman who knows about how to live beyond the Wall."

Gairth's eyes lit up. "One of the madwomen!"

"She's not mad. She's wiser than you or I about some things. If we can make it out past the Wall safely, then I can come back and do the same thing again. Someday maybe we can have a whole village—men and women and animals and crops and children of our own. Come on." He led the way down the steps into the garden.

"And then the airplanes will come," Mooly said mournfully, "just like it says in the White Book. First the sickness, and then the flying coaches dropping fire, and then the time of Harmony will descend 'like soft rain upon the thirsty world.'"

"You may be right," Danlo said. "On the other hand, you might be the one to think of a way for us to hide from the airplanes. If you don't come with us. . . ." He looked around in the darkness for some sign of Linnie. It would be like her to slip away from her pursuers and circle back to where she knew she would find him. But the only sound was the song of crickets. "Others have done it. The Body had far more planes at the time of the Great Cleansing than it has today, and still some escaped. And we have a great advantage that they didn't: We know the nature of those who are hunting us.''

"I gotta go make sure my mom is okay.''

"We'll wait here,'' Danlo said. "Don't dawdle. If anybody comes, we'll be gone.''

The big boy slipped away across the garden toward the lighted windows. Danlo frowned at the silent darkness. His nerves screamed at the delay, but if the proctors were prowling the streets for Linnie, the garden was as safe a place as any. Besides, he didn't know which direction to go. How was he to find Linnie? The coach had been seized, so she would know better than to rendezvous with him there. Possibly she would strike out on foot, intending to get past the edge of town and wait for him in the fields beside the main road. But it would be too easy to miss her in the dark. Could he afford to wait in Yubasty until sunrise? And how, from a hiding place, would she recognize him even in daylight if he were driving a coach? He was almost grateful when Gairth interrupted his litany of perplexities with a question. "What I'd like to know,'' Gairth said, "is *why?* Why don't you care about the harmony of the Body?''

"The world is a far larger place than you think. And we're not alone in it. When I thought we were alone, I thought, as you do, that the way of the White Book was the only way, even when it was hurtful to—to one whom I loved. Now I think we have to find a new way. The Body must learn to live in peace with nulls. Killing them has warped us so badly that I weep to think of it.''

"I still think you're crazy,'' Gairth said. "You want to know why I want to come? Because it'll be more fun watching you being crazy and getting dragged away by the proctors than laying around watching that mountain of underwear pace up and down.''

"Somebody's coming,'' Danlo whispered. "Three or four of them.'' He grasped Gairth's elbow and they stepped off the path, among the bushes. As far as he could tell, the newcomers had not kenned him. He went into them a bit more deeply. Smug satisfaction. They were coming back to take a closer look at their captive. Coming to the rear of the proctor station, to the garden gate.

Mooly bustled up. "Hey, I thought for a second you guys were gone.''

"Ssh!''

"My mom's okay, no thanks to you.''

"We'll have to go over the wall," Danlo told them. "Or else—
Can you stand perfectly still and not make a noise?"

"What's the matter?" Mooly still hadn't gotten the idea.

"Somebody's coming. Don't move. Don't talk. Don't even
cough."

The garden gate swung open. Danlo concentrated on becoming
entirely transparent in the ktess, having no thoughts at all. Mooly
made a tiny noise that might have been the beginning of a sneeze,
but stifled it. Four men came up the gravel path in single file.
"Good night's work," one of them said. Another grunted assent.
They passed the motionless figures and reached the door.

"Hold a minute. Goodwoman, are you unwell?"

"My son. He—"

"Come on," Danlo whispered. "Quickly!" He went across the
lawn on the balls of his feet, aiming straight for the gate. Gairth
dashed soundlessly past him, but Mooly was making a distressing
amount of noise.

Behind them the cry went up. "Hey! There they go!"

Danlo plunged out the gate and looked swiftly up and down the
street, not knowing which way to turn. Gairth had already decided
for him. He followed the boy as best he could, leaving Mooly to
bring up the rear.

Ahead of them, two people came out of doorways, clearly
alerted to intercept them, but Gairth dodged between two buildings. When Danlo regained sight of him he was scrambling over
a fence. They reached back down together and hoisted Mooly up
by the elbows.

They were at the rear of a private yard. Gairth led the way down
the areaway between two houses. "Watch out," he cautioned.
"Garbage cans."

"You woke her up, didn't you," Danlo said bitterly. "To tell
her you were going."

"Sure I did. What did you expect?"

"A little common sense, I suppose." To Gairth he said, "Do
you know where we're going?"

"Out of town, I guess. You tell me which direction. Or do you
want to get a coach?"

"We'll need a coach."

Mooly said, "What we need is one of those airplanes!"

The boy might be right. But that was a bow that had only one
arrow. "First we have to find my friend. Then a coach." Maybe,
he considered, he could locate mentally those who were leading

the search for her, and learn where she had last been seen. But first they had to put some distance between themselves and the proctor station. A cry was going up behind them. Soon it would be ahead of them. They crossed an empty street, and climbed another fence, and startled a couple of cats, and worked their way under a hedge on their elbows. Twigs clawed at Danlo's face like skeletal fingers.

Mooly was huffing. "C'mon, guys," he said. "I gotta rest for a minute. I gotta." Danlo ignored him. After several more fences and narrow misses with garbage cans, they peered out at a front gate and saw a man standing in the white pool under the streetlight at the nearest corner. He was wheeling slowly to look north, east, south, west, north again. At the corner beyond him, a second man was doing the same. The Body had thought of a way to watch for fleeing nulls. They were caught in a net.

The boys looked to Danlo. "We've got to know where we're running to," he whispered. "Just a minute." He closed his eyes and cast loose. The grid of sentinels, one on every corner, winked into view. A yard-by-yard, building-by-building search was fanning out from the proctor station, several dozen strong, and all who were able joined in, hoping to stumble upon a fresh trail. One elderly woman armed with a flowerpot was creeping down her own cellar stairs, quaking but determined, not ten yards from where the fugitives stood.

His own face, he saw, had been passed on by Pal Cottis, along with the faces of the nulls. But what about Linnie? He cast further.

With a cold shock he saw why her face was not paired with his in the sending. She had been captured. She had been prowling near the proctor station when half a dozen youths confronted her and chased her into a blind alley. He saw the scene clearly, in the form in which one of the young men had shared it with a joddie. She had kept them at bay for several minutes with the spear, and when reinforcements arrived and they finally summoned the courage to press in on her, two had been stabbed, one badly. She had broken a third man's arm before they subdued her.

Was she alive, or dead? He followed the trail from mind to mind. It led back to the proctor station. At this moment five joddies and two dozen other men were crowded into the duty room, jostling one another around the table, their sweat thick and close. The carved animals had been pushed aside. In their place, Linnie lay sprawled on the table. Two men gripped each of her limbs, but she writhed in defiance, tried to kick, tried to scratch. A purple welt was raised above one eye, and her upper lip was puffy. She was mouthing words, and Danlo felt the men's astonishment. Not only had they found a new wild woman running loose in the very heart of the Serral Valley, but she was speaking words they could understand. "Linnie strong woman," she said. "Bad men kills children. Linnie takes. Danlo takes." Then she lapsed into her own tongue.

"Hey, are you all right?"

Gairth's voice. Danlo dropped back into his own body. He had swayed, nearly swooned; the boys were holding him up. The dark bushes pressed close, and the houses in whose windows no lights burned. "Too many," he said, shaking his head. "There are too many of them. We'll never be able to—"

"What are you talking about?"

"They've taken her. They've got her."

"Got who? Oh, the madwoman. Who's got her? The proctors?"

"Proctors and joddies and some others. They've taken her back to the station."

"So what are we gonna do?" Gairth asked.

"I don't know." Danlo felt like crying. "I don't know. We can't let them keep her. But there are too many of them, and they're alerted now. We'll never get her out of there." He gripped his head fiercely in both hands, as if it were a ball that was about to be snatched from him.

"I thought you were gonna take us away someplace," Mooly said plaintively. "To the mountains or somethin'."

"Shut up, pie-face. Can't you see he's thinkin'?"

But what was he to think about? Drained already from losing Julan, he had no more resources. He sat down heavily on the ground. It was cold and damp, but he scarcely noticed. He had realized this might happen, had steeled himself to leave Linnie. His first loyalty was to the nulls. Yet he found that he could not desert her.

"We could find someplace to hide and wait," Gairth suggested. "Maybe by tomorrow they'll figure we're gone, so they'll only leave a couple of proctors watching her."

"Maybe. I'd rather not wait that long. Certainly not in town."

"Well, then let's get out of town and come back tomorrow night."

"We may have to do that. But there's something I want to try. First we need a coach." A four-seater, at least. Danlo cast about in the ktess. A coach might be parked nearby, but unless somebody was actively thinking of it, he could spend half an hour sorting through their memories without stumbling upon it. Nothing, nothing, nothing. Then the man standing at the nearest corner wheeled in his surveillance, and his eyes flicked across a curve of glass and metal. Yes—the rear of a vehicle protruded beside a house. "Wait here." Danlo knelt and crawled forward on his belly until he could see the man at the corner. He watched with his eyes and tried to correlate what he was seeing directly with what he was seeing through the ktess. Ah—the coach was in the block to the southwest of the intersection. They would have to cross one street, in clear view, to get to it.

He crawled back to the boys, stood up, and brushed himself off. "Can either of you drive a coach?"

Gairth shook his head. Mooly shrugged indecisively. "I guess I could. I done it a couple of times," he said. "But you can drive, can't you?"

"I won't be able to, not until we get out of town. Come on." Danlo led the way back through the yard and up over another fence. They emerged beside a street that crossed the previous street at right angles. This one was wider, a broad tree-lined boulevard. Two watchers were in view, one at either end of the block. "We're going to have to get across," Danlo said.

Gairth studied the watchers. "We'll never make it," he said. "Even if we could run with no noise, there's not enough time while both their backs are turned."

"I'm going to try something. When I give the signal, I want you to both run across. Run as quiet as you can, and wait for me in the lane between those two houses."

Gairth looked distinctly dubious, but crouched in starting position for a sprint. Mooly's hands clenched and unclenched. "I know they're gonna catch us," he said. "I just want you to know, I appreciate what you're tryin' to do for us. I don't know why you're doin' it, but I'm glad."

"You just do as well as you can," Danlo told him. "We're not caught yet. Ready?" Both boys nodded. Danlo closed his eyes and sought out the men at the nearest corners. Holding two of them in mind at once was easier than he had expected. He waited patiently until a moment when both of their backs were turned, and then gently rode in upon them, slowing their sense of time, draining away the rhythm of their turning. He twitched his hand vigorously without opening his eyes, and heard soft footsteps dashing away.

He held the men in suspended motion for as long as he dared.

One of them was sleepy, and would happily have stood unmoving for an hour, but the other was restive. A twinge of suspicion lurked at the edge of his mind, threatening to surface. Danlo stilled the suspicion for a few seconds, and then let them both go. They went back to rotating as if they had never paused. The street between them was empty.

He drifted back toward the bright knot of activity in the proctor station. Pain and confusion exploded toward him. He found Pal Cottis's mind, dipped into it, and looked out through Pal's eyes. One of the joddies was bleeding from a long scratch down the side of his face. Beyond him, Linnie crouched in a corner, her eyes wild, fingers stiffened into claws. Three of the proctors advanced on her warily.

Trembling, Danlo restrained himself. The station room was full of joddies. He could only destroy whatever chance he had by trying to help her now. In a few minutes, when the coach was in position to pick her up. . . .

He returned his attention to the watchers at the corners. Did he dare play the same trick again? No—a joddie was monitoring the grid of watchers, and had nudged them all to keep to the rhythm. What, then? They were looking for a tall, thin man and two boys. Could he arrange their minds so that they didn't see a tall, thin man? What about a short, plump woman? He conjured up his memories of the farm woman who had fed him on his first day back among the Body, her round shape and the placid warmth of her ktess. He concentrated, wrapping himself as completely as he could in the other personality. Armored in it, he touched the watchers' visual centers, overlaying the impressions coming from their eyes with another set. Then he stepped boldly out and walked slowly, complacently across the street.

Both men saw him without seeing him, and turned away, satisfied. He slipped into the lane on the other side, straightened his shoulders, and let out a shaky breath.

Gairth and Mooly stared at him, mouths agape. "How did you do that?" Gairth demanded. "Nobody but a joddie could do something like that."

"I'm doing things that I never thought I could. I guess when you don't have any choice. . . . Come on, we've got to get that coach."

The boxy six-passenger vehicle glowed dull silver in the light from a nearby window. Danlo climbed in behind the boys and eased the door shut. "Do you think you can drive this?" he whispered.

Mooly looked at the controls with an unconvincing mixture of bravado and discomfort. "It's, ah, not exactly like the one I drove," he said. "I guess I can do it, though. What are we gonna do? We're not gonna go back into the station, are we?"

"I hope not."

"I'm not going back in there," Gairth said stubbornly. "I'm starting to think it would be neat to stay alive. I think we ought to just let them do whatever they like with the madwoman. Why do we need her? We can get out of town while they're busy worrying about her."

"There has been enough killing," Danlo said wearily.

"Who says they're gonna kill her? They'll probably just put her with the other ones, and keep on studying them like they've been doing."

"Eventually they'll kill them all," Danlo said. "And I *cannot* stand by while anybody else is killed. Do you understand that?"

"People get killed all the time."

"I'm only responsible for the deaths that I could have prevented."

"So you're gonna get us all killed. That's really smart."

"Keep your voice down. There are ears in that house." Danlo tilted his head toward the nearest dwelling, which lay a scant twenty feet beyond the coach. "If you need a more practical reason, consider this: We have twice the chance of surviving next winter if she's with us. Five times the chance." He held up his hand so that Gairth could see the scars. "Wild dogs. They run in packs. They would have torn me to pieces. She knows how to build weapons. I don't."

Gairth would not meet his eyes. "I still think it's a bean-brain idea."

"I can't force you to do anything. But I can walk away and leave you. You won't get far before the proctors find you. You can't even cross the street without my help. And she's a good person. I think you might like her."

"I want to try," Mooly said. "If you say we got to do it, I say let's try." He nudged the other boy's shoulder. "Come on Gairth."

Gairth scowled and rolled his eyes, as if he couldn't believe what he was hearing. "Okay, yeah. You did it for us, I guess we can do the same thing for her. Or try."

Chapter ║ 21

MOOLY'S hands were slick on the steering wheel. He had been sort of exaggerating a little about knowing how to drive. He had felt sure they would be caught before the crazy old man could find them a coach, and just as sure that the old man wouldn't really let him drive it. But he didn't want to let on that he had been lying. Also, he didn't want to disappoint the old man—well, not really old, but a lot older than Mooly—after he had gone to all that trouble to get them out of the station, and after Mooly had nearly fluffed the whole thing by waking his mom up, which had, he admitted to himself, been a real bonehead move. Anyway, Mooly had sat in the front passenger seat plenty of times and watched the coach driver work the pedals, and it didn't look that hard. This one would make the coach go forward, and this other one would make it stop. Now where was the switch to turn on the motor? The switch had to be here somewhere, but there were lots of switches. The public coaches had always been turned on already when he got on board.

"Once we get rolling," Danlo said, "I won't be able to keep them from seeing us. So I'm going to try something else. It will take all my concentration, so don't be surprised if I just sit here with my eyes closed. I'll be busy. Try not to distract me. What I want you to do is drive straight down to the proctor station, go in, and find Linnie—that's the wild woman. Tell her you're with me. Say 'Danlo friend.' She'll understand that. Pick up her bow and arrows, if you see them, but don't waste time looking for them. They'll look like sticks. The bow is a curved stick with a string on it, and the arrows are sticks with feathers."

"If somebody tries to stop us," Gairth said, "I'll smack 'em a good one."

"No," Danlo said firmly. "Do whatever you can to get around them, but please—don't hurt anybody. If I ken somebody trying to stop you, I'll try to confuse them or trip them, but I don't know how well I'll be able to manage. I've never tried anything like this before. You understand what to do?"

Gairth nodded eagerly, but Mooly was uncertain. "What if

something happens? What if they've taken her downstairs and locked her up?''

''You're on your own. If I can speak to you through another mouth, I will, but don't count on it.'' Danlo looked tired. ''Let's get started.''

Mooly tried a switch at random. A jet of soapy water squirted on the windshield.

Danlo and Gairth looked at him. He felt his face burning. ''Wrong one,'' he said.

He found the wiper switch and got the water wiped away. He also found the switches for adjusting the angles of the seats, turning the interior lights on and off, raising and lowering the windows, and starting and stopping the music. ''Just getting used to where everything is,'' he said. Eventually he located the starter switch, and the motor purred to life. He touched the speed pedal as lightly as he could. The motor raced, but the coach failed to move.

''I think you have to release the brake,'' Danlo said. ''And you'd better put it in reverse, if you don't want to crash through that fence.''

''Okay. Yeah. I knew that.''

''You might want to turn on the headlights too,'' Gairth added.

Mooly fiddled with the gear lever until he found a position where the engine strained against the brake in the other direction. Then he unlocked the brake. With an abrupt lurch, the coach leaped backward into the middle of the street. Mooly stomped on the stop pedal, and the coach rocked to a halt. He looked to Danlo for advice, but Danlo had closed his eyes and sagged sideways in his seat, as if he were asleep.

''Put it in gear,'' Gairth said, pounding with his palms on the back of the seat. ''Let's get rolling.''

The coach surged forward. Mooly hunched over the wheel and peered out at the night. At the last possible second he realized that the innocent mound of clothing lying motionless in the center of the intersection was the body of one of the watchers. He jerked on the wheel, and the coach careened around the inert form. ''Slow down!'' Gairth cried. ''Slow down!'' Mooly put his foot on the stop pedal, and the tires screeched on the pavement. Two tires bounced up over the curb and back down. He wrestled with the wheel and got the coach aimed more or less down the center of the street.

"Some driver you are," Gairth said disgustedly. "Why don't you pull over and let me try?"

"No way! He said for me to do it."

At the next corner they passed another fallen figure. "You think they're dead?" Mooly asked.

"Nah," Gairth said. "You heard what he said about hurtin' people. He's just makin' 'em go to sleep or something."

In the half-dozen blocks back to the proctor station, they passed nobody who was awake. Mooly risked taking his eyes off the street to glance back at Danlo. The old man had slumped lower when they hit the curb. His face was waxy. "Is he okay?" Mooly said. "He looks sick."

"What do you want me to do, take his pulse? He said for us not to distract him."

The coach rocked to a halt behind the proctor station, a few yards from the garden gate. Gairth popped the door open and jumped out. Mooly paused to look at Danlo. "I sure hope you know what you're doin', old man," he said softly.

They dashed across the garden, but stopped in alarm when a joddie crossed the path between them and the lighted rear door of the station. They stood frozen until the joddie passed from view among the fruit trees. Mooly moaned. "What are we gonna do? They're gonna be too strong for him, I just know it. We better go back to the coach and wait until everybody is asleep."

The joddie crossed the path again. He was weaving drunkenly, and his arms windmilled. High, wordless sounds escaped his lips.

"Come on," Gairth said, gripping Mooly's elbow. "Whatever he's doin', it's workin'. That guy's not gonna stop us."

They made a wide circle around the joddie and peered cautiously through the door. One man lay fallen just inside; they had to step over him. Several others beyond him were in the same state. A joddie sat in a chair against the wall. His eyes were open wide, and his tongue and jaw worked wordlessly. His fingers were making tiny convulsive motions in his lap.

"Here," Gairth said. "Take one of these." He had found the wild woman's bow and two containers of arrows.

The thunder of feet rumbled down the hall, accompanied by high cries of desperation or pain. Mooly tensed to run, but the commotion grew fainter, not louder. He stepped to the hall door and risked a look.

A knot of men had reached the far end of the hall, the front door of the station. Amid three red robes, half a dozen blue shirts, and a great many writhing arms, a flailing half-naked form was being carried. The front door banged open and the group disappeared from view.

"You think that was her they were carryin'?" Mooly asked.

"It wasn't the Egg Bunny."

"You think we oughta go after 'em?"

"Go ahead if you want to," Gairth said. "I'm gettin' outta here!"

Mooly hovered indecisively. He didn't want to let Danlo down, but whatever Danlo was doing to immobilize the men in the station, it obviously wasn't working as well as it ought to, if a bunch of them could run off. So probably Gairth was right. Behind him he heard scuffling, and turned. One of the fallen proctors had gotten to his feet; he clamped a meaty hand on Gairth's collar. The bow and arrows clattered to the floor. Another proctor was on his knees, blinking groggily and shaking his head. Mooly scooped up the bow and brought it around in a whistling arc that connected solidly with the side of the first proctor's head. The bow cracked, and the man staggered backward. Gairth wriggled free. Not stopping to grab the arrows, Mooly slipped between the two proctors and followed Gairth to the back door. He was still holding the bow, but it had snapped in the middle, so he cast it aside.

They sprinted across the garden. Mooly was imagining that the coach would be gone, or surrounded by proctors, but when they burst out of the gate, there it was, cool and inviting under the street light, door still standing open. He banged his knee scrambling in. As he leaned over the seat to look at Danlo, the gate slammed open again and three proctors rushed toward the coach.

"Yikes!" Gairth crowded in behind Mooly. "Drive, drive, drive!" Mooly's feet fumbled on the pedals, a moment that seemed to stretch out forever. The coach leaped forward as one proctor's arm plunged through the open door. Mooly was too busy steering to see what happened to the arm or its owner. When he looked around, Gairth was reaching out carefully over the blur of pavement to bring the door shut. In the rearview mirror, the proctors were running uselessly after the coach, falling behind.

"I should have kenned it sooner." Danlo's voice was a hoarse croak. "There was no need to put you in danger, but I was busy dealing with the watchers. Even before they saw that we were coming, they were getting ready to move her."

"Should we follow them?"

"They put her in one of the fast coaches," Danlo said. "We'll never catch them."

"We can try." Mooly knew the suggestion was hollow, but he hated to hear anybody sound so discouraged. "Anyway, I have to drive somewhere. Where should we go?"

"What does it matter? Useless, useless."

"Do you want to head for Serameno?" Mooly demanded. "Or toward the mountains? You have to tell me what to do!" But Danlo said nothing. Mooly felt abandoned. Though he had known this old man with the crazy ideas less than an hour, he had started to rely on him. Danlo could do things that were impossible, unthinkable. But Mooly couldn't, not by himself.

Ahead, a group of men, seven or eight, stepped out into the street. Mooly bore down on them without slowing. "Hey, are you gonna do something? Get them out of the way!" Danlo seemed not to hear, and Mooly had no time to repeat the request. The men were strung out across the street, not leaving enough room for the coach to go around on either side. Evidently they trusted that he wouldn't actually drive over any of them, which was odd considering that he had hit the proctor in the head with the bow, but maybe the proctor was still unconscious—or dead—and nobody knew about it yet. The men were right, though. Mooly didn't want to hurt them. He slowed and stopped, and they ran toward the coach. He put it into reverse and started backing up. It was hard to steer while backing up. The coach careened from one side of the street to the other, and it made so little speed that the men were closing the gap. He backed onto a lawn so he could turn around, cranked the wheel hard, and headed back the way they had come. But before he could reach the end of the block, another pack of men appeared ahead, larger than the first one. They spread out across the street, stretching their arms out toward one another. Since he had no other choice, Mooly aimed right down the middle, and at the last possible moment the men directly in his path scattered and leaped aside. He heard, or felt, a soft *thwup*, as if the front fender had brushed a shoulder or a hip. Danlo said, "Ouch!" In the rearview mirror one man had sprawled on the pavement, and others were running to his aid.

"It's his own fault," Mooly said, trying to smother the feeling of guilt.

"The joddies may not have left him any choice," Danlo said.

Mooly took a couple of corners at random. The sentinels were no longer posted in the centers of the intersections, and no more

groups emerged to block the coach, but one or two people stood at
every corner and watched them pass. Some of the people shouted
and waved their arms. The fugitives were in a fishbowl; wherever
they turned, eyes followed them. Mooly wondered whether Danlo
had gotten tired of putting everybody to sleep, or whether he
couldn't because the joddies had figured out how to stop him, or
whether he just didn't care anymore, now that the wild woman had
been taken. But Mooly was afraid to ask. "I still think we should
go after your friend," he said. "They have to stop eventually,
don't they? Why don't we follow along and catch them when
they're off guard? Where are they taking her, did you find that
out?"

"Serameno. To the Jewel of the One."

Gairth said, "To keep her with the other wild women. Sure."

"This is all because of my own poor judgment," Danlo said.
"We could have gone to Serameno first, and tried to free Linnie's
companions before the One was alerted. If we had succeeded,
Linnie would have had others standing by her when she was
discovered. I judged that entering the Jewel would be too difficult.
And that was before I became known. Now it's impossible."

"I'm glad you decided to help us first," Gairth said. "If you
hadn't, we would have been dead before you got around to us."

"That was my thinking too." Danlo sighed. "I'm only one
man. I can't stop all the killing by myself. Now it appears that I
won't be able to stop any of— Brace yourselves. More trouble."
Another coach emerged from a side street just behind them and
raced after them.

"Do something!" Mooly tried to press down harder on the
pedal, but his foot was already jammed to the floor.

"I'm trying. They've got—" The other vehicle collided jar-
ringly with the coach's right rear, and Mooly had to fight the
wheel to keep from running up the sidewalk into a tree. As he
rolled on at top speed, the rear wheels shuddered and shook. He
cast a terrified glance back over his shoulder. The other coach was
following them. It swung to the side to come around them.

"They're gaining on us," Mooly shouted. He could guess why
Danlo was having trouble diverting the other driver; he had
glimpsed two joddies riding in the passenger seats.

The other coach swung sideways and nudged them, not gently,
toward the curb. Ahead loomed a narrow bridge across a canal.
Mooly saw that he would have to stop to avoid being run into the
bridge rail. He swung the wheel the other way, forcing the second

coach toward the opposite rail. Metal banged against metal with a teeth-snapping impact, clashed again grindingly. Brakes squealed, and the other coach smacked solidly into the rail. Over his shoulder Mooly saw slats flying as the vehicle tilted and slid into the canal.

Gairth whooped. "All right! Great driving!"

Mooly swung the coach onto the main road that led east toward Grawly. "We're almost to the edge of town," he said. The road unfolded before them, smooth and empty in the moonlight. Blocks of houses on either side alternated with patches of orchard.

"We're gonna make it!" Gairth said.

"Yeah," Mooly said, "if the wheels don't fall off." The coach was vibrating rather alarmingly.

"You're right," Danlo said. "We need a better coach. Turn off on one of these streets."

"I don't know if we ought to," Mooly said. "Maybe we should just keep going. What if they send three coaches after us at once? Last time we got lucky."

"We don't have any choice. Even if this one doesn't fall apart, they know what it looks like."

"And they can ken you," Gairth said. "What's the difference what it looks like?"

"They can't ken me. Not always. I can block them, or make them think I'm somebody else. Turn here."

"I guess you're right." Mooly swung the coach into the next side street. The rear wheels shuddered. He watched the cross streets nervously for more vehicles. In his imagination they leaped at him at every corner, but the street remained empty. They passed more groups of watchers, but none tried to stop them. A fire horn was hooting in the distance.

"Down that way." Danlo pointed. "There's one." Another six-passenger coach, this one parked at the curb.

"If we just switch," Gairth said, "they'll know which one we took when they find this one. What we've got to do is leave this one somewhere else."

"Useless," Danlo said. "Look." The front doors of houses were flying open on both sides of the street. People rushed toward them. Mooly jammed down on the stop pedal, and the damaged coach screeched to a halt beside the new one. A young woman brandishing a garden rake reached them first. She swung the rake hard at the coach window. The tines whacked against the clear plastic. As she brought the rake up for a second blow, Danlo shut his eyes. She dropped to the pavement, and the rake clattered free.

Those nearest the coach swooned, but more were running forward behind them. Mooly clenched his hands, afraid to open the door. The circle of sleep widened. Danlo was breathing raggedly. People appeared at the corner in threes and fours, running toward them, then stumbled and fell and lay quiet. A couple of coaches appeared and proctors tumbled out, but they too succumbed before they could reach the fugitives. The Body was throwing a mob at them, but Danlo was neutralizing it. When Mooly saw that nobody was getting near them, he opened the door cautiously and slid out. "Come on," he said.

"He's not movin'," Gairth reported.

"Well, then we gotta carry him." Mooly climbed into the back of the coach. He got one of Danlo's arms draped over his shoulder, and the two boys maneuvered Danlo's dead weight out onto the street. Danlo swayed and moaned. "In the rear seat. Come on." Gairth fumbled at the door of the new coach, but Mooly said, "No, forget it."

"What do you mean?"

"Look for yourself." Mooly indicated the street around them. A maze of bodies lay sprawled in all directions. "No way we're gonna get out of here without driving right over people." The idea of hard tires rolling over soft bodies, the crunch of bones, didn't appeal to him. "We'll have to run."

"With him like this?" Gairth seemed close to tears. "We can't even *walk*."

A new coach appeared at the next intersection. More proctors, Mooly figured—but when the door popped open, nobody spilled out. The driver waved at them. Beckoned. "With her," Danlo mumbled. Mooly and Gairth looked at one another, perplexed.

A girl got out of the new coach and dashed toward them, treading lightly around the sprawled bodies. Long blond hair streamed out behind her. "Come on!" she called. "What are you waiting for?"

"I think she wants to help us," Gairth said.

Though it was hard to be certain in the dim light from the nearby houses, Mooly had the impression that the blond girl was very beautiful. "I'll get his legs," she said, squatting. "You guys get the rest of him." Among the three of them they hoisted Danlo and picked their way back toward the girl's coach at an awkward trot.

Gairth said, "You're not—are you like us?"

"Am I a null? No."

"Then why are you—?"

"I'll explain later. Let's get him in the back. Careful." They slid Danlo into the rear seat of the girl's coach, and Gairth climbed in beside him.

The girl turned to Mooly. She was definitely beautiful. "You're Mooly Farn, right? I'm Ainne Murrinder." She held up her palm. Her hand was small and firm and cool, and Mooly flushed, feeling that his was hopelessly pudgy and sweaty. Ainne seemed not to notice. "You're going to have to drive some more. He needs help."

"He's okay, isn't he?"

"He's fine. He's just busy. If I don't help him, things are going to get worse real fast. Let's get going."

"Sure. Whatever you say." Mooly got behind the wheel of the coach. He was relieved to find that the controls of this one were much like the controls of the other. The lights flared, the engine purred, and they slid away from the curb. "Just one thing: Where are we going?" Ainne didn't answer. Her eyes were already closed. "Hey! Where are we going?"

"Serameno," she murmured. Mooly swung the coach around and headed south.

"This is crazy," Gairth said.

"Yeah," Mooly said. "But fun. I think."

"Yeah." Gairth laughed. "Who woulda thought?"

Mooly kept stealing glances at Ainne. The blond hair hung in a loose halo around her face, and he caught a trace of perfume. She was definitely the most beautiful girl he had ever seen. Once in a while her face twitched. He wondered what she and Danlo were doing in the ktess. He felt jealous that they could share, and hopelessly inadequate. Even if he hadn't been a null, she would never have looked at him twice. But here they were, flying through the night together.

His eyes felt sandpapery. It must be after midnight. He yawned hugely. The streets were quiet. After a couple of wrong turns he reached the main north-south highway, the Innersay, and swung onto it. They passed the outskirts of town, and the last of the street lights slid away. The road stretched out straight through acre upon acre of field. Night receded from the little pool cast by the headlights, and closed in again swiftly behind.

Danlo groaned and sat up. "That's the worst of it," he said. "For a while, anyway."

"Plans?"

"You're my daughter," Danlo said. "I can change how they see my face. We can get into the city untroubled. These two under a blanket on the floor of the coach. The Joddirate will guess where we're going, and why, but they won't know how we'll strike, or when." He laughed bitterly. "*I* don't know how either. It's impossible. For a city the size of Serameno, multiply what we just went through by a hundred. For the Jewel itself— Oh. Turn here."

Mooly slowed the coach, and they jounced down off the pavement onto a gravel side road. "They've blocked the road up ahead," Danlo said. "A barricade of coaches. No way through. Your driving frightened them, so they pulled back to where they could mass their resources."

"Shouldn't we turn around and go some other way? Maybe up to the mountains?" Mooly didn't really want to go into Serameno. Now that they had a new ally, his interest in the wild woman had receded.

"They've blocked all the roads out of Yubasty," Ainne said.

The coach lurched up a little hill. In the distance, an irregular clot of lights showed where the highway was blocked. Figures milled in the glare. "Shut off the headlights," Danlo snapped. Mooly fumbled at the controls, and darkness engulfed the coach. "They saw us. No, it's all right."

"I can't drive in the dark," Mooly said. "We'll run into a ditch."

"This road only goes another half-mile anyway," Ainne said. "We may as well leave the coach here."

Mooly stopped the coach, and they all got out. He was glad to be done with driving for a while. His nerves were scraped raw. He stretched and took a deep breath of the night air. A blanket of stars glittered overhead. The others were making good time down the road, and he had to trot to catch up. "Hey, are we gonna walk all the way to Serameno?"

"Once we get past where they've blocked the road," Danlo said, "we should be able to find another coach. Unless they think to pool all the coaches, and set people watching them. If they do that, we'll have to arrange for one of the coach-watchers to be careless." Now that he had recovered from the shock of losing the wild woman, he seemed alert and confident again. Mooly wondered a little whether that might be only a show.

"More trouble," Ainne whispered. "Okay, you two. There's a farmhand up there watching the road. We're going to walk on the shoulder, in the grass, and he's going to think he's seeing a family of deer. So walk slow and quiet, like deer, and whatever you do, don't say a word!''

They went single file along the grass between the road and the fence, Ainne leading, then Gairth, then Danlo, Mooly bringing up the rear. At first Mooly didn't see the farmhand, but then a darker shape coalesced out of the darkness, leaning on a gatepost. The fugitives approached the watcher without changing their pace. Even though he had seen Danlo perform this trick earlier, Mooly's heart was hammering. The farmhand was smoking a pipe; the sweet, pungent smell of pipeweed drifted toward them, and when he scraped a match and applied it to the bowl, his face shone in the ruddy glow.

They would have to pass within ten feet of him. As they neared, he chuckled. ''Nice night for a stroll,'' he said softly. The back of Mooly's neck prickled, and his thighs tensed to run. ''Just mind you stay out of my garden,'' the man went on, ''or we'll have some nice roast venison for supper tomorrow.''

Mooly relaxed a little. He walked with his head down, and tried to avoid looking directly at the man. They passed the man, and went slowly on.

Gairth missed his footing in the grass, and stumbled and fell. ''Ouch! Damn! Oh—''

''Hey! What— Ohhh.'' The farmhand slumped to the ground.

''Too late,'' Ainne cried. ''They picked it up. Run!''

But when Gairth tried to stand, he stumbled again. ''Hurt my foot,'' he said.

''Lean on me,'' Danlo said. They climbed a low fence and set off across a field as fast as they could, Gairth limping awkwardly as Danlo hurried him along. The ground was uneven, and Mooly stumbled several times, but didn't fall.

In the distance, a low roar swirled. Ainne streaked ahead. ''Trees! Hurry!'' But the field was large, the thin fringe of trees a long way off. The roar got louder, and flashing lights pierced the sky. An airplane was approaching from the direction of the highway, flying low and slow, searchlights swinging in arcs across the fields. Mooly ran faster. ''Why not—make the pilot—sleep?'' he gasped.

''Then the plane crashes,'' Ainne called over her shoulder. ''People get killed.''

Mooly wasn't sure, by this time, that he cared whether people got killed, but it wasn't his decision. The plane got closer, the lights glared brighter. But then he was under the shelter of the trees. He stopped and turned to watch as Danlo helped Gairth, who was hopping on one foot, across the last few yards of open ground.

They stood huddled together while the plane's roaring downdraft made storms among the branches, while the glint of lights played like angry lightning in the clouds of stirred-up dust. Dead leaves swarmed around them like bees.

After a while the plane moved on, and Ainne said, "They didn't see us." Mooly looked down at her, and discovered that his arm was wrapped tight around her shoulders. Hers was around his waist. He flushed in embarrassment and hurriedly let her go. She smiled up at him, a sad little smile. "It's all right," she said. "I'm scared too."

Chapter || 22

"OH, and some wrapping bandage," the vintner said. "My eight-year-old fell out of a tree." He shook his head bemusedly. *Children chaos hopeless.* "Twisted his ankle."

Confusion. "Think we've got some," the shopkeeper said. "But you said you're from Lirmorr. You came all the way to Serameno for a bandage?" The shopkeeper, a small man with a sharp face and a birdlike tilt of the head, paused with his hand, which held a fine stainless-steel sheath knife, suspended over the sack he was packing for his customers.

"Camped by the river," the vintner said. "Family trip. Fell just this morning."

The vintner's daughter, sixteen years old and improbably beautiful with her long blond hair and finely chiseled features—though in the shopkeeper's wistful view all sixteen-year-old girls were improbably beautiful—came up bearing a collapsible fishing pole and a kit with hooks and line, floats and flies and sinkers. It was the finest fishing kit in the shop, and the shopkeeper could not stifle a pang of regret that it was being looked at by out-of-towners rather than by one of his regulars. The vintner's daughter, who was really quite self-possessed, pretended not to have noticed the inharmonious feelings. "You said you'd show me how to fish, Daddy."

"Did I? Well, bring it along. If we don't get the use of it that it deserves, we can always bring it back." He patted her shoulder indulgently, and she handed the pole and kit to the shopkeeper, who found room for them in the sack. The vintner, except for his stiffly rayed snow-white hair and kindly demeanor, looked rather like the fiendish Danlo Ree, whose face had been shared in a barrage of sendings since yesterday morning. It was on the tip of the shopkeeper's tongue to mention this resemblance, but a moment later he couldn't remember what he had been about to say. Nothing important, surely. He hunted up a roll of wrapping bandage and put it in the sack. "Anything else?"

"No, I think not. Many thanks, goodman shopkeeper. You are admirably supplied."

The shopkeeper inclined his head. "My pleasure." As the vintner and his daughter passed out into the street, the shopkeeper tugged at his earlobe. Now who had that fellow reminded him of?

Danlo handed the sack to Ainne, smoothed back his hair, and pulled a wide-brimmed hat from a pocket. After snapping the hat open, he adjusted it at a rakish angle that screened the upper half of his face from view. She handed the sack back to him and they proceeded down the street at a sedate pace. "Amazing how distorted they've got my face," he said softly. "You'd think I'm eating the children."

"The whole thing," Ainne said. *Stirring/burst.* "Hornet's nest."

They had waited all day yesterday, hidden in a haystack, while mobs of searchers prowled the fields around Yubasty. Hordes of wild women coursed through the Body's imaginings, crept invisibly toward proctor stations from one end of the Valley to the other. Nulls had been reported missing from stations in two more towns, which mystified Danlo but gave him some comfort. Possibly he was not alone in wanting the slaughter to end; possibly others, emboldened by his action, had taken action of their own. More likely, fantasies were mingling in the ktess with fact. That pleased him as well. "The more they imagine," he said, "the more likely they are to misguess what we're about. Whole city's on edge. Can't remember when traffic was this bad." The street was a snarl of coaches, carts, bicycles. Tempers were frayed.

"You've been away," Ainne said.

"So have you." *Child missing.*

"Been thinking about that. My mother has high hopes for me." *Civil Council. Nausea.* "Not sure she knows you were the one that came to the farm. Even if she does, she might keep quiet hoping I'll come home without ever connecting with you—or, if

we do connect, that I'll get over my impetuousness without it
becoming known. She won't be able to keep it from Uncle Foony,
but he's on her side. And she knows I can keep secrets. I can see
how she'd look at it. She'd think that nobody need know who
might later influence my future.''

"Do you want to keep it secret?"

Ainne shared disgust, and a vision of a man on his hands and
knees in a garden clutching a dinner fork in one hand and a fan in
the other. It was a picture from a children's tale—"The Man Who
Tried to Help the Seed Grow"—about lack of faith. Danlo
acknowledged the rebuke, and she changed the subject: "That's
the tools, and the clothes, and the supplies. We can't carry any
more than we've got now."

"Hoping we won't have to carry it all."

"Always hope. Ready for next?"

Uneasiness. Danlo shared a vision of stepping off a cliff into
a fog-filled abyss.

Ainne said. "No other way down."

Confidence restore need.

Long wait/elsewhere look. "It's got some chance of working.
You said it last night: The biggest factor we've got in our
favor—the only factor, almost—is that they've never had to face
anything like this before. They have no idea what to expect, or
what to do about it. So we try something crazy. The crazier it is,
the further off balance we throw them, and the better chance we've
got. Olivia knows I can't take on the whole Council of the One
when they're in their usual state of composure. Not even sure how
powerful they are—I've always stayed away from them. You
they'd snap like a twig."

The vintner and his daughter boarded a public coach and rode
out to the warehouse district, sitting in companionable silence and
exchanging only a few polite flickers of thought with their fellow
passengers. As the clean, orderly streets rolled by, Danlo felt a
nostalgic ache. He had lived in Serameno for twenty years, when
he was not travelling. He considered the city his home. Yet
suddenly he was a stranger.

At a corner where farm produce trucks rumbled past, they
disembarked. When the coach had glided away, they set off down
an alley between two rather grimy buildings. From the ktess they
knew no fugitive nulls had been found, so they were not surprised
when they rounded the end of the building and found the truck
parked where they had left it. They had appropriated it before

dawn from a truck yard along the highway. It was large, ancient but well maintained, its bed outfitted with open cages of wire mesh for hauling live animals—pigs or turkeys, probably. The cages were too big for rabbits but not big enough for sheep.

"Tarp," Danlo said.

"I'll look." Ainne cast her mind outward.

Danlo stepped up into the cab and lifted the sack of equipment over the back of the seat. "Last load," he said. "Get it stowed in the backpacks."

Gairth's head poked up from beneath a blanket. "About time you got back. We're *suffocating* in here. Can we sit up for a minute?"

Danlo scanned the area. Stockers and counters in the nearby buildings. The truck was visible from several windows, but no eyes were turned their way. "All clear."

Mooly sat up, his hair rumpled. "Can I get out and stretch my legs? I got a bad cramp."

"Too risky. After dark."

Ainne climbed into the cab. "Found a good one. Down about three blocks. Big enough to cover the whole thing, and they haven't used it in so long they'd almost forgotten it's there. Best of all, it smells of tar. That's why they don't use it."

"Get them to bring it outside?"

"Too big for two of us to lift," she said.

"We can't wait for dark. Have to have them load it for us, drive out to some isolated spot where the boys can help lift it over the top."

Ainne nodded. "I'll drive." *You invisible.*

Danlo climbed behind the seat and hunkered down under the blanket with Mooly and Gairth. They were right—on such a warm day it was very stuffy under the blanket, especially given the oppressive residue of animal manure and the close-pressed bodies of two boys who had hiked for miles the night before last and not changed their clothes since. It reminded Danlo uncomfortably of being herded and penned up by the wild women. He stilled his mind, so that to any onlooker Ainne would seem to be alone in the truck.

The truck swayed and creaked. He watched through Ainne's eyes as she rounded a corner and rolled up beside two broad-shouldered stockers, who were carrying the ends of a long rolled tarpaulin. She gave them her brightest smile and said, "That's perfect! Can you slide it in the back for me?"

"Glad to, missy." The truck creaked some more. One of the stockers was curious why a young girl would be driving a truck full of empty animal cages. A moment later, he was not curious.

Once they were rolling again, Danlo crawled out from behind the seat, leaving the boys to their misery. While Ainne concentrated on driving, he let his mind roam. They entered a main boulevard. "There's one," he said, nodding toward a side street where the joyful fantasies of a waking dreamer flickered through the ktess. A minute later, "Another down that way."

Abundance.

They had to drive east for half an hour to find a spot screened by a stand of eucalyptus trees, where Mooly and Gairth could get out. Mooly stamped up and down waving his arms. Gairth tried to walk, winced, and leaned on a fender while he held one foot clear of the ground. Ainne got out the bandage and efficiently set about wrapping his injured ankle. Mooly looked at her kneeling before the other boy, flushed, and stalked away into the trees. When he came back, Danlo enlisted his help dragging the tarpaulin out of the truck. Then Mooly and Ainne climbed the latticework of cages, and Danlo and Gairth handed up two corners of the tarp. When they had it arranged smoothly over the tops of the cages, they tied the edges to the bed of the truck. They left the rear tied at only a couple of spots, so that they could get in and out easily. Gairth slipped inside. "It's gonna be hot in here," his muffled voice reported. "Hotter than in the cab." He lifted the flap and peered out. "And the stench is pretty bad."

"Good." Danlo rubbed his hands together. "You can ride back there, or in the cab. At least there's room back there to stretch out. But once we get back to town you won't be able to switch back and forth."

"Cab," Gairth said. "I want to know what's goin' on."

"Cab," Mooly agreed. So they arranged themselves under the blanket behind the seats, and the truck rolled back toward Serameno.

They left the highway and cruised down a street of small shops. Danlo was sitting up beside Ainne now. They both kenned the dreamer before they saw his sparkling robe. He was spinning out a rapidly shifting dream of flying through waterfalls, of old comfortable rooms, of machines that made waterfalls and the antique brass levers and dials on the machines. The waterfall became a foaming river. Ducks that were children quacked and splashed.

Half a dozen people had gathered around the dreamer to bask in his phantasmagoric effusion. One by one Danlo joined them and reminded them of appointments elsewhere, teased a flicker of boredom until it flamed into restlessness. The little throng dispersed, leaving the dreamer swaying by himself on the sidewalk.

Danlo hopped down out of the cab, and Ainne drove on. He approached the dreamer, whose eyes were slits in a blissful face. The warmth of the visions was enticing, but Danlo ignored it. He touched the dreamer's elbow. *Sadness lift in dear one. Come with.*

The dreamer said, "Mmmmm." His head swung in slow easy arcs from side to side. He allowed Danlo to steer him down the street and around the corner.

The truck stood waiting, the rear flap lifted. Danlo and the dreamer sat on the rear bumper, the dreamer waiting patiently for whoever was to come and be soothed. At a moment when nobody was in sight, Danlo put the dreamer into a sudden dreamless sleep and tipped his body back into the truck. Ainne grasped him under the arms and dragged him out of sight.

Danlo scrambled into the truck and let the flap down. In the fragrant half-darkness they opened one of the animal cages and stuffed the dreamer into it. They had to tuck his knees up beneath his chin and fold his elbows tight.

Ainne had a thought. "Naked?"

"Naked would be better, yes." When the dreamer awoke, they wanted him to be in as much distress as possible. So they hauled the recumbent form out and removed the robe. The dreamer's flesh was pasty, as if he ate only sweets and never exercised. Lying on his side in the cage, he looked so pitiful that Danlo felt a pang of remorse.

"We're not going to hurt them," Ainne said.

"To a dreamer, flesh-pain may be less real than other kinds."

"They can be healed. There's no way to heal beheading."

They slipped under the flap and got back into the cab. "Better if your face isn't seen," Ainne said. "Let me get the next one." So Danlo drove. When they spotted another dreamer, Ainne jumped down and sent his audience drifting away while Danlo found a quiet spot for the truck and kept the first dreamer firmly asleep. During the course of the afternoon they gathered a total of seven in this manner, five men and two women, and packed them all naked into the cages. The dreamers were restive in the heat and bad air, and Danlo had to flit from mind to mind to keep them from rousing.

Their search brought them to the curving drive through a wooded park near the river. Traffic was light, and broad oaks and rolling lawn stretched out in both directions. Families strolled in the late afternoon glow, and smoke from barbecues tinged the air. "Hungry," Ainne said. "Enough?"

"Twenty might not be enough. Let's see if we can find one or two more before dark."

Around the next curve the soft spell of a dreamer beckoned. Danlo found a place to park, and Ainne hopped out and disappeared down a path. He got out and untied the rear flap. His wait was interrupted by her summons: *Quick-come. Peculiarity.* He kenned her excitement, and wariness. He poked his head back into the cab. "Stay down, boys," he said. "Back in a minute."

"What's goin' on?" Mooly asked. "Somethin' wrong?"

"Don't know." He pulled the wide-brimmed hat low and loped down the path, slowing to a walk when a group of picnickers saw him and asked, *Emergency? Assistance need?*

Decline with thanks. Where was she? There. The dreamer sat placidly on the ground beneath a tree, but Ainne was not alone with him. Standing next to her was a skinny, bald man in his fifties. The bald man's eyes had a wary, haunted look. He was dressed in an ordinary shirt and trousers, and he was barefoot. His fringe of gray hair was shorn so close that Danlo took him at first for a vacuist. When he kenned the man he recoiled in confusion, and nearly lost his grip on the dreamers in the truck. The man had the mind of a very frightened twelve-year-old boy. Also, he was a joddie.

Ainne looked pleased. "His name's Eppy. Thought you might like to meet him. Eppy, this is—"

"Dappa Snee." Danlo held out his upraised palm, and after a worried moment the bald man pressed his palm against it. "We won't hurt you, Eppy." Danlo looked a question at Ainne: *What?*

Deep-ken.

Sleepers watch. After letting Ainne take over the monitoring of the bodies in the truck, Danlo delved deeper into Eppy's mind. Eppy offered no resistance. He was an open book.

The story, what little Danlo could ken, was as bizarre as anything he had ever encountered. Eppy might be a grave danger to them, but he might just as easily be a treasure of incalculable value. He knew where the captured women were being kept! For forty years an iron discipline had held his mind in two separate compartments, the outer never knowing that the inner existed. Somehow that discipline had crumbled, leaving him dazed and disoriented. At any moment he might flip back into his other state, become a powerful joddie named Epigrass. But at the moment, he was a little boy. So they left the dreamer where he sat dawdling, spraying the ktess with languid fireworks and snatches of song, and led Eppy back toward the truck. He went with them trustingly. "Ever since yesterday I've been walking around the city," he said softly. "This is Serameno, isn't it? I've never been here. I mean, I've read all about it a hundred times, but it doesn't. . . . When I came across that man back there, all the pretty things he was thinking, I started to feel better. I've been following him all day. I still don't see what could have happened. I was in my tree house reading, and then all of a sudden—" He held out blue-veined hands. "Look at me. I'm *old*."

They shepherded him into the cab of the truck, where he perched between them, hunched forward, hugging his knees. "I turned into a character in a book I was reading," he said in a desolate tone. "How can something like that happen?"

Danlo calmed him while Ainne probed his mind. Behind the seat something rustled, but Eppy didn't notice. Several minutes passed before Ainne said, "It wasn't a book. You did something in your mind, a long time ago, to keep a part of yourself safe. After you did it, you deliberately forgot that you did it. That was the only way to keep it safe. The part of you that was kept safe is called Eppy."

"*I'm* Eppy."

"That's right. You're Epigrass, and you're Eppy. You're a joddie, and you're the boy who grew up to become the joddie." *Sameness* "There's only one of you. All the things you read in the book, they were really happening, just at the moment when you read about them."

"It was a *history* book." Eppy was close to tears. Then he frowned, and twisted his neck to look back. "Why are all those people sleeping in the back of the truck? They're not comfortable."

"We'll let them out before long." *Overriding need.* "Maybe you could help us too, Eppy. Do you remember reading about the wild women?"

Eppy nodded. "Sure. Lots. I liked them."

"How did you feel when you saw them locked up?"

"I didn't like it. I told Epigr— I wished for— I was trying to— I don't know."

Danlo sorted through the joddie's cloud of memories. "That's right. You suggested to Epigrass that he try to help them. And he did. He took your suggestion. Do you remember? He got them some cookies, and later a bath and fresh clothes."

"Yeah. That was fun!"

"The reason he took your suggestion," Danlo said, "is because he's you. He's not a character in a book. He never was. The 'book' was his way of letting you share his life. After he tried to help the women, the One summoned him. Do you remember that?"

Eppy pressed his eyes shut and shuddered.

"It's all right," Ainne said. She put her arm across the joddie's shoulders.

"I almost—he almost— It was all I could do to get out of there without them kenning. I was so— Eppy was— How can I explain it? I don't know what words to use."

"Maybe it's time for you to become one person again," Ainne said gently.

Epigrass started crying. "I'm—he's—ohh." He sobbed and snuffled and choked and coughed. Danlo and Ainne sat with their arms around him, shared the pain, and guided him in discovering himself. The sun set in a red blaze, and twilight deepened around the truck. After a while he wiped his face with his hands and said, "I never knew. All those years and I never knew he was there, inside me. It wasn't the women that caused the contagion of individualism. They only accelerated it. I started it myself."

"It's not a contagion," Danlo said. "The Body needs *more* individualism."

"We'll tear ourselves apart. This is known."

"It's not known, it's feared. If we allow individualism, we'll become something new, something that the One has prevented us from becoming. And the change will be painful, yes. Already there have been deaths. But the only alternative to pain is to continue in fear, and the fear ends by causing even more pain. You see?"

Epigrass shook his head. He was excited by Danlo's vision— the Eppy part of him was excited—but the controlling part, the dweller in the Jewel, was more cautious. "What will we become? What can we possibly become, if we plunge ourselves into anarchy?"

"Whatever we want to become," Ainne murmured.

"Stopping the killing is only the beginning," Danlo said. "A necessary beginning. The Cleansings more than anything else have numbed the Body. We dare not look outward, when this fearful thing lies within."

Epigrass shook his head again. "I like what you're saying. But it's impossible. The One *cannot* be opposed."

"You yourself have opposed them for forty years, in their midst, and they never knew it."

"In a small way. A very small way."

"As others have, and do, and will, in small ways. Now the small ways are joining to become a single large way."

"Why risk telling me all this?"

"You can help us. We've come for Linnie and her friends—the ones you call the wild women."

Epigrass laughed. "You must be the one that took those two nulls out of the proctor station in Yubasty. Ridiculous. A futile exercise."

"Not futile as long as they're free. And far from futile, since it shows how vulnerable the One has become."

"Not vulnerable. A little slow to react. But vulnerable?" Epigrass was recovering his composure. He kenned the truck bed again. "I see. You think you can disrupt—hmm. No, it's got no chance of working. You don't know what you're up against. Even if a feedback resonance should start among the dreamers, which is far from certain, the One can dispense with them in seconds. A minute at most."

"Then what would you recommend? Should we wait until the women are moved to some more accessible location? Could you move them?"

"Even if I were willing to help you, I've been removed from authority. Smaun would block anything I tried, and the weight of the One behind him."

"Wait until Smaun moves them?"

"He won't. He wants to kill them as soon as possible. And I imagine he'll do it right there. Now that he's got one that they suspect was travelling with you, why should he risk moving them as long as you're loose?"

"There's got to be a way," Ainne said.

"Why all this trouble to do something impossible? I can see you have compassion for the women. I do too. But if I go along with what you were saying about how the Body has to change, then the best way to bring about that change is to remain free yourselves, not to get locked up and Renewed.''

"Good ends," Danlo said, "can't be achieved through bad methods. If we begin by ignoring our convictions whenever following them would be difficult, we'll get nowhere. Nothing I've done in the past three months has been possible.''

"And sooner or later, one of the impossible things that you try is going to turn and bite you.''

"I've been bitten.''

"I mean fatally.''

"It may happen. But we have no way of knowing in advance which undertaking will be fatal. If I accept your argument, I'll never try anything.''

"There's got to be a way," Ainne said again.

Epigrass glanced again toward the back of the truck. His nostrils flared as he drew a breath, and his eyes narrowed as he let it out. "You've heard of the Great Panic of 850? Yes. A sudden, self-reinforcing instability in the One. Very distressing. What they don't teach in school is that that wasn't the first time; it was the fourth. In 619, 732, 734, and 850. Each time it was thought the process was understood, and new controls were put in place to insure that it could never happen again. There have been minor quiverings in recent years, but they've been dealt with. By now, the One is surrounded very thoroughly by control mechanisms.''

"Mechanisms?"

"In the ktess. Individuals who respond to specific inputs by sharing specific outputs. There's a school of thought that holds that by their nature such controls can't work, that rigidity lends energy to the oscillations once they begin. I don't know much about that; it's not my specialty. But I'm wondering whether the unexpected input from your dreamers might trigger a new episode of self-oscillating panic. That would change the picture very considerably.''

The light of hope glimmered for Danlo. "Do you think that's likely? How can we make it more likely?''

"Not my field. I'm in eccentrics, not dynamics. My impression is that nobody knows what sets off a panic. Lots of theories, but of course there's no way to test them without causing terrible damage. At best, I think it's unlikely. All I'm saying is that your weapon—'' Epigrass nodded toward the truck bed. "—isn't quite as impotent as I estimated at first. Another problem, though. In a panic, you'll be just as impaired as anybody else.''

"Perhaps. Will you share the route to where the women are kept?"

Up to now Epigrass had been discussing wild discord, but only in theoretical terms. Now Danlo was asking him to make an active choice. Danlo waited, doing his best to be patient. Attempting to join a joddie, even one in such a vulnerable state, was a very bad idea, especially if he hoped for the joddie's whole-hearted cooperation. He kenned Epigrass's inner struggle, the idealistic little boy warring with the efficient, practical adult.

"There's one thing you should consider," Ainne said. "Your old life is finished. You can't go back. At the very least, you'll be given Guidance. Eppy will be gone."

Epigrass vibrated inwardly. Part of him had never known Eppy existed. To that part, Ainne was talking about a nonexistent loss. Still—to find an unsuspected part of yourself, a vulnerable part that needed your protection, and then to let it be destroyed . . .

"The same thing will happen to you when you're caught. You'll both be Renewed. If I do help you, what alternative can you offer?"

"Only this," Danlo said. "Now, at this moment, we're free to act. Eppy has never been free to act. Neither has Epigrass. So we can offer you something precious that you've never known. What will happen to any of us an hour from now, or a day, or a week, can't be known, much less controlled. Tomorrow we will have as much or as little freedom as we have tomorrow. It may be more than your fear whispers, but that's immaterial. Today—today we have all the freedom that we have today. That is the alternative."

"I want to. Part of me knows you're right. But you're asking me to help destroy the harmony that I've served all my life!"

"A harmony that kills without compunction," Danlo said. "I'd prefer to think only about releasing those who are held prisoner. But if what we're doing has any impact on the One, it will not be to destroy it. We'll be releasing it, as you've been released, from the bondage of an illusion. The One has become stagnant. How it might change, what new dream might arise to replace the illusion, we can't guess. But change it must."

Epigrass shared a vision of the Council of the One sitting around their long table, most of the joddies fat and all of them seemingly in a stupor in the midst of opulence. Danlo laughed. "How well do you suppose they'd survive a month in the mountains?"

"How did you survive? If I'm to throw in with you, I need to know more."

Danlo shared a kaleidoscope of sensations from his months with Linnie—the wood smoke, the sore muscles, the endless array of animals intent on their own business, the sense of union with nature that came in the magnificent isolation of the mountains. "Nobody can make you twelve years old again. But we can give you the chance to do things that a twelve-year-old would enjoy. Hike, build a house out of sticks, cook over an open fire."

"I'm not handy with physical things," Epigrass admitted. "Not after all these years."

"Would you like to learn?"

Epigrass sighed. "I fear I've lived too long in buildings. I don't think I could ever live like that."

"Then you'll be given Guidance whether you help us or not. So it comes down to a question of what you believe in. Do you *want* to help?"

Epigrass shared a vision of Terana standing by the barred window, crying. "If you can free them—but even that won't do any good!" *Airplane factories endless.*

"That's another cause for fear, yes. There's no shortage of them. If we can free the women, they can return to their homeland and warn their people. Their ancestors survived once; they can do so again."

"He wants to help," Ainne said quietly. So Danlo shared further—his anger at the Cleansings, the dawning of his understandings that a life outside the Body was possible, his conviction that somehow the Body must learn to live in harmony with the nulls. His desolation at losing Linnie.

"Yes. I see."

"You could be of the most use if you could rebuild the separation between Epigrass and Eppy. Let Eppy go back to his tree house." The joddie felt rising panic. Danlo went on soothingly, "It's only temporary. Now that Eppy knows the truth, he can come out any time he wants to. In the meantime he can read what's going on in his book and tell Epigrass what to do. All Epigrass has to do is follow those inner promptings. It's very much like what Ainne and I do, I think, and it hasn't hurt us. If you can manage that, you might even be able to release the women and take them to safety without our having to use our weapon." Danlo tilted his head toward the rear of the truck.

"They won't come with me peaceably. They might have yesterday, but I shudder to think what Smaun may have done to them by now."

"Then I'll come with you. Assuming that Linnie's been put with them, when she sees me she'll know we mean no harm."

"It might work," Epigrass conceded. "If that's the plan, we can release the dreamers. They're *very* uncomfortable back there."

"Don't want them wandering around," Danlo said. "Even though their impressions will be confused, somebody might put the picture together. Besides, we may yet need them."

From behind the seat, a strained voice said, "In about ten seconds I'm gonna pee my pants."

Epigrass started. Danlo chuckled. "You didn't think we'd sent them off into the mountains alone, did you?"

The boys sat up. Mooly, groaning prodigiously, crawled over the seat and half-fell out the door. Gairth examined Epigrass, his eyes narrowed speculatively. "You trust this guy? He's some kind of joddie, right?"

"Some kind, yes. An unusual kind."

Mooly leaned in the door, looking relieved. "Are we gonna go get the women now?"

"In a couple of hours," Epigrass said, "the Jewel will have settled down for the night. That's the best time to get in and out unobserved."

"It's a poor plan," Danlo observed, "to start something when you're tired and hungry—especially when it's something you can't stop once it's started. How early do they stir awake?"

"Seven."

"Then we'll go in at six. In the meantime, some supper and sleep. Let's find a hostel and get a big meal to take out. It's the last we'll see of stove-cooked food for a while."

"Unless we're caught," Gairth said. "More likely, we'll all be eating tomorrow night in a proctor station. If they bother to feed us."

Chapter || 23

AS the first soft gray of dawn flushed pink above the mountains, the truck rolled toward the Jewel of the One. Mooly hunched forward over the wheel and squinted out the windshield. He kept expecting a vehicle to leap at them out of a side street, or a surging mob to block the way, but the broad avenues of Serameno remained nearly deserted—the odd early riser taking a morning constitutional, an occasional delivery truck, and not much else. The truck's engine rattled and sputtered, and the fragrances of spring rolled in through the window at his elbow. Beside him Danlo, Epigrass, and Ainne sat quietly. He wanted to say, "This *is* going to work, isn't it?" But he knew any reassurance they could give would be hollow. Also, he didn't want to distract them. They might already be busy doing whatever they planned to do.

Gairth, wedged behind the seat, said, "This *is* going to work, isn't it?"

Danlo turned to look at Gairth, and turned away again without replying. Mooly was glad he had kept his mouth shut.

Gairth said, "I was just askin'."

The Jewel stood near the center of a broad swath of park called the Hub of Roads. They were still several blocks short of the edge of the park when Ainne said, "Watchers."

"Where?" Mooly looked around wildly.

"Not here," Danlo told him. "The One has posted proctors around the perimeter of the Jewel. Twelve—no, eighteen of them."

"If they were expecting trouble," Epigrass said, "they'd have done more than that."

"That may be enough to stop us. How close can we get?"

"They'll be monitored," Ainnie pointed out, "to make sure they haven't all dozed off at once."

"And they'll have the schedule," Epigrass said. "They'll know we're not a regular delivery."

"Will they?" Danlo chuckled softly. "Seems to me the Council unexpectedly ordered up a load of fresh rabbits for breakfast this morning."

"Might work. Rabbits?"

"Oranges, then. Table linen."

Mooly turned onto a broad boulevard lined by twin rows of ancient oaks. Ahead, the gleaming edifice of the Jewel flashed among the trees, opposite the high, brilliantly colored arches of the Amphitheater. "What do I do?" he asked. "Just drive straight up the front steps?"

"Turn here," Epigrass said. A narrow service road curved out of sight behind a grassy knoll. Mooly guided the truck onto it. Blocks of white stone flanked the immaculate strip of pavement. The blocks slipped past much too quickly; whatever was about to happen, Mooly wasn't ready for it. His guts had turned to jelly. By now the three adults were busy in the ktess; they sat very still, and twice Danlo grunted softly.

The outer wall of the Jewel was hexagonal. Three of the sides were solid honeycombs of windows and balconies, but the other three were each split by a wide squared-off arch. The open sides alternated with the solid ones, so that the service road, when the truck rounded the knoll and the Jewel hove fully into view, pointed straight toward one of the arches that were invisible from the boulevard side. More than a dozen coaches were scattered across a parking lot. Mooly sped along the edge of the lot toward the opening.

He had seen pictures of the Jewel in his schoolbooks, but he had never visited it. He hadn't realized it was so large. It was the diamond in the belly-button of his world, and he was sneaking in like a wayward child, the way a child might steal its mother's jewels, only far worse. Shame warred with awe in his breast.

Three proctors stood in the mouth of the Jewel, dwarfed by the arch. The truck rolled toward them. "Is it okay?" Mooly said.

"So far," Danlo muttered.

"They'll wave us through," Ainne said. As she had predicted, the nearest proctor smiled and motioned the truck past. Mooly pasted a smile onto his lips and waved back casually. The proctor had a rifle tucked under one arm, and metallic objects were clipped to his belt. Mooly shivered; he had never seen a proctor carrying a weapon before.

The dawn had barely penetrated the depths beneath the arch, but in seconds the truck emerged in one of the six huge wedge-shaped courtyards of the Jewel. They had names, Mooly remembered, but he didn't know which one this one was. Unity, Service, Sharing, Repose, what were the others? It didn't matter. Between hedges manicured into fantastic shapes and flower beds bursting with color, walkways of white stone meandered. Above, the arms of the Jewel frowned down, hundreds of windows in patterned arrays. A few were lighted. How many eyes might be looking down on the truck? And what had Danlo arranged that they should see? How many minds could he throw into illusion at once? Not many, surely. Not the minds in this place.

Mooly stopped the truck at the lip of a wide loading dock. Danlo's eyes opened. He looked around and took a breath. "All right. This may even turn out to be easy." He looked at Mooly. "Are you ready?" Mooly pressed his lips together and nodded, not trusting his voice. "Let's go, then." Danlo opened the passenger door and stepped down.

They had discussed the strategy after supper. If possible, they would locate the women and bring them to the truck without rousing anybody. The dreamers in the truck would be wakened only if no other option remained. Their first idea was that Danlo and Epigrass should go after the women while Ainne stayed in the truck with Mooly and Gairth. But if an emergency arose, the One would concentrate its energies on the truck, so keeping two of the adults, or even three, at the truck would be better. Either Danlo or Epigrass had to go into the Jewel, because they were the only ones that the women would recognize. If Linnie was being kept with the others, Danlo would be a better choice; if she was being kept isolated, Epigrass would be preferable. They judged that penetrating the ktess of the One far enough to learn where she was being kept was too dangerous, so they had to guess. Epigrass suggested that the One had no special reason to isolate Linnie—that, on the contrary, Smaun could expect to learn from the conversation when she was reunited with others. Besides, Epigrass was afraid that if he went into the Jewel, the familiar hallways would waken old reflexes that would betray them all. So he shared with Danlo the turnings of the hallways that led to where the captives were held. Mooly wanted very much to stay with the truck, because he wanted to be able to drive away at the first sign of trouble. But Danlo needed a null for a companion; if panic erupted in the ktess, a null would be unaffected by it, and could think clearly and act. Gairth's ankle was still swollen, so he would have to stay at the truck.

Two days ago, Mooly reflected, I didn't even know this crazy old guy, and here I am. What is it about him? He makes you believe you can do impossible things. No, it's more than that: He makes you believe that even if you can't do them, you ought to try. Well, it's not like I had a lot to lose. If they catch us doin' this, they'll only chop my head off, and they were gonna do that anyway.

Danlo opened a door at the end of the loading dock. Mooly hustled to follow. They trotted down a narrow, ordinary hallway and emerged in a vast cavern ablaze with light. Mooly nearly bumped into Danlo, who had stopped to gaze upward. Sweeping stairways curved around one another on spider-thin supports. Chandeliers twinkled in rainbow hues, and sheets of mirror multiplied the vista.

"Up that way," Danlo whispered, pointing to a stairway. Their footsteps blossomed into fading echoes. Out of the corner of his eye Mooly thought he saw a red-robed figure standing on one of the high balconies, but when he turned to look the balcony was empty. They climbed past one landing and then another. Mooly was breathing hard, and when he looked down, the yawning chasm dizzied him. In the mirrors, the square-edged pattern of polished white floor tiles seemed to stretch out forever.

Danlo paused with his hand on the rail. A tremor passed through him.

"What is it?" Mooly asked.

Danlo gasped, made a gargling noise, and slumped to the stairs. Mooly was so scared he thought he might faint. What was he supposed to do now? He leaned over Danlo and shook his shoulder. "Hey. Hey!" Danlo didn't respond. Mooly shook harder. "Hey, is this the right floor?" They had briefed him on the route, but panic had churned his mind into a hopeless jumble. "Is that the hall? Which way do I go? You gotta tell me!"

He gazed around wildly. The cavernous hall was still deserted, but somebody might come along at any moment. Danlo's body would be clearly visible. Mooly put his hands under Danlo's arms and dragged him the last half-dozen steps to the next landing. The mouth of the hallway offered concealment, so he dragged Danlo in that direction and propped him in a sitting position against the wall. Danlo's head sagged on his chest. His face was chalky, and Mooly wondered whether he might be sick.

What now? Search this level. If he didn't find them, try the floor above. But how would he know when he found what he was searching for? This hallway alone had a dozen doors, all alike. If he started opening doors at random, he might surprise somebody, and he didn't want to do that.

At the end, the hall made a T with another hall. He tried to remember: Was he supposed to go left and then right, or right and then left? Before he reached the corner, he heard somebody screaming. He looked back at Danlo, but Danlo lay motionless. The raw, high-pitched sound seemed to have words embedded in it, but Mooly couldn't make them out. The hair on the back of his neck prickled. At the corner the sound was louder, and it was coming from the right, so Mooly went left. Then he halted. Epigrass had said proctors were stationed outside the door of the women's room. With nobody else in the halls, the screaming might be coming from one of them. Wishing he had some other choice, he turned around and went toward the sound.

He approached the next intersection cautiously and peered around the corner. Yes, two blue-shirted proctors were halfway down this hall. One had fallen to his knees and was beating his upraised fists against the wall. The other, still standing, staggered drunkenly as he clawed at his own cheeks with his fingers. Mooly's heart thudded in his throat. What was he supposed to do—walk right past them? His legs balked. Long seconds passed while he tried to force himself to step out boldly. This is stupid, he told himself. This is really stupid. None of us are going to get out of here until after I go down there. Okay, I'm gonna do it now. Okay. Now.

He bolted out into the hallway and headed toward the proctors at a dead run. At first he thought they hadn't seen him. But as he approached, the one who was standing reached out a hand as if to block him. Mooly put his shoulder down and plowed into the proctor, who sailed backward and landed hard on his tailbone. Incongruously, he started to cry.

The door they had been guarding looked much like all the other doors, except that a small gray box was mounted on the wall next to it, a small box with two square buttons. Mooly tried the door. It was locked. He pushed one of the buttons and tried again. The door sprang open.

Two women were half-sitting up in bed. A third stood at the window; she looked across at Mooly, a hunted gleam in her eyes. These had to be the right women, but there were supposed to be four, and he didn't see the fourth one. Damn! And what was he supposed to do now? This was the part where one of them was supposed to recognize Danlo. Mooly stepped into the room. ''I'm—''

Out of the corner of his eye he saw a large, dark shape, and something hit his head just above the ear. Sparks exploded. He fell to his knees and sprawled on his side. Around him pattered rapid footsteps. He forced his eyes open, expecting to see a proctor standing over him. The room was empty.

He scrambled to his feet. In the hall, the screaming had stopped. Both proctors were standing up. They reached toward him, groping like blind men. The women—four of them—were retreating rapidly down the hall. The fourth one must have been hiding beside the door!

Unfortunately, they were headed the wrong direction. ''Hey,

wait! Come back!'' They ignored him. ''I'm with Danlo! One of you— Linnie! Linnie! Danlo!''

The women reached a corner, and three of them vanished around it. The fourth, hampered by a bad limp, slowed further, hesitated, and looked back at Mooly.

''Danlo! He's back this way!'' He gestured wildly.

Heavy hands gripped his shoulder. He was spun around. The proctor's face, eyes glazed, was inches from his. The proctor was taller than Mooly, and fifty pounds heavier. Mooly tried driving his fist into the proctor's stomach, but the blow felt feeble, and the man seemed not to notice it. The second proctor moved in beside him and fumbled for a grip on Mooly's shoulders. They both pressed down, as if to bear him to the ground. He tried to push them away, but he couldn't get any leverage. He jammed the heel of one hand upward, aiming for a chin, but the blow slid harmlessly along the proctor's ear. The other one got behind him and wrapped an arm around his neck. He kicked with his knee, and got a sharp poke in the kidney. He tried to run, and couldn't take a step. The proctors were grunting, and Mooly could smell their sweat. He was afraid they would fall on him and smother him.

So this was how it ended. He had done his best, and he had failed. He had failed Danlo, and put his own head back on the block. Not only that, but he would never see Ainne again. He squeezed his eyes shut against the tears.

One of the proctors lurched sideways. Something hit Mooly's legs, and he fell in a tangle of bodies and limbs. There seemed to be more than three people in the tangle. He opened his eyes expecting to see more proctors—and found himself entwined with one of the women. She pushed him away and got to her knees. Two other women had grabbed a proctor by the shoulders; they ran him headfirst into the wall, and he sagged to the floor.

Mooly got to his feet. Evidently using Danlo's name had been the right thing to do. All four women were there. Their eyes were on him. He had always envisioned them wearing their bizarre native garb, but they were dressed in overalls of various colors, and shod in sandals. The one with the bad leg made little circular motions with an open hand and said, ''And? And?''

''Oh. Ah, this way. Danlo is down this way.'' He started moving. ''We came to get you. We've got a truck and everything. We gotta hurry, though.'' They were following him, but hanging back. They jabbered at one another. He quickened his pace. ''Which one of you is Danlo's friend?''

The woman with the bad leg said, "Danlo friend." She jabbered some more at the others, and their reluctance evaporated. Mooly skidded around the first corner, and they followed, matching his pace.

Blocking the hall was a group of seven joddies. Mooly slowed, but the largest of the women let out a full-throated screech and thundered past him. The joddies blinked and waved their arms in a vague, nervous way, as if they were under water. The large woman thumped two in the chest, one with the heel of each hand, and they buckled like cardboard. Mooly took aim at a tall gangling fellow with pop-eyes and kicked him hard in the stomach. Something spun him sideways and a fist smacked the corner of his mouth. He saw another fist coming, ducked, and tackled a pair of red-robed legs.

Hands seized his shoulder and pulled him to his feet. The women were standing, though one of them, the round-faced one, was cradling an elbow and rubbing it. The joddies lay sprawled like bowling pins. Several were moving slowly, but they weren't getting up. Mooly touched the side of his mouth, and winced. His lip was split. "C'mon," he said. "Let's go." The women needed no urging.

When they rounded the next corner, Mooly expected to see Danlo propped against the wall, where he had left him. But the hall was empty. Mooly slowed, confused, and let the women get ahead. Was this the wrong hall?

One of the women cried aloud. Mooly emerged onto the long balcony of the main hall and found the women clustered around Danlo. On his hands and knees, Danlo was moving groggily toward the railing. The woman with the limp knelt and hugged his head and shoulders against her breast. His arms and legs were still trying to crawl. Linnie said something in a high, anguished tone. The only words Mooly recognized were "white hair, white hair." Of course. When she had last seen Danlo, he hadn't yet disguised himself by dyeing his hair. Maybe she had never seen hair dye; she must think he had suddenly grown old.

Mooly stepped to the railing and looked out apprehensively. The glittering cavern was still deserted. No, it wasn't. A red-robed figure dashed at top speed across the floor far below, and disappeared into a hallway. A moment later another appeared, at a balcony opposite Mooly and two levels higher. Without pausing, this joddie leaned over the rail, tipped outward, and pitched headfirst into the void. He fell silently, robes fluttering, and landed with a small, sickening crunch on the white tile. Mooly stared down at the splash of red.

A hand shook his elbow. The big woman glowered at him and said something. "We're going down there," he said, pointing. "I don't think Danlo's going to be able to walk. Can you carry him?" He mimed picking up a body, and the big woman nodded and grunted. They got Danlo's weight distributed among three of them and started down the stairs. His arms still thrashed feebly, and he said something unintelligible in a harsh, strained voice. Mooly wondered—if the same thing was happening to Epigrass and Ainne, would Gairth be able to protect the truck by himself? The proctors would surely have surrounded it by now, or driven it away.

Before they reached the floor, three proctors—no, four—appeared at a balcony near the end of the hall, pointed at them, shouted, and dashed toward another stairway. No, five. Encumbered by Danlo, the women couldn't move quickly. The proctors would intercept them before they reached the hall that led toward the loading dock. Worse, it appeared from the speed with which they moved that these five had somehow evaded the panic that was sweeping the ktess. Or else the One had quelled the panic. How could four unarmed women and a teenager, burdened by an unconscious body, defeat an equal number of trained men? They couldn't. Mooly remembered the stick-weapons he and Gairth had found in the proctor station in Yubasty. There was no chance of finding the other women's weapons in this maze, if they had been kept at all. But something else might serve.

Rather than descend to the ground floor, he led the party off the stairs at the second floor. No side halls radiated from this landing. A long wall was set with doors at regular intervals. He pushed open the nearest door and groped for a light switch. "Got to find weapons," he said. "Sticks, knives, anything." He aimed the words at Linnie. He wasn't sure she was listening; she was stroking Danlo's hair. But she stopped long enough to raise her head and bark something at the others.

Mooly's fingers bumped the switch, and soft blue light flooded the room. The large, high-ceilinged space was broken up into alcoves by colorful free-standing screens. Low, comfortable-looking padded chairs were set around round tables. Except for their embroidered cloths, the tables were bare, and the chairs looked too heavy to lift. On several pedestals, taller than the tables and not surrounded by chairs, stood objects of wood and metal.

The nearest piece was an abstract spider-web of miniature girders. He grabbed a vertical bar and tugged. The sculpture scooted a couple of inches. It weighed as much as he did, and the bar was firmly welded in place. The big woman positioned herself at the other side, but between them they only managed to tug the piece back and forth.

They scooped Danlo up again and crossed the room swiftly. Detouring around the screens and tables, they were soon out of sight of the door. Mooly wished he had thought to pull the door shut, so the proctors couldn't see where they had gone. Too late now. He wondered if there was another way out of this room, or if they had walked into a trap.

Beyond the next door lay the gleaming counters and ventilator hoods of a kitchen. With a cry of triumph, one woman grabbed a skillet from its wall hook and swung it in wide arcs. Another seized a long twin-pronged fork. Mooly frowned uncertainly at the wicked-looking fork; he knew Danlo didn't want to see anybody hurt, but this didn't seem like the time to raise that sort of objection—if the woman even understood his words, which he assumed she wouldn't. He rummaged in a drawer. Could he force himself to stab anybody with a butcher knife? Probably not. But maybe he wouldn't have to. If he waved the knife as if he meant to use it, maybe the proctors would back off. He chose the two largest knives in the drawer and gripped one in each fist.

At the far side of the kitchen lay another doorway. The servers would bring food deliveries up the back way, Mooly reasoned. Probably straight from the loading dock! He pointed with a knife. "That way. Let's go."

A single light burned at the far end of the narrow passage. Mooly led the way. The woman with the skillet, the round-faced one who had hurt her elbow, dogged his heels, and the others followed close behind, awkwardly carrying both Danlo and their improvised weapons.

The stairs were as narrow as the passage, but better lighted. Mooly hurtled downward at top speed. The first flight ended in a closed landing. He turned and started down the second flight. At the bottom, before he reached it, two proctors appeared. He managed, barely, to stop without piling into them. He was jostled painfully from behind. A third proctor wedged himself between the first two, and they glared up, their faces glistening with sweat.

Mooly swallowed, and raised the knives. "Don't make me, guys." One of the proctors took a step upward. Mooly tensed, and the man halted. "Back off. Back off, we're comin' through. You're not gonna stop us." Mooly made a small, experimental lunge with the knives. The proctors barely flinched, and held their ground. Mooly's hands were so sweaty he thought he might drop the knives. He didn't know what to do. He couldn't attack a grown man with a knife, let alone three men. But if he didn't attack now, more proctors were sure to arrive.

Fingers gripped his left wrist, and the knife was pried from his hand. Linnie slipped past him on the stairs, holding the knife low and well out from her body. On his other side, the big woman took the other knife. The two of them advanced on the proctors steadily, relentlessly. The women with the skillet squeezed past him, and the woman with the fork.

Mooly decided he didn't want to watch. He turned away, feeling ill. Danlo was lying on the stairs, head pointed downward. Mooly bent and got his arms under Danlo's. At the foot of the stairs scuffling noises erupted—quite a lot of scuffling noises, and the unmistakable *bong* of a skillet. Mooly dragged Danlo down one step, another. He turned to check his footing just in time to see Linnie, standing behind a proctor, haul his head back by a copious handful of curly hair and pull the butcher knife across his throat. Blood gushed over her hand. She looked up at Mooly, her head and jaw moving slightly, irregularly, like leaves in a breeze. He couldn't read her expression. Shame? Fear? Hope? "Danlo friend comes. We goes now." She pulled the knife free of the proctor's throat and let go of his hair, and he collapsed.

The women helped him lift Danlo. He couldn't stop staring at the proctors, all three of whom were lying dead in pools of blood. He was urged on, and stumbled away down the hall. He thought he might throw up, or faint, but he kept moving.

They passed through a dim, fragrant warehouse and emerged on the loading dock. They were at the far end, well away from where the tarp-covered truck was still parked. On the ground around the truck more than a dozen people lay sprawled, red-robed, blue-shirted, or dressed in the gray uniforms of servers. One of the joddies nearest the truck managed to get to his feet, tottered a couple of steps, and fell, his limbs contorting in spasms. None of the recumbent were still; they writhed, jerked, squirmed. Some were crawling toward the truck, some away from it. Two more proctors staggered across the courtyard from the direction of the arch, but as they neared the truck what remained of their coordination abandoned them. They fell, struggled to their knees, fell again.

Mooly didn't want to wade through them to reach the truck. Hands would clutch at his ankles, pull him down. Besides, they would have to drive over people to get away. Not that Danlo's prohibition on violence mattered, after what the women had just done, but maybe they could retreat to the parking lot beyond the arch and take another vehicle. Not without the others, though. Where were they? Still in the truck? He cupped his hands around his mouth. "Hey! Hey, Gairth!"

Linnie pointed. "Look." From behind a hedge near the edge of the courtyard, an arm waved frantically.

They set Danlo on the edge of the loading dock, clambered down, and picked him up again. Behind the hedge, Gairth was standing over Ainne's unconscious form. He grinned broadly. "Boy, I thought you guys were *never* gonna make it!"

"Where's Epigrass?"

"He's still in the truck. When I saw people comin', I figured they were after the guys in the back, so it'd be safer if we got out of there, but he was too heavy to move."

"I was thinkin' maybe we ought to leave the truck where it is," Mooly said. "We could get one of those coaches out of the parking lot. If we do that, though, we gotta get Epigrass first. Maybe it'd be easier to take the truck, huh? Maybe the wild women could drag everybody out of the way, so we wouldn't have to drive over them." He realized that they were waiting for him to make a decision. He had no idea what to do. He bent down and patted Danlo's cheek. "Hey, wake up. Hey." Danlo didn't respond.

Mooly stepped out from behind the hedge to survey the courtyard. One of the proctors who had come from the arch was still crawling toward the truck, on his knees and one hand. With the other hand he was fumbling at his belt. Fifty yards of open ground separated the truck from the hedge, and hundreds of windows overlooked the span. What if a proctor with a rifle had found his way to one of the windows? Mooly shuddered. Behind him, Gairth said, "Just before she conked out, she said something about how we should watch for a plane."

"A plane?" Ignoring the danger from the windows, Mooly scanned the sky. Not a bird. Not a cloud. A plane would be better than a coach, that was for sure. But he didn't see any plane.

His eye was caught by motion closer to the ground. The proctor who had been crawling toward the truck rose to his knees and threw something, something small and dark, and fell on his face. The small, dark thing bounced across the lawn and rolled under the truck.

Mooly turned back toward Gairth. "I don't see any—"

There was a muffled *whump*. Gairth said, "Oh, Frank. No."

Smoke engulfed the truck. Smoke and flame. Bits of hot metal rained down around Mooly. Several people started screaming, possibly the dreamers inside the truck but probably not. "They killed 'em," he said to nobody in particular. "The shirkers killed 'em all, just to stop the panic attack."

"Well, if they stopped it," Gairth said, "we're in *big* trouble."

Mooly laughed bitterly. "We weren't in big trouble already?"

"You know what I mean. Once the One gets coordinated, every grownup in Serameno'll be heading this way. They'll tear us limb from limb."

"So where's the shirking plane?" Mooly squinted at the sky again. Except for the rising column of greasy brown smoke, it was empty.

Chapter ‖ 24

THE green miles unrolled beneath the wings, tidy fields criss-crossed by straight strips of road, an ordered world basking in a spring afternoon. Luth Vardiki guided the plane easily, one casual hand resting on the wheel.

"Beautiful view," said Oxar Blennish.

"From up here, all views are beautiful."

"Even the wild lands? I suppose if you're high enough, you can't see." *Unchecked nature. Boundless wreckage.* Oxar leaned back comfortably in the front passenger seat and tapped his fingers lightly on the long thin cane propped between his knees. His opaque glasses reflected the cloud-scattered sky above the distant Sernada.

"Wildness even here." Luth nodded down at the irregular bends and mud banks of the Serameno River.

"What was that?" Oxar shared a scattered glimpse of the sharp

V-shaped wake of the boat that Luth's eyes had flicked across. "Look down again—I want to remember it."

Luth guided the plane in a lazy circle while he watched the boat out the side window. He felt a flash of irritation; he didn't like being Oxar's eyes. Oxar radiated a gentle other-shame, and Luth countered with mild but unwavering defiance.

"What's the difference?" Oxar said. "We're all one. You know who you remind me of? Danlo Ree. And look what happened to him. You ought to have a joddie adjust your attitude."

"You knew him well."

Oxar shrugged. "As well as anybody. I'm honored that the One wants me at hand while he's being hunted. This business in Yubasty yesterday—they wouldn't have bobbled it if I'd been there. I'd have told them, 'He'll slam the door on you. He'll go around the back way while you're still pounding at the front.' Sensible they've called for me. Who knows what he might try next? Strange, strange man, even before this business. Used to sneak out before dawn to go to Cleansings. Afterward he'd be all stirred up. But somehow I could never ken more than bits and snatches. He had a trick of keeping his thoughts hidden."

Luth felt a flash of envy.

Oxar laughed indulgently. "Think that if you like. Look at the trouble it's landed him in. If it had been known how wayward he'd become, he could have been Guided. Letting nulls loose from a proctor station—beyond belief. Bringing a wild woman down into the middle of the Valley. How many more might be skulking in the bushes? And what was he doing, all those months beyond the Wall? Frank only knows how he managed to survive." Oxar shared his own highly colored vision of the wilderness. It bristled with dangers.

"We'll learn when he's caught." But the thought saddened Luth. He imagined Danlo striding across the mountains, leading a band of nulls.

Oxar's fingers drummed on the cane. "Dangerous thinking."

"Is it? Why? Why shouldn't I think what I like?" Nulls roaming free. A phrase floated up in Luth's mind: *We can build a bridge that a few.* . . .

"Inharmonious. Wayward. What's this about a bridge?"

Luth struggled to remember. Danlo Ree, and building a bridge. And hiding eggs under hats. He could see Danlo's face, but not as Oxar shared it. Outdoors, at dusk. Danlo holding up a tiny ball of paper. A licorice wrapper.

Oxar's head swiveled toward Luth. "Oburn. He *was* there."

"Don't know what you're talking about." Suddenly Luth didn't ant to remember. He turned his thoughts deliberately toward the onstruction of the plane—flaps, linkages, fuel lines. Low on fuel? o, the gauge showed more than half-full.

Oxar tsk-tsked. "A joddie'll have it out of you. Makes sense at he'd seek you out. The mad scheme he must have hatched, he ould use a pilot. And what luck to stumble onto you! Wayward, ayward, wayward. Your flying days are over, Goodman Vardiki. Vhen the One learns you've been contaminated by Ree's foul inking, you'll be Guided into furniture-building, I've no doubt."

"I've never met the man!"

"You *say* you haven't. How are we to know he didn't teach you e same trick he uses himself?"

"Wish he had." Luth's mind was in turmoil. He remembered nly scraps, but sensed that more hovered just out of reach. He vanted to dredge it up, but not while Oxar was sitting next to him, mirking and chuckling. "You've never liked me," Luth said in a ow, even voice. "You're making something out of nothing just to iscredit me. Planting thoughts in my mind, for all I know."

"I don't dislike you," Oxar claimed, disingenuously. "I just on't trust you."

"At the moment," Luth said, looking down at the distant andscape, "you don't have much choice but to trust me, do you?"

Oxar chuckled again, a little less smugly. "You won't do nything foolish. What would you do? Turn off the engines? 'ou'd die as surely as I. You wouldn't want that."

Luth imagined opening the door and pitching Oxar out.

Oxar's ktess convulsed with vertigo. "You wouldn't," he said uickly.

It was Luth's turn to laugh. "How can you be sure? If I can hide ny thoughts from you. . . ."

Oxar edged sideways in his seat. He envisioned groping for the un locker in the rear of the cabin, defending himself from Luth vith a rifle.

"Useless," Luth told him. "The arms master took them three lays ago, to put in planes that had border duty."

Oxar got up and edged toward the rear of the plane. He meant o shut himself in the rear compartment, behind the heavy partition hat was designed to keep the passengers and pilot safe from orisoners, should any be taken in the wilderness. "The door locks rom this side," Luth said. "Ride back there if you like. But you're right. I wouldn't throw you out. I might want to, but I wouldn't.''

Oxar sank back into his seat, but kept a tense grip on his cane. ''Wayward. Furniture-building. Or maybe cleaning drains.''

The engines thrummed. The outskirts of Serameno slid by below, houses and trees and a schoolyard thronged with children. Luth thought they would probably stop playing ball and point up at the plane, but he was too high to see.

The rest of the flight passed in stiff silence. Luth landed, as on every flight into Serameno, at the large truck yard on the north side of the city where mechanics who knew the planes were kept posted. As he reduced airspeed and pulled back on the lever that swiveled the engines upward for vertical descent, he debated letting Oxar disembark and then taking off again alone. It was a pointless gesture; where would he go? But he was in a mood for pointless gestures. Whatever might have happened in Oburn—and Luth still remembered no more than he had in that first confused burst—Oxar was probably right that the One would not want him in possession of an airplane. At least not until Danlo was safely locked up. The unfairness of it galled him. To be grounded for something he couldn't remember, something that might never have happened. . . .

Two joddies stood waiting, the skirts of their robes fluttering wildly in the backwash of the propellers. As the landing gear bumped the pavement, Luth's defiance evaporated. He went through the shutdown routine as usual. The engines rattled and died. The corners of Oxar's mouth tilted up in a small, satisfied smile.

They climbed out of the plane, and the joddies greeted them with formal bows. ''Goodman rememberer,'' the shorter of the two murmured. ''Most prompt.''

''Anything to help.''

Luth looked around idly. A second plane was visible through the open door of a large shed; one of its engine housings was open and two mechanics were busy with wrenches.

The joddie introduced himself and his companion. ''Brother Topal, Brother Emsh. Way prepared.'' He indicated a small coach parked in front of a huge freight truck.

One of the mechanics waved at Luth, but Luth didn't respond. He turned away and followed in the joddies' wake like a toy duck on a string, neither feeling nor thinking much of anything, and climbed into the back of their coach.

Oxar was asking the joddie about the new wild woman. "Speaks?"

"Badly."

"Chance to see?"

Complexity of decision. "Smaun consulted."

Luth only blinked, it seemed, and the coach was rolling up the wide, smooth drive at the front of the Jewel, where shallow steps led beneath the arch into the Courtyard of Joy. The coach stopped, and he got out along with the others. His arms and legs were farther away than usual; they moved smoothly, but he could barely feel them. At the top of the steps one of the joddies went with Oxar. The other escorted Luth through a door, down several halls, and through another door into a room. Luth sat down in a chair. *Wait here.* The door closed. He waited.

After a while he started to think about the schoolyard they had flown over. He imagined little arms reaching up toward the plane. He imagined swooping down, reaching out, grasping an arm, and hauling the child aboard without ever touching the ground. It was a pleasant fantasy, so he kept imagining it.

They won't let me, though, he said to himself. That's why they brought me here. Not so they can teach me to fly better. I already fly better than anybody. They're going to keep me here so I can't fly. He couldn't remember why they were going to do that, but it sounded right. The room was warm and comfortable. He got up and wandered around. There wasn't much to see, not even a window to look out of, only three chairs and a table and a picture of Frank and Olivia on the wall.

After he had circled the room fifteen or twenty times, he noticed that there was a door in one wall. The door scared him. He certainly, absolutely didn't want to go out that door. He didn't even want to get near it. He sat down again. But he kept looking at the door out of the corner of his eye. What was it about the door that was so scary? He couldn't figure it out. If he opened the door—what? So it was scary. That didn't mean it would actually hurt him. Luth wasn't bothered by things that were scary. He liked them. That was why he had volunteered to be a pilot. The more he thought about the door, the more he wanted to see what was on the other side. He turned his chair so he could look at the door. It was an ordinary blank-looking door, with an ordinary round doorknob. Almost anything might be on the other side. Wild animals, or knives and fire, or some of the poison gas that he had heard the One was experimenting with, that made you cough your lungs out.

He didn't want to breathe poison gas, so he looked around for another door. There wasn't one. Which meant, he reasoned laboriously, that he had to have come in through that door. So probably there wasn't any poison gas on the other side. Maybe he could hold his breath and open it just far enough to sniff the air and take a peek for other dangers.

He stood up, tiptoed toward the door, and reached for the knob. The knob grew pointed teeth and snapped at his fingers. He flinched back. Teeth? Had it actually grown teeth, or had he only been afraid that it would? He stared at the knob and pushed his hand toward it very slowly. It was hard to look at the knob; his eyes swam with the effort, but he kept concentrating. No, there were no teeth. He got his fingers around the knob. It burned his skin with acid. No, it wasn't acid at all, just smooth cool metal. He turned the knob, remembered the poison gas, and quickly gasped down a lungful of air.

The wedge of corridor that appeared was empty of knives and wild animals. He took a cautious sniff. It seemed, briefly, to bite his nose with the reek of fumes, but he took another sniff anyway, and this time smelled nothing. He let his breath out slowly and stood peering out the door.

Probably they had electrified the floor, so if he stepped outside he would fry. No, that was only another fear. He was getting used to the game now. He poked one toe out the door and gingerly tested the floor. Sparks failed to fly. All right, then. His head felt clearer now, as if he was waking up from a nap. Had he really sat in that room for an hour, afraid to open the door? Yes. And if the joddies found him roaming the halls, they would put him back in the room. They would make his fear so overpowering, he might never be able to go outdoors again. He started down the hall, moving lightly but not wasting time. Actually, they didn't have to see him; they could ken him from any room in the Jewel. How could he stop them? For a moment he felt real fear. But a strong emotion would betray him more swiftly than anything else. Think about engineering diagrams. The tail flaps are connected to the controls in the cockpit by a combination of mechanical and hydraulic linkages. The mechanical linkage consists of twined strands of aluminum wire, alloyed with. . . .

He chose halls at random, moving in what he hoped was the right direction, swinging his arms and walking purposefully. A dozen times his thoughts strayed from aircraft construction, and he dragged them back. Twice he passed servers, but they glanced at him and passed on. When he saw daylight glowing through a glass door ahead, he quickened his pace. The golden rectangle grew. It engulfed him. He pushed the door open, skipped down the steps, and paused, only for a moment, to take a deep breath and look up at the sky. The wide squared-off arch yawned invitingly, and he angled toward it. A minute later he was across the boulevard, striding through the park that surrounded the Amphitheater. He allowed his concentration to stray.

Sooner or later, he knew, the joddies would find him. The world was full of joddies. They might even have kenned that he was leaving the Jewel, and let him go, knowing they could haul him back whenever they were ready to look into his waywardness.

Danlo Ree, though, seemed actually to be able to elude them. He had managed it so far, anyway. A hot flush of admiration swelled in Luth's chest. He would like to meet the man. Oxar seemed to think he had done so already, and couldn't remember. Odd. Oburn. A licorice wrapper. Luth searched his pockets. Usually he carried licorice. Today he had none.

He jammed his hands deep into his pockets and ambled along a curving paved path that wandered among a stand of ancient trees. Mothers pushing strollers and watching toddlers were in the park this afternoon, and young couples enmeshed in their own affection, and here and there a student sprawled on the lawn with books and papers. An old woman was scattering crumbs for the pigeons.

Oxar had said the One wouldn't let him fly anymore. Another of Oxar's petty digs? No, the joddie who had put him in that room wanted to keep him there, so they must have kenned something serious. Luth felt cheated; they meant to punish him, as if he were a child, for something that he hadn't done!

Luth knew nobody in Serameno, and he had no business to attend to. Guided only by an urge to stay out of the little room with the doorknob that had teeth, he wandered until sunset, found a hostel, ate dinner without tasting it, and retired to the room that the hosteler showed him. He leafed through the well-thumbed paperbound copy of the White Book that he found on the bedside table. "Each will be called," Frank Rettig had written, "to serve according to his true nature. The talents of none will be wasted." All very well in theory, but in practice it was the joddies who determined what one's talents and true nature were. Determined or decreed. Luth put the book down. What could he possibly do in the morning? Go back to the Jewel and insist that flying was his true nature. Assure them that he would do whatever was required if only they would let him fly. But would they trust his assurances?

He switched out the light, stripped off his pants and shirt, and lay down. A night breeze whispered in the gauze curtains at the window, and the cool radiance from a light in the yard shifted in the folds of cloth.

He was not alone in the room. He sat bolt upright.

A girl sat in the chair opposite. She glowed brighter than the light in the curtains, and the breeze did not stir her long blond hair.

The Jewel, she said. *Six-fifteen tomorrow morning. Remember what I'm saying. Six-fifteen, no later. We'll be counting on you to fly us out.*

"Who are you? What–"

There may be a disruption. It may be unpleasant. You'll have to fight it. We'll help if we can.

"Who's 'we'?"

Instead of an answer, his mind filled with a crisp image—a blue rose in a drift of crimson snow. When he could see again, the girl was gone. "Wait!" he cried uselessly. A blue rose. He remembered now. Talking with Danlo outside the Sharing Hall in Oburn. Danlo telling him he ought to envy nulls. Asking for his help. Had he agreed? Yes. Foolish. Terribly rash. And look at the trouble it had landed him in already, before he had even done anything. He ought to go straight back to the Jewel now, let them probe his mind to the bottom. If he willingly gave up this new information, they might let him go on flying.

He hugged his knees and beat his head against them. The idea of meekly submitting to the joddies made him nauseous, as if his skin were covered with filth. And how could he ever love flying again if he betrayed a man he admired, a man who had trusted him?

Of course, he didn't have to actively betray Danlo. He could simply do nothing. The girl had said to pick them up at the Jewel, which was ridiculous. Not even the infamous Danlo Ree could get into and out of the Jewel without being captured. By the time Luth woke in the morning, the crisis would be over, and the One might choose to concern itself no further with the personal failings of a single wayward pilot. Once Danlo was safely locked up, Luth's failure to come forward would be of no consequence.

He lay down and closed his eyes, but he might as well have been lying on rocks. He squirmed and fidgeted. His eyes flew open. He wrestled with the pillow. He shut his eyes again and willed his limbs not to twitch. They twitched.

"So little of your life is your own," Danlo had said. "Most of it belongs to others. Take that little piece that's your own, and make it count for something." The little piece that was his own, Luth saw, was the flying. Flying already counted for something, he told himself indignantly. Just soaring above the world, going where there were no roads—wasn't that enough? Danlo meant that he should use the flying in the service of something further. The joddies would demand the same. They would expect him to hunt down wild nulls, drop explosives on them. He couldn't avoid using the flying in the service of one vision or another. So which vision did he prefer?

He rolled out of bed and pulled on his trousers.

The hour was late, and few coaches roamed the streets. He didn't trust himself to sit next to anybody without inadvertently sharing, so he walked, and rested, and walked some more. The truck yard was miles from the hostel. The plane might not even be there, by now. Or the mechanics might have taken an engine apart. Just as likely, a joddie would be waiting, to gently stop him before he could get into the air. It was a long walk—he had plenty of time to imagine things that could go wrong. He went through the same turmoil before every flight in a new plane. The difference was that this time he was half-hoping something *would* go wrong. If it did, he would be relieved of the awful burden of having to choose whether to defy the Body.

He thought again about the doorknob with teeth. They had given the Wall that sort of teeth. As long as he was part of the Body of Harmony, he would be stuck in that stifling little room. He would never breathe fresh air, or roam the sky. Seeing it that way made the decision easy. He walked faster.

The sky overhead had paled and the east was brightening by the time he approached the truck yard. Dim blue lights on poles still glowed, but they cast only faint shadows across the pavement. Eight or nine large haulers were parked in a loose row with their noses pointed toward the street, and between the big sheds an assortment of vans, pickups, and hauler cabs without freight beds created a maze of metal and glass. The plane, if another pilot hadn't been called to fly it elsewhere, lay at the center of the maze.

Luth cast about in the ktess, hoping to find the yard deserted. He kenned two minds, fuzzy balls of warmth in the silent darkness. No, there were three; he had missed the third one for a moment because it belonged to a thicker. Probably a mechanic named Tombly, a little broad-faced, smiling man whom Luth had seen around the yard. Thickers had trouble coordinating their work with others, so it was not surprising that Tombly would be here early, to work alone. The other two were sharply aware. Not wanting to attract their attention, Luth turned his mind again to airplane parts. But even that topic might be inadvisable. He switched to fishing. He had been ocean-fishing often when he was younger, had loved standing in the prow in heavy seas to watch the foaming green walls advance, the breathless moment when the boat slid down the trough to slap water and dash salt spray.

He sauntered across the yard, aiming not directly at the plane but toward Tombly, a course that would take him along the edge of the landing area. While he had loved the sea, he had hated the nets. A pole, bait, man against fish, that was the fair and sporting way, not scooping them up by the thousands. They flopped across the deck in a helpless silver carpet, were poured into the hold like a flood with staring eyes and gasping mouths.

Wings, engines tilted up, a light in the cabin. He did his best not to care, not to let his pulse quicken. Diving off the side of the boat one summer morning, treading water, watching the hills of home rise out of the swell, sink down again. He left the landing area behind. Tombly was in the shed just ahead.

The gloom within the shed was fleeing before the advancing day, though night still haunted the rafters, which were black with years of grime. Tombly was on his back underneath a twelve-seater; as Luth entered, he rolled out, got to his feet, and wiped his hands on his coveralls. "Goodman flier," he said, nodding. "Early to be off."

"This business about Danlo Ree. Has anybody put in fresh fuel cells, Tombly?"

"Don't know. I can if you like. Usually it's a two-man job, though. Could you lend a hand?"

"You're alone out here? Thought I kenned—"

"Oh, the proctors." Tombly's broad, freckled face bobbed up and down.

"Proctors?"

"Surprised, eh? They're keeping a watch. Over the plane, I mean. Don't know what that's about."

Luth frowned at the grease-spotted pavement for a moment. "Saw another plane this afternoon, over in the aircraft shed."

"Number Seven," Tombly agreed. "Engine overheating, I heard."

"They get her put back together?" He might not need to tangle with the proctors at all.

Tombly shook his head. "If it was a rush job, somebody ought to of told them before they went home. Proctors giving you a bad time about something?"

"No, I'm curious about Number Seven, that's all. I want to take a look at her while you're fueling Number Four. What time is it?"

Tombly glanced at the clock on the workbench. "Five of six."

"Tell the proctors they can go home." Luth patted Tombly's shoulder. "I'll look after the plane."

Tombly shrugged. "Whatever you say, goodman. Don't know that you ought to take Number Four out, though. She hasn't been checked over since you flew in yesterday. Should I send for the flight mechanics?"

"No need. She was fine yesterday. Just get her fueled."

The mechanic strode rapidly away on his stubby legs. Luth waited for a few seconds and then followed. He had been able to fool Tombly because Tombly was a thicker. Fooling a thicker was bad manners, but it had been done out of necessity, not to make fun of the man. All the same, the trick wouldn't work with the proctors. If he approached the plane, they would ken his intention at once. They might ken it now, if their minds turned in this direction.

There was only one way he could wrest the plane away from them. He stood quietly, watching the dawning sky and thinking about fishing, until Tombly emerged from the aircraft shed at the wheel of a fuel cart. The cart rumbled across the pavement toward Number Four. Luth kenned the proctors' surprise. One of them rose and climbed down out of the plane to talk with Tombly. Luth started walking rapidly toward the aircraft shed.

He navigated among the haphazardly parked trucks while keeping his mind turned receptively toward the proctors. *Who told you—* Tombly's response was too weak to ken. *Here? Where?*

The moment for secrecy was past. Luth sprinted for the aircraft shed. The proctors' shock washed across him. The one on the ground sprang into motion, running straight toward him, and the other clambered out of the plane to follow. He had only a few seconds' lead.

In the light that spilled through the wide door, Number Seven cast a lopsided shadow. Luth ducked under the gaping engine housing, clawed at the door, and hoisted himself inside. No time to switch on an interior light; in the half-darkness he dove at the gun locker and jerked it open.

Three rifles. He grabbed one and fumbled in the canvas ammunition bag for a full clip. Footsteps scraped on the pavement outside, rang on the ladder. Luth had been trained to use the weapons, but not to load one in the dark. The clip wouldn't fit. He turned it around the other way, pushed it in, and felt a satisfying snap.

The first proctor burst through the door. "Don't even think about it," Luth said, swinging the barrel around.

"You won't hurt me." The proctor took a step forward, and held out his hand. "Give me the gun."

"Ken me." Luth held the barrel pointed unwaveringly at the proctor's gut. He hoped his intention was just as steady. If he was willing to shoot, he might not have to, but he had to be willing to. If they kenned that he wouldn't shoot, they would simply take the gun away. *Contempt. Stepping on a snail.*

"All right."

"Back up." Luth scrabbled with his free hand in the bottom of the locker, and made sure all the clips were in the canvas bag. "Back up, I said." He got the bag over his shoulder. "I'll kill you where you stand if you don't move." His finger tightened on the trigger. The proctor shuffled backward toward the door and groped blindly for the ladder with his foot.

Luth kenned that the other proctor had started back across the yard toward Number Four. *Stay where you are.* The other proctor broke into a trot. Luth saw his intent: to smash the plane's controls so it couldn't be flown. *I'll kill this one unless you—* Blank disbelief.

"Your pardon, goodman." Luth pulled the trigger. The rifle recoiled hard against his hands, and the first proctor flew backward out the door. Luth felt the fiery pain rip through his own guts, and gasped. Still in agony, he ducked out the door and jumped to the ground, his body already turning to swing the rifle toward the open doorway of the shed. He landed in a crouch and saw, beneath the engine housing, the second proctor's running legs, fifty yards away, mere steps from the other plane. He squeezed the trigger. The proctor disappeared around the side of the plane. In the ktess, a door swinging open, the back of the pilot's seat.

Touch the hardware and you'll die. Believe it. Leave it as it is and you'll not be harmed.

The second proctor hesitated. Luth prodded the first one with his toe. The hole in the front of his shirt was ringing with blood, and more blood was pooling beneath the body. He was still alive, but not by much. *For Olivia's sake, drive this one to the hospital.* Hesitation. Uncertainty.

Luth ducked under the wing and trotted toward Number Four, rifle at the ready. The sky was bright, and gold was creeping upward in the east. Tombly had not moved from beside his fuel cart. "Get a coach," Luth called. "A man's been shot." Even if he had to kill the second proctor, maybe the first one could be saved.

Tombly scampered to obey. The second proctor came around the side of the plane, moving carefully. Luth stood aside, but kept the rifle pointed. "Go ahead. Help him."

"What kind of man *are* you?" The proctor's face was a mask of pain and confusion.

"A man who loves freedom."

"A killer." The word dripped revulsion.

"Maybe both." Luth climbed into the plane, and sat down, and balanced the rifle across his lap where he could easily fire at anybody who tried to climb through the door. He started through the checklist. Electrical power on, oil pressure, hydraulic pressure, instruments. Suddenly he felt sleepy. Understandable—he hadn't slept all night. It was 6:03. He could catch a quick five-minute nap and still be. . . . His head had almost slumped against the wheel before he realized what was happening and shook himself convulsively. Somewhere nearby, a joddie had been awakened by the proctor's pain. The joddie, perhaps without knowing the details of the situation, was taking the precaution of putting Luth to sleep.

Skip the start-up routine, in that case. Luth hit the power switch, and the engines hummed to life. Dream-phantoms swam between his eyes and the control panel. Forget the engine warm-up too; he pulled back on the throttle, the engines screamed, and the plane rose into the air.

As it rose, his head cleared. The joddie, sensibly, was withdrawing rather than risk causing Luth to crash. The plane rose rapidly. The cold engines shrieked and shuddered, but the blades bit the air with full power.

The Jewel lay to the southeast. Luth aligned the nose with the compass dial and tilted the engines forward.

Streets and buildings slid beneath him. Sunrise, blinding, shone in his face, and the haze over the city shimmered. He leaned sideways to peer out. Where was the Jewel? The buildings looked unfamiliar, but Serameno was full of buildings. After a minute, when he still didn't see it ahead, he checked the compass. The heading was correct. Was that open patch of green ahead the Hub of Roads? It seemed too broad and irregular. He looked left and right, feeling uneasy, and reached up to tap the compass with a fingertip.

He could feel the smooth glass face, and hear his finger tap, but his hand was invisible. The compass sat steady on a southeast heading. He held his hand up in front of it. No hand.

He swung the plane in a bank to the right, and the compass didn't change. He wasn't seeing the real compass, then. So he wouldn't use it. Where was he? He stayed in the bank until the plane had described a complete circle. The mountains and the sun were in that direction, so that must be west. No, east. They were playing tricks with his thinking, too. All right, then. Most of the city lay off that way, and the Jewel lay at the center of the city, so forget the compass and forget the mountains. Just fly toward the center of the city.

For a minute or so the flight went smoothly. He had just started to relax when a wave of uneasiness rolled through the ktess, thick and greasy. It was visceral. His skin crawled, and his breath caught in his chest. He ignored it. He kept his hands on the wheel, his eyes ahead, and waited for it to pass. Instead, it grew stronger. He felt trapped. He couldn't breathe! A suffocating stench filled the plane, and his arms and legs were tangled in something he couldn't see. He stretched vigorously and gasped for air.

Screaming. The high, anguished keen of a thousand invisible throats. He looked wildly around the plane, knowing he would see nobody. Wherever he turned, his vision was overlaid with a grid of wire fencing. He wrapped his fingers around the wire and wrestled with it.

Incredibly, the feelings mounted further. Dimly Luth could see that he wasn't piloting the plane. It sailed on through the sky on a heading of its own. Altimeter. How high was he? *If you want to make sure I crash, just keep doing what you're doing.* If anybody kenned him, they made no response. Altimeter. Five hundred feet. Take it up to two thousand. Safer. Falling off a cliff into an abyss, falling forever onto bloody knives. His fingers found the throttle. Up. Severed arms, bloody shoulder-stumps, cut-off cocks and balls. Drowning in a sea of sewage. How high was he now? Three hundred feet. Throttle. He had let go of the throttle. There. Up. Up.

Spiders and rats crawling on his face. He tried to brush them off. They wouldn't brush off. He pawed harder.

For a time—he had no idea how long—he was entirely lost in gibbering panic. Horrible things that had no names swam through him and gnawed on his bones. Then something like a cool hand touched his forehead. He found that he was on his hands and knees on the floor of the plane. The engines were still humming.

A voice as cool as the hand insinuated itself into the fever in his brain. *You've got to fight against it.*

He was eating a raw rat, a raw live rat crawling with flies, dripping filth.

Fight it. I can't fly the plane. You have to. None of it is real. It can't hurt you. Just let it come and go.

The rat felt very real. It slid down his throat, swelling until it plugged his esophagus. He gagged. The cool hand came on his forehead again. He could see the back of the pilot's seat. His seat. He got his hands wrapped around the seat and pried himself up off the deck.

The world rushed by, terrifyingly close beneath the window. This was no phantom from the ktess: He was a scant fifty feet above the rooftops. He half-fell into the seat, still gagging on rat shit, rat hairs, flies on his tongue, and pulled back on the throttle. He was headed straight into the fanged mouth of a mile-high demon. No, the demon was in his head; out the window, only bright morning sky awaited. The demon didn't go away, nor did his terror of it, but he found that now, somehow, he could stay in his seat, keep his hands on the controls, and watch what lay ahead. His bowels were being sliced open with a rusty sword. Mountains on his left, suburbs and open fields below. He had crossed the city. The Jewel lay at his tail. Octopus tentacles were growing from his skin, crawling under his clothes. He brought the plane around in a wide bank.

The white hexagon of the Jewel wavered in the distance, half-visible among the glistening gray tentacles that groped across the window leaving trails of ooze. As the Jewel got bigger, the horror got worse. He had to bank away. Well, if he couldn't fly in directly, maybe he could circle in on it, get used to the distress a little at a time. He banked again, keeping the Jewel in view out the left-hand window. His bones had turned to glowing coals. His flesh was sizzling and charring from the inside out. Huge blisters swelled and burst on his skin, his tongue blackened and shriveled, his hair smoked and sparked. When he rubbed his hands through his hair to brush away the sparks, the hair fell out in burning clumps. He kept the Jewel on the left, and angled the plane a little toward it. Check the altimeter. Four hundred feet. He was going to throw up the rat he had eaten. He could feel it clawing its way up his gullet, entrails dangling. Somebody had attached a giant clamp to his skull, and they were tightening it. The pressure was obscene. His skull was about to crack open like a walnut and splatter brains across the cabin. The Jewel was still on the left, but he couldn't get any closer in. He couldn't. The pressure was still building, and it wasn't going to stop. He tried to bank tighter, and screamed aloud and fought with the wheel, which had come alive and squirmed out of his hands. Ease up. Keep it at a distance. He wrestled the wheel under control. He was still a mile out from the Jewel. The clock on the control panel read 6:27. He circled, and sweated, and scraped the spiders off his face.

A paroxysm of fiery pain convulsed the ktess. He rose out of his seat and screamed again. His knee hit the wheel, and the plane angled sharply to the right, throwing him down across the seat. He banged his head on something, and when he struggled back into the seat the ground was spinning toward him at a crazy angle. The fire went on, to a renewed chorus of shrieks, but he was too busy to pay attention. He pulled the plane out of its dive without actually brushing the treetops but with no room to spare. Now which direction was the Jewel? The burning sensation was cleaner, somehow, than what had been happening before, and the pressure was gone from his head. He spotted the white hexagon ahead, and risked angling more directly toward it. He could breathe. The plane was filled with smoke and the odor of charred flesh, but the spiders and the knives were gone.

He was approaching the Jewel from the rear. As he got closer he saw a small band of people running in a slow, burdened way across the grassy knoll beside the parking lot. An arm waved at the plane.

He reduced air speed as he came around above them, and tilted the engines up and let the plane settle toward the ground. The ground came up faster than he expected. It met the plane with a teeth-jarring thump.

He popped the door open. Wind from the propeller battered his face. Hurrying toward him was an odd assortment—two teenage boys, one large, olive-skinned and pink-cheeked, the other small, red-haired, and limping, four women with a wild, determined cast to their eyes, one of them also limping, and two bodies being carried like sacks of grain, a girl with long blond hair and an older man with a stiff hairdo of pure white. The man's face was dangling upside down; it took Luth a moment to realize he was looking at Danlo Ree.

The large boy looked up at Luth, exhausted and wary. "You better be who you're supposed to be."

"Get in." Luth made way. The woman who was not helping carry Danlo or the blond girl climbed in first. She was holding two butcher knives in one hand; before she could turn to reach for the girl's arms, she had to set them on the deck. Both blades were smeared with blood. "Need a hand?" Luth asked. She ignored him.

The cabin was too small to hold them all. They propped Danlo and the girl up in two of the seats, and the large boy and one of the women sat beside them. The other three women and the red-haired boy climbed into the rear compartment, behind the partition. "Belt yourselves in," Luth said as he seated himself at the controls.

"They don't understand you," the large boy said. "Linnie—tell them. Straps. Buckles. Oh, never mind. Grab something. Hold tight."

One of the women used a string of words Luth didn't understand. He was vaguely aware that they were nulls. So were the boys. He revved the engines, and the plane lifted. Nulls. Not children, either. Grown women. Gradually it penetrated. His passengers were the wild women. And carrying bloody knives. A terror that had nothing to do with the ktess bunched his shoulders. He looked back. They weren't creeping toward him with murderous intent. The three in the rear compartment were standing up, their faces pressed to the windows. They nudged one another, pointed, exclaimed. The fourth had Danlo's head cradled in her lap; she was stroking his hair and crooning to him, so softly that Luth almost couldn't hear her voice over the drone of the engines.

The plane sped eastward, into the rising sun. Luth waited apprehensively for a renewed assault in the ktess. He had passengers now who would die in a crash. But the terrible flood of panic had subsided.

The large boy climbed into the front seat beside him and raised a palm in greeting. "Hi. I'm Mooly Farn."

"Luth Vardiki." Luth pressed his palm against Mooly's.

"I guess I'm sort of in charge—until Danlo wakes up, I mean. Can you tell what they're doing? Him and Ainne? That's Ainne back there. Are they okay? You're not a null, right?"

"Right." Luth cast his mind toward Danlo, and recoiled from a blast of icy air. He probed deeper. Crags. Glaciers. And something warm and soft and enticing within, or behind, or around them. He pulled back with an effort. "Don't think I ought to focus on it. I've got to fly the plane."

"Yeah." Mooly perked up as he looked around. "This is pretty neat, hunh? You think you could teach me to fly?"

"Probably. Not much point, though. Fuel cells will give out in a couple of hours."

Mooly looked crestfallen. "Oh. Is that enough time for us to get over to the other side of the Wall?"

"Time and to spare. Had you thought about what you're going to do when you get there?"

"You're coming with us, right?"

Luth considered the question. "I can't go back. I shot a proctor."

"You *shot* a *proctor*? You mean with a gun? You mean, like an accident?"

"No. On purpose. I didn't want to, but I don't suppose that makes any difference."

Mooly pointed across at Luth's side window. "What's that out there? Looks like another plane."

The metallic speck was less than a mile away. It angled toward them on an intercept course. Number Three, probably. It had been posted to border watch in this area.

Land immediately.

"They want me to set down," Luth said.

"You're not gonna do it, are you?"

"They may not leave me any choice." Like the lost Number Two, Number Three had outside weaponry mounted in its nose.

"Danlo'll stop them," Mooly said stoutly. "Just keep flying."

You do yourself no favors. Land at once and you'll not be disciplined.

But what would be done to his passengers? Luth watched the miles unroll before the plane. They were over foothills now, and more rugged country rose ahead. He wondered why his mind was not being invaded. Maybe Danlo and Ainne were blocking whatever the joddies tried to do. Or maybe there was no joddie in the other plane, and those on the ground were being passed over too quickly to organize such an assault. All he had to do was hold to his present course. They would pass just north of the Belonging Reservoir and be over the Wall in ten minutes. Probably the other

lane would follow. What then? "Did Danlo say where in the
nountains we're headed?"

"Not that I ever heard."

*This is your final warning. Land without delay, or you will be
hot out of the sky.*

"They say they're going to shoot at us," Luth told Mooly.
"Should we land?"

"How far are we from the Wall?"

"Fifteen, twenty miles."

"We better go as far as we can before we go down. If we have
o walk the rest of the way—"

The window beside Luth shattered in spreading rays and
oncentric circles, and something small and hard spanged and
attled around inside the cabin. Wind whistled in the hole.

"Can we shoot back at them?"

"No external weapons," Luth said. "You ever fire a rifle?"

"No." Mooly looked a little green.

Several low thuds in quick succession. Luth glanced back over
is shoulder, and saw new bullet-sized holes in the fuselage. The
lanes, he knew, had been built to attack tribes who were equipped
vith hand weapons. The fuselage was too thin to withstand
gunfire. "We'd better go down." He shared the thought of
ompliance as strongly as he could, and banked into a downward
piral.

The plane shuddered. It was responding to the controls sluggishly, and he was drifting to the right faster than he expected.

The needle on the r.p.m. gauge for the right engine vibrated like
a tuning fork, and the temperature gauge next to it was rising fast.
Luth pulled the wheel to the left and eased up on the throttle, but
he plane shook harder. "They hit one of the engines," he said.

Below, the waters of the reservoir spread out, smooth and
nany-fingered between the hills. He cut the right engine to
half-power and pulled out of the spiral. They were heading west
again, away from the Wall, but he didn't dare try to change course
until they got over dry land.

The plane rocked up and down violently. Luth cut the remaining
power to the right engine. He gnawed at his lower lip, and gripped
he wheel hard. He had practiced landing on one engine, but only
under controlled conditions, and with an ambulance crew standing
by.

The huge curve of the ancient dam slid by, and they were over
he spillway gorge. A narrow ribbon of water snaked past far

below. He couldn't set down in the gorge, but a wide, fla
promontory on the north side looked possible. He reduce
airspeed as much as he dared and began to tilt the engines back
The damaged engine failed to tilt, but that didn't matter. The goo
one tilted.

Without the stabilizing force of the second engine, the plan
began to spin. He jammed the tail flaps hard in the opposit
direction, but they didn't help much. Fifty feet above the ground
thirty, and the world beyond the windows whirled in a blur
"Hang on!" he shouted. "Here we go!"

They hit the ground hard and skidded sideways toward th
gorge. Luth was thrown and shaken hard against his seat belt
When the bouncing motion stopped, he unbuckled it and stood up
His head was still spinning, but while the deck canted, it wa
stationary. He leaned across to look out the window on the othe
side. They had stopped a scant ten feet from the drop-off. Not fa
away, the other plane was descending in controlled fashion.

"We better get outta here," Mooly said. Without waiting fo
Luth's response, he tried to open the outside door. The leve
moved only an inch. He put his weight on it and grunted.

Luth picked up the rifle and looked back at his passengers
Ainne had rolled off the seat onto the floor. Linnie was bent low
over Danlo so that her loose hair obscured his face. In the rea
compartment, Gairth and the other women were struggling with
the inner door, which had slid shut in the crash.

Mooly stepped back and kicked at the outer door. Luth wedge
in beside him and they both kicked, more or less in unison. Th
door gave a little. "Again." This time it flew open.

Luth stepped to the sill. "Help them get that one open," he said
jerking his head at the rear compartment. He jumped down to th
ground, which was a good deal closer than usual. The right wing
torn nearly off, sagged from a few remaining bolts. He peered ove
it. The other plane had landed. He rested the rifle on top of th
wing, took careful aim, and fired at the center window on the side
that he could see. The window blossomed with shatter fractures
Stay inside, he shared. *We don't want any more bloodshed.*
He waited for a response, waited for the door to open. The othe
plane was silent. He kenned four people inside. The pilot, Ka
Smeds, he had gone through training with. The other three h
didn't know. They were angry and determined. *Don't let them d
anything foolish, Kar.*

You're the one being foolish.

Mooly poked his head out the door. "It's jammed real good," e reported. "They're stuck back there."

"Well, keep trying."

"There's another thing."

Luth kept his eyes on the other plane and his finger on the igger. "What?"

"It's Danlo." Mooly's voice broke. "I think he's dead."

Chapter 25

HE Jewel was indeed a jewel. As they climbed the broad, urving stairway in the glittering central hall, Danlo was inundated ith admiration for all that was beautiful and noble about his orld. He was an interloper here, a cockroach. Around him a housand trained minds throbbed quietly, like the hum and crackle n the air at an electric power plant.

Mooly was huffing. At the second landing he slowed and ooked down over the rail into the bright abyss. His eyes widened, nd he swallowed. Danlo hoped the boy's courage wouldn't fail. Ie hoped, too, that he could repay that courage with something etter than the edge of an axe.

Behind and below him he kenned Epigrass and Ainne. The hread of thought that connected them was tenuous, only enough o assure him that the truck hadn't been noticed. Ahead, down a ide hall, two men were awake. Proctors standing at a door. They vould be the guard posted over—

A mind blazed out at him, brilliant as a searchlight. *What's his?*

Nearby, a joddie had awakened and sensed the intrusion. Danlo eached out in the ktess, aiming for the joddie's sleep center. He night as well have been trying to touch a creature with a dozen urms. No matter how he groped, the effort was batted away. As he probed deeper, the beam of the searchlight that shone on him proke apart into a thousand luminous strands of thought. He had tepped into a room full to bursting with candles, with mirrors that hrew back flame upon flame. The light flowed into forms, antalizing, familiar, and yet, unfamiliar. I must be larger, he told iimself. I must encompass more. He is a man, as I am a man. Vhatever he can ken, I can ken by kenning him.

The forms snapped into crisp focus. The joddie's name wa
Clemino. Danlo looked out through his eyes as he sat up in bed
saw the dark cubicle, felt the coverlet between his fingers
Clemino had already alerted a second joddie, and a third: i
moments the alarm would spread throughout the Jewel. *Mis
taken,* Danlo/Clemino shared. *No cause for alarm. Go back t
sleep.* The nearest minds paused, confused, but beyond them th
ripple of wakening still spread.

Wanting to alert Ainne, Danlo tried to retreat from Clemino'
mind. The strands of light through which he had pushed wov
themselves into a springy mesh that resisted his efforts. Unable t
retreat, he went deeper. He came to the place where Clemino'
certainty of purpose resided, and sowed doubt, spurred unreason
ing fear. Clemino shuddered like a tree trunk in a windstorm, an
Danlo was able to pull free.

He sought his own body, and couldn't find it. No time to search
Two dozen minds were awake now, and waking others. The floo
was unstoppable. He shouted mentally in Ainne's direction
Wake the dreamers! Wake them all! He couldn't tell whethe
she had heard.

Several joddies focused on him, their joined minds a mois
warmth that offered no gaps at all through which he might breal
free. He threw up the strongest shield he could muster. The
poured around the edges like water, like smoke, like bright-eye
snakes undulating toward him, fanged mouths grinning; a doze
snakes, a hundred. He turned to run, and a curtain of snakes wa
coming at him from the other direction.

Was this a nightmare being directed at him by a few joddies, o
was each joddie as he woke appearing somehow in the form o
another snake? No time to puzzle that out. He grabbed writhin
handfuls of snakes and flung them away, but more pressed in
tighter, tighter. Their jaws nipped at him, and lances of pai
sheared through him. He was sinking in a seething cauldron o
snakes.

Become another snake, then. Don't fight them, leave then
nothing to attack. He imagined himself limbless, sinuous. H
undulated among them, mimicked their rhythms. The pain re
ceded. The roiling mass of snakes began to blur. It was hot
turbulent smoke. He gathered himself into a tight ball and plunge
downward through the smoke.

Wind roared in his ears, and there were voices in the wind
wordless voices crying anger and anguish. He fell faster, spinnin

izzily, his mind expanding in terror as he awaited the crushing low when he hit bottom. The wind buffeted him, tore at him, hot nd freezing, hard and sharp as teeth. The wind was inside him, all rough him. He was a whirling vortex, a roaring.

If I am the wind, I can direct the wind. He willed the wind to row still.

It grew still.

A light sprang up. He was standing in a room. It couldn't be a eal room, because it turned to mist at the edges of his vision, but vherever he turned his gaze it was chiseled with incandescent etail—chairs, lamps, bookcases, a richly patterned purple carpet, nd beyond the windows a blurred, shifting pattern of sunlight and oliage. He had never suspected that such a 'place' could exist in ie ktess. What other realms, exotic or dangerous, might lie hidden ere? The room might be sustained by some individual's mental ffort, or by the habit of a thousand minds whose attention was irected elsewhere. However it was being created, it was as real or him as the Jewel had been moments before.

He was alone in the room—and then, without transition, he was ot alone. Behind an old-fashioned wooden desk stood Frank ettig. Frank eyed Danlo with something like paternal irritation. Ie looked much as he had in the later pictures—stout through the niddle, with tangled gray brows above icy blue eyes. His hair, in concession to modern fashion, fell in loose waves to his houlders. A crisp blue-white aura crackled around his head. The nes that bracketed his mouth were harder than in the pictures, the vattles beneath his chin heavier.

"So. Our wayward counter. You've been causing quite a ommotion." Frank spoke slowly and deliberately, in the deep, asal voice Danlo had heard in the recordings, though of course he poke in the modern way rather than in ancient English. His lips noved as if he were speaking aloud. "We should have made you joddie, I see that now. Too late. You'll have to be destroyed."

Danlo knew he should be terrified, but the fear was muted by we. To speak directly with Frank—! "I'm honored that you hould concern yourself with my small comings and goings. But ou needn't. Why not simply let me go? My friends and I mean no arm to the Body."

One corner of Frank's mouth rose in a crooked smile. "Surely ou don't think me so naïve. If you still cherish innocent itentions, it's only because you haven't thought things through. 'he forces you have set in motion are profoundly disruptive."

"I have only come to rid you of something that you don't wan
You have no use for the women, or for the children either."

"The use I have for them," Frank said heavily, "is to see ther
Cleansed."

"Let me cleanse the Body of them, then. Let me take them an
be gone."

Frank laughed. "How little you understand. For nulls quietly
vanish is hardly the same as a good Cleansing."

"You make it sound almost as if you enjoy the bloodshed."

"Enjoy? No. I see the necessity."

"You've done things the same way for a thousand year:
You're not willing to consider change."

"Changes are considered every day. Changes for the better are
in due course, adopted. Changes that would threaten the stabilit
of the Body are rejected."

"I am not a threat."

"You are certainly a threat," Frank said. "Even if you don
admit it to yourself. And I think you do. I can ken you, you know
You have no more secrets from me than a frog laid open on
dissecting table."

Frank's mind reached out toward Danlo's in a moment c
delicate silence that rolled with deep thunder. Danlo teetere
unsteadily on the edge of a vast labyrinth of shadows. He haule
himself back from the precipice—and tipped headlong and fell i

Walls of rough gray stone pressed close to his left and right. A
the end of the corridor Frank stood smiling, haloed by the golde
light of the room where they had been speaking. Danlo heade
toward him. The corridor suddenly twisted like a snake, and h
was going in another direction. He came to an intersection, an
glimpsed Frank down the passage to the left, and turned, but Fran
was gone. Danlo came to a flight of stairs, and went down—but
moment later he was going up. Through a stone archway he sav
himself walking away at an impossible angle.

Behind him came the clicking and scrabbling of claws on ston
and the rasp of hoarse harsh breath. A huge wolf bore down o
him, a wolf as tall at the shoulder as Danlo, eyes bloodred, teet
bared, all bunched muscle and raging hostility.

Danlo ran. The wolf pursued. It was gaining on him, its breat
hot on his neck and foul-smelling. He couldn't tire physicall
since his physical body wasn't running, but still he was weary. H
wanted to let the beast take him. The labyrinth stretched o
forever. Why go on struggling?

For the children, that was why. To save the children.

His hand, brushing the stone wall, found a door handle. He yanked, and slipped through the door, and slammed it.

The wolf crashed into the door. The door bulged inward. The wolf yammered hysterically, howling and barking all at once, and launched itself against the door again. The latch snapped, and the wolf's snapping muzzle poked through. Danlo leaned all his weight against the door, and felt his feet slipping backward.

Another door was behind him. He retreated through it and shut it. The wolf howled and snarled. Its claws scratched in a frenzy. He backed through another door, and another, and another. As he shut each one, the wolf's cries and thrashing diminished.

After a dozen doors, the wolf was gone. But Danlo was still lost in the gray stone labyrinth, in a long passage as featureless as any of the others. Explore it, find a way out? He would never finish. Corridors would rearrange themselves behind him. And the wolf would be back. He needed a better strategy.

The wind was inside me, he remembered. That was how I controlled it—by being larger than it was, by containing and directing. He brought the labyrinth into himself, all of its twists and turns, its hidden chambers. Region by region, he collected it. The process seemed to take either seconds or centuries. Which way was in, which out? He had been turned inside out. The recesses of his mind stretched to the edges of the world, while his exterior was as small and hard as a grain of sand.

Eventually he caught a glimpse of the room where Frank was standing behind the desk. He hesitated—and felt the labyrinth spread out again to the horizon. No, he would have to gather that room to himself along with the rest. I am this, too. . . .

He was standing in the room with Frank, exactly as before. The indistinct foliage wavered beyond the windows, and the pattern on the purple rug was etched with gold sparks. The labyrinth might never have existed.

Frank chuckled. "You're very good. Better than you could possibly realize. Not that it will make the slightest difference in the end. You're only one miserable little man. All the same, I'm curious. I wonder if you're some sort of mutant. The way you erect partitions within your mind, so that actions that I can't anticipate come from behind them—I've never seen that before."

"I'm nobody special," Danlo said. "If I can do it, anybody can."

"Oh, no. That's quite impossible. The ktess is open. It's continuous. There can be no barriers."

"I've met two others who can act in secrecy. And I think the joddies must do it from time to time. Am I right?"

Frank winced, and put his hand to his head. "What?" The room dimmed, and Frank's body stretched and wavered like a sheet of rubber. "Oh, not again. They've lost centrality. They're gibbering like children. Damn! This is your doing, isn't it?"

Danlo dragged his mind away from a place where the sound of marching feet was blossoming into tall, oily plants. How much time had passed on the outside? By now Epigrass and Ainne must have awakened the dreamers. From Frank's comment, the dreamers might have triggered the large-scale instability that Epigrass had predicted. But what did that mean, here in the deep recesses of the ktess? Might Frank himself fly to pieces?

Apparently, the crisis wasn't that profound. The room steadied. There was less furniture in it than before, and the dappled light beyond the windows had winked out, leaving flat blackness. "Order will be restored," Frank said. "It always is. This is no worse than an upset stomach. Well, no, it is worse than an upset stomach. Far worse. What were we talking about?"

"Your desire to release the women and let us depart unharmed."

"A cheap strategem. I'm not that seriously impaired. No, we were talking about blockages in the ktess. I'm using one right now, to keep the little storm of unpleasantness your friends have brewed from sweeping us apart. And of course the joddies channel a great deal of thought from place to place. Quite naturally they deflect it from those who would be distracted by it."

Danlo smiled. "As you say. Quite naturally."

"I don't know why I should bother to discuss it with you." Frank sounded irritated. "No, I do know. So little anymore catches my attention. You've caught my attention. I hope you're pleased. You've achieved that much. It's all you're going to achieve."

"Since I do have your attention, then—why not stop the terrible cruelty? The Body gains nothing by killing children."

Frank seemed older suddenly. He stared down at his desktop, as if remembering. "You think you're the first person ever to protest? There have been dozens. Impassioned mothers who swayed whole towns. Once a head of the Joddirate. He slit his own throat rather than acknowledge my wisdom." His eyes darted out

Danlo from beneath the shaggy brows. "You call it cruelty. Would you like to see cruelty?"

"I have seen enough."

"No. No, you haven't. Not nearly enough." The room vanished. Danlo found himself in a dimly lit, foul-smelling place. Or rather, he didn't find himself. He had no sense of inhabiting a body, nor did he see Frank, but Frank's invisible presence was close beside him, thick and hard like a lump of clay. The place was an alley between buildings—but not an alley like any Danlo had ever seen. The pavement was littered and slimed with filth, and the crooked walls were spotted and peeling. Several people lay in doorways, or sprawled against the walls. Their eyes were dull, their faces caked with dirt. *This was a place called Mexico City,* Frank said. *I fought in a war not far from here, when I was young.*

A woman hobbled up the alley toward where they watched. She was dressed, or at least wrapped, in rags, and she walked in a stoop, without ever straightening up. A torn gray shawl covered her head. She walked like an old woman, but as she got closer Danlo saw that her hair was black and her face, though drawn in pain, was unlined. She coughed, and coughed again. Her thin frame shook. She spat. The dark gob of her spittle mingled with the wet filth, but even in the poor light Danlo could see that the spittle was bloody.

This is what the world was like, Frank said. *She breathed gas in the war. Not enough to kill her. Only enough to torment her for months and then kill her.*

It could never have been like this, Danlo protested. *This is a fantasy.*

It was like this. Worse, some places. Other places it wasn't so bad yet, but it was getting worse. Before much longer it would have been like this everywhere. You saw how dirty the wild nulls were, how they fought with one another. Their world is a garden, thanks to me. But do they appreciate that? No. They'll breed until it's like this again, if we don't stop them.

It's not a garden for them, Danlo said. *They're suffering. We could ease their suffering.*

You're mistaken. Suffering will always exist. The important question is how to structure the suffering so that it works for you rather than against you.

The street scene winked out. Danlo found that he had a body again—or rather, a semblance of a body. His real body must still

be in the Jewel, but he had no sense of contact with it. He and
Frank were walking along a dirt road in the country. It was not a
road that could ever have existed. The colors were all wrong—the
sky purple and blotchy, the plants reddish with fleshy stems and
no leaves, the soil yellow-green. Water was pooled in the low
places in the road, as if from a recent rain, and the edges of the
pools danced with bright shards of light, like ribbons of broken
glass.

"A certain amount of suffering is not only necessary but
healthy," Frank said in a reasonable tone. His hands were clasped
behind his back, and he frowned at the ground as he walked, as if
he was looking for something he had dropped. "People need
bloodshed. So I wouldn't prevent the Cleansings even if I could.
I think sometimes we've grown too soft; I wouldn't want us to get
any softer. If people never saw blood spilled, they would find
ways to spill it. Ways that you would like far less. You must know
how it heals. How many Cleansings did you attend? Fifty? Sixty?
You were anointed with the blood."

"I was trying to recover something I had lost," Danlo said
stiffly. "Something that had been taken from me."

"You think you had no other reason? How little you know
yourself. No, a Cleansing isn't cruelty, not really. What happened
in that city a thousand years ago—that was cruelty, because it was
uncontrolled. People did those things to one another. They could
have stopped, but they didn't know how to stop. So they went on,
century after century, all around the world. They maimed and
killed one another in a thousand ways, not just poison gas, not just
starvation and disease. They were creative about cruelty—and just
as creative about the reasons they invented to justify it. You have
never had to see all that. I spared you it. But I lived my whole life
in the midst of it, and I am quite careful not to forget. If I forget
everything else, I will remember the cruelty."

He stopped and turned to fix Danlo with an unblinking gaze.
"Would you like to see more? Would you like to see babies blown
up by explosives? Women who were raped until they died?"

"What is 'rape'?"

"Rape is—never mind. You wouldn't believe me. Would you
like to see men rotting on sharpened stakes because they fell into
traps in the jungle? I saw that myself, more than once. No, I can
see you're too squeamish. Perhaps I'll tell you things that I read
about but never saw. Did you know there used to be men who beat
their wives with their fists?"

"Their neighbors would stop them. The proctors would stop them."

Frank laughed again. "How little you know! When the women tried to get the proctors of that time to protect them, the proctors laughed at them and sent them back to their husbands. Or should I tell you about death squads? Death squads were bands of armed men who roamed the countryside. They killed thousands of people every year for the flimsiest of reasons, or for no reason at all. They spread terror across the world, and nobody could stop them. There was a word, in fact: 'terrorist.' One whose life was dedicated to provoking terror in others.

"And if you think the cruelty perpetrated by the nulls ended with the Great Cleansing, you're mistaken. We were hundreds of years reclaiming the land of the Serral Valley from the terrible chemicals they had spread everywhere. They pumped poisons into the soil and the water, left more poisons stored in leaking drums from one end of the world to the other. The people who made the poisons knew they were causing dreadful afflictions, though they pretended not to know. They *refused* to stop, and they were so powerful that nobody could force them to. You can't even conceive of such a thing, but it's true. And yet you tell me we're being too cruel by ridding ourselves of a few nulls! In the world in which I grew up, such cruelty would never even have been noticed. And it's *precisely* the Cleansing of the nulls that stands as our only barrier against the return of that plague of cruelty. If we let them live, they will spread across the world until they overwhelm us. Our peace and happiness will be swept away, replaced by endless cruelty. Is that what you want? What you truly want?"

Danlo's resolve faltered. Maybe Frank was right; maybe he was bringing a dreadful future to birth. "No, it isn't. But you're trying to hold me responsible in advance for the actions—the possible actions—of generations yet unborn."

"I'm trying to show you, little counter, that your own actions have consequences."

"I can't control all the possible consequences. I don't think either of us can know with certainty what the consequences might be. There's only one thing I'm certain of: Killing the children is wrong. There has to be some other way. There is no justification strong enough for the killing of a child."

Frank shrugged. "Children die all the time. Some before they're born, even. They're born, they grow old, they die. All of them die,

sooner or later. If you'd lived as long as I, you'd have learned t
take the long view. You act as if moral absolutism were a shin
new toy that you'd just discovered. If you play with it for a whil
I assure you, it will tarnish.''

"What about the Great Cleansing? Wasn't that an act of mora
absolutism? And what about the people we killed in the Grea
Cleansing? Wasn't our cruelty to them as extreme as anything the
could ever have perpetrated?''

"That was necessary," Frank said gruffly. The blood-colore
trees were darkening, and the sky flickered. "It was a historica
imperative.''

"Do you remember the Great Cleansing as vividly as yo
remember the woman in the alley? Would you like to show m
that cruelty?''

Frank looked away. "I choose not to dwell on it. It was lon
ago, and no longer has any relevance. What we have today—''

"In the Great Cleansing, how many people did you kill wit
your own hands? How many did you stand by and watch die, whe
you could have saved them?''

"They were nulls." Frank grew. He was twice Danlo's heigh
a vast gray bulk. His fingers reached out toward Danlo like fa
sausages. "You are only one misguided man," Frank boomed
"You have no understanding of these matters.''

Danlo backed up to keep out of reach of the groping sausages
"How many died in the Great Cleansing? Thousands? Millions
How many millions? I am a counter. Tell me the number.''

The wind sprang up. The trees swayed and clacked against on
another. "Six billion," Frank said. "But half of them wer
starving already.''

"We killed six *billion* people? How many deaths does tha
come to for each day of tranquillity among the Body? Shall we d
the calculation?''

Frank lunged at him. He staggered back, and fell. Frank towere
over him. "This is not to be thought of." Spittle flew from Frank'
mouth. "Not think! Not think!" Frank's fingers closed aroun
Danlo's torso, thick and oily, and pressed and squeezed. Danl
sank into a foul, suffocating soup of nausea. He struck out, but hi
arms were feeble, weightless things. The sausage fingers clampe
tighter, and the nausea spread and turned gluey. He had to vomit
He could not survive for another second without vomiting. Bu
there was nothing to bring up, and he had no throat to expel i
from.

There are places within me, he thought dimly, that you can't get
o. All I have to do is transfer myself into one of those places, and
'ou'll be left holding air. But where were the places? He had no
ense of anything but Frank—Frank surrounding him, suffocating
iim, grinding him to a smear of grease. He was on his stomach on
he ground, and Frank's bloated form was a crushing, impossible
veight on top of him. Frank's fingers spread through his body like
at roots through the soil, violating him, spreading a foul burning
eek.

At the edge of his vision, a many-colored sparkling ribbon
vrithed, shimmering. It was the edge of one of the pools of water
hat he had seen earlier in the road. He crawled toward it with
painful slowness, inch upon inch, carrying Frank's hideous
veight. Frank's fingers had reached his bones. They were tying his
bones in knots, squeezing out the marrow.

Beneath the surface of the pool flashed a circus of interlacing
ight. Pinwheels threw off sparks, and scintillating lattices opened
vithin one another to infinite depth.

The pinwheels spun at him. They were many-bladed whirling
knives, slashing, impossible to dodge. But anything was better
han being crushed by Frank. Gratefully, Danlo tipped over the
edge and into the pool.

The spinning knives plunged into him. The pain sheared
hrough him, but it was a clean pain. The knives severed the
entacles that Frank had sunk into him, and suddenly he was
falling, and Frank's weight was gone.

A moment later the blade-wheels were gone too, flown past him
and away. Cool air buoyed him, or something like cool air. He
spread his arms and legs and glided like a bit of fluff. Agitation
crackled through the ktess, rough and irregular. He touched a
surge of it, and drew back quickly. The panic caused by the
dreamers was still raging, but he had withdrawn somehow into a
region so deep that he could remain unaffected by it—for a while,
anyway. Distantly he heard Frank's anguished wail. Or was it the
howling of a wolf? The sound crawled across his skin like ants.

He floated onward. Where was he? Still in Serameno? How
much time had passed? Minds glowed on all sides like globes of
light, some flickering feebly, some blazing like beacons. As he
tumbled among them he focused on one at random and it cleared,
mist evaporating from a window. A man at the top of a ladder,
afraid to come down. Another: a woman, her belly surging with

guilty laughter. One of her hands streamed blood, and the floor around her feet was jewelled with broken glass.

One of the globes pulsed in a seductive rhythm. He drifted closer and peered into it. From within, trapped inside a soap bubble, Frank Rettig bared sharp teeth in a snarl. Frank lunged, and Danlo recoiled. He spun away as fast as he could, vibrating in panic. When he dared turn to look back, Frank had not followed. The ktess undulated, surrounding him like a great slow river of light, a river jolted by lightning flashes and turbid with fear.

Wandering wasn't accomplishing anything. He ought to return to his body and see if Mooly needed help. But where *was* his body? He searched within himself for a somatic connection, and couldn't find one. A twinge of panic convulsed him.

Forget about Mooly and the others, then. As long as Danlo could evade Frank he wasn't defeated. He could plant a seed of rebellion in every mind he came to. *We must not kill.* A simple idea, one that would be remembered. *The killing must stop.* We must learn to care for the nulls, just as we care for the blind, the deaf, the crippled. He probed the nearest mind, planted the seed, and slid out again. It was as easy as putting people to sleep. He chose another and did the same thing. But there were so many minds! How long before the joddies beat off the panic and joined forces to find and stop him? Rising higher, he looked down on the ktess. A single idea. He folded it into the ktess like an egg into cake batter, into a hundred minds at once. **We must not kill, not ever again.**

Would it be enough? What could a hundred, or five hundred, do against the combined force of the trained minds that sustained Frank Rettig and his mania? The new thought would be diluted, guided, beaten down.

There was a solution. He saw it, and trembled, because he saw in the same instant that Frank was right. Danlo could enable those he touched to hold fast to the idea that killing was wrong—but only by showing them how to hide their thoughts from one another.

Any thought, no matter how wayward, could be hidden just as easily. And that could only lead to chaos. To the shattering of the Body of Harmony.

But what else could he do? If the preservation of order meant killing children, he would have to trust chaos. He reached out to the same hundred minds and placed a second thought beside the first. **You can hide your thoughts from one another. This is how.**

The technique of separating the outer mind from the inner, which he had never dared share before, he now gave freely. He touched a hundred more minds, and placed the two thoughts side by side: We must not kill. To hide your thoughts, build a barrier *here*. And another hundred minds, and another.

Some would not have the inner strength to utilize the technique. Those who did might misuse it to hide more damaging desires. But at least those who wanted to keep the nulls alive would be able to screen their intentions from the joddies. Imperfectly, perhaps, but what with the upswing in waywardness, the joddies would have their hands full. And once it was known that the technique existed, it would spread. Those whom Danlo touched would teach others.

A woman strode toward him across the void, tiny at first but growing rapidly. He squirted away, and she followed, closing the gap without effort. "Come back here," she said. "Where have you been? What are you doing? You won't believe the trouble that's been stirred up." She was tall and slim, with a suggestion of heaviness in the bones of her face. Her hair was piled in a tower of curls that ended in coiling streamers of fire. "I thought you were going to help with this, Frank."

"You're Olivia," he said warily. "And you think I'm Frank."

"I don't *think* you're Frank, you *are* Frank, insofar as either of us is anybody in particular. Open your— Oh."

Without meaning to, he dropped the barrier with which he had been holding himself apart from her. Portions of his mind merged with portions of Olivia's, so that he saw himself through her eyes. She was right. She knew her husband. He was not Danlo Ree, not entirely. He was Frank Rettig. But parts of Frank were missing. Something alien had been spliced into their place. He had been subverting his own purposes without knowing it.

Olivia reached out mentally and tore him in half.

The part that was Danlo tumbled away. It exploded in sheets of fiery pain. It whipped across the ktess like a loose fire hose, ripping minds from their moorings, seeking blindly amid the roaring flame, the bath of acid, for the scarred stump that had been itself.

Nothing. Everything. The ragged edges of stone house bleeding eye sockets wild dogs fangs broken bowl smashed skull Linnie rabbit bones dark birds. What was that obscure irritant? He swam up out of the pain. Julan's voice? No, the blond girl. What was her name? Ainne. Ainne's voice, distant and garbled like the remains of something small and broken. "Beat your heart," she was saying. "Please, listen to me. Beat your heart. Breathe. You have to do it yourself. If she comes back while I'm still doing it for you, you'll die."

Chapter || 26

CARING was lifting an impossible weight with arms that had been asleep for a week. Don't care, then, he told himself. Just do it. He reached out, found the connections within himself, and knitted them, one by one, together. His body was no more than an irritant at the edge of his awareness, but he could sense that his autonomic functions had started operating on their own. He was under water; no, worse than water, he was swimming through mud. Slowly the mud thinned. A beacon glowed before him: Ainne was a bright, fuzzy-edged globe that glowed with silver fire and fluttered with the exuberance of youth. Around her in the dim and cluttered void of the ktess the vicious red obsessions of the dreamers churned and jostled.

"I thought you were gone." Her silent voice vibrated through him as if he were a taut string. "You were gone, for a long time. I couldn't ken you anywhere. Then I found your body, and you weren't in it."

"I was—absorbed somehow by Frank. Or I absorbed part of him. We should have known we'd attract Frank and Olivia. What's going on now in the Jewel? Have you been able to keep track?"

"The joddies are still trying to mount a defense against the dreamers. I don't know how far the panic has spread. Clear across Serameno, anyhow. Epigrass has made himself a channel for it, and he's directing most of it away from us. Every time it starts to settle down, he whips it up again. I'm not sure how he'll survive being so completely insane. I've been knocking down anybody that tries to get near the truck. The panic helps me, as long as I don't get sucked up in it. I'm not sure where your body is. Can you get an impression?"

With difficulty, he isolated the physical sensations. Stiffness in his limbs. Arms around him. Uneven movement. Head lower than torso. "Being carried. Down stairs, I think."

"By one person, or more than one?"

"More than one. He must have found them!"

"Olivia did something to you, didn't she? I caught the edge of it. I was afraid she was going to do it to me next."

"She's probably busy trying to heal Frank. I was inside him. I became part of him, without knowing it. Frank didn't know it either. He knew I was there, but he thought he was dealing with *me,* when he wasn't, exactly. He was doing something to himself—fighting with himself, toward the end. Then the part that was me got away from the other part, and— Oh."

"What?"

Danlo chuckled. "I acquired one or two of Frank's skills while we were enmeshed. Afterward I was able to make some changes. Some people are going to feel differently about the killings than they did before."

"That won't matter," Ainne said bitterly. "He can just change them back."

"I showed them how to hide their thoughts from one another. He'll have a harder time undoing that."

"Maybe. We ought to be—oh. I'm not—"

Ainne spun away from him, sucked into an invisible whirlpool. She cried out, and the words were torn to meaningless scraps that flitted away like frightened birds. He plunged after her, desperate not to lose the contact, but a barrier pushed him back. Soft as mattress padding, it wrapped around his face, smothering him. He tried to push through, and the barrier wrapped him tighter. He turned in another direction, and it was there too. He couldn't breathe! Physically suffocating? He had lost touch with his body again. No, this smothering was interior, and that made it ten times worse. Smothering. Itching and smothering. The air was all ants, and the ants were on fire, he was being crushed by an impenetrable wall of ants. He contracted into a small hard ball, made himself as cool and smooth and heavy as steel, let the hordes of fire-ants march around him. After a time they blurred into a red mist, and he fell free.

The articulated brightness of minds on all sides, as before. Now which one was Ainne? He cast about swiftly, and didn't ken her. How about his own body, then? That might orient him. He located a body, entered it, and discovered it wasn't his. It was young and female, and quite pregnant. He left it quickly and drifted on. Would he even know his body if he found it? What did it feel like? What distinguished it from other bodies? He tried again. Male this time, but standing on a street corner looking up at the sky. Vivid in memory: an airplane roaring low overhead.

A fresh onslaught of pain flashed through him. He moaned, and thought he heard the sound through physical ears. His own ears? The smell of charred flesh was strong. An instantaneous, palpable impression: a boy sitting among the branches of a tree, a book in his lap, the book ablaze, the boy, horrified, holding up the flaming stumps of his hands. The boy flew past and was gone, but the pain intensified. It rolled like a boulder downhill, crushing, crushing.

He collected himself with an effort. What had he been doing? Trying to find Ainne. He conjured up her face, her hands, her voice, narrowed his focus until she filled it. Something tugged at him. Yes—here was her body. He found the farmhouse and family easily among the memories. Keeping part of his attention fixed on her latent essence, he quested outward for a congruent pattern.

He heard her whimpering before he found her. She was in what appeared to be a small village square. She was wielding an axe. A young man knelt in front of her, arms bound behind him, his head laid on the block. On the other side her parents stood, their arms linked, smiling and nodding encouragement. She raised the axe and chopped at the young man's neck. Her parents smiled. Ainne's mouth welled blood. It spilled down her chin. She swung the axe again. The boy crawled away from her. She pursued him, chopping and chopping, grunting like an animal. Her parents smiled serenely and nodded encouragement.

Danlo tried to get between Ainne and the boy. She swung at him, and the axe bit into his shoulder. He cried, "No!"

"No," she echoed. "No. No. No." She swung the axe at herself. Her parents smiled. She chopped at her own foot, chopped again, severed it at the ankle. Her parents smiled and nodded. She chopped at herself again and again in a mounting frenzy.

Danlo got behind her and reached for the axe. She turned on him and swung the gleaming blade, her mouth spouting blood, her eyes glazed and blank. He backed away. She started hacking at her own shoulders, at her head.

The mother said gently, lovingly, "She's such a good girl."

Bits of Ainne sailed outward in lazy arcs. Danlo tried to enter her mind to calm her, and recoiled. She seethed inside, a nest of snakes drowning in venom. Somehow, something had breached her defenses. Olivia or the dreamers, it didn't matter which. The nightmare was her own. The axe whirled, ripped through her. Efficiently, tirelessly, she dismembered herself. The parents were gone now, and the young man. The axe blurred into a boiling silver cloud, and Danlo couldn't reach her through the cloud.

After what seemed to be a long time, the cloud dissipated in a bitter smell of overheated metal. Bits of Ainne, not flesh but her essence, tumbled slowly away from one another, sparks drifting on the wind.

Her physical body still lived. It lay like an empty house, shutters drawn, furniture covered with dusty dropcloths. A rumbling vibration filled it. He opened her eyes. She was lying down. Sideways oblongs of light were filled with sky, and below them a deck of corrugated metal. He could hear other people nearby, so he closed her eyes again. He didn't want to be distracted by questions.

One by one, he remembered each slash of the axe, and traced the bright filaments, the memories that had turned to pain. He brought them back and placed them reverently in Ainne's center. The fragments were drifting apart faster now, and he had to fly after them. How many had there been? Twenty? Fifty? He searched for more, spreading himself wide across the ktess. There, a wistful sadness like the sound of a waterfall. There a bitter, cynical shrug. He gathered them all.

What he collected lay colorless and inert within her, pieces of a puzzle that would never be put back together. Eventually he saw that he was not going to find any more. Ainne's sorrow had merged with the world's. He returned to her body and centered all his attention in it. Gray ash, the remains of a fire. He needed to breathe on it delicately, feed it twigs. He imagined, as vividly as he could, a butterfly, and sent it fluttering into the center of the gray. Flowers, their fragrances, buds opening. A wind-up duck he had had when he was a toddler. Sunlight spreading downward through the forest canopy in broad, dusty beams. What else would a little girl growing up on a farm be fond of? Lightly he riffled through her inert memories: A horse. A white horse. Galloping on a white horse, and laughing.

Deep within her, something flickered. He cupped it close. Songs—what would her favorite songs be? The song didn't matter, the feeling was what mattered. He went through his own favorite, a six-voice arrangement of "The Flower Fields Rolling," lingering on every exquisite chord. The flicker of life grew. Julan on the day when they were married, a wreath woven into her hair. Being indoors, warm and cozy beside the fire, while rain poured outside. Hot chocolate and buttered biscuits. Biscuits with honey.

"Oh."

"Lie still. You'll be all right."

"What—where—?"

"Don't try to remember. Just rest."

"You're the man from the mountains. You went off to—"

She shuddered as chunks of memory broke loose within her. He warmed her with his presence, wrapped himself around her mentally. He hoped it would be enough.

After a minute she calmed. "Did we get out of Serameno?"

"I think so," he shared. "I think we're in a plane. I think maybe everything is going to be all right." But was it? For several minutes he had been kenning a new threat. Now that her need for him was less intense, he was able to stretch guardedly in that direction. A second plane, paralleling their course. Threatening to turn its weaponry on them. Ainne was aware, but dazed and listless. He would have to cope with this danger alone.

He shifted toward the occupants of the other plane and reached for their sleep centers. A rubbery barrier rebuffed him. Either he was too tired by now to act effectively, or Olivia had found a way to block him. What other options did he have? Could he cast some sort of illusion—convince them that Luth's plane was descending so they would go after it?

Before he could act, an angry yellow glow burst inside him. It plucked at him as if he were a giant harp-string. His sense of contact with his surroundings snapped and was gone. The deep, resonant vibration drew him, struggling, up a column like a tall round chimney, a column corrugated with circular ribs. As the chimney narrowed, the ribs rippled in waves and pressed against him rhythmically, squeezing him in iron bands. He tried to sink back down the column toward his body, but he had no power of motion.

At the top he was ejected into a vast, jumbled place. He sorted out the impressions: A windowless, cornerless chamber lined from floor to ceiling with cushions and mirrors. The cushions were covered with sumptuous fabrics in iridescent weaves. The mirrors, set in jagged frames at crazy angles, glittered coldly.

Olivia reclined among the cushions. She was wrapped to the ankles in a tight-fitting green dress studded with a multitude of tiny buttons as hard and black as snakes' eyes. She smiled at him, but with little warmth. "You still haven't given up this ridiculous scheme. I don't know why I should expect you to be sensible—no,

I do. It's because you're a counter. You must understand the value of order. Yet here you are, stirring up trouble."

"It is not I who stir up trouble."

She dismissed this with a languid wave. "Your little friends haven't been hurt. They're odd playthings, but if you'd like to keep them, perhaps I'll let you."

"They're unhurt because you haven't been able to get at them. Was it you who did that to Ainne?"

"A troublesome girl. What happened to her was no worse than she deserved. Just now you and I have more serious matters to discuss. Anomalous phenomena require attention." The words 'anomalous phenomena' had a rubbery echo, as if four or five mouths had spoken at once. "I know you'll be eager to help. You understand how vital it is that I be impressed by your cooperative spirit."

"What can I do?" He was not agreeing to do anything, but he was curious why she was being friendly instead of attacking him. The more he learned, the better chance he would have against her.

"We have not been able to undo the mischief that you did when you had access to portions of Frank. Certain ideas, tendencies—we thought we had isolated them, but they've broken through. They're spreading."

"I don't know what I can do." The soft luxury of the cushions beckoned. He hesitated, but he was tired. He lay down and stretched out, heedless of the sharp edges of the mirrors.

"Perhaps more than you realize. I'm hoping, dear little man, to understand you. Really understand you, through and through. You hold the key to everything that has happened. I've been speculating that you might feel, on some level, a profound contempt for your fellows. Is that it? Do you simply reject the notion of belonging to the Body?"

"I think I appreciate the value of belonging in a way that you wouldn't understand. It's been a long time since you've been alone."

"Mmmm. Do you like this place? You don't ever have to leave if you don't want to." Her fingers brushed the back of his hand. The touch seared, but he couldn't tell whether it was fire or ice. One mirror showed the curve of Olivia's bare shoulder from behind. In another a pattern of black circles, the buttons on her skirt, rippled against shimmering green. They shifted as she settled deeper among the cushions. Did he want to leave? Why should he? A dusky incense had sprung up, cloyingly sweet—or was it as dry as old paper? The contours of Olivia's body beneath the clinging fabric were a profound mystery, yet not even remotely a mystery.

What was odd was that while he was lying close enough to reach out and stroke her, her image was in all the mirrors and his in none. There were more mirrors than before, and not so many cushions. A couple of the glass edges pressed against his back, his legs, but he felt too comfortable to move.

"You are going to help us," Olivia murmured. "I'm sure of it. Already I feel very close to you. Perhaps I'll let you continue to exist, even to have some limited autonomy—under close guidance, of course. That would be amusing." Her voice caressed him like fur. Under the green dress her body had grown less rounded, more angular. Her hip jutted like bare bone. He was looking at reflections, at her back, her shoulder, a falling curling lock of hair. He was afraid to shift his attention back to her face. "You could advise the One on questions of right and wrong. I understand you have some thoughts on the subject. If you'd enjoy having your opinions considered, you need only agree to work with us."

He turned his attention deliberately away from the reflected Olivias and toward the edges of the mirrors, where narrow ribbons of rainbow shimmered. "Why should you want my help? You've dealt with emergencies before."

"True. Frank and I together. But Frank is not himself. Parts of him have been contaminated through contact with you—and of course the panic and instability disturbed him. At present I'm stretched quite thin. If I knew I could count on you not to stir up further trouble, it would put my mind at ease." The cloth of the green dress rustled and whispered like dry leaves, or like something slithering along the ground beneath a cover of dry leaves.

"Why should I want to put your mind at ease?" He found that he was standing again, though he had not risen. The heavy glass mirrors loomed above him menacingly, leaning inward, swaying unsupported in midair. He could see his own reflection now. He was gray and shrunken, and the reflections had no arms.

"Because I'm your soul, little man. We're wasting time."

"In a thousand years, I'd think you would have learned patience." While he fenced verbally with Olivia, Danlo studied the mirrored chamber. The mirrors moved, slowly but not aimlessly. They were coming closer.

"In a thousand years I have learned when to act and when to wait. This is a time to act. You are trying my patience. You can help me voluntarily, or you can force me to destroy you, which I will certainly do if you don't cooperate.''

"You want me to help you unravel the ideas I planted."

"Precisely," she said silkily. "It will be so easy for you. Just open yourself to me, so that I can make use of the resources you're hoarding.''

By not looking at her face, he could catch glimpses of it. It flickered and fled from one mirror to another, always ahead of his gaze, or behind. Her face was a naked skull.

"You will open yourself, you know. You trust me," the skull murmured. "In a very real sense, we have always been one, you and I. You imagine that I'm trying to harm you only because you have been warped by your own unfulfilled need to merge with the Body. How could I do less than love you? Whatever your shortcomings, whatever your weaknesses, you are a part of me. You will be cherished and forgiven. Ken me. Merge with me. When you see my intentions, you will trust me.''

"I don't doubt your intentions." Danlo began walking, slowly and carefully, among the heavy mirrors. The skull drifted after him. "Frank was contaminated," Danlo said, "by his contact with me. He thought he was fighting me, when he was fighting himself.''

"These distinctions are somewhat arbitrary. But yes. He entered a state of internal dissociation due to his contact with you." The skull was larger now, and closer behind him. The green dress and the body beneath it had vanished.

"How can you be certain that the same thing won't happen to you?" Danlo walked faster. "If I open myself to you, how can you be sure you won't be destroyed?''

"Because I know myself," the skull said. "Women are more practical. Frank's weakness has always been that he won't acknowledge the hidden side of himself. His denial created a chink in his armor that you could burrow into.''

"So Frank has been hiding thoughts from himself for a thousand years." Danlo chose a turning at random among the mirrors. "No wonder the hiding of thoughts became a contagion the moment the technique was revealed. It's Frank you should blame, not me." He chose another turning. The skull was at his heels.

"Word-play," the skull said. "Blame is not important. The restoration of the Oneness of the Body is what is important.''

"The Body has been chopping off parts of itself for a thousand years. They can never be restored."

"Toenail-parings," the skull said nastily. "And you're a cyst. I think I'll dig you out now."

Danlo dodged down a narrow, crooked path between mirrors. The mirrors slid across one another, edge to edge like scissor-blades. He slipped into a closing gap, turned, and dove through another as it opened. The skull advanced toward him from a hundred directions, and he could not tell which was the real skull and which were reflections. He stopped, confused, chose a direction, dived, and ran headlong into a mirror. It shattered, and the fragments clashed around his head like bright knife-shaped birds. He was falling into a dazzling forest of razors. He shouted, "You can't have me!" but the words were severed from one another. Each flew into its own mirror. He was inside-out, everywhere and nowhere. He was stretched to the ends of the world, sliced into ribbons, stretched again, chopped apart. He dissolved.

A hundred mirrors. A hundred Danlos, each behind a mirror, all staring out, motionless. In a little clearing in the forest of mirrors, the skull hovered, flame dancing behind its empty eyes. The Danlos watched it, thinking nothing, feeling nothing. They had, perhaps, a lingering awareness of one another—dim, peripheral, a wisp as tenuous as a teaspoonful of fog.

"You see how it is." The skull giggled. "You don't exist anymore. Try to have a thought. You can't do it. You can't even try. You can't even *want* to try. No action, nothing to be reflected, only the reflection itself. Soon that too will fade." The skull sighed. "We'll have to repair the damage the hard way, the slow way. But we *will* repair it. The Body will be as it has always been. Poor, wretched little counter. You've accomplished exactly nothing."

The skull did not vanish, for to vanish is to remain present in memory. Without memory, nothing can vanish. So there had never been a skull among the mirrors. A peal of shrill laughter hung in the air like dirty smoke.

The mirrors began to drift apart. Each Danlo, pressed flat behind a mirror, watched its other selves recede, and did not reach out to draw them together, and did not know that they were called Danlo, and did not mourn for anything. The air that was not air turned gray and then blue-gray, and each of the flat panels tumbled slowly into the deepening gloom.

Stray scraps, reflections, flashes of form. A room. Hair. Voices. In every mirror different glimpses, coming and going without being noticed. Shaving. The brash morning nonsense of a mockingbird. Lou Carrodos spading up the flower garden behind his kitchen. Lou was still a little shaken up by the awful malaise that had poured through the ktess earlier, but he trusted that Frank and Olivia had put things right. Pip Sith yawning as he opened the doors of his dress shop. Sellie Murtager swinging up into the cab of her truck for the morning run. She clipped the mug of tea in its holder and adjusted the rearview mirror. A pair of haunted eyes behind the mirror, looking out at her? No, only the empty parking lot. Powl Trasnic tickling his wife as she stood at the stove. She pretended to push him away, then let him kiss her. Sweetness of toothpaste. Gaby Nickle getting out of a coach at the edge of a river gorge, looking across the gorge at a pair of planes, one with a broken wing. Rahl Clathers sitting in one of the planes, hands gripping a rifle. The other pilot had plainly gone corker. Shooting at them! Well, let him. He would run out of bullets soon enough, and the other plane wasn't going anywhere.

Resoluteness of ending. Pac Endiby looked at Rahl and raised his eyebrows. "Crowd," he said, pointing across the gorge. More than a dozen vehicles had stopped at the edge of the highway, and the braver souls were climbing down the slope. "Be across before long."

Rahl nodded. No sense letting Vardiki injure more innocents with his rifle. As proctors, their duty was to take it away from him. Besides, Pac and Rahl and Kar and Bith wanted to capture the fugitives themselves. They wanted their names to be sung.

Behind Vardiki, one of the nulls had climbed out of the disabled plane. He was holding a limp form with long blond hair, a life-sized rag doll, as if he were dancing with it.

Rahl opened the door. Vardiki fired, and the bullet spanged off of the top edge. Rahl winced.

The boy turned, and the rag doll swung so that its beautiful woman-child face lolled into view.

Ainne.

A searchlight snapped on in an empty room. Lost scraps surged toward one another like papers sucked into a whirlwind. Part of Rahl's mind tugged, yearning toward Ainne. The tug swelled, thoughts tumbling like dust-motes in a boiling raindrop. Pressure in his head, impossible pressure. The raindrop burst out of him in a brilliant arc across the ktess. It exploded in Ainne, gathered force, leaped again.

Danlo coughed weakly. The spasm ripped at his lungs. He coughed again. Arms were supporting his shoulders. He found an arm of his own and pushed downward, taking a little of his own weight. A voice, tinny with distance yet shockingly loud: "Hey, he's not dead! He's wakin' up!"

He shuddered from head to toe, and concentrated on breathing. HIs eyelids were coated with glue, but he got them open. A face hovered above him, upside down. Linnie. She was crying. A low stream of words in her own language, and then, "Linnie carries Danlo. Linnie carries Danlo."

"Carry—" He coughed, and knife-pains tore at his lungs. "Carry the children. They need you." He struggled to sit up. She helped him, and clung to his back, sobbing. "Run," he said. "Run. All of you. I'll stop them."

Mooly leaned in the door. "We can't run. They're stuck back there." He pointed at the rear of the plane, where Gairth and Big Awa were straining against the jammed door.

"Break it. Free them." He tried to get to his feet, and couldn't. Mooly extended a hand and pulled him upright. He stepped down from the plane and stood, tottering, in the sunlight. He had no sensation in his legs, but for now they obeyed him. Ainne was awake, but dazed. Her wide green eyes gazed at him almost without recognition. He turned to Luth, whose rifle still rested on the broken wing. "There is to be no more killing."

"We didn't start this."

"Who started it makes no difference. I'm ending it."

"You mean for us to let them take us?"

"No. They won't harm you."

"I've kenned them," Luth said forcefully. "I know what they mean to do."

"Yes. Give me the rifle." Danlo held out his hand.

Luth was locked in bitter indecision.

"I can force you," Danlo said. "I'd rather not."

Luth lowered the rifle and presented it to Danlo. It was so heavy Danlo nearly dropped it. "Boy," he said to Mooly. "Take this. Throw it over the edge."

Mooly looked from Danlo to Luth, and shrugged. "Sure." He accepted the rifle and heaved it. It spun end over end into the gorge.

The door of the other plane opened. Danlo took a couple of

steps in that direction. Mooly put out a hand to restrain him, and on the other side Linnie gripped his shoulder.

"There's nothing more you can do for me," he said. "Free the others, and go. Hurry."

Somehow he shook them off. He shuffled slowly toward the three proctors who had emerged from the other plane. "You'll have to let them go," he said, quietly but firmly. "There is to be no more killing." Two of the proctors raised their rifles.

Chapter ‖ 27

MOOLY felt as if he couldn't move, as if time had stretched out and left them all suspended forever beneath the great empty bowl of sky. Ainne stood beside him, one hand raised to her mouth. On the other side, Linnie, bent forward at the waist, had stretched out both arms toward Danlo. Luth's back was to Mooly, broad shoulders in a black aviator jacket beneath glistening black curls. Behind the proctors the other plane rested, sleek and compact, and beyond it in the distance the gray curve of the dam filled the gorge. The morning sun beat on their faces and cast the proctors' shadows long across the ground.

Two rifle shots cracked, nearly together. Danlo flew backward and sprawled crooked in the grass.

Mooly's throat burned. He was supposed to lead us! You weren't supposed to do that! Linnie growled and took a step toward the proctors, but Mooly gripped her shoulder to restrain her. He wanted to jump on the proctors too, and beat them with his fists, but he knew he'd never get close enough. He didn't want to watch Linnie get shot too.

What happened next was very odd. The proctors lowered their rifles. They looked bewildered. Two of them let their weapons fall to the ground, and the third turned and pitched his down the slope into the gorge. One of them sat down in the grass, another turned and wandered away. The third simply stood like a statue, looking distractedly at the ground, not at the fugitives.

Luth turned. "They don't want to stop us anymore. He fixed them somehow, didn't he?"

Ainne nodded, slowly at first and then with more force. "Yes. Yes. It's more complicated than that. He—"

Linnie broke free with a little cry, and ran and knelt over Danlo's body. "Why couldn't he have fixed 'em a minute sooner?" Mooly demanded.

"It wouldn't have made any difference," Ainne said.

"What do you mean? They wouldn't have shot him!"

"It wouldn't have made any difference," she repeated. "His body died ten minutes ago."

"Then how—"

"I don't know. He wasn't there. He wasn't anywhere. And then—" She gestured at the thing that lay collapsed and broken in the grass.

Mooly looked out across the gorge. Twenty coaches had stopped there, and more were arriving. People were pouring like ants down the far slope. "What about them?" He pointed. "It sure doesn't look like he fixed them."

Ainne's brow creased. "This is hard. I don't have—it isn't— Oh. That's Olivia. They still want to take us in."

"Or tear us apart," Luth added. "Lot of hostility."

"We better get goin', then!"

"First we have to get that door open." Luth strode toward the plane.

Mooly had forgotten that Gairth and three other women were still trapped in the rear of the plane. Luth ducked inside. Mooly stepped to the edge of the gorge to look down. The leaders of the mob had nearly reached the bottom, where a bright ribbon of water meandered. More vehicles were coming from both directions, stopping haphazardly and blocking the highway as the occupants spilled out. Shouting echoed thinly across the gap.

Ainne was beside him. "Can't you do something?" he asked.

"Olivia is over them like a cloud. I'm trying to make them forget about us, but I'm too weak. I feel like when the doctor takes a cast off your arm."

Banging came from the plane.

"Maybe they can't swim," Mooly said hopefully. Far below, two men waded out into the river. Halfway across, the water reached only to their chests. "Doesn't look like they'll have to."

Ainne made a small, meaningless noise. She was staring hard at the dam. "All of them," she murmured. "All of them. Hurry."

Long seconds passed. Mooly wanted to know what Ainne was doing, but he figured he shouldn't interrupt her. He thought about picking up one of the proctors' rifles and firing it down into the gorge—not to hit anybody, just to scare them. He was afraid it might make them more angry. He didn't especially want to be torn limb from limb.

"Watch." Ainne pointed at the base of the dam, where the broad concrete troughs of the spillway, streaked green and brown from centuries of algae, fed a steady stream into the gorge. The stream gushed faster. "I made the dam-keeper open the pipes," she said. Dirty white foam boiled at the lower ends of the troughs. The roar of rushing water grew until it covered the shouting from the other bank. The foam kicked splatters of spray into high arcs, and the concrete mouths at the top of the spillway spewed a solid torrent. The slick swell of new water advanced downstream toward the crossing point, covering the crowns of boulders and carrying muddy debris.

That ought to stop them, Mooly thought. Or most of them. If it reached them in time. Several people were already on the near side of the gorge, starting the climb, and seven or eight more were in midstream. The spillway was almost half a mile away. The swell hadn't yet reached the crossing point; the mob might not even have noticed it.

The roaring sound faltered and died. Mooly looked back at the dam. The flow at the top of the spillway had slowed to a trickle. A dirty brown trickle. A ripple of mud or sand cascaded down the ramp. "He closed 'em again," Mooly said.

"No."

"Then what?"

"I'm not sure. I don't—"

In the midst of a crooked spume of spray, a rattle of stones pitched out of the mouth of the spillway, mostly small chunks but a couple of large ones. Above, the smooth, concave face of the dam sagged slightly. Mooly blinked and shaded his eyes with his hand. It wasn't just his eyes. Cracks were spreading upward from the spillway, thin and dark and many-branching.

Across the gorge, somebody screamed.

The dam settled further, and its base bulged, slowly at first, like a balloon swelling. A low rumble reached them. Then the base exploded outward. Huge jets of spray spurted between hurtling chunks of debris. The upper rim of the dam dropped and disappeared beneath a dirty white cataract, and a solid wall of water and shattered concrete roared down the gorge.

Mooly felt fingers digging into his arm. Ainne was holding onto him. The people on the far slope were scrambling upward, but in seconds the flood reached them. Those nearest the bottom vanished beneath the ugly brown torrent. Ainne's eyes were squeezed shut. Mooly leaned forward to peer down the slope on this side, and saw no survivors, only one of the proctors from the other plane, who was standing motionless just above the new waterline. On the other side, those who were safely above the flood stood pointing, hugging one another, averting their eyes. Through the gap in the dam the waters of the reservoir poured, thundering, and away to the west the swollen river rampaged toward the sea.

"It was an old, old, dam," Ainne said, almost too quietly for Mooly to hear. "The dam-keeper knew it was a bad idea to open all the floodgates at once. I made him do it anyway." She hung her head, and her mouth trembled.

"You did what you had to do."

Her eyes were haunted. "I hope you'll keep telling me that. Maybe someday I'll believe it."

"You did."

"All I did was gain us some time. I'm not sure how much time. We'd better get moving." She went to Linnie and put her hand on Linnie's shoulder.

Mooly climbed into the disabled plane. He had to step around another of the proctors, who was sitting in the shade beneath the wing, picking idly at a clump of grass.

Luth had improvised a crowbar by unbolting a seat. The crowbar was jammed into a narrow slot at the edge of the rear compartment's door, and Luth was braced against the side of the plane, pushing on the crowbar with both feet, his face tense with effort. Behind the glass, two of the women were risking their fingers tugging in the same direction.

"Why not just break the window?" Mooly asked.

"Unbreakable. Designed for holding prisoners. Throw your weight into this with me."

Mooly wedged himself in beside Luth, set one foot on the crowbar, and pushed as hard as he could. With a shearing screech, the gap beside the door widened by several inches. The crowbar clattered to the floor. The smallest of the women tried to sidle through the gap, but it was still too narrow.

Luth grabbed the edge of the door and pulled it toward him. It gave a little. Mooly braced his back and pushed the edge of the door with his foot while Luth rocked it in and out. Half an inch at a time, it moved. The small woman jabbered at them, and they stepped away. This time she slipped through easily.

Gairth followed. He laughed nervously. "I thought we were gonna die back there."

"You almost did," Luth told him.

They worked at the door for another minute, until the gap was wide enough for the other women. Then they all piled out into the sunlight. Linnie's eyes were stricken and empty, and Ainne's arm was around her. Gairth gazed open-mouthed at the remains of the dam. Luth pointed east. "We're only about ten ground-miles from the Wall," he said, "around the north edge of the reservoir. But it's all up and down. Take us all day." He turned to Ainne. "Is there anybody out there that's going to try to stop us?"

She was silent for a minute. "I don't think so. They can still bring in coachloads if they decide to, or hunt us from another plane. But maybe—" She glanced toward the gorge, and shuddered. "—maybe the joddies have had enough for a while."

They ransacked the proctors' plane quickly, and amassed a pile of survival gear, which they distributed among themselves. Mooly hooked a water bottle to his belt, and tucked the folding tent under his arm. The medicine kit had a handle. When he found some binoculars, he felt weighed down, so he handed them to Linnie. She started crying. He didn't know what he had done wrong. He thought maybe she didn't want them, so he tried to take them back, but she hugged them with both arms and rocked back and forth and wouldn't let go.

When they got to the top of the first hill, Mooly turned to look back. Two planes, one crippled and one whole, lay like bright toys on the wide ledge. The wind riffled the grass around them in slow waves. Between them, a body lay crumpled.

The hikers skirted the broad, muddy bank of the shrunken reservoir. The sun climbed, and beat down on them. The proctors' water bottles had been empty. Mooly was thirsty, but walking out on the mud didn't look like a smart move. Eventually they came to where a creek splashed down toward the reservoir, and they drank and filled the bottles. A little further on they came to a cluster of buildings, with docks that extended out into the mud and boats lying crooked alongside the docks. They detoured around the place. A couple of people came out of the buildings and looked at them, but nobody tried to come after them.

Much of the land through which they were walking was lumber forest. They crossed logging roads and passed swaths of bare stumps and other areas thick with freshly planted saplings. Because Gairth's ankle was still swollen, they had to move slowly.

The wild women ranged among the trees, and came back with long, straight poles, to the ends of which they lashed the butcher knives and the two-pronged fork.

Mooly saw a dark speck overhead, and his heart hammered. "Everybody! Under the trees!"

Luth shaded his eyes. "It's only a hawk."

"Why is it all of a sudden they're not comin' after us?"

"It's Danlo," Ainne said. "He—did some things. Changed some things. Right now there's a big struggle going on in the ktess. I'm staying clear of it, but several people are feeding me bits and pieces. Olivia is still furious, but some people out there who might always have agreed with Danlo, if they'd had the chance, are starting to make their presence felt. The One has plenty to worry about without chasing us."

"Anyway," Luth added cynically, "what's their hurry? They can hunt us down almost as easily tomorrow or next week."

Ainne looked at him. "Regret?"

Luth thought for a minute. "No. Fear."

"Good. Fear will keep you alert."

"What about you?" Mooly asked Ainne. "Are you sorry you're doing this? You could have had a pretty good life, not like Gairth and me."

"I'm only sorry Danlo didn't come along a year sooner. But if he had, I might have not been ready, or willing. After what they did to Borry, I could never have had 'a pretty good life,' but I had to try to go on the old way for a while before I understood that it was never going to work. This is a lot scarier, and it'll probably be a lot harder, but I won't have to spend the rest of my life being poisoned by anger. Besides, Danlo went through a lot—he died—to give us this chance. We have to do it. Not just for ourselves but for the ones who come after." She brushed her hair back behind her ears, caught it at the nape of her neck, and wrapped the long white-gold fall of it around her hand and twisted it down across her shoulder and breast. "This is going to get caught in the bushes. I should cut it."

"It's too beautiful," Mooly protested. "Don't."

Ainne didn't respond. She only walked along, fingers twisting in her hair, lost in thought.

At the top of every rise Mooly strained his eyes looking ahead for the Wall. By midafternoon he was starting to wonder whether they would have to find a place to sleep and go on in the morning. Or maybe it didn't make any difference. If they got to the Wall today, they would still have to find a place to sleep on the other side. Mooly had never worried before about where he was going to sleep. He remembered complaining to his mother that the bed was too small, and smiled wryly. He had a bigger bed now. The whole world was his bed. Not a comfortable one, but he could stretch out as far as he liked.

Linnie and the other women talked for a long time. The talk wasn't all friendly. At one point the large woman shouted and waved her arms in Linnie's face, and Linnie bared her teeth and shouted back. The round-faced woman interrupted in a low, firm voice, and they quieted down.

When the exchange ended, Linnie hobbled over to walk beside Mooly. "Danlo friend."

"Yeah?"

"My friends, we talks. Linnie talks about red bowl."

"Red bowl?"

"Man eats from red bowl, *onka bairanan cheassimidu* eats— what word, what word?—dreams." She looked at him expectantly.

Mooly turned to Ainne. "Do you know what she's talkin' about?" Ainne shrugged. To Linnie he said, "Sorry. Eating dreams from a red bowl?"

Linnie shook her head energetically. "Man eats from red bowl. *Onka bairanan cheassimidu* eats dreams. What this word?" Her fingers scampered rapidly up her arm. "Insect. Fire insect." Mooly looked at her in perplexity. She went on: "Linnie talks to Linnie friends. Talks with red bowl and big bird throws fire from sky. Linnie friends walks to Ranoima later, carries Danlo words."

"Your friends are going to walk somewhere."

"Ranoima. Linnie home." She waved her arm eastward. "Far. Many, many, many days walks."

"Your friends are going to walk to your home. And carry. . . ."

"Carries Danlo words. With red bowl, with big bird comes."

"Okay, I guess." Mooly was lost. He hoped Linnie wasn't as crazy as she sounded.

"Linnie not walks fast." She slapped her bad leg. "Linnie stays with Danlo friends. Linnie shows Danlo friends, shows how hunts, now makes fire."

Ainne moved close to Linnie. "You're going to stay with us?" She drew a circle with her finger around herself, Mooly, Gairth, and Luth. Linnie nodded emphatically. "This is very good."

Linnie nodded. "Good. Linnie shows how makes houses for

children. Not stone house. Good house.'' She turned away and covered her face with one hand. She was crying again.

While they walked, they ate some of the dried food from the survival pack. Afterward, Mooly's stomach still grumbled. He hoped Linnie would catch them something to eat. He resolved to watch close to see how she did it.

Toward the end of the afternoon they came to the foot of a wide ridge that rose like a ramp. At the eastern end, a mile or so away, the ridge was crossed by a brown-gray ribbon. Mooly pointed. ''There it is!''

Gairth whooped. ''All right! We made it! We're out of danger.''

Linnie looked at him strangely. ''Danger is animal claws, bites? Hungry, no food?''

Gairth averted his eyes. ''Yeah, okay. I see what you mean.''

She nodded. ''Danger *starts* now.''

The ridge was treeless, while the draw beside it was choked in brush, so they took the easy route. Mooly was still nervous about being pursued by planes, and kept craning his neck to look back. They had covered more than half the remaining distance to the Wall when he saw, lower down the slope, a couple of specks that hadn't been there before. The setting sun was in his eyes, so it was hard to be sure. He stopped and squinted. The specks were moving. People on foot, several of them.

He touched Ainne's shoulder and pointed. ''I know,'' she said. ''They've been back there for quite a while.''

''Oh, Frank. Shouldn't we run?''

''I don't think we need to. We can go on to the Wall, if you like, and wait there.''

''*Wait?*'' Gairth yelped.

Ainne smiled. ''You'll have to learn to trust me about some things. Linnie knows about some kinds of dangers. I know about others.''

Mooly kept looking over his shoulder, but their pursuers didn't seem to be gaining on them. The Wall, when they reached it, wasn't as high as he expected, only eight or nine feet. Little green plants were growing in chinks in the stonework. He found footholds and handholds and hoisted himself up. The top was wide enough to walk along. It stretched away to the north and south, dipping up and down across the hills like an empty highway. He turned and sat with his legs dangling. To the west, the sun was setting in a red blaze. Beyond the foothills the Serral Valley lay spread out, broad and flat, layered in bloody haze. At his back the ancient forest whispered in a breath of evening breeze. He reached down to give Ainne his arm. She swung up easily and sat beside him.

Out of the heavy red glow of sunset, up the ridge toward them, people were coming. Not many; ten or fifteen, in twos and threes. The nearest were a man and a woman, and between them, holding one of her parents' hands in each of hers, a little girl. Both the man and the woman had large packs strapped to their backs. They trudged steadily. The little girl was skipping. Behind them others came, carrying tools, sacks, a coil of rope.

Mooly started to relax. "They're not comin' after us, are they?" "No."

"So are they bringin' us stuff, or what? We can't possibly carry all that stuff."

"We won't have to," Ainne said. "They're coming with us."

Chapter || 28

WHAT I miss most is seeing the world. Touching it, smelling it, the wind on my face. I can catch glimpses filtered through others' senses—commandeer a pair of eyes, if I like, for a few minutes. But the immanence is missing. And the continuity. More often than in their eyes, I am a passenger in their memories, their plans, their lusts and fears. The void in which I float is cluttered with the furniture of their lives. The furniture of my life, now. The food and drink. I savor it, having no other.

I wonder, for the hundredth time, what I am. A tendency? An opportunity? A free-floating scrap of defiance? I feel that I am autonomous, that I act—but that may be an illusion. Do the figures one meets in dreams think they are autonomous? I have asked them, but they are capricious. If they answer at all, they answer in riddles. Occasionally, in my wanderings, I encounter myself. It's an odd experience, always surprising but not unwelcome. I absorb myself, and grow larger.

I was able to release a girl not long ago. In my last glimpse of her before the old man whose body I had borrowed turned away, she had a canvas pack on her back, a big pack for such a small girl, and she was fastening a knife to her belt. She had leaned sideways to fumble at the knife with both hands, and a lock of hair hung down across her face. I think about her often, standing like that, so young and frightened and brave. I don't know what she'll find when she reaches the mountains. The reports I hear are fragmentary, and contradict one another. The planes go out, but they find nothing, or the scattered ashes of long-dead fires. Sometimes they go out and don't come back.

I would like very much to make contact with Ainne, but I have avoided trying. If I succeeded in opening a channel, others might use it, for other ends. I would like, too, to know whether other groups have survived the way Linnie's people did. The world is large, and the Body has not yet been able to launch any image-taking satellites.

I bear some of the blame for this, of course. When I am not freeing children, I visit the factories where they make the planes. It's hard to build a plane that will fly well. There are so many things that can go wrong—a wing joint welded so that it will crack under stress, a screw in an engine whose threads are stripped, an instrument that gives unreliable readings, a leaky oil line. I feel badly about those who fly out into the mountains and don't come back, but I like to think that they may have landed safely, and found others who can help them, and now don't want to come back.

Olivia is still—always—enraged at me. Or rather, she stirs up rage in the Body, having no rage of her own. She thwarts me where she can, as I thwart her. But she cannot rid the Body of me. She gathers those who love her, swells their numbers, feeds their love, and I find no welcome among them, but as long as I find a welcome anywhere, her work unravels around the edges. I remind them what the Great Cleansing was really like. I whisper to them that we are no better than the savages we supplanted. I pass on to them the taste of raw freedom.

I suppose we might go on like this, Olivia and I, for as long as the Body of Harmony is One. How long will that be? If the children flourish in their new home, if Linnie's people grow in numbers, the Body might someday dissolve. Olivia and I might cease—perhaps gradually, perhaps suddenly—to exist. I suppose I ought to fear that, but I will leave the fear to Olivia. She has a talent for it. Long before then, the Body could break in half, with each of us confined to one half. We might reinvent war.

I have not seen Frank for a long time. How long? Time is difficult to gauge here. The old public ceremonies became battlegrounds of dissension, and have mostly been abandoned, but many among the Body still call forth Frank and Olivia in torchlit gatherings in the fields. There is no shortage of joddies to help them. I am not welcome at such rituals, so I don't know whether the Frank who appears at them is the real Frank or a temporary simulacrum compounded by the joddies. Or is there a difference?

If there is a real Frank, where has he gone? Perhaps, as before, I have become Frank, without ceasing to be myself. Since I don't know what my 'self' is, I don't know whether such a thing is possible. Or perhaps—and I think this more likely—Frank has withdrawn from the Body. He might have focused himself in some single mind and entirely dominated it, or in a small group of minds, loyal believers who have isolated themselves in the Northern Forest, or in the desert. When he has laid new plans, he may return. He could still cause great suffering. And how would I stop him? He has been at home in this place-that-is-not-a-place far longer than I. He knows its ways.

Another Cleansing is scheduled soon, in Saffersisko. A large one—five children. I will be there, the day before, and find friends, and help them do what they can. Perhaps, when the morning comes, the Hand of Cleansing will not need to put on his blindfold, or take his axe down from the wall.

275